"In the beginning of a change,
the patriot is a scarce and brave man, hated and scorned.
When his cause succeeds however,
the timid join him, for then it costs nothing to be a patriot."

Mark Twain

Acknowledgement

I acknowledge all efforts by alternate media and most conspiracy theorists for persistently chasing the 9/11 case with unfolding truth, news, pictures, and fact sheets including analysis without resting the case. Complete 9/11 timeline from Cooperative Research History Commons was a great resource base for investigation and analysis. I also acknowledge Wikipedia for summarizing most of the alternate theory along with the official claims all in one place. I acknowledge with gratitude all photographers who shot pictures of 9/11 US domestic disaster, graphic artist David Dees, and all who relentlessly worked over the internet to convey the messages for worldwide audience. My special thanks to Joe Vialls for bringing out the "Home Run"- *Electronically Hijacking of Passenger Jet Aircrafts* and publishing it online for universal access and review; Steve Kangas for his Timeline of CIA atrocities; Global Outlook - the publisher of 9/11 truth quiz; Dr. Daniele Ganser for his 'Able Danger adds twist to 9/11; Jim Hogue for interviewing former FBI translator courageous Sibel Edmonds for her fight against the unlawful gag order for 9/11 cover ups; as well as many online articles. I also thank my free pet lovebirds who gave me much needed company throughout the lonely mission towards everlasting peace exposing truth and bringing equal justice to all. Finally, the book would not have been possible without constant inspiration, scholarly help and encouragement from my darling wife – Dr. Radha Banerjee Sarkar.

Let us prepare ourselves for the journey remembering the warnings and advices of our founding fathers and leaders who fought to preserve American democracy and true Statesmanship in the world for global enlightenment. Kolki

Real Path To 9/11

A barrier to peace

Good environment

And universal well being

"The greatest tragedy is not the brutality of the evil but rather the silence of the good" -- *Martin Luther King Jr.*

From Kolki

The Author of "Poems by Kolki – Absolutely Humane"

Dedicated to all victims of 9/11 and related pre-emptive abuse and destructions throughout the world including helpless pilots, law enforcement officials as well as fire fighters

"If our government had merely [done] nothing, and I say that as an old interceptor pilot—I know the drill, I know what it takes, I know how long it takes, I know what the procedures are, I know what they were, and I know what they've changed them to—if our government had merely done nothing, and allowed normal procedures to happen on that morning of 9/11, the Twin Towers would still be standing and thousands of dead Americans would still be alive. [T]hat is treason!"
Col. Dr. Robert Bowman

"In the councils of government, we must guard against the acquisition of unwarranted influence, whether sought or unsought, by the military-industrial complex. The potential for the disastrous rise of misplaced power exists and will persist."

Dwight D. Eisenhower,
Farewell Address to the Nation, January 17, 1961

Transportation Secretary Norman Mineta's Testimony to 9/11 Commission which was censored from the report:

"During the time that the airplane (AA 77) was coming into the Pentagon, there was a young man who would come in and said to the Vice President, 'the plane is 50 miles out, the plane is 30 miles out.' And when it got to 'the plane is 10 miles out', the young man also said to the Vice President, 'Do the orders still stand?' And the Vice President...said, 'Of course the orders still stand. Have you heard anything to the contrary?'"

Norman Mineta testimony to 9/11 Commission

Smoking Gun

Standard order was to shoot down any non-military aircraft entering the "Prohibited" airspace over Washington, in which **"Civilian flying is prohibited at all times"** ("Pilots Notified of Restricted Airspace; Violators Face Military Action," FAA Press Release, September 28, 2001).

Yet no military action was taken to evacuate and save Pentagon! That's Treason!

Cold blooded murderers?

(The US taxpayer's groomed domestic treasoners with Neoconian ideology wanted maximum casualty from the well planned spectacular New Pearl Harbour)

The 9/11 Commission concluded that in spite of an unprecedented attack threat in the months before 9/11, US "domestic agencies never mobilized in response to the threat. They did not have direction, and did not have a plan to institute. The borders were not hardened. Transportation systems were not fortified. Electronic surveillance was not targeted against a domestic threat. State and local law enforcement were not marshalled to augment the FBI's efforts. The public was not warned." [9/11 Commission, 7/24/2004, pp. 265]

9/11 Similarity with Reichstag Fire that brought death to German Democracy:
[Ref: http://en.wikipedia.org/wiki/Reichstag_fire]
On the night of February 27th, 1933, Berlin was rocked by a fire that blazed through the Reichstag Building, the German House of Parliament. The building was absolutely gutted. Called out to watch the massive bonfire, Adolf Hiltler exclaimed, "This is a God-given signal." He was, in fact, delighted with what he saw. The very next day, Hitler met with President von Hindenburg, and pressured him into giving him dictatorial powers. This was a vital step for the Nazis. Now Hitler no longer relied upon the votes of the deputies in the Reichstag, where the Nazis did not enjoy a majority.

The following day, Chancellor Hitler took the radical steps of denying all legal guarantees of personal liberty, freedom of speech and the right of assembly by official decree. This step sent a shiver up many Berlin spines, as the people saw the destroyed Reichstag building as a symbol of the death of German democracy.

9/11 gave the Bush Administration unquestionable extra-judicial authority.

9/11 wasn't 'Bolt From The Blue' - rather 'Age Old Power Play' of the Elites for Dominating the New World

The actions of the Reagan Administration during the Iran-Contra scandal revealed "a pattern of conduct and a state of mind among important people in this administration which must be described as an American style of fascism. I would prefer to avoid that term, but it is the only one in the modern political vocabulary that adequately describes the situation."

William Pfaff, *Chicago Tribune*, March, 1987

"This present window of opportunity, during which a truly peaceful and interdependent world order might be built, will not be open for too long - We are on the verge of a global transformation. **All we need is the right major crisis and the nations will accept the New World Order.**"

David Rockefeller, *September 14, 1994, United Nations conference*

"Moreover, as America becomes an increasingly multi-cultural society, it may find it more difficult to fashion a consensus on foreign policy issues, **except in the circumstance of a truly massive and widely perceived direct external threat.**" (p. 211)

Former National Security Advisor **Zbigniew Brzezinski**, Book, The Grand Chessboard

January 26, 1998, PNAC Letter to President Clinton urging him to initiate military action to remove Saddam Hussein

The Honorable William J. Clinton
President of the United States
Washington, DC

Dear Mr. President:

We are writing you because we are convinced that current American policy toward Iraq is not succeeding, and that we may soon face a threat in the Middle East more serious than any we have known since the end of the Cold War. In your upcoming State of the Union Address, you have an opportunity to chart a clear and determined course for meeting this threat. We urge you to seize that opportunity, and to enunciate a new strategy that would secure the interests of the U.S. and our friends and allies around the world. That strategy should aim, above all, at the removal of Saddam Hussein's regime from power. We stand ready to offer our full support in this difficult but necessary endeavor.

The policy of "containment" of Saddam Hussein has been steadily eroding over the past several months. As recent events have demonstrated, we can no longer depend on our partners in the Gulf War coalition to continue to uphold the sanctions or to punish Saddam when he blocks or evades UN inspections. Our ability to ensure that Saddam Hussein is not producing weapons of mass destruction, therefore, has substantially diminished. Even if full inspections were eventually to resume, which now seems highly unlikely, experience has shown that it is difficult if not impossible to monitor Iraq's chemical and biological weapons production. The lengthy period during which the inspectors will have been unable to enter many Iraqi facilities has made it even less likely that they will be able to uncover all of Saddam's secrets. As a result, in the not-too-distant future we will be unable to determine with any reasonable level of confidence whether Iraq does or does not possess such weapons.

Such uncertainty will, by itself, have a seriously destabilizing effect on the entire Middle East. It hardly needs to be added that if Saddam does acquire the capability to deliver weapons of mass destruction, as he is almost certain to do if we continue along the present course, the safety of American troops in the region, of our friends and allies like Israel and the moderate Arab states, and a significant portion of the world's supply of oil will all be put at hazard. As you have rightly declared, Mr. President, the security of the world in the first part of the 21st century will be determined largely by how we handle this threat.

Given the magnitude of the threat, the current policy, which depends for its success upon the steadfastness of our coalition partners and upon the cooperation of Saddam Hussein, is dangerously inadequate. The only acceptable strategy is one that eliminates the possibility that Iraq will be able to use or threaten to use weapons of mass destruction. In the near term, this means a willingness to undertake military action as diplomacy is clearly failing. In the long term, it means removing Saddam Hussein and his regime from power. That now needs to become the aim of American foreign policy.

We urge you to articulate this aim, and to turn your Administration's attention to implementing a strategy for removing Saddam's regime from power. This will require a full complement of diplomatic, political and military efforts. Although we are fully aware of the dangers and difficulties in implementing this policy, we believe the dangers of failing to do so are far greater. We believe the U.S. has the authority under existing UN resolutions to take the necessary steps, including military steps, to protect our vital interests in the Gulf. In any case, American policy cannot continue to be crippled by a misguided insistence on unanimity in the UN Security Council.

We urge you to act decisively. If you act now to end the threat of weapons of mass destruction against the U.S. or its allies, you will be acting in the most fundamental national security interests of the country. If we accept a course of weakness and drift, we put our interests and our future at risk.

Sincerely,

Elliott Abrams   Richard L. Armitage   William J. Bennett

Jeffrey Bergner   John Bolton   Paula Dobriansky

Francis Fukuyama   Robert Kagan   Zalmay Khalilzad

William Kristol   Richard Perle   Peter W. Rodman

Donald Rumsfeld   William Schneider, Jr.   Vin Weber

Paul Wolfowitz   R. James Woolsey   Robert B. Zoellick

Notes: Then President Clinton ignores PNAC recommendation and faces Monica Lewinsky *Scandal (Orchestrated by PNAC sympathisers in FBI, Justice Department, Senate, Congress and Media!)*
Ref: http://www.cnn.com/ALLPOLITICS/1998/resources/lewinsky/timeline/

The NEOCONS' document
'Project For the New American Century (PNAC)'
argued in Rebuilding America's Defense (Page 51/63)

"Creating Tomorrow's Dominant Force - the process of transformation, even if it brings revolutionary change, is likely to be a long one, absent some catastrophic and catalyzing event like a new Pearl Harbor".

Most signatories of the PNAC were either member of the Bush Administration or Pentagon as follows:

[Donald Rumsfeld   Vin Weber   George Weigel   Paul Wolfowitz
Elliott Abrams   Gary Bauer   William J. Bennett   Jeb Bush
Dick Cheney   Eliot A. Cohen   Midge Decter   Paula Dobriansky
Steve Forbes   Aaron Friedberg   Francis Fukuyama   Frank Gaffney
Fred C. Ikle   Donald Kagan   Zalmay Khalilzad   I. Lewis Libby
Norman Podhoretz   Dan Quayle   Peter W. Rodman   Stephen P. Rosen
Henry S. Rowen]

Thus, 9/11 was a requirement for re-establishing American Supremacy throughout the world, as viewed by this group of people.

NORAD Hijacking Protocol

Before 9/11 and on 9/11 throughout the disaster saga

NORAD hijacking protocol before 9/11: **Per 1st Air Force's own book about 9/11, the "sector commander [at NEADS] would have authority to scramble the airplanes.").**

But,

Protocols in place on 9/11 stated that if the FAA requested the military to go after an airplane, **"the escort service will be requested by the FAA hijack coordinator by direct contact with the National Military Command Center (NMCC)."** But the FAA hijack coordinator, Mike Canavan, was silent in Puerto Rico without backup.

[Source: 9/11 timeline with live commission's interview and NORAD's document]

NORAD – North American Aerospace Defense Command
NEADS – Northeast Air Defense Sector (USA)

"There is no way that an aircraft . . . would not be intercepted when they deviate from their flight plan, turn off their transponders, or stop communication with Air Traffic Control ... Attempts to obscure facts by calling them a 'conspiracy Theory' does not change the truth. It seems, 'Something is rotten in the State.' "
- Capt. Daniel Davis

September 20, 2001 Letter of PNAC to President George W. Bush

http://www.newamericancentury.org
Toward a Comprehensive Strategy
Project for the New American Century
1150 17th St NW Suite 510 Washington, DC 20037 September 20, 2001
The Honorable George W. Bush President of the United States Washington, DC

Dear Mr. President,

We write to endorse your admirable commitment to "lead the world to victory" in the war against terrorism. We fully support your call for "a broad and sustained campaign" against the "terrorist organizations and those who harbor and support them." We agree with Secretary of State Powell that the United States must find and punish the perpetrators of the horrific attack of September 11, and we must, as he said, "go after terrorism wherever we find it in the world" and "get it by its branch and root." We agree with the Secretary of State that U.S. policy must aim not only at finding the people responsible for this incident, but must also target those "other groups out there that mean us no good" and "that have conducted attacks previously against U.S. personnel, U.S. interests and our allies." In order to carry out this "first war of the 21st century" successfully, and in order, as you have said, to do future "generations a favor by coming together and whipping terrorism," we believe the following steps are necessary parts of a comprehensive strategy.

Osama bin Laden We agree that a key goal, but by no means the only goal, of the current war on terrorism should be to capture or kill Osama bin Laden, and to destroy his network of associates. To this end, we support the necessary military action in Afghanistan and the provision of substantial financial and military assistance to the anti-Taliban forces in that country.

Iraq We agree with Secretary of State Powell's recent statement that Saddam Hussein "is one of the leading terrorists on the face of the Earth...." It may be that the Iraqi government provided assistance in some form to the recent attack on the United States. But even if evidence does not link Iraq directly to the attack, any strategy aiming at the eradication of terrorism and its sponsors must include a determined effort to remove Saddam Hussein from power in Iraq. Failure to undertake such an effort will constitute an early and perhaps decisive surrender in the war on international terrorism. The United States must therefore provide full military and financial support to the Iraqi opposition. American military force should be used to provide a "safe zone" in Iraq from which the opposition can operate. And American forces must be prepared to back up our commitment to the Iraqi opposition by all necessary means.

Hezbollah is one of the leading terrorist organizations in the world. It is suspected of having been involved in the 1998 bombings of the American embassies in Africa, and implicated in the bombing of the U.S. Marine barracks in Beirut in 1983. Hezbollah clearly falls in the category cited by Secretary Powell of groups "that mean us no good" and "that have conducted attacks previously against U.S. personnel, U.S. interests and our allies." Therefore, any war against terrorism must target Hezbollah. We believe the administration should demand that Iran and Syria immediately cease all military, financial, and political support for Hezbollah and its operations. Should Iran and Syria refuse to comply, the administration should consider appropriate measures of retaliation against these known state sponsors of terrorism.

Israel and the Palestinian Authority Israel has been and remains America's staunchest ally against international terrorism, especially in the Middle East. The United States should fully support our fellow democracy in its fight against terrorism. We should insist that the Palestinian Authority put a stop to terrorism emanating from territories under its control and imprison those planning terrorist attacks against Israel. Until the Palestinian Authority moves against terror, the United States should provide it no further assistance.

U.S. Defense Budget A serious and victorious war on terrorism will require a large increase in defense spending. Fighting this war may well require the United States to engage a well-armed foe, and will also require that we remain capable of defending our interests elsewhere in the world. We urge that there be no hesitation in requesting whatever funds for defense are needed to allow us to win this war. There is, of course, much more that will have to be done. Diplomatic efforts will be required to enlist other nations' aid in this war on terrorism. Economic and financial tools at our disposal will have to be used. There are other actions of a military nature that may well be needed. However, in our judgement the steps outlined above constitute the minimum necessary if this war is to be fought effectively and brought to a successful conclusion. Our purpose in writing is to assure you of our support as you do what must be done to lead the nation to victory in this fight.

Sincerely,

William Kristol, Gary Bauer, Jeffrey Bell, William J. Bennett, Jeffrey Bergner, Eliot Cohen, Seth Cropsey, Midge Decter, Thomas Donnelly, Aaron Friedberg, Hillel Fradkin, Francis Fukuyama, Frank Gaffney, Jeffrey Gedmin, Reuel Marc Gerecht, Charles Hill, Bruce P. Jackson, Eli S. Jacobs, Michael Joyce, Donald Kagan, Robert Kagan, Jeane Kirkpatrick, Charles Krauthammer, John Lehman, Clifford May, Richard Perle, Martin Peretz, Norman Podhoretz, Randy Scheunemann, Gary Schmitt, William Schneider, Jr., Richard H. Shultz, Henry Sokolski, Stephen J. Solarz, Vin Weber, Leon Wieseltier, Marshall Wittmann.

Note: The same NEOCONS who asked for the 'New Pearl Harbour' similar to 9/11 advised /urged then President George W. Bush, Jr. to implement all the other agenda, immediately following the unprecedented domestic disaster, including enormous military spending for hegemony, unconditional support for Israel, and bribing other countries to be part of the new destructive and abusive military ambition ignoring civilized rule of law and international institutions.

Let us review some more sayings by important leaders and philosophers

"We are apt to shut our eyes against a painful truth...for my part, I am willing to know the whole truth; to know the worst; and to provide for it." - **Patrick Henry,** 1st Post Colonial Governor of Virginia, USA

"The liberty of a democracy is not safe if the people tolerate the growth of private power to a point where it becomes stronger than their democratic State itself. That, in its essence, is Fascism - ownership of government by an individual, by a group or by any controlling private power." –

Franklin Delano Roosevelt, 32nd President of USA

"Fear can only prevail when victims are ignorant of the facts."
- **Thomas Jefferson,** 3rd President of USA

"These are the times that try men's souls. The summer soldier and the sunshine patriot will, in this crisis, shrink from the service of their country; but he that stands it now, deserves the love and thanks of man and woman. Tyranny, like hell, is not easily conquered." - **Thomas Paine, The American Crisis, 1776**

"Be isolated, be ignored, be attacked, be in doubt, be frightened...but do not be silenced" - **Bertrand Russell**

Preface

I am writing this book as a conscious world citizen who believes in truth and equal justice for all as the very basis of establishing and maintaining a true democratic free world. 9/11 saga unfolded in front of my televisionic eyes from the beginning when I was watching morning News on CNN which started broadcasting the first plane hit the World Trade Center (North Tower) right around 8:50am, 4 minutes after the apparent collision. I was worried about the crew and the passengers and was hoping fast rescue operation like in Hollywood movie. But nothing was happening except waiting when the second plane hit the other tower which CNN could telecast as it was coming in and almost missed the building absence of a sharp last moment manoeuvre to hit the target (South Tower)! As a novice pilot I was wondering how this was possible by human operators controlling such massive moving vehicles in balance! Then with utter disbelief I watched one tower came down entirely and then the other one. As an engineer I was bewildered how these all were possible except my recollections of planned demolitions I watched in Atlantic City and Las Vegas!

I was very shocked thinking of all the passengers, crew, and people in those two buildings and surroundings! In fact I was once interviewed for a job in 53rd floor of the World Trade Center (WTC) by Morgan Stanley and had been three times at the top with my friends and even parents. So I was very disturbed and wrote to politicians and leaders expecting first recovery of the buried alive inside the debris. Then watched with frustration how slow the rescue process was using people in line clearing site by hand and tub. Foreign rescuers in Canada and elsewhere were eager to extend help but were turned down from the well guarded FBI crime scenes!

Being a good corporate citizen in North America for 20 years and a reborn student at the University of Victoria pursuing Ph.D my focus shifted from my main thesis in Electromagnetics to the research of 9/11 American domestic disaster. I chose to call it a disaster and not external attack until proven beyond reasonable doubts following existing legal system's proof of conviction.

As I read through news filtering yellow journalism propaganda from the very beginning many anomalies were obvious from the official statements and reasoning including passenger lists, flight recorders and shooting down of Flight 93 over Pennsylvania. Watched non-democratically installed Ex-president George W. Bush warned media and senators not to indulge in outrageous conspiracy theories. Watched helplessly the Anthrax attack and scare that followed 9/11 targeting democratic senators and media critical to the new Supreme Court installed administration. Watched how quickly they manoeuvred military efforts in Afghanistan while the fire in WTC still burning underneath. Watched how coherently administration, military, CIA, FBI and media were blaming Bin Laden and Al-Qaeda for everything without addressing any trivial anomalies. Watched also curiously how few world citizens were trying hard for attentions towards the anomalies which were absolutely missing from main stream media or buried under a pile of commercial propaganda. I salute and send my regards to all who have been contributing over the internet and alternate news media constantly to bring justice home for real solution to terrorism.

9/11 disaster didn't kill only the ill-fated crew and passengers of Boeing 757s and 767s, workers & visitors in WTC and the victims in Pentagon. It also managed to kill decorated fellow Golden Gate University alumni army Lieutenant General Timothy Maude , the highest ranking person killed at the Pentagon and John P. O'Neill, a former Assistant Director of the FBI, who was closely involved with prior terror related alleged convictions against Al-Qaeda looking for evidences that fit in.

I waited for the much delayed inquiry commission, which then President George W. Bush and Vice President Dick Cheney were vehemently against, knowing well the 9/11 Commission was nothing but a decent way of cover ups and face saving like most other Government installed commissions keeping the real criminals in power running our once free country. The assassination of Daniel Pearl and related indifference from the Pentagon and US administration really triggered my writings and campaign for peace and justice. I tried my best using all my corporate analytical and management skills and electromagnetic vision of seeing things beyond to prosecute this case so that world citizen can say with certainty that the only outrageous conspiracy theory is the US Government and Media version warranting immediate opening of a thorough and full public investigation respecting the founding fathers and their wisdoms. **Kolki**

"If they were to do real investigations we would see several significant high level criminal prosecutions in this country. And that is something that they are not going to let out. And, believe me; they will do everything to cover this up."

-Sibel Edmonds, former FBI translator

"Some of the biggest men in the United States, in the field of commerce and manufacture, are afraid of something. They know that there is a power somewhere so organized, so subtle, so watchful, so interlocked, so complete, so pervasive, that they better not speak above their breath when they speak in condemnation of it." - **Woodrow Wilson**, "The New Freedom", 1913

Table of Contents

Table of Contents (Cont.)

Table of Contents (Cont.)

Introductory

We will find out analyzing facts and anomalies in this book that 9/11 never could happen the way it happened without then President George Bush Jr.'s authorization changing existing North American Air Defense (NORAD) protocol[1] inactivating NORAD's authority to scramble fighter jets against any suspicious airplanes, especially flying without transponder[2], in the North American Airspace! The newly authorized Federal Aviation Authority (FAA) Hijack Coordinator, Mike Canavan[3], was sent to Puerto Rico without backup where he was out of contact throughout the 9/11 operation enabling the success of the well coordinated precision Remote Control Military Plan, like the Operation Northwoods.

The signatories of the 'Project of the New American Century (PNAC)', including Vice President Cheney and Defense Secretary Donald Rumsfeld, masterminded 'The New Pearl Harbor' on 9/11 using Air Force to remotely hijack well known fully automated military/commercial jets, Boeing 757 & 767, locking on the transponders from Pentagon running airplane crash simulation from the National Reconnaissance Office (NRO), in Chantilly Virginia, making the patriotic pilots watch helpless destructions in utter disbelief!

There were no physical hijackers! The fake calls and rumors were part of the planned implementation script as originally envisioned in the Operation Northwoods against Cuba (March 13, 1962) and rehearsed as exercise before 9/11! All alleged hijackers names were given to CIA by Israeli, British, and German Authorities long before September 11, 2001, for the well conceived spectacular 9/11 implementation plan allowing foreigners with fake names perform their duties inside USA which can be later used by FBI and CIA for the eventual framings and cover ups! The actual 9/11 masterminders used the Saudi visa express facility which allowed known criminals (at least the names) enter and leave countries including USA and Britain with full knowledge of CIA, MI6, FBI and Mossad so that those names with pictures can be used to frame and blame Islamic militants who apparently never took or could take any of those flights as confirmed by all 9/11 flight's passenger lists! Providing photo Id with name as in the ticket was always a norm before boarding the flight in all US Domestic airports. The FBI doctored lists couldn't tally the full proof commercial head counts inside each flight.

That is the main reason why massive warnings from major world intelligences were ignored by CIA, FBI, NSA, Pentagon, Bush Administration and responsible Senators and Representative in Congress as well for the successful implementation of the spectacular New Pearl Harbor following PNAC prescription!

Well choreographed and timed mysterious Bin Laden videos may help International Republican Party re-elect NEOCONS dominated U.S. administration fooling Americans but none of them can ever address the well documented **9/11 anomalies** illustrated in this book!

Many questions got buried under the massive noisy propaganda and preparations for the illegal wars against Afghanistan and Iraq, Anthrax attacks, swift congressional passages of bills empowering President with dictatorial authority and Pentagon with unquestionable military spending, Washington DC sniper[11] and Virginia Tech massacres[12].

As we go through this book, it would be obvious that 9/11 wasn't an isolated event like a bolt from the blue. Rather it was a well planned multinational coordinated precisely enacted military operation by the very people whom the citizens trusted putting them in charge of protecting the nation from domestic or foreign threats paying them huge salary out of US Tax money to live a well connected respectable life! **Without coherent betrayal and deceiving at the highest levels of the Government and Media for the anticipated evangelic military and commercial gains no one on this planet could hurt the 9/11 victims and buildings if America simply followed the existing day to day security measures and procedures before and on 9/11.**

It is time for the North American Politicians, NORAD officials, true patriotic high level Military Authority and prudent Journalists & Media personnel to come forward and tell the world what really happened on 9/11 in the name of maintaining US/NATO/Israeli military supremacy on Earth, Space and Cyber Space per PNAC! Anyone who remains silent and tries to make others silent imagining its all good for the Americans and long term Western Hegemonic Economy committing the greatest crime against humanity letting democratic mass murderers be the worst Frankenstein ruling our world with terror toward overall destruction for the benefit of few. Hope the universal loving power helps our leaders rise to speak truth under oath enabling United Nations (UN) and International Court of Justice help the Americans with the much deserved open investigation of the disastrous events of September 11, 2001, on U.S. soil.

References:
1. NORAD Protocol from 9-11 Timeline, http://www.kolki.com/peace/NORAD-Hijacking-Protocol.htm
2. Home Run, http://www.kolki.com/peace/Home-Run.doc
3. Mike Canavan, 9-11 Timeline, 9-11 Commission, http://www.kolki.com/peace/MikeCanavan.doc
4. http://en.wikipedia.org/wiki/Daniel_Pearl
5. http://www.fas.org/irp/world/pakistan/isi/
6. The Role of Pakistan's Military Intelligence (ISI) in the September 11 Attacks, **Michel Chossudovsky Professor of Economics, University of Ottawa,** http://www.globalresearch.ca/articles/CHO111A.html
7. http://web.utk.edu/~rkirk1/Hoover.html
8. http://news.bbc.co.uk/1/hi/world/americas/3516233.stm
9. http://www.btinternet.com/~nlpwessex/Documents/armitageISlatta.htm
10. US Planned Attacking Afghanistan in July 2001, BBC; http://news.bbc.co.uk/2/hi/south_asia/1550366.stm
11. Snipers bring fear to Washington, BBC, http://news.bbc.co.uk/2/hi/americas/2570477.stm
12. Virginia Tech Massacre, http://www.rense.com/general76/reallife.htm

Let us begin with a poem

"Truth"

the very reason of our journey

Truth
(Dedicated to all victims of lies in our heavenly world)

I can speak truth openly without thought of humiliation!
Because I don't belong to an institution!
No one paid me to act honest in sophistication!
Certainly not gaining anything for self gratification!
Have no intention to campaign for future election!
Why can express myself before media characterization!
Unconcerned with worries of journalistic speculations!
Not lobbying on behalf of any platform with affiliation -
Finally, speech is not my professional transaction!

We are taught to be truthful throughout childhood
But we learn the adjustments reaching adulthood!
Soon get used to diplomacy embedding falsehood
Often knowingly withhold truth for livelihood!
Cautiously avoid inquisitive child throughout parenthood
Nation's intelligence hides truth to save Nationhood -
Elected officials forget hands still on the holy book!

When people get used to lying under condition -
An honest and just society only lives in imagination!
Guarding truth is a game in corporate competition!
Military ensures national security blacking out documentation!
Celebrities learn to lie looking smart with fashion!
Religious leaders make stories during Evangelic mission!

Truth seekers try in vein to remind implication -
Avoiding truth only leads to eventual self destruction!

Why September 11 Was Chosen To Attack America?

Rather the main question is why major yearly US military exercises were preponed suddenly on the week of 9/11/2001 from normal yearly schedule towards end of October? And why FEMA and Transportation department set up command center at Pier 29 for counter Bio Terror attack exercise on September 12, 2001, in New York City, which will be used as the Emergency Command Center following 9/11 disaster and loss of New York City command center due to predicted World Trade Center collapse?

September 11, 1922, One of the things that the League of Nations did during its short period of existence was to grant Great Britain a special "Mandate" to establish a homeland for the Jewish people in the territory of Palestine, which had been taken from the newly defeated Turkish Empire. History records that the administration of this mandate effectively began with the swearing into office as High Commissioner and Commander in Chief for Palestine of the Right Honourable Sir Herbert Samuel, in Jerusalem, on September 11, 1922.

September 11, 1922, The final achievement of Brandeis and American Zionism in the post-war period was the passage by Congress on September 11, 1922 of a joint resolution favouring a Jewish homeland in Palestine. The words of the resolution practically echoed the Balfour Declaration.

The **Balfour Declaration of 1917**[1] (dated 2 November 1917) was a formal statement of policy by the British government stating that

> *"His Majesty's government view with favour the establishment in Palestine of a national home for the Jewish people, and will use their best endeavors to facilitate the achievement of this object, it being clearly understood that nothing shall be done which may prejudice the civil and religious rights of existing non-Jewish communities in Palestine, or the rights and political status enjoyed by Jews in any other country."*

September 11, 1941, Construction begins on the Pentagon.

September 11, 1941, Charles Lindbergh spoke about the danger of Jewish power in the media and government. The shy 39-year-old -- known around the world for his epic 1927 New York to Paris flight, the first solo trans-Atlantic crossing -- was addressing 7,000 people in Des Moines, Iowa, on September 11, 1941, about the dangers of U.S. involvement in the war then raging in Europe.

"The three most important groups pressing America into war, he explained, were the British, the Jews and the Roosevelt Administration. Their greatest danger to this country lies in their large ownership and influence in our motion pictures, our press, our radio, and our government. ... For reasons which are understandable from their viewpoint as they are inadvisable from ours, for reasons which are not American, [they] wish to involve us in the war. We cannot blame them for looking out for what they believe to be their own interests, but we must also look out for ours. We cannot allow the natural passions and prejudices of other peoples to lead our country to destruction."

September 11, 1973: President Salvador Allende of Chile was assassinated and his country was taken over by a United States covert intelligence CIA backed coup.

September 11, 1994: A lone pilot crashed a stolen single-engine Cessna into a tree on the White House grounds just short of the President Clinton's bedroom. **(Notes: White House and Pentagon are covered as military airspace with shoot down authority! The question is how and why that plane was allowed to enter without military intervention?)** Coincidentally, in December 1998 Clinton ordered four days of concentrated air attacks against military installations inside Iraq.

In 1998, Clinton appointed Richard Clarke—who until then served in a drugs and counter-terrorism division of the CIA—to lead an interagency comprehensive counter-terrorism operation, the Counter-terrorism Security Group (CSG). The goal of the CSG was to "detect, deter, and defend against" terrorist attacks. Additionally, Clinton appointed Clarke to sit on the cabinet-level Principals Committee when it met on terrorism issues.

Clarke was demoted when the Bush administration took office. Condoleezza Rice kept Clarke on staff but she downgraded his position so that as national counterterrorism coordinator he no longer reported directly to Cabinet-level officials. Clarke's January 2001 request for urgent cabinet level meeting about future Al-Qaeda strikes was postponed till September 4, 2001, only to be attended by a group of deputy secretaries.

On March 24, Richard Clarke delivered a persuasive performance in front of the commission investigating the Sept. 11 attacks. Clarke—who has worked for Ronald Reagan, George H.W. Bush, Bill Clinton, and George W. Bush, serving as counterterrorism chief for the last two—apologized for his failures in fighting al-Qaeda. Then he slammed the Bush administration for paying insufficient attention to the terrorist threat in the summer of 2001. His new book, Against All Enemies, makes similar points at greater length.

Excerpt from a book 'Against All Enemies' by Richard Clarke:

Pages 23-24: Resolved to attack al-Qaeda on the evening of Sept. 11. That night, Bush spoke to his staff: "**I want you to understand that we are at war and we will stay at war until this is done. Nothing else matters.**" When Donald Rumsfeld pointed out the legal problems posed by some proposed attacks, Bush said, "**I don't care what the international lawyers say, we are going to kick some ass.**"

When the US Commander in Chief should have focused on the rescue efforts in WTC and Pentagon as well as immediate opening of 9/11 investigation to diagnose the true causes that led to the success of 9/11 so that future events can be deterred effectively, he indulged into attacking Iraq framing reasons!

But let us take a look at what then President Bush was doing on Sept 12, 2001, evening when the fires in WTC and Pentagon were still burning!

Page 30-32: **Bush Considered attacking Iraq on the evening of Sept. 12.** At one point, Bush pulled a few of his advisors into a conference room:

"Look," he told us. "I know you have a lot to do and all ... but I want you, as soon as you can, to go back over everything, everything. See if Saddam did this. See if he's linked in any way."

I was once again taken aback, incredulous, and it showed.

"But, Mr. President, Al Qaeda did this."

"I know, I know, but ... see if Saddam was involved. Just look. I want to know any shred."

"Absolutely, we will look ... again." I was trying to be more respectful, more responsive. "But, you know, we have looked several times for state sponsorship of Al Qaeda and not found any real linkages to Iraq. Iran plays a little, as does Pakistan, and Saudi Arabia, Yemen."

"Look into Iraq, Saddam," the President said testily and left us.

This hint of attacking sovereign Iraq in some pretexts is nothing short of war crimes by international standards set following World War II.

References:

1. Balfour Declaration of 1917,

    http://en.wikipedia.org/wiki/Balfour_Declaration_of_1917

"In wartime, truth is so precious that she should always be attended by a bodyguard of lies" - Winston Churchill

9-11 Preparation

9-11 preparation started right after signing of the "Project of the New American Century (PNAC)" by key US administration, military, and corporate supremacy think tanks of neoconian ideology of enacting 'New Pearl Harbour' for 21st Century World Supremacy - **"Creating Tomorrow's Dominant Force - the process of transformation, even if it brings revolutionary change, is likely to be a long one, absent some catastrophic and catalyzing event like a New Pearl Harbour"**.

CPD The Committee on the Present Danger

CPD logo. [http://en.wikipedia.org/wiki/File:CPD_logo.jpg]

A group of hardline Cold Warriors and neoconservatives revive the once-influential Committee on the Present Danger (CPD) in order to Promote their anti-Soviet, pro-military agenda. The CPD is an outgrowth of the Coalition for a Democratic Majority (CDM), itself a loose amalgamation of neoconservatives and Democratic hawks[1].

Spreading Propaganda - According to a 2004 BBC documentary, the CPD will produce documentaries, publications, and provide guests for national talk shows and news reports, all designed to spread fear and encourage increases in defense spending, especially, as author Thom Hartmann will write, *"for sophisticated weapons systems offered by the defense contractors for whom neocons would later become lobbyists."* [Common Dreams (.org), 12/7/2004; BBC, 1/14/2005]

They sent a letter to then President Clinton (see pages 9-10) asking him to undertake necessary measures outlined in PNAC for continuous American military supremacy throughout the world ensuring no one can rise as competition against American economy and military guaranteeing success of corporations and military industrial complex.

Ex-President Clinton declined to sign and approve huge military spending in peace time and was charged with Sexual Harassment case the day after. The military and oil industry machine and their media became active to elect a president who will resonate with their mission, orchestrating most sophisticated voting fraud doctoring paperless electronic voting machines and complicating ballots!

The military and oil industry machine and their 'lawyer & media' managed to stop Florida State vote counts blessed by like minded judges in the Supreme Court making George W. Bush Jr. illegal non-democratic president of America.

Right from the beginning of the George W. Bush's presidency NATO, CIA, FBI, MI6, Mossad started converting US-made NATO supported Al-Qaeda to virtual military wing to enact terrorism wherever needed to justify pre-emptive US-NATO-Israeli military actions – with utmost secrecy and convenient high-tech intrusive technology and propaganda.

They revived "Operation Northwoods" to inflict "Pearl Harbour" like American catastrophe to justify war time military spending and authoritative power that can unilaterally declare wars in any part of the world bypassing United Nations and undermining International Court of Justice.

They discontinued "Able/Danger" Pre-CIA OSS type intelligence data gathering operation against Al-Qaeda and started breeding already tracked members inside USA, Britain, Canada, Germany and Pakistan to frame them as the 9/11 hijackers, forging passports, opening bank accounts in their name and transferring funds.

APRIL 4, 2001: BUGGING TECHNIQUES REACH NEW HEIGHTS

One of the approximately 30 radomes at the Echelon station in Menwith Hill, England. A radome covers an antenna to protect it from the weather and disguise the direction it is pointing. [Source: Matt Crypto / Public domain]

The BBC reports on advances in electronic surveillance. The US's global surveillance program, Echelon, has become particularly effective in monitoring mobile phones, recording millions of calls simultaneously and checking them against a powerful search engine designed to pick out key words that might represent a security threat. Laser microphones can pick up conversations from up to a kilometer away by monitoring window vibrations. If a bug is attached to a computer keyboard, it is possible to monitor exactly what is being keyed in, because every key on a computer has a unique sound when depressed. [BBC, 4/4/2001] Furthermore, a BBC report on a European Union committee investigation into Echelon one month later notes that the surveillance network can sift through up to 90 percent of all Internet traffic, as well as monitor phone conversations, mobile phone calls, fax transmissions, net browsing history, satellite transmissions and so on. Even encryption may not help much. The BBC suggests that *"it is likely that the intelligence agencies can crack open most commercially available encryption software."* [BBC, 5/29/2001]

In May 2001 Bush administration hired **Dr. Dov Zakheim as the Comptroller** of the Pentagon [http://judicial-inc.biz/Dov_zakheim.htm]. He was the Corporate Vice President of Systems Planning Corporation which specialized in Remote Control Flight Termination from the ground [http://www.sysplan.com/Radar/FTS]. He also brought with him extensive knowledge of WTC building structures and security.

On May 8, 2001 Vice President Richard B. Cheney was placed in charge of anti-terrorism training and military preparedness exercises by then President Bush. This gave him command authority during the 9/11 alleged attacks when as many as nine **war game exercises** involving military and intelligence agencies were occurring simultaneously. [http://911proof.com/9.html]

In May 2001 Medics Were Trained for Airplane Boeing 757 Hitting Pentagon *(9/11 Script Rehearsal?)* [HistoryCommons.org]
The Army's DiLorenzo Tricare Health Clinic (DTHC) and the Air Force Flight Medicine Clinic, both housed within the Pentagon, held a tabletop exercise along with Arlington County Emergency Medical Services. **The scenario practiced for was of an airplane crashing into the Pentagon's west side—the same side as was impacted in the attack on 9/11.** [US Department of Health and Human Services, 7/2002, pp. B17; Goldberg et al., 2007, pp. 23 and 107] Reportedly, the purpose of the exercise was "to fine-tune their emergency preparedness." [US Medicine, 10/2001] **According to US Medicine newspaper, the plane in the scenario was a hijacked Boeing 757.** [US Medicine, 1/2002] **Flight 77, that targeted the Pentagon on 9/11, was a 757.** [New York Times, 9/13/2001]

Since July 2001 US Military started preparing for Mass Casualty **(MASCAL Training Exercise** Held at Fort Belvoir, Virginia, near Washington DC).** It was "designed to enhance the first ready response in dealing with the effects of a terrorist incident involving an explosion." [MDW News Service, 7/5/01]. But **they were not preparing to deal with the causes to stop the alleged terrorist incident!**

Historic Fort Belvoir is a beautiful army installation, with a unique and complex global mission. Fort Belvoir is home to one Army major command headquarters and elements of 10 others; 19 different agencies and direct reporting units of the Department of Army; eight elements of the U.S. Army Reserve and the Army National Guard; and 26 Department of Defense (DOD) agencies. Also located here are a Marine Corps detachment, a U.S. Air Force activity, and an agency from the Department of the Treasury. **Imagine together they couldn't stop the bomb explosion in nearby Pentagon around 8:32am on 9/11 and subsequent American Airlines Flight 77 hitting the newly furbished Navy Command Center around 9:37am.**

World Trade Center ownership changed hands along with security: On the 23rd July, 2001, just seven weeks prior to 9/11, the Port Authority of New York and New Jersey signed a deal with a consortium led by Larry Silverstein for a 99 year lease of the World Trade Center complex. The leased buildings included WTC One, Two, Four, Five, and 400,000 square feet of retail space. The Marriott Hotel (WTC 3), U.S. Customs building (WTC 6) and Silverstein's own 47-story office building (WTC 7) were already under lease. Silverstein was seeking $7.2 Billion from insurers for the destruction of the center but rewarded with 5.5 Billion.

BEFORE SEPTEMBER 11, 2001: ECHELON INTELLIGENCE NETWORK USED ON AL-QAEDA disinformation propaganda

An Echelon station in Menwith Hill, Britain.
[Source: BBC]

By the 1980s, a high-tech global electronic surveillance network shared between the US, Britain, Canada, Australia, and New Zealand is gathering intelligence all over the world. The BBC describes Echelon's power as *"astounding,"* and elaborates: *"Every international telephone call, fax, e-mail, or radio transmission can be listened to by powerful computers capable of voice recognition. They home in on a long list of key words, or patterns of messages. They are looking for evidence of international crime, like terrorism.*" [BBC, 11/3/1999] One major focus for Echelon before 9/11 is al-Qaeda. For instance, one account mentions Echelon intercepting al-Qaeda communications in Southeast Asia in 1996[1]. A staff member of the National Security Council who regularly attends briefings on bin Laden states, *"We are probably tapped into every hotel room in Pakistan. We can listen in to just about every phone call in Afghanistan."*

Sincere serious warning were conveyed to US intelligence and administration from most capable nations on earth about the up coming possible 9/11 attack. The Russian president even spelled out the detail. Then CIA director was absolutely sure about the attack. US Counterterrorism czar[2] predicted spectacular attack. Thus the question remains unanswered why USA remain unprepared despite so many viable cooperation to save the nation?

Ernst Welteke. *[Source: Publicity photo]*

EARLY SEPTEMBER 2001: ALMOST IRREFUTABLE PROOF OF INSIDER TRADING IN GERMANY

German central bank president Ernst Welteke later reports that a study by his bank indicates, "There are ever clearer signs that there were activities on international financial markets that must have been carried out with the necessary expert knowledge," not only in shares of heavily affected industries such as airlines and insurance companies, but also in gold and oil. [DAILY TELEGRAPH, 9/23/2001] His researchers have found "almost irrefutable proof of insider trading." [MIAMI HERALD, 9/24/2001] "If you look at movements in markets before and after the attack, it makes your brow furrow. But it is extremely difficult to really verify it." Nevertheless, he believes that "in one or the other case it will be possible to pinpoint the source." [Fox News, 9/22/2001] Welteke reports "a fundamentally inexplicable rise" in oil prices before the attacks [Miami Herald, 9/24/2001] and then a further rise of 13 percent the day after the attacks. Gold rises non-stop for days after the attacks. [Daily Telegraph, 9/23/2001]

On September 10, the day before 9/11, FEMA and other emergency response personnel set up a command post at Pier 29 apparently to conduct a counter-bioterrorism exercise code named "Tripod II" scheduled for September 12, 2001. But the best educated reason for their presence on Pier 29, after careful analysis of the post 9/11 events, would suggest their preparation for the massive rescue operation needed after the spectacular remote controlled airlines crashes and subsequent controlled demolitions of the World Trade Center. It may also be speculated that they were there as back up operation to spread massive bio-terror using Anthrax and other agents just in case something goes wrong with the implementation of well planned 9/11 script, since the White House was ready with CIPRO.

The treasoners with Neoconian ideology among the higher ups inside CIA-MI6-Mossad who were spreading the rumour of Al-Qaeda attack using US taxpayers paid NSA sponsored Echelon information gathering and false flag spreading installation in Britain while elements within covert CIA, Military, FBI, NSA, FAA, FBI, Pentagon, White House, Senate and Congress coordinated the précised plan of remote control hijacking of Boeing 757 and 767 passenger jets using 'FAA approved & installed" augmented GPS and military flight termination technology, targeting world trade center and Pentagon precisely.

"Despite repeated assertions by President Bush and his top advisers that their global campaign against terrorism will be a 'new kind of war', the biggest recipients of the new weapons spending sparked by the September 11 attacks will be the usual suspects: big defense contractors like Boeing, Raytheon, Lockheed Martin and Northrop Grumman. Once emergency anti-terror funding and supplemental appropriations to finance the war in Afghanistan are taken into account, this year's Pentagon budget could hit $375 billion, a $66 billion increase over last year"[3].

End Notes:

1. History of Commons,
http://www.historycommons.org/entity.jsp?entity=james_baker]
2. Czar - http://en.wikipedia.org/wiki/Tsar
3. William Hartung, Pentagon Spending Spree, Multinational Monitor Magazine, November 2001
http://www.thirdworldtraveler.com/Corporate_Welfare/PentagonSpendingSpree.html

"In the big lie there is always a certain force of credibility; because the broad masses of a nation are always more easily corrupted ...they more readily fall victims to the big lie than the small lie... It would never come into their heads to fabricate colossal untruths, and they would not believe that others could have the impudence to distort the truth so infamously." --- **Adolf Hitler**

Let us read another poem

"Lies"

the very reason for this research

Most world leaders end up lying, once in a while, under oath to satisfy the desires of the power behind the throne or 'Vicar of Christ' insulting honest law abiding citizens; but George W Bush lied 935 times[1] under oath yet avoided Congressional impeachment or media assassination!

"A sophisticated false-flag operation like 9-11 has an organizational structure with three basic levels: architectural, operational, and working. Atta and the 19 Arabs blamed as the hijackers of 9-11 were part of the working level, and were simply part of the deception. That is, after all, how false-flag terror works." - **Andreas von Buelow**, the former head of the parliamentary commission that oversaw the German intelligence agencies.

"The deathly precision and the magnitude of planning behind the attacks would have required years of planning. Such a sophisticated operation would have required the 'fixed frame' of a state intelligence organization, something not found in the 'loose group' like the one allegedly led by Mohammed Atta while he studied in Hamburg. The nebulous Al Qaeda and the Taliban of Afghanistan clearly lacked the 'fixed frame' of a state intelligence organization. Many people would have been involved in the planning of such an operation and the absence of leaks was a further indication that the attacks were 'state organized' actions." - **Eckehardt Werthebach**, the former head of the Verfassungsschutz, the domestic branch of German intelligence

1. Bush, aides made 935 false statements in run-up to war, CNN, January 24, 2008.

Lies
(Dedicated to all souls suffering from wars and/or scars of supremacy)

Presidents, Prime Ministers, Constitutional Monarchs
Always lie under oath to justify wars!
During speeches praising heroic efforts
Without explaining the mission under cover
Hiding true intention raising patriotic fever!

Politicians lie or avoid truth afterwards
Thinking its good for economy and the voters!
Making humans the only animal of The Creator -
Who enjoy killing own kind as predators!

Citizens kill citizens with license
Sufferers become labelled as insurgents!
Reporters report from a distance
Daring ones get abducted, beheaded in cyberspace -
Sensitive true media get bombarded, displaced!

Peace lovers cry, walk with candle and incandescence
As bodies, buildings, beings get annihilated!
People pray, some ignore, some rejoice -
As occupiers kidnap, assassinate, activists providing solace!

Pope tries to mediate in vain -
UN efforts get side tracked for convenience!
Evangelists delighted glorifying revenge!
Buddha sighs, Jesus asks for forgiveness -
Mohammed in disbelief! God bewildered helpless!

9/11 Motives

"Creating Tomorrow's Dominant Force - the process of transformation, even if it brings revolutionary change, is likely to be a long one, absent some catastrophic and catalyzing event like a New Pearl Harbour" – Rebuilding America's Defenses[1], page 51/63, PNAC signatories.

Newly confirmed Defense secretary Donald Rumsfeld, a member of PNAC, predicted New Pearl Harbour during his inaugural speech in January 2001. Notably, Mr. Rumsfeld had been a prominent member of the secret Shadow Government** along with the newly elected Vice President Dick Cheney since its inauguration in 1980 under then President Regan.

But the actual planning for the New World Order under Bankers and Military elites started long before at the secretive aristocratic Bilderberg conference in 1991 in Baden, Germany, attended by many dignitaries around the world including Bill Clinton & Dan Quayle.

David Rockefeller, then Chairman of Bilderberg, summarized their goal during the meeting as follows:
"We are grateful to the Washington Post, the New York Times, Time Magazine and other great publications whose directors have attended our meetings and respected their promises of discretion for almost forty years.

It would have been impossible for us to develop our plan for the world if we had been subjected to the lights of publicity during those years. But, the world is more sophisticated and prepared to march towards a world government. The supranational sovereignty of an intellectual elite and world bankers is surely preferable to the national autodetermination practiced in past centuries".

The Clinton-Gore era military cuts and base closures agonized many pro-military higher ups in US Government and media, although the fruits of the cuts yielded to peace time balanced budget and surplus civilian economy.

2000 Presidential Candidate George W. Bush's hard-line rhetoric on Defense issues raised high hopes among Defense contractors letting the industry donate more than four times as much to the Bush campaign compared to Al Gore's presidential bid, and favouring Republican candidates for Congress by almost a two-to-one margin.

"But Bush dashed the arms makers' hopes for a quick payoff in February 2001 when he announced that he would not seek additional increases in Pentagon spending beyond those already recommended by the outgoing Clinton administration until Secretary of Defense Donald Rumsfeld had completed a comprehensive review of U.S. military strategy"[6].

Secretary of Defense Rumsfeld tapped Dr. Stephen Cambone[2] as a special assistant to the secretary and deputy Secretary of Defense. In July 2001, he was confirmed as principal deputy undersecretary of Defense for policy, a position that would require some deftness in implementing the so-called Revolution in Military Affairs.

Ironically for the defense industries, the new path towards the military's technological leap forward meant more cutbacks, **"Cambone was demanding force structure cuts, with briefing charts that showed how the Army could cut two divisions, about 40,000 soldiers. The Navy could afford two less carrier battle groups. Maybe the Air Force didn't need the new F-22[3] stealth fighter"[2].**

To add fuel to the fire **Defense Secretary Rumsfeld exposed missing 2.3 - 2.6 Trillions from Pentagon Fund** (CBS, September 10, 2001), triggering possibilities of more audit and accountabilities. Also the newly refurbished Navy Command Center (NCC) grew independent building worldwide command, control, and monitoring facilities parallel to National Security Agency (NSA). **9/11 destroyed NCC entirely along with the adjacent budgeting/auditing /personnel unit killing 125 people including** Lieutenant General Timothy Maude.

As a grand finale Bush administration infuriated the Christian Fundamentalists (Zion's 70+ million US Christian soldiers) by putting the final touches on a 'Middle East initiative', which included **recognition of a Palestinian State, endorsement of the Mitchell Plan, and position statements about Palestinian refugees and the status of Jerusalem.** This initiative was to be shared with the Saudi Ambassador to the United Nations on Sept. 13, 2001, with a formal presentation to the U.N. General Assembly by the then Secretary of State Colin Powell on

September 23, 2001. But the evangelists with influence in all aspect of US Government were entirely opposed to the two state solutions.

9/11 destructions and related propaganda of fear ensured more generous military funding and F-22 became part of United States Air Force (USAF) service beginning December 2005. Lockheed Martin Aeronautics[4] became the prime contractor and was responsible for the majority of the airframe, weapon systems and final assembly of the F-22. Program partner Boeing Integrated Defense Systems[5] provided the wings, aft fuselage, avionics integration, and all of the pilot and maintenance training systems. 9/11 also forced the Bush administration to take hands off approach towards the fate of Palestinian Statehood leaving helpless Palestinians at the mercy of powerful abusive Israeli military and intelligence forces. Finally 9/11 gave Vice President Cheney the authoritative power to reign USA and the World activating all arms of the dormant the shadow government.

"Despite repeated assertions by President Bush and his top advisers that their global campaign against terrorism will be a "new kind of war," the biggest recipients of the new weapons spending sparked by the September 11 attacks will be the usual suspects: big Defense contractors like Boeing, Raytheon, Lockheed Martin and Northrop Grumman. Once emergency anti-terror funding and supplemental appropriations to finance the war in Afghanistan are taken into account, this year's Pentagon budget could hit $375 billion, a $66 billion increase over last year"[6] – without a meaningful 9/11 congressional and/or public investigation.

"Most of this new funding will be used to bankroll long-standing pet projects of the military-industrial lobby, not to finance equipment or techniques designed for the fight against terrorism. As one Pentagon official told Defense News, much of the initial anti-terror funding 'will have nothing to do with retaliation in response to the Sept. 11 attacks. The funding will go to the [military departments'] wish lists for things we'll have several years from now."[6]

Within days following September 11 spectacular disasters, **Congress signed off**[6] on **a $40 billion package for reconstruction and anti-terrorism efforts**. Stock analyst Paul Nisbet predicted a $400 billion military budget was now within reach. Boeing vice chairman Harry Stonecipher told the Wall Street Journal that "*the purse is now open*," so the Pentagon will no longer have to make the "hard choices" among competing weapons projects that were present prior to September 11.

This Defense industry robbery exploiting ironic US calamities certainly reminds the world of the warning from Ex-President Eisenhower:

"In the councils of government, we must guard against the acquisition of unwarranted influence, whether sought or unsought, by the military-industrial complex. The potential for the disastrous rise of misplaced power exists and will persist."
Dwight D. Eisenhower,
Farewell Address to the Nation, January 17, 1961

References:

1. New American Century, PNAC,
   http://www.newamericancentury.org/RebuildingAmericasDefenses.pdf
2. Who is Steve Cambone, Armed Forces Journal,
   http://www.armedforcesjournal.com/2006/04/1813786/]
3. F-22 Raptor, http://en.wikipedia.org/wiki/F-22_Raptor
4. Lockheed Martin Aeronautics,
   http://en.wikipedia.org/wiki/Lockheed_Martin_Aeronautics
5. Boeing Integrated Defense Systems,
   http://en.wikipedia.org/wiki/Boeing_Integrated_Defense_Systems
6. William Hartung, Pentagon Spending Spree, Multinational Monitor Magazine, November 2001
   http://www.thirdworldtraveler.com/Corporate_Welfare/PentagonSpendingSpree.html

** **End Notes**: "Cheney and Rumsfeld worked through the 1980s and 1990s on emergency nuclear-response plans which allegedly suspended the American constitution and also Congress. Through these decades Rumsfeld was CEO of a major pharmaceutical firm, and in the later 1990s Cheney was CEO of Halliburton; but their private status did not deter them from continuing to exercise a supra-constitutional planning power conferred on them by Ronald Reagan.

Few Americans know that these rules, originally dealing with a nuclear attack on America, were extended by Reagan Executive Order 12656 to cover "any occurrence, including natural disaster, military attack, technological emergency, or other emergency, that seriously degrades or seriously threatens the national security of the United States." And few Americans realize that at least some of these rules, known technically as Continuity of Government or COG rules, were invoked before 10:00 AM on September 11, 2001." - **Professor Peter Dale Scott, "Road To 9/11".**

Bin Laden Guilty or Innocent?

If we believe in innocent till proven guilty, then we must consider evidence against Bin Laden which the Taliban wanted to have before handing over Bin Laden.

Although then CIA director claimed moments after the 2nd airliner crashed WTC south tower "its Bin Laden's finger prints all over" FBI till date has no evidence to connect Bin Laden to 9/11!

• **To date[1] - The FBI's *Most Wanted List* does not mention that Osama bin Laden is wanted for 9/11 because the FBI has "no hard evidence" connecting him with the attacks.**

FBI says, "No hard evidence connecting Bin Laden to 9/11"

"On June 5, 2006, the Muckraker Report contacted the FBI Headquarters, (202) 324-3000, to learn why Bin Laden's Most Wanted poster did not indicate that Usama was also wanted in connection with 9/11. The Muckraker Report spoke with Rex Tomb, Chief of Investigative Publicity for the FBI. When asked why there is no mention of 9/11 on Bin Laden's Most Wanted web page, Tomb said, "The reason why 9/11 is not mentioned on Usama Bin Laden's Most Wanted page is because the FBI has no hard evidence connecting Bin Laden to 9/11."
Surprised by the ease in which this FBI spokesman made such an astonishing statement, I asked, "How this was possible?" Tomb continued, "Bin Laden has not been formally charged in connection to 9/11." I asked, "How does that work?" Tomb continued, "The FBI gathers evidence. Once evidence is gathered, it is turned over to the Department of Justice. The Department of Justice then decides whether it has enough evidence to present to a federal grand jury. In the case of the 1998 United States Embassies being bombed, Bin Laden has been formally indicted and charged by a grand jury. He has not been formally indicted and charged in connection with 9/11 because the FBI has no hard evidence connected Bin Laden to 9/11." - Muckraker Report (06/06/06)

Here is an excerpt from an interview with Osama bin Laden that was published in a Karachi-based Pakistani daily newspaper, Ummat[2], on September 28, 2001 -

"I have already said that I am not involved in the 11 September attacks in the United States. As a Muslim, I try my best to avoid telling a lie. I had no knowledge of these attacks, nor do I consider the killing of innocent women, children and other humans as an appreciable act. Islam strictly forbids causing harm to innocent women, children and other people. Such a practice is forbidden even in the course of a battle. It is the United States, which is perpetrating every maltreatment on women, children and common people . . ."

The US State Department issued the annual report on terrorism in April 2001. However, as CNN described it, *"Unlike last year's report, bin Laden's al-Qaeda organization is mentioned, but the **2001 report does not contain a photograph of bin Laden** or a lengthy description of him and the group."* [CNN, 4/30/2001]

At the new Bush administration's first Deputy Secretary-level meeting on terrorism [Time, 8/4/2002] **Deputy Defense Secretary Paul Wolfowitz said the focus on al-Qaeda was wrong.** He stated, *"I just don't understand why we are beginning by talking about this one man bin Laden,"* and *"Who cares about a little terrorist in Afghanistan?"* [Clarke, 2004, pp. 30, 231; Newsweek, 3/22/2004]

In July 2001, shortly after a pivotal al-Qaeda warning given by the CIA to top officials [JULY 10, 2001 HistoryCommons.org], **Undersecretary of Defense for Intelligence Steve Cambone expressed doubts.** He spoke to CIA Director George Tenet, and, as Tenet later recalled, **"he asked if I had considered the possibility that al-Qaeda threats were just a grand deception, a clever ploy to tie up our resources and expend our energies on a phantom enemy that lacked both the power and the will to carry the battle to us."** Tenet claimed he replied, **"No, this is not a deception, and, no, I do not need a second opinion.... We are going to get hit. It's only a matter of time."** [TENET, 2007, PP. 154]

Thus it seems that then CIA Director George Tenet wanted the 'deception' to be 'the reality' on 9/11 advancing neoconian ideology. It would be obvious later on reading 'What is Al-Qaeda' that **Irrespective of the Origin it became covert wing of US/NATO/Israeli Intelligence using private mercenaries like Black Water!**

Reference:
1. Killtown, http://killtown.911review.org/oddities/2006.html#Osama_FBI#Osama_FBI
2. Ummat Interviews Usamah Bin-Ladin, 28 September 2001, Ummatt http://911review.com/articles/usamah/khilafah.html

Let us take a quiz on 9/11 (September 11, 2001)
From www.GlobalOutlook.Ca
9/11 Truth QUIZ –
*What You Need to Know About What Really
Happened on September 11, 2001*

1. *Did you know that* a third World Trade Center high-rise building also fell on September 11th? WTC Building 7 was a 47-storey, steel-framed skyscraper located a full block away from the Twin Towers and it was not even hit by any plane. Nonetheless, it fell at near free-fall speed straight down into its own footprint at 5:20 p.m. that afternoon.
YES NO

2. *Did you know that* the owner of Building 7 Larry Silverstein, said "We've had such a terrible loss of life that maybe the smartest thing to do is pull it [Building 7] and they made that decision – to pull – and then we watched the building collapse" and yet *The 9/11 Commission Report* never mentioned a thing about Building 7? [N.B. 'Pull' is an industry term for using controlled demolition.]
YES NO

3. *Did you know that* 'Lucky' Larry Silverstein was awarded 4.68 billion dollars in insurance claims for the Twin Towers which he had just leased six weeks before 9/11 from the Port Authority of New York who declined to spend the multi million dollars required to remove the asbestos and bring the Towers up to code required by law?
YES NO

4. *Did you know that* fire has never caused any steel-frame building to collapse in the history of architecture, except on 9/11 when 3 skyscrapers fell at near free-fall speeds despite the fact that there were 47 massive steel columns in the core of each of the Twin Towers and 25 in WTC7?
YES NO

5. *Did you know that* most of the WTC steel was quickly shipped overseas – before any independent investigation – and melted down? (This is unprecedented and contrary to federal crime scene laws.)
YES NO

6. *Did you know that* fighter jets routinely are scrambled the minute any airplane loses contact with the FAA or deviates from its flight path and this, on average, takes 20 minutes?
YES NO

9/11 Truth QUIZ (Cont.)

7. *Did you know that* in the nine months preceding 9/11 there were 67 jet fighter scrambles of wayward airplanes and that on average 100 intercepts occurred each year prior to 9/11?
YES NO

8. *Did you know that* the Secret Service broke established protocols by allowing President Bush to remain in a well-publicized classroom photo-op for at least 8 minutes after it was revealed to him that "America was under attack" when Andy Card informed him that the second plane had hit the second tower?
YES NO

9. *Did you know that* the SEC (Securities Exchange Commission) has never revealed the unidentified traders who made millions of dollars in profits by short-selling the stocks of American and United airlines that were impacted by the attacks?
YES NO

10. *Did you know that* there were countless warnings of "impending terrorist attacks" from at least 11 countries prior to 9/11 and that the threat level for such an attack was 'blinking red' according to George Tenet, Director of the CIA?
YES NO

11. *Did you know that* Attorney General John Ashcroft, San Francisco Mayor Willie Brown, author Salmon Rushdie and (according to *Newsweek*) a group of high-ranking generals at the Pentagon were warned not to fly on 9/11 but would not reveal who told them?
YES NO

12. *Did you know that* in September of 2000 a group known as The Project for A New American Century (PNAC), many of whom would become key officials in the Bush administration, wrote that their proposed massive military build-up would proceed slowly "absent some catastrophic and catalyzing event - like a new Pearl Harbour"?
YES NO

13. *Did you know that* at least 6 of the alleged 9/11 hijackers were reported to be still alive according to BBC and UK print media reports in the weeks following 9/11?
YES NO

9/11 Truth QUIZ (Cont.)

14. *Did you know that* the FBI has said that there is no evidence to link Osama bin Laden to 9/11 and that Osama is not wanted for the crime of 9/11 on the FBI's *Ten Most Wanted Fugitives* list? [See details in Issue # 12, p. 124 or at www.FBI.gov/]
YES NO

15. *Did you know that* Bruce Lawrence, the leading scholar of Osama bin Laden stated that the December 2001 confession tape, which the Bush White House flaunts as evidence, is fake?
YES NO

16. *Did you know that* Colin Powell promised a White Paper proving that Osama bin Laden and al Qaeda were responsible for 9/11 back in 2001 – but never produced that White Paper?
YES NO

17. *Did you know that* the Bush administration resisted the formation of the 9/11 Commission for 441 days? Or that similar investigations, such as those for Pearl Harbour, the JFK assassination and the space shuttle disasters, all started within one week?
YES NO

18. *Did you know that* "The Jersey Girls" – four courageous 9/11 widows – finally forced the 9/11 Commission into existence and presented many questions the Commission said they'd answer, 70% of which were ignored? And that under the leadership of Bush administration insider, Philip Zelikow, the final report failed to address any evidence which contradicted the official story?
YES NO

19. *Did you know that* no official agency (the FAA, FBI or the airlines) has ever released a list of the 9/11 passengers which includes the names of the hijackers, but within hours of the attacks, the FBI released a definitive list of the 19 so-called hijackers?
YES NO

20. *Did you know that* multiple air Defense drills (war games) were planned for (or were underway during) the morning of 9/11 and that these exercises left only a few pairs of fighter jets available to protect the entire North East Air Defense Sector of the United States leaving Washington and
NYC vulnerable to an attack?
YES NO

9/11 Truth QUIZ (Cont.)

21. *Did you know that* there was no visible airplane debris where Flight 93 supposedly crashed near Shanksville, PA – only a smoking hole in the ground, much like a bomb crater, with a pile of scrap metal dumped into it, but that there was debris from the aircraft found 8 miles away at New Baltimore? And that Shanksville Mayor Ernie Stull said three times in an interview with
Gerhard Wisnewski for a 2003 German documentary that there was "no airplane"?
YES NO

22. *Did you know that* office furniture burns at low temperatures of 600 to 800°F, and that jet fuel, an ordinary hydrocarbon has a maximum burning temperature of 1200°F, but that steel melts at 2750°F?
YES NO

23. *Did you know that* tests have shown that cellphone calls cannot be made at altitudes over 8,000 feet for any meaningful duration and, that more significantly, United Airlines Flight 93 was proven to be flying at 35,000 to 40,000 feet high when many of the supposed calls were made?
YES NO

24. *Did you know that* a bomb reportedly went off in the North Tower in the basement a few seconds before the first plane hit according to Willie Rodriguez, a janitor who became known as *the last man out* and was awarded a medal by President Bush for his bravery in rescuing dozens of people from the North Tower before it collapsed?
YES NO

25. *Did you know that* Hani Hanjour was known as an incompetent pilot to his trainers and yet he pulled off an unprecedented 270° – 330° turn at 500 – 530 mph, diving 7,000 ft. in 2.5 – 3 minutes, crashing Flight 77 into the least populated, most reinforced section of the Pentagon?
YES NO

26. *Did you know that* the mainstream media in the US is owned and controlled by six major corporate conglomerates (see p. 2.) and that there has been very limited and sporadic coverage of alternative views about 9/11? Any time they are raised, the MSM accuses the questioner of being a 'conspiracy theorist' or even a 'traitor' (as you will see in the following set of 46 articles).
YES NO

TOTAL SCORE (Give yourself one mark for each YES.) =
9/11 Truth QUIZ (Cont.)

How did you score?
1 - 6 You may be suffering from corporate controlled mainstream media brainwashing.
7 - 12 Your brainwashing is wearing off.
13 - 18 You're on your way to becoming a 9/11 Truther. Keep digging.
19 - 24 You should be leading the 9/11 Truth movement in your community and helping spread the word about what really happened on 9/11.
25 - 26 You might consider running for President of the United States and restore the justice, freedom and democracy for which the Republic stands.

End Note[1]:
British businessman **Cecil Rhodes** advocated the British Empire **re-annexing** the United States of America and reforming itself into an "Imperial Federation" to bring about a hyperpower and lasting world peace. In his first will, of 1877, written at the age of 23, he expressed his wish to <u>fund a secret society</u> (known as the **Society of the Elect**) that would advance this goal:

"To and for the establishment, promotion and development of a Secret Society, the true aim and object whereof shall be for the extension of British rule throughout the world, the perfecting of a system of emigration from the United Kingdom, and of colonisation by British subjects of all lands where the means of livelihood are attainable by energy, labour and enterprise, and especially the occupation by British settlers of the entire Continent of Africa, the Holy Land, the Valley of the Euphrates, the Islands of Cyprus and Candia, the whole of South America, the Islands of the Pacific not heretofore possessed by Great Britain, the whole of the Malay Archipelago, the seaboard of China and Japan, the ultimate recovery of the United States of America as an integral part of the British Empire, the inauguration of a system of Colonial representation in the Imperial Parliament which may tend to weld together the disjointed members of the Empire and, finally, the foundation of so great a Power as to render wars impossible, and promote the best interests of humanity."

Rhodes Scholarship was introduced in 1902 to achieve that goal.

1. http://en.wikipedia.org/wiki/New_World_Order_(conspiracy_theory)

Now let us dive into

Simple Proof

to establish that we have a case

[Without 9/11 Open Public Investigation American Government Is Corrupt and Criminal Regime Making All Talk About World Peace, Security, and Multi-Faith Moot Points. Kolki]

Simple Proof Why UN Must Help 'The Americans' Establish 9/11 Truth with Open Public Investigation Immediately To End Global 'War on Terror'!
Or
Simple Proof How American Media and Politicians Could Have Impeached Bush Administration Right After 9/11 Preventing Global 'War of Terror'!
Or
Simple Proof Why Blaming Islam For 9/11 Tragedy Without Open Public Investigation Is the Worst Racist Hate Crime for Genocide in Human History!

[NORAD: North American Air Defense; NEADS: North Eastern Air Defence; FAA: Federal Aviation Authority; NMCC: National Military Command Center; NRO-National Reconnaissance Office; NSA: National Security Agency; WTC-World Trade Center; ISI: Inter-Services Intelligence; PEOC: President's Emergency Operations Center; NCC: Navy Command Center; UN: United Nations; CFR: Council On Foreign Relations]

[Abstract: On February 14, 2005, a car bomb explosion killed former Lebanese Prime Minister Rafik Hariri and several other people in his convoy. Following the incident USA/NATO along with the European Union called for an inquiry into the matter resulting in immediate UN Security Council Resolution 1595 for setting up an international commission of investigation. Ironically the same US Administration and Government opposed and/or derailed 9/11 public investigation to investigate killings of approximately 3000 citizens including firefighters, US military personnel and destruction of the World Trade Center Complex and part of the Pentagon housing the state-of-the-art Navy Command Center (NCC). To this date, most of the 9/11 anomalies contradict the faith based official speculative reasoning of the massively planned precisely enacted terrorism inside USA evading super power intelligence, evasive FBI, counter terrorism protective measures, pre-emptive media, aggressive military, and vigilant NORAD. This well researched paper would expose factually that US military, CIA, FBI, President, Vice President, FAA, NORAD and Counter Terrorism, even key Senate and Congressional members were directly responsible for the success of 9/11 attack on WTC and Pentagon inflicting related deaths, destruction and sufferings for world citizens. To respect rule-of-law and proof-of-conviction, better late than never, like Hariri Tribunal, UN and European Union must help 'The Americans' establish 9/11 Truth once for all with open public investigation Immediately to diagnose the very reason for the expensive and devastating ongoing global 'War on Terror'!]

Ever wondered as an American or world citizen why the deified protectors of America like **Superman**, **Batman**, and **Spiderman** couldn't save New York City and Pentagon on 9/11/2001? Then you should have also wondered where they were hiding during the Anthrax attack on Democratic senators and media critical to the legitimacy of the Bush Presidency stopping Florida State vote counts! Well, they were fooled like other ordinary citizens because they couldn't recognise evil within trusted law enforcements, agents, military, and government(s)! That is why all efforts of congressional and public inquiry were unitedly evaded, blocked, and finally disinformed citizens through a much delayed poorly funded *($3 Million -> $15 Million; compared to $80 Million spent for investigating President Clinton's White Water deal and personal sex life)* face saving biased commission which carefully ignored honest testimonials, trivial evidences, and conveniently adjusted timelines to support the Government Conspiracy Theory blaming alleged dead hijackers with box cutters for the massively well planned, well financed, well coordinated, well guarded precision destruction (3000+ victims) on US soil.

Let us hear **Sibel Edmonds**, former FBI translator, **"If they were to do real investigations we would see several significant high level criminal prosecutions in this country. And that is something that they are not going to let out. And, believe me; they will do everything to cover this up."**
[http://www.kolki.com/peace/FBI-Translator-Sibel-Edmonds-Interview.htm]

Let us also hear from Senator John McCain (R-Arizona) who sponsored legislation creating the 9/11 commission: **"But getting White House cooperation will not be easy, The Bush administration slow-walked and stonewalled the congressional inquiry. I don't see how you can have a thorough investigation without talking to the people who were in charge throughout the time period prior to 9/11"** [Craig Cox, Utne.com].

A thorough review of how Government procedures normally worked in USA including Federal Aviation Authority, Military, CIA, FBI, NSA, Counter Terrorism and NORAD (Joint North American Air Defense), would make it obvious that neither GOD (?) could do 9/11 nor the Russian Army. Bin Laden might have thought about it like many victims of US Foreign Policy Blunders around the world but simply didn't have the means, expertise, massive manpower to plan and accomplish something like 9/11 in broad day light, especially on 9/11/2001 when military and NORAD were at the highest state of alert and readiness. Thus the official version is a conspiracy against Bin Laden and Islam for convenience of war on terror to kill ancient people and destroy their land for Evangelical Crusades, private military & oil industry gains, and NATO expansion!

Let us begin this article with a quote from NEOCONS' favourite Winston Churchill's dictum that, "In wartime, truth is so precious that she should always be attended by a bodyguard of lies." NEOCONS' dossier 'Project of the New American Century (PNAC)' was all about starting wars for the century concocting 'New Pearl Harbour'! It was no wonder that Bush Administration lied 935 times before illegal invasion of Iraq as well. Irish statesman John Philpot Curran once said, "*The condition upon which God hath given liberty to man is eternal vigilance*".

Here is a short list of outstanding questions about 9/11 to remind the world why citizens must be vigilant:
It has been more than seven years since 9/11/2001 and still most of the basic questions about the success of that spectacular event remained unanswered: [Ref: 9-11 Commission Report, various 9-11 Timelines, http://patriotsquestion911.com/, 9/11 Research http://911research.wtc7.net/index.html, History of Commons and many truth related sites, articles as well as media reports including Wikipedia]

    • **Why NORAD hijacking protocol was changed before 9/11 especially sending the new responsible coordinator Mike Canavan to Puerto Rico without back up?** [http://www.kolki.com/peace/NORAD-Hijacking-Protocol.htm]

The **most important Government Action** which led to the success of the 9/11 destruction inside USA was the change in NORAD hijacking protocol before 9/11:
Per 1st Air Force's own book about 9/11, the "sector commander [at NEADS] would have authority to scramble the airplanes.").

But, Protocols in place on 9/11 stated that if the FAA needed the military to go after an airplane, "**the escort service will be requested by the FAA hijack coordinator by direct contact with the National Military Command Center (NMCC).**" But the FAA hijack coordinator, Mike Canavan, was silent in Puerto Rico without backup.
[Smoking Gun]

    • **Why Vice President Dick Cheney would order Flight 77 to hit Pentagon** as per then Transportation Secretary Norman Mineta's testimony: "during the time that the airplane was coming into the Pentagon, there was a young man who would come in and said to the

Vice President, 'the plane is 50 miles out, the plane is 30 miles out.' And when it got to 'the plane is 10 miles out," the young man also said to the Vice President, 'Do the orders still stand?' And the Vice President...said, 'Of course the orders still stand. Have you heard anything to the contrary?"? [Smoking Gun]

Standard order was to shoot down any non-military aircraft entering the "Prohibited" airspace over Washington, in which "Civilian flying is prohibited at all times" ("Pilots Notified of Restricted Airspace; Violators Face Military Action," FAA Press Release, September 28, 2001).

(Note. Yet no military action was taken to evacuate and save Pentagon despite Defense Secretary Donald Rumsfeld's conviction to Representative Christopher Cox (R) after watching the second plane (UA175) hit WTC south tower, "Believe me, this isn't over yet. There's going to be another attack, and it could be us!")

• Why US military and NORAD preponed scheduled yearly Military Exercises (Practice Armageddon, Global Guardian, Vigilant Warrior, Amalgam Warrior and Vigilant Guardian – running war games including airliner crashing) from October 22-31, 2001, to the week of September 11, 2001? [Smoking Gun]

• How AA 77 Boeing 757 Passenger Jet Hit Pentagon Surrounded By Absolute Military Airspace, When E-4B National Airborne Operations Center Was Flying Over Equipped With Most Sophisticated Military Options Ready For Actions As The Global Guardian?
Shortly before Flight AA 77 hit Pentagon around 9:37 a.m. an E-4B National Airborne Operations Center (NAOC) took off from an unspecified airfield outside of Washington, DC. E-4Bs are militarized versions of Boeing 747. The E-4B launched from outside Washington was supposed to be using and testing its sophisticated technology and communications equipment.
[OMAHA WORLD-HERALD, 2/27/2002; VERTON, 2003, PP. 143-144]

[Note. This E-4B (NAOC) would have been directing PEOC and NMCC coordination and, by 9:37 a.m., Military, FAA, NORAD, PEOC, NMCC and Secret Service would have been in full gear to intercept and/or destroy any passenger jet flying over military airspace especially without active transponder. This is nothing but cold blooded treason to destroy NCC and Pentagon accountabilities guiding AA 77 hit target precisely!]

• **Why Vice President Dick Cheney warned President Bush that hijackers had access to the transponder of Air Force One suggesting hijackers were capable of remote hijacking even Air Force One?**

• **Why then Defense Secretary Donald Rumsfeld would say in Iraq "**...the people who attacked the United States in New York, **shot down** the plane over Pennsylvania and attacked the Pentagon...."?

• Why 9/11 Commission Report would stress Flight 93 crashed when Donald Rumsfeld, President and Vice President stated clearly that it was shot down?

"Well, I discussed it with the president. Are we prepared to order our aircraft to shoot down these airliners that have been hijacked? He said yes... I--it was my advice. It was his decision."(**Vice President Dick Cheney**, September 11, 2001, source CBS News Archives)

"That's a sobering moment, to order your own combat aircraft to shoot down your own civilian aircraft. But it was an easy decision to make, given the--given the fact that we had learned that a commercial aircraft was being used as a weapon. I say easy decision. It was--I didn't hesitate; let me put it to you that way. I knew what had to be done."(**President George W. Bush**, September 11, 2001, source CBS News Archives)

• **How and why Cessna trained box cutter armed hijackers would hit Pentagon precisely destroying the newly refurbished Navy Command Center (NCC) capable of intelligence gathering similar to NSA, the Army Budget Office having books of $2.3 trillion missing from Pentagon and US Army's Deputy Chief of Staff for Personnel?**
[http://911research.wtc7.net/talks/noplane/distraction.html]

• **Why FBI higher ups tried so desperately before 9/11 to stop fellow FBI Agents from searching suspected Al-Qaeda Zakarias Moussaoui's laptop, yet charged him for masterminding 9/11 afterwards?** (**Note.** A simple pre 9/11 search would have exposed the covert spectacular implementation planed by people from inside!) [Smoking Gun]

Dave Frasca of the FBI's Radical Fundamentalist Unit (RFU) denied a request from the Minneapolis FBI field office to seek a criminal warrant to search the belongings of Zacarias Moussaoui, who was arrested on August 15 as part of an intelligence investigation. [US District Court FOR THE EASTERN DISTRICT OF VIRGINIA, ALEXANDRIA DIVISION, 3/9/2006]. A criminal warrant to search Moussaoui's belongings would be granted only after the 9/11 attacks (SEPTEMBER 11, 2001).

• **Why alleged mastermind Zakarias Moussaoui's diary had US private Mercenary company Blackwater's telephone number?**
[http://www.kolki.com/peace/Zacaria-Moussaui.doc]

• **Why Pakistan's ISI Director Lt. Gen. Mahmood Ahmed who allegedly transferred 100,000+ to alleged 9/11 mastermind Atta's Florida Account was entertained by the higher ups in Bush Administration, Pentagon, and Key congressional members including Christopher Cox and Joe Biden, before, on, and after 9/11?**
[Smoking Gun]

• **Why Osama bin Laden Periodically Underwent Dialysis with Approval of the ISI (CIA & MI6's Main Link to Al-Qaeda)? Has Bin Laden Been in Secret US Custody Since 9/11?**
Indian sources claimed, "Bin Laden, who suffers from renal deficiency, has been periodically undergoing dialysis in a Peshawar military hospital with the knowledge and approval of the ISI, if not of Pakistani President Musharraf himself." [SAPRA (NEW DELHI), 7/2/2001]
Jane's Intelligence Digest later reported the story adding, "None of these details will be unfamiliar to US intelligence operatives who have been compiling extensive reports on these alleged activities."
[JANE'S INTELLIGENCE DIGEST, 9/20/2001]
CBS later reported bin Laden had emergency medical care in Pakistan the day before 9/11. [CBS NEWS, 1/28/2002]
[Notes: Naturally an emergency patient would be under ISI-CIA-MI6 custody explaining US Military indifference to hunt bin Laden!]

• **Why on August 31, 2001, Transportation Department Held Plane Hijacking Exercise similar to 9/11 including cell phone calls?**
According to Ellen Engleman, the administrator of the DOT's Research and Special Programs Administration, "This was actually much more than a tabletop exercise, during that exercise, part of the scenario, interestingly

enough, involved a potentially hijacked plane and someone calling on a cell phone, among other aspects of the scenario that were very strange when 12 days later, as you know, we had the actual event [of 9/11]."
[MINETA TRANSPORTATION INSTITUTE, 10/30/2001, PP. 108]
[Note. Rehearsals like this as well in Pentagon directly contradicted then Secretary of State Condoleezza Rice's statement that no one could ever envision planes would be used as missiles?]

• **Why FAA would set up communication channel with the White House just prior to Flight 11 hit WTC North Tower letting President Bush view the first plane crash videoed by French crewmen blocks away from WTC?**

Shortly before the first WTC plane crash, the FAA opened a telephone line with the Secret Service to keep the White House informed of all events. [*Sources:* Richard ("Dick") Cheney] A few days later, Vice President Cheney stated, "The Secret Service had an arrangement with the FAA. They had open lines after the World Trade Center was ..." (He stopped himself before finishing the sentence.) [MSNBC, 9/16/01]

Coincidentally two (2) French documentary filmmakers were filming a documentary on New York City firefighters about ten blocks from the WTC ended up recording the 9/11 Saga right from the first WTC crash. They continued shooting footage non-stop for many hours, and their footage was first shown that evening on CNN. [New York Times, 1/12/02] President Bush later claimed that he saw the first attack live on television. [Wall Street Journal, 3/22/04]
[Notes. The president can only see it on CCTV on Limo via FAA Channel!]

• **Why FAA rescinded rule allowing guns in cockpits just two months before the 9/11 disaster?** (Is it so that the alleged Hijackers with box cutters theory be viable?) [http://911research.wtc7.net/sept11/disarm.html]
For 40 years prior to 9/11/01, a Federal Aviation Administration (FAA) rule had allowed commercial airlines pilots to carry firearms in the cockpit. Just two months before 9/11/01, the FAA rescinded the rule.

• **Why all 9/11 flights were delayed approximately 14-40 minutes from scheduled take offs? Was it for the convenience of remote hijacking** strategy? [http://www.kolki.com/peace/9-11-Flights-Delayed.htm]

• **Who Sent False Bomb Threats To 9/11 Related Air Traffic Controllers (ATCs) Derailing Focuses On The Hijacked Airliners And Ensuring SOS Transmissions From Ill-fated Pilots Remain Unattended?**
[James Hillston, "From Takeoff to Takeover: Putting It All Together," *Pittsburgh Post-Gazette*, 28 October 2001]
CNN reported that, while Flight 11 was heading toward the World Trade Center, "[S]ources say there were bomb threats called in to air traffic control centers adding to the chaos." One center receiving such threats was the FAA's Boston Center, which handled air traffic over New England and monitored flights 11 and 175. Cleveland Center, which would monitor Flight 93, receives similar threats. According to Newsweek, "Officials suspect that the bomb threats were intended to add to the chaos, distracting controllers from tracking the hijacked planes." [NEWSWEEK, 9/22/2001; CNN, 9/30/2001]
[**Notes.** The remote High-Tech flight terminators covered themselves from all possibilities of losing remote control which could have facilitated control back to pilots, even momentarily, to notify ATCs that there were no physical hijackers on board and the planes were being flown as drones disabling transponders and cockpit microphones!]

• **Why President Bush's Longboat Key Resort had tight overnight security on September 10, 2001, including Surface to Air missiles, but Pentagon couldn't fire the anti-aircraft missile to stop Flight 77 from crashing!**

• Why Securacom, a Kuwait-American owned foreign company, where Marvin P. Bush, the ex-president's younger brother, was a principal, provided security for the World Trade Center, United Airlines, and Dulles International Airport on 9/11?
[http://www.commondreams.org/views03/0204-06.htm]

• **If Israel could warn its Odigo Headquarter (two blocks from WTC) employees at 6:45am on 9/11 then why CIA, FBI, Counter Terrorism and Key Congressional members couldn't warn WTC and Pentagon Employees as well as fellow Americans overall?**
At 6:00 a.m. Israeli Company Odigo, one of the world's largest instant messaging companies, received warnings of imminent attack in New York City at its headquarters in New York two blocks from WTC. ""Instant Messages To

Israel Warned Of WTC Attack," *Washington Post*, 27 September 2001. [http://www.historycommons.org/entity.jsp?entity=odigo_inc.]

• Why President Bush would think that CIA briefings before 9/11 warning about upcoming attack were '**covering ones Ass**'?
[Notes. Was it because he knew that those were false flags for future cover ups?]

A CIA briefer went to Bush's Crawford ranch to read to the president a briefing called, "**Bin Laden Determined to Strike in US**" (2 redacted pages out of 11 reported). After the briefing, Bush told the CIA man, "**All right. You've covered your ass, now.**" Bush then went fishing.

• **Why CIA didn't go public with its absolute warning of the upcoming Spectacular event briefed only to key administration and congressional members?**

• **Why all CIA helicopters and resources were sent to Monterey, California before 9/11 despite CIA's absolute knowledge and urgent briefings of the upcoming attack?**

• **Why former Counter Terrorism Czar Richard Clarke didn't go public with the eminent massive spectacular threat briefed during CIA briefings?**

• **Why key Congressional and Senate leaders didn't go public with the threat mentioned during the pre-9/11 CIA briefings?**

• **Why New York/ New Jersey Port Authority sold public property WTC to Silverstein Properties and West Field America just 6-weeks prior to 9/11** [Notes. Deal brokered by former Bilderberg Chairman and current Steering Committee member David Rockefeller who is also the Chairman of CFR and Trilateral Commission.**)?**
Journalist Joseph Kraft, a former member of both the CFR and the Trilateral Commission, said the Council "comes close to being an organ of what C. Wright Mills has called the Power Elite – a group of men, similar in interest and outlook, shaping events from invulnerable positions behind the scenes."[WikiCFR]

• **How the 47-storied WTC7 was wired for controlled demolition** (5:20 p.m.) **within less than 7 hours** since the claimed free fall (in ten seconds) of WTC Towers (South Tower at 9:58:59 a.m. and North Tower at 10:28 a.m.)? [Smoking Gun]

• **Why BBC would broadcast World Trade Building 7 collapsed at 4:57pm EST repeating it at 5pm on 9/11 when the building actually collapsed at 5:20pm?** (Was BBC following script for the event as well?)

• **Why none of the hijacker's name appeared on the airlines passenger lists?** (A photo ID check showing name on the ticket was always a norm)
[The original airliners passenger and crew lists from all 4 flights of 9/11 added to 266 people on board. Yet when one adds up the 4 official death manifest lists published on CNN.com, there are only 229 names. Somehow 37 people are missing including all 19 alleged hijackers. There is not even a single Arabic name there]

• **Who jammed Air Force One and Secretary of State Collin Powell's phone lines during the 9/11 Saga**, the worst crisis inside USA?
The then Secretary of State Colin Powell in Lima, Peru, abruptly ended his breakfast with the Peruvian president after getting word of the second strike on the trade center (WTC) and made plans to return to Washington. ... He had a seven-hour flight, with poor phone connections, ahead of him. Ex-President Bush, the Commander-in-Chief, also complained about poor connection on Air Force One. Communications with Washington were so poor that President Bush told 9-11 commission was "deeply dissatisfied" with the technical problems, at one point resorted to using a cell phone. [9-11 Timeline; 9-11 Commission]
[Notes. Who were jamming these important secured phone lines during spectacular much anticipated national emergency; Alleged dead hijackers armed with box-cutters or high-tech pre-emptive military?]

• **Why military cargo C-130 was sent to check on hijacked airliners UA 93 and AA 77 instead of scrambling fighter jets per routine NORAD procedure?**

• **Why President Bush didn't act as the Commander-in-Chief right**

from the beginning of the event? (**Notes.** He asked Vice President Cheney what he should do! Was it because Richard B. was in charge of the Shadow Government in place already?)

Intelligence expert James Bamford describes Bush's reaction: "Immediately [after Card speaks to Bush] an expression of befuddlement passe[s] across the President's face. Then, having just been told that the country was under attack, the Commander in Chief appear[s] uninterested in further details. He never ask[s] if there had been any additional threats, where the attacks were coming from, how to best protect the country from further attacks.... Instead, in the middle of a modern-day Pearl Harbour, he simply turn[s] back to the matter at hand: the day's photo op." [Body of Secrets, James Bamford, 4/02 edition, p. 633] Bush continues listening to the goat story. Then, in an event noticeable in its absence, as one newspaper put it, "For some reason, Secret Service agents [do] not bustle him away." [Globe and Mail, 9/12/01]

• **Why none of the crew could inform ground control 'I have been hijacked'?**

"In the event of a hijacking, all airline pilots are trained to key an emergency four-digit code into their plane's transponder. This would surreptitiously alert air traffic controllers, causing the letters 'HJCK' to appear on their screens." [CNN, 9/13/2001; NEWSDAY, 9/13/2001; NEWS (PORTUGAL), 8/3/2002; 9/11 COMMISSION, 7/24/2004, PP.17-18] "The action, which pilots should take the moment a hijack situation is known, only takes seconds to perform." [CNN, 9/12/2001; CHRISTIAN SCIENCE MONITOR, 9/12/2001;] "Yet during the hijackings of flights 11, 175, 77, and 93, none of the pilots do this." [CNN, 9/11/2001] [Smoking Gun] [**Notes.** This only happens when planes are remotely controlled locking on the transponder - be it Boeing or Global Hawk drone!]

• **Who keyed on Flight 175's cockpit microphone before departing from Boston Logan Airport?**

At 8:41 a.m. the FAA's New York Center requested information about Flight 11 over the radio. Flight 175 responded: *"[...]ah we heard a suspicious transmission on our departure out of Bostan ah with someone ah, ah sound like someone sound like someone keyed the mike and said ah 'everyone ah stay in your seats'"*[2]

[Notes. This can only be explained as remote hijacking testing to ensure Flight 175 could be taken over later! Since Cockpit microphones were disabled in all hijacking cases along with the transponders on 9/11 resulting in Pilot's silence, all hijacking related messages from unknown sources to selected ATCs and/or Flight 175 couldn't come from the cockpit(s); thus they were nothing but acting per New Pearl Harbour script faking physical hijacking from secret location(s)!]

• **Since the alleged hijackers were mostly from Saudi Arabia why US didn't threat and attack Saudi Arabia?**

• **Since money was transferred to alleged mastermind's Florida account from Pakistan's intelligence boss why US didn't warn and attack Pakistan instead of Afghanistan?**

• **Why FBI higher ups ordered agents to prepare for the disaster and not stop it from happening?** Acting FBI Director Thomas Pickard held a periodic conference call with the heads of all FBI field offices. This was to bring to light of all the increased threat reporting. *However, **he did not task the field offices to look into whether any plots were being considered within the US; nor did he tell them to take any action to disrupt any such plots**.* [9/11 COMMISSION, 7/24/2004, PP. 259]

• **Why both President Bush and Vice President Cheney would vehemently oppose judicial, congressional, and public inquiry regarding pre-9/11 CIA briefings and possible pre-knowledge inside Administration, Pentagon, CIA, FBI, FAA, and NSA?**
'President Bush personally asked Senate Majority Leader Tom Daschle Tuesday to limit the congressional investigation into the events of September 11, congressional and White House sources told CNN. (John Karl and John King, 1/29/02)'.
"The vice president expressed the concern that a review of what happened on September 11 would take resources and personnel away from the effort in the war on terrorism," Daschle told reporters.
(Notes. **Coincidentally Anthrax was sent to Tom Daschle afterwards!**)

• **Who sent special US military grade Anthrax to Senators connected with Judiciary Committee and Media critical to Bush Presidency?**

[http://www.kolki.com/peace/Anthrax-Proof-UN.htm]

• **Who were short selling stocks related to all 9/11 targets, airliners, related corporations and insurances with definite pre-knowledge?** [Notes. Since computer keeps records as well as audit log of each stock related transaction and knows details of each transaction executor, it would have been a matter of days to expose the identities of all the sources]

People with foreknowledge of the 9/11 attacks short sold reinsurance company stocks that were insuring either or both the airplanes and the buildings involved in the attacks. [AGENCE FRANCE-PRESSE, 9/17/2001] The Securities and Exchange Commission (SEC) later announced that they were investigating the trading of shares of 38 companies in the days just before 9/11. [ASSOCIATED PRESS, 10/2/2001; SAN FRANCISCO CHRONICLE, 10/3/2001] There was a sharp increase in the short selling of American and United Airlines stocks on the New York Stock Exchange prior to 9/11. [REUTERS, 9/20/2001; SAN FRANCISCO CHRONICLE, 9/22/2001]

• **Why <u>Medics Were Trained in May 2001 For Airplane Boeing 757 Hitting Exactly The West Side of Pentagon</u>?**
The Army's DiLorenzo Tricare Health Clinic (DTHC) and the Air Force
Flight Medicine Clinic, both housed within the Pentagon, held a tabletop exercise along with Arlington County Emergency Medical Services. The **scenario practiced for was of an airplane crashing into the Pentagon's west side—the same side as was impacted in the attack on 9/11. [<u>US DEPARTMENT OF HEALTH AND HUMAN SERVICES, 7/2002, PP. B17; GOLDBERG ET AL., 2007, PP. 23 AND 107</u>] According to US Medicine newspaper, the plane in the scenario was a hijacked Boeing 757. [<u>US MEDICINE, 1/2002</u>] Flight 77, that targeted the Pentagon on 9/11, was a 757. [<u>NEW YORK TIMES, 9/13/2001</u>]**

• **Why CIA destroyed Al-Qaeda harsh interrogation video after hiding them from the 9/11 commission?**
George Tenet was CIA chief when the tapes were made, and Porter Goss headed the agency when the tapes were destroyed. Destruction of evidence is a felony in a civil society! Both of them had meetings with then **ISI Director Lt. Gen. Mahmood Ahmed (the alleged fund transferer to alleged Atta's Florida account)** before, on and after

9/11.
Thus without 9/11 investigations some high level criminals enjoying public life as celebrities with legal immunity!
[http://www.consortiumnews.com/2009/030209a.html]

• **Why US military destroyed Able/Danger database that was tracking alleged Al-Qaeda members, including alleged Atta, inside USA since 1999.** Able Danger was an 18-month highly classified operation tasked, according to Army reserve Lieutenant-Colonel Anthony Shaffer, with "developing targeting information for al-Qaeda on a global scale", and used data-mining techniques to look for "patterns, associations, and linkages". He said that he himself had first encountered the names of the four alleged hijackers in mid-2000.

It will be obvious as we step through this article that *9/11 wasn't failure of intelligence or administration; it was well choreographed successful military coup coordinating like minded high level officials* and their network while instantly blaming Bin Laden without any open public investigation and proof-of-conviction to start long intended wars against Afghanistan and Iraq for oil and NATO/Israeli supremacy! That is the only reason why both President and Vice President vehemently preached against congressional as well as public investigation to identify the cause of 9/11 disaster even blocking pre 9/11 CIA briefings that particularly and specifically described the upcoming event.

> • 'President Bush personally asked Senate Majority Leader Tom Daschle Tuesday to limit the congressional investigation into the events of September 11, congressional and White House sources told CNN. (John Karl and John King, 1/29/02)'

> • "The vice president expressed the concern that a review of what happened on September 11 would take resources and personnel away from the effort in the war on terrorism," Daschle told reporters.

Just imagine that a cancer patient is not being diagnosed because doctors believe that the cancer might spread further if the case is investigated! Also imagine a suspected serial killer is not being interrogated/tried because the killer would be more violent inflicting more casualties! It is more than seven years and US as well as world citizens have no idea how the mass killers successfully planned and implemented the 9/11 type massive destruction in broad day light inactivating or incapacitating all normal procedures and accountabilities! Yet Iraq and Afghanistan have been invaded killing and displacing millions, insulting United Nations, and bypassing rule-of-law and proof of convictions while terrorizing the world with rumours and unilateral actions by US/NATO/Israeli military administrations.

That is why it is the most important and urgent world issue to open 9/11 public investigation immediately supervised by a neutral international body like UN coordinating with the International Court!

Let us review history of private US Defense industry, military ambition, and NECONS/Evangelic suggested methodology for world supremacy:

"In the councils of government, we must guard against the acquisition of unwarranted influence, whether sought or unsought, by the military-industrial complex. The potential for the disastrous rise of misplaced power exists and will persist."
Dwight D. Eisenhower,
Farewell Address to the Nation, January 17, 1961

On March 13, 1962, a top secret document outlining the key components of Operation Northwoods was presented by the then American Joint Chiefs of Staff, Army Gen. Lyman L. Lemnitzer, to the Secretary of Defense Robert McNamara with suggestions including:
- Staging the assassinations of Cubans living in the United States,
- Developing a fake "Communist Cuban terror campaign in the Miami and other cities of Florida, as well as Washington DC,"
- Sinking a boatload of Cuban refugees (real or simulated),"
- Faking **remote controlled** Cuban air force attack on a civilian jetliner, and
- Concocting a "**Remember the Maine**" incident by blowing up a U.S. ship in Cuban waters and then blaming the incident as Cuban sabotage.

Now let us review NECONS document for Rebuilding America's Defense (Page 51) as part of the 'Project For the New American Century (PNAC)',

"Creating Tomorrow's Dominant Force - the process of transformation, even if it brings revolutionary change, is likely to be a long one, absent some catastrophic and catalyzing event like a New Pearl Harbour".

Signatories -

[Donald Rumsfeld   Vin Weber   George Weigel   Paul Wolfowitz   Elliott Abrams   Gary Bauer   William J. Bennett   Jeb Bush Dick Cheney   Eliot A. Cohen   Midge Decter   Paula Dobriansky   Steve Forbes Aaron Friedberg   Francis Fukuyama   Frank Gaffney   Fred C. Ikle Donald Kagan   Zalmay Khalilzad   I. Lewis Libby   Norman Podhoretz   Dan Quayle   Peter W. Rodman   Stephen P. Rosen   Henry S. Rowen]

Thus, 9/11 disaster (spectacular as predicted by then Counter Terrorism Czar Richard Clarke) in US soil was a requirement for re-establishing American Military Supremacy throughout the world in peace time, as viewed by this group of people and their network.

Now let us hear Excerpt from then Secretary of Defense Donald Rumsfeld (who also predicted New Pearl Harbour during his acceptance speech in January, 2001) in CNN's 'Lary King Live' regarding his 9/11 morning meeting with a congressional delegation including Deputy Defense Secretary Paul Wolfowitz, and Representative Christopher Cox (R) -

"I had said at an 8:00 o'clock breakfast that sometime in the next two, four, six, eight, ten, twelve months there would be an event that would occur in the world that would be sufficiently shocking that it would remind people again how important it is to have a strong healthy Defense department that contributes to -- That underpins peace and stability in our world".

Also

The same Secretary of Defense would predict moments before Flight 77 hit Pentagon to Christopher Cox, the defence policy committee chairman of the House of Representatives who was watching TV coverage of WTC, **"Believe me, this isn't over yet. There's going to be another attack, and it could be us."** [Telegraph, 12/16/01]

Thus, many actions and events revealed during 9/11 commission's interrogations including emergency drills prior to and on 9/11 by key Government, Administration, Military, Intelligence, Law Enforcement, Media and influential powerful private citizens somehow lead to impressions that many of them were following the well choreographed script for the success of much needed 9/11 disaster for stronger private allied (NATO) power in peace time.

Thus without 9/11 investigation we may have been being ruled by mass murderers who committed treasons as politicians campaign for 'tough on crime' to put more ordinary felons and resentors in private prison cells!

We will now dive into simple proof how easily US administration, military, intelligence, federal agencies, and law enforcement could have stopped 9/11, but they didn't rather watched the military success of New Pearl Harbour for invading Afghanistan and Iraq while enhancing NATO/Israeli security and evangelical monarchist supremacy around the world.

But first we must address the reasons for the unprecedented silence from the main stream media, rather betrayal to help covering up the worst State-sponsored War Crime in human history insulting and frustrating law abiding good honest citizens of America and around the world:

The most puzzling question to world citizens must have been why main stream media had been silent about obvious 9/11 anomalies yet vocal against the truth seekers! Here is the answer:

> • Let us hear from the American God Father (Ex-Chairman & current steering committee member of secretive private world power Bilderberg as well as Chairman of the secretive Trilateral commission) David Rockefeller:
> "We are grateful to the Washington Post, the New York Times, Time Magazine and other great publications whose directors have attended our meetings and respected their promises of discretion for almost forty years."
> Speaking at the June, 1991 Bilderberger meeting in Baden, Germany (a meeting also attended by then-Governor Bill Clinton and Dan Quayle).

- Operation MOCKINGBIRD — in late 40s the CIA began recruiting American news organizations and journalists to become spies and disseminators of propaganda. The effort was headed by Frank Wisner, Allan Dulles, Richard Helms and Philip Graham. Graham had been publisher of *The Washington Post*, which became a major CIA player. Eventually, the CIA's media assets would include ABC, NBC, CBS, *Time, Newsweek*, Associated Press, United Press International, Reuters, Hearst Newspapers, Scripps-Howard, Copley News Service and more. By the CIA's own admission, at least 25 organizations and 400 journalists became CIA assets [Ref: A Timeline of CIA Atrocities by Steve Kangas]. (Now extrapolate the scenario in 2001 after 50 years)

- In an October 1977 article published by Rolling Stone magazine, Washington Post Reporter Carl Bernstein (famous for unfolding the Watergate Scandal) reported that more than 400 American journalists worked for the CIA. Bernstein went on to reveal that this cozy arrangement had covered the preceding 25 years. Sources told Bernstein that the New York Times, America's most respected newspaper at the time, was one of the CIA's closest media collaborators. Seeking to spread the blame, the New York Times published an article in December 1977, revealing that "more than eight hundred news and public information organisations and individuals," had participated in the **CIA's covert subversion of the media.**

- **Yellow Journalism:** When Robert Parry reported the first breaking stories about Iran-Contra for Associated Press that were largely ignored by the press and congress, then moving to Newsweek he witnessed a retraction of a true story for political reasons. In '**Fooling America: A Talk by Robert Parry**' he said, *"The people who succeeded and did well were those who didn't stand up, who didn't write the big stories, who looked the other way when history was happening in front of them, and went along either consciously or just by cowardice with the deception of the American people."*

It's all started with the fathers of Yellow Journalism, William Randolph Hearst and Joseph Pulitzer, back in 1898 before the Spanish War to arouse Americans with fabricated stories for the rallying cry *"Remember the Maine! To hell with Spain."*

Artist Frederick Remington found little to report about Spanish atrocities and wrote to his boss: "**There is no war, Request to be recalled.**" Hearst sent a cable in reply: "**Please remain. You furnish the pictures, I'll furnish the war.**" Hearst was true to his word. For weeks after the *Maine* disaster, the *Journal* devoted more than eight pages a day to the story. Not to be outdone, other papers followed Hearst's lead. **So it is not a secret how private Media monopoly could spread gossips and rumours for ideological advantages   blocking   real   news   and   derailing   real   issues.** [http://www.smplanet.com/imperialism/remember.html]

Now let us now go straight to the very trivial proof before getting lost in the forest of the much delayed disruptive commission report and official disinformation of well rehearsed coordinated lies through loyal media whose allegiances are towards the NATO/Israeli alliance supervised by the global Monarchial alliance secretive Bilderberg under the blessed guidance of Evangelical Holy See.

1. **Mr. Dick Cheney**, supreme court installed Ex-Vice President (known as Robert B. in CIA's covert Allec Station) **could have saved Pentagon**, it's newly upgraded **U.S. Navy Command Center (NCC)**, and **125 fellow Americans** at the Pentagon including fellow alumni of Golden Gate University Lieutenant General Timothy Maude!

   But he didn't perform as US Vice President that morning when Americans needed him most! **Let us again hear from Transportation Secretary Norman Mineta testifying before 9/11 Commission** (his recollections at the White House PEOC after he arrived at about 9:20 a.m.), "during the time that the airplane was coming into the Pentagon, there was a young man who would come in and said to the Vice President, 'the plane is 50 miles out, the plane is 30 miles out.' And when it got to 'the plane is 10 miles out," the young man also said to the Vice President, 'Do the orders still stand?' And the Vice President...said, 'Of course the orders still stand. Have you heard anything to the contrary?" [Smoking Gun]

   [During the September 11, 2001 attacks, the Executive Briefing Room adjacent to the PEOC was occupied by Dick Cheney, Lynne Cheney, Condoleezza Rice, Mary Matalin, Lewis "Scooter" Libby, Joshua Bolten, Karen Hughes, Stephen Hadley,

David Addington, and Secret Service agents.[1]]

Secretary Mineta arrived at PEOC around 9:20 a.m., by then all pertinent military, civilian officials, and secret service knew of World Trade Center crashes as well as Flight AA 77 and Flight UA 93 hijacking in progress!

The standard order was to shoot down any non-military aircraft entering the **"Prohibited"** airspace over Washington, in which **"Civilian flying is prohibited at all times"** ("Pilots Notified of Restricted Airspace; Violators Face Military Action," FAA Press Release, September 28, 2001).

Since the attacking airplane was not intercepted and destroyed firing Anti-aircraft missile from Whitehouse or Pentagon, even though the Vice President knew of it, "the orders" might have been to allow the plane to hit the Pentagon at 9:37am since the military machinery for implementing the "New Pearl Harbour" was in the process and a bomb had already destroyed NCC around 8:32am per implementation script. So the remotely hijacked Flight 77 had to hit Pentagon at the programmed GPS coordinates performing miraculous manoeuvres as part of Global Guardian War Games supervised from E-4B National Airborne Operation Center Surveillance above and monitored from big screens of NSA and Pentagon!

This is nothing but treason and was more than enough to impeach Bush administration just after 9/11. The inaction from the Congress and Senate, which tried to impeach President Clinton for personal sex life, can be also interpreted as treason!

2. **President Bush could have sent Fighter Pilots from Long Island New York base** to intercept both planes before they hit WTC since FAA security line was open with Whitehouse and Flight 11 was hijacked around 8:20am, saving both towers and all the people along with it as well, not to mention, saving dear tax dollars from the disaster related expenditures and subsequent 13% rise of military spending.

But He Didn't! He went to the Emma E. Booker Elementary School to read "My Pet Goat" to a class of minority children accompanied by all key White House staff enjoying gentle ride in tax payers paid most sophisticated high-tech limo equipped to receive any emergency briefings and ready for any presidential order including military!

In preparation for the president's visit to the Colony Beach and Tennis Resort, all guests were cleared out of the building "to make way for the invasion of White House staffers, aides, communications technicians—even an antiterrorism unit." *Overnight, snipers and surface-to-air missiles were located on the roof of the Colony and adjacent structures, to protect the president. "The Coast Guard and the Longboat Key Police Department manned boats that patrolled the surf in front of the resort all night.* Security trucks with enough men and arms to stop a small army parked right on the beach. An Airborne Warning and Control System (AWACS) plane circled high   overhead in the clear night sky."
[SAMMON, 2002, PP. 13 AND 25; SARASOTA HERALD-TRIBUNE, 9/10/2002]

Thus it is obvious that Ex-President Bush made himself well guarded against 9/11 with pre-knowledge from CIA briefings but left Americans uninformed, unwarned, and unguarded!

3. **FBI higher ups could have stopped 9/11 disaster simply by allowing fellow FBI agents search suspected Al-Qaeda mastermind** Zacarias Moussaoui's belongings **including Laptop.** [Smoking Gun]
But FBI Radical Fundamentalist Unit Headquarter vehemently opposed search warrant from the FBI Minneapolis field office for the suspected terrorist mastermind Zacarias Moussaoui's belongings! Minneapolis division chief Coleen Rowley said, "I feel that certain facts... have, up to now, been omitted, downplayed, glossed over and/or mischaracterized in an   effort to avoid or minimize personal and/or institutional embarrassment on the part of the FBI and/or perhaps even for improper political reasons." She asked, "Why would an FBI agent deliberately sabotage a case? The superiors acted so strangely that some agents in the Minneapolis office openly joked that those higher-ups 'had to be spies or moles... working for Osama bin Laden.'

Immigration and Naturalization Service agent Steve Nordmann, one of the officers who arrested Zacarias Moussaoui (AUGUST 16, 2001), pressed for a warrant so that law enforcement bodies could search Moussaoui's computer files. He would later write of his regret that they were not allowed to access Moussaoui's laptop. More details were not known as Nordmann died in a motorcycle accident in 2003 and would not testify at Moussaoui's trial. [STAR-TRIBUNE (MINNEAPOLIS), 6/28/2003; ST. CLOUD TIMES, 9/7/2003]

Kathleen McChesney. *[Source: FBI]* FBI agent Robert Wright was continuing to protest and fight the cancellation of the Vulgar Betrayal, the most significant US government investigation into terrorist financing. In January 2001, he claimed that his supervisor told him, **"I think it's just better to let sleeping dogs lie."** FBI agent John Vincent backed up the allegation. [ABC NEWS, 12/19/2002]

At a conference held in Washington, DC, on July 11, 2001, Assistant FBI Director Dale Watson, the head of the Counterterrorism Division, warned that a significant terrorist attack was likely on US soil. He said, **"I'm not a gloom-and-doom-type person. But I will tell you this. [We are] headed for an incident inside the United States."** [NATIONAL GOVERNORS ASSOCIATION, 7/10/2001 🔁; REUTERS, 7/12/2001; NEWSDAY, 4/10/2004]

After 9/11, FBI translator Sibel Edmonds made allegations of serious FBI misconduct, **"In July or August 2001, an unnamed FBI field agent discovered foreign documentation revealing certain information regarding blueprints, pictures, and building material for skyscrapers being sent overseas. It also revealed certain illegal activities in obtaining visas from certain embassies in the Middle East, through network contacts and bribery."** FBI translation unit supervisor Mike Feghali decided not to send translated information back to the field agent aiding in the success of 9/11. The revelation had been blocked from public by a congressional gag order but in January 2005 an internal government report determined that most of Edmonds' allegations have been verified and none of them could be refuted. [EDMONDS, 8/1/2004; ANTI-WAR (.COM), 8/22/2005]

4. **CIA could have stopped 9/11 disaster warning public and exposing ISI Director's Alleged 100,000+ Fund Transfer from Pakistan to Able-Danger tracked alleged Atta's account in Florida! But they didn't! They let the**

remotely hijacked Boeing 757 and 767 hit precisely programmed targets only to label them as attacks! [Smoking Gun]

In May 2001, then CIA Director Tenet Secretly Visited Pakistan and had a long meeting with then ISI Director **Lt. Gen. Mahmood Ahmed** who allegedly sent 100,000+ to alleged Atta's account in Florida before his week long trip (Sep 4-13) to Washington DC for mysterious meetings at the Pentagon and National Security Council" as well as meetings with CIA Director Tenet (SEPTEMBER 9, 2001), unspecified officials at the White House and the Pentagon, and his "most important meeting" with Marc Grossman, US Under Secretary of State for Political Affairs. [NEWS (ISLAMABAD), 9/10/2001]

Shortly after a pivotal al-Qaeda warning given by the CIA to top officials (JULY 10, 2001), Undersecretary of Defense for Intelligence Steve Cambone expressed doubts. He spoke to CIA Director George Tenet, and, as Tenet later recalled, "he asked if I had considered the possibility that al-Qaeda threats were just a grand deception, a clever ploy to tie up our resources and expend our energies on a phantom enemy that lacked both the power and the will to carry the battle to us." Tenet claimed he replied, "No, this is not a deception, and, no, I do not need a second opinion.... We are going to get hit. It's only a matter of time." [TENET, 2007, PP. 154] [SMOKING GUN]

On august 15, 2001, CIA Counterterrorism Head Cofer Black claimed, "we are going to be struck soon"!

CIA secretly warned FAA about imminent, spectacular attack from Muslim Fundamentalists shortly before September 6, 2001, yet let its emergency planes and helicopters moved to Monterey California as well as failed to recall fighters sent from North Eastern military bases to Iceland and Saudi Arabia.

Let us hear CIA Director George Tenet again, "As a result of the intelligence community's efforts, in concert with our foreign partners, by September 11, Afghanistan was covered in human and technical operations." They also covered Saudi Arabia and Iceland with

US fighters while leaving America and Americans unprotected despite all pre-knowledge of the imminent spectacular event specifically targeting WTC and Pentagon as well as possibly The White House!

5. **Senate And Congress Could Have Stopped It Going Public With CIA Warnings About Imminent Attack, But They Didn't.**
On the morning of 9/11, David Welna, National Public Radio's Congressional correspondent, said, "I spoke with Congressman Ike Skelton—a Democrat from Missouri and a member of the Armed Services Committee"—who said, "just recently the Director of the CIA [George Tenet] warned that there could be an attack—an imminent attack—on the United States of this nature. So this was not entirely unexpected." [NPR, 9/11/2001]

CBS News reported that **Attorney General Ashcroft had stopped flying commercial airlines due to a threat assessment**, but "neither the FBI nor the Justice Department... would identify [to CBS] what the threat was, when it was detected or who made it." [CBS NEWS, 7/26/2001]

This must have been an urgent issue for Congressional inquiry since pertinent Senate and Congressional Chairs (Members) were receiving CIA briefings of imminent Spectacular attacks inside USA. Again, it's nothing but treason from within.

On July 5, 2001, the government's top counter-terrorism official, Richard Clarke stated to a group gathered at the White House: "Something really spectacular is going to happen here, and it's going to happen soon." The group included the FAA, the Coast Guard, the FBI, the Secret Service, and the INS. Clarke directed every counter-terrorist office to cancel vacations, defer non-vital travel, put off scheduled exercises and place domestic rapid response teams on much shorter alert.
[Notes. Once again counter terrorism Czar didn't want to counter upcoming "spectacular" disaster inside but prepared for rapid response contributing to the success of 9/11].

6. **FAA Could Have Stopped 9/11 by Warning Airliners And Pilots with Pre-Knowledge and Ensuring Back Up Hijacking Coordinator to Guarantee Effective Functional Protocol! But They Didn't!** Flight 11 was hijacked around 8:20 a.m. Normally NORAD would have scrambled fighter jets within 10 minutes! But NORAD failed to get authorization from NMCC since new FAA hijack coordinator was out of contact since 8:30 a.m. creating an invincible wall between NORAD and NMCC.

Protocols in place on 9/11 stated that if the FAA requested the military to go after an airplane, *"the escort service will be requested by the FAA hijack coordinator by direct contact with the National Military Command Center (NMCC)."* [FAA, 11/3/98] Acting FAA Deputy Administrator Monty Belger stated essentially the same thing to the 9/11 Commission, "The   official protocol on that day was for the FAA headquarters, primarily through the hijack coordinator ... to request assistance from the NMCC if there was a need for DOD assistance." [9/11 Commission Report, 6/17/04 *Sources:* Monty Belger] However, the hijack coordinator, FAA Office of Civil Aviation Security Director Mike Canavan, was in Puerto Rico and claimed to have missed out on "everything that transpired that day." The 9/11 Commission failed to ask him if he had delegated that task to anyone else while he was gone. [9/11 Commission, 5/23/03; 9/11 Commission   Final Report, 7/22/04, pp 17] (Note. *This rigid presidential directive incapacitating vigilant NORAD was the main reason for the success of 9/11 New Pearl Harbour which then CIA director labelled instantly as attack by invisible finger prints of Bin Laden without waiting for physical evidence and logical analysis because framing and blaming Bin Laden was the goal*!)

7. NORAD Could Definitely Stop 9/11 Simply Following Standard Hijacking Protocol Of Scrambling Fighter Jets Immediately To Intercept Hijacked Airliners! But The Protocol in Place on 9/11 created a deliberate gap in the chain of commands since the new Hijacking Coordinator was silent in Puerto Rico without a backup!

NORAD was at the highest state of alert as Lieutenant Colonel Dawne

Deskins and other day shift employees at NEADS started their workday. NORAD was conducting a weeklong, large-scale exercise called Vigilant Guardian. [Newhouse News Service, 1/25/02] Deskins was regional mission crew chief for the Vigilant Guardian exercise.
[ABC News, 9/11/02] Vigilant Guardian was described as *"an exercise that would pose an imaginary crisis to North American Air Defense outposts nationwide"; as a "simulated air war"; and as "an air defense exercise simulating an attack on the United States."*

8. **Us Military Definitely Could Stop 9/11, But Every Evidence Would Suggest 9/11 Was A Sophisticated High-Tech Military Coup Coordinating Like-Minded High Level CIA, FBI, FAA, NSA, Pentagon, Bush Administration, Senate and Congressional Committee Chairs along with NATO and Israeli Intelligences**
[http://www.kolki.com/peace/Army-Inaction.htm]

They preponed yearly Dooms-Day Exercises jointly with NORAD from the week of October 22nd - 31st, 2001 to the week including September 11, 2001. NORAD was conducting a weeklong, large-scale exercise called Vigilant Guardian described as stated above.
[Newhouse News Service, 1/25/02] [ABC News, 9/11/02]

At the Fort Belvoir, an army base 10 miles south of the Pentagon, Lt. Col. Mark R. Lindon was conducting a "garrison control exercise" at 8:30 a.m. when the 9/11 attacks begun. The object of this exercise was to "test the security at the base in case of a terrorist attack." *Yet no fighters we scrambled from the base to save Pentagon.*

As the 9/11 attacks were taking place, a large military training exercise called Global Guardian, an annual exercise, was "in full swing" sponsored by US Strategic Command (Stratcom) in cooperation with US Space Command and NORAD.
[Omaha World-Herald, 9/10/02; Omaha World-Herald, 2/27/02]
Note: *Yet military (NMCC) didn't ask NORAD per modified hijacking protocol to scramble fighter jets intercepting hijacked airliners!*

Admiral Richard Mies, Commander in Chief of US Strategic Command

(Stratcom) at the Offutt Air Force Base near Omaha, Nebraska, was directing Global Guardian military exercise "in full swing" when the 9/11 attacks begun. [Omaha World-Herald, 9/10/02] Because of Global Guardian, bombers, missile crews, and submarines around America were all being directed from Stratcom Center, a steel and concrete reinforced bunker below Offutt. [BBC, 9/1/02; Omaha World-Herald, 2/27/02; Omaha World-Herald, 9/10/02; Bulletin of the Atomic Scientists, 11/12/97; Associated Press, 2/21/02 (B)] This bunker was staffed with top personnel who were at a heightened security mode because of the exercise.
[Air Force Weather Observer, 7/02; Associated Press, 2/21/02 (B)] Barksdale Air Force Base in Louisiana, an important node in the US Stratcom, was aiding Global Guardian beginning at 8:30 a.m. on 9/11.
Note. *Ironically President Bush would be forced to visit both Air Force Bases before returning to Washington, DC, as newly indoctrinated Commander in Chief!*

During the hour or so that American Airlines Flight 77 was under the control of hijackers, up to the moment it struck the west side of the Pentagon, military officials in [the Pentagon's NMCC] were urgently talking to law enforcement and   air traffic control officials about what to do." [New York Times, 9/15/01 (C)] Yet, although the Pentagon's NMCC reportedly knew of the hijacking, NORAD reportedly was not (authorized) notified until 9:24 a.m. by some accounts, and not notified at all by others. [9/11 Commission Report, 6/17/04; NORAD, 9/18/01] Note. **NORAD didn't need notification because they could see all Flights without transponders immediately on their screens for scrambling fighter jets. But under protocol in effect on 9/11 NORAD needed NMCC authorization after notifying FAA. But the FAA Hijack coordinator Mike Canavan was sent to Puerto Rico without a backup creating inactions! This was again nothing but treason contributing to success of 9/11.**

Cold blooded murder of fellow military personnel by emergency military Administration in place during 9/11 saga! Let us re-visit then Defense Secretary Donald Rumsfeld's amusing inactions before AA 77 hit Pentagon. He made these comments to Christopher Cox while watching

CNN news about WTC crashes, "Believe me, it isn't over yet. There's going to be another attack, and it could be us". With confidence like that the first thing would have been done evacuate Pentagon and military readiness to shoot down any passenger plane over restricted Pentagon and White House air spaces. Ironically, he insisted not to evacuate even after the programmed Bomb blasts and AA 77 crash.

9. **World Trade Center Demolition?**
On September 11th 2001, BBC World reported at 4:57pm Eastern Time that the Salomon Brothers Building (more commonly known as WTC7 or World Trade Building 7) had collapsed. This even made the 5pm EST Headlines! But what was bizarre was that the building did not actually collapse until 5:20pm EST suggesting strongly BBC was also part of the New Pearl Harbour implementation script. [Smoking Gun]

WTC complex owner Larry Silverstein rushed immediately calling his people over cell phone to pull it down, which he admitted on a September 2002 PBS documentary, 'America Rebuilds' that **he and the NYFD decided to 'pull'** *WTC 7* **on the day of the attack**. The word 'pull' is industry jargon for taking a building down with explosives.

Official explanations for the dramatic free fall of Twin Towers and WTC7 had been very consistent, twin towers fell from the heat of the burning fuel causing also the fall of WTC7 in a similar fashion.

But **2004 Democratic Presidential candidate John Kerry** directly contradicted the official story about WTC7 when questioned by members of 'Austin 9/11 Truth Now': "I do know that that wall, I remember, was in danger and I think they made the decision based on the danger that it had in destroying other things, that they did it in a controlled fashion."

Pulling down WTC7 is another smoking gun because wiring a massive 47 storied building like WTC7 would require weeks of expert preparations suggesting all three buildings were wired for controlled demolitions synchronizing with the remotely hijacked GPS controlled precisely programmed crash of Flight 11 and Flight 175 (Boeing 767).

10. **How feasible were Remote Controlled Military Hijackings and GPS Programmed Precise Targeting voiding the need of physical hijackers?**

Well, in a world where people look for all answers to media Mr. Bush could suggest in a speech immediately after 9/11 "**new technology, probably far in the future, allowing air traffic controllers to land distressed planes by remote control.**" [NEW YORK TIMES, 9/28/2001] WHAT MR. PRESIDENT FORGOT TO TELL THE WORLD THAT THE TECHNOLOGY WAS ALREADY OPERATIONAL WITHIN MILITARY AND DEFENCE INDUSTRIES FOR YEARS BEFORE 9/11.

But during 9/11 saga, Mr. Cheney told Mr. Bush not to come to the White House from Florida because hijackers knew the transponder code for the Air Force One! **That is really the smoking gun suggesting remote military hijacking** because only military has knowledge and access of the Air Force One transponder code needed for remote controlling the plane in case of emergency!

The simple unnoticed and unexplained fact was that British-US military had been flying drones for intelligence gathering since Word War II and technology has been advancing since then at a rapid speed throughout cold war which eventually led to the successful unmanned take-off and landing of Boeing 737 size **military Global Hawk** that flew remote controlled GPS programmed trans-Pacific flight from Edward Air force Base, USA, to Edinburgh, South Australia, on April 24, 2001, 5-months prior to 9/11.

US Department of Defense (DOD) DARPA initiated projects to take control of the hijacked airliners collaborating with Defense Contractor Giants Honeywell, Boeing and later on Raytheon since early 70s, successfully implementing the methodology by early 90s. Since then hundreds of auto landings have been tested beginning with Boeing 737 at the NASA's Crows Landing Flight Facility in California and later integrating augmented GPS into Boeing 757 and 767 flight management systems.

Silence from helpless pilots during the entire hijacking drama suggests that the controls were taken from the ground piggybacking Primary Channel and keying the cockpit microphone, disabling Transponders in the process in all hijacking occasions!

[http://www.kolki.com/peace/Home-Run.htm]

All 9/11 flights were delayed for remote hijacking convenience! But they lost control of Flight UA 93 when pilot took back control of the plane! [http://www.kolki.com/peace/9-11-Flights-Delayed.htm]
All Cell Phone calls and sounds depicting 9/11 hijackings were well rehearsed acting originated from the secret Remote Control Centers and their microphones following New Pearl Harbour script.
09:36 A.M.: MINUTE(S) BEFORE AA 77 HIT PENTAGON (9:37 A.M.) REMOTE HIJACKERS GOT BACK CONTROL OF FLIGHT UA 93
09:45 A.M.: SECRET SERVICE ORDERED COMPLETE EVACUATION OF THE WHITE HOUSE [Notes. UA 93 was reprogrammed to hit the White House now since they made AA 77 hit Pentagon at the precise point; UA 175 was also remotely hijacked (8:45 a.m.) minute(s) before AA 11 hit WTC North Tower (8:46 a.m)]
09:56 A.M.: CHENEY OBTAINED BUSH'S ORDER TO SHOOT DOWN UA 93 OVER NOISY TELEPHONIC COVERSATION [Notes. Remote Hijacking Was Losing Control]
10:00 A.M.: FLIGHT 93 TRANSPONDER GAVE BRIEF SIGNAL [Notes. Pilot Got Back Control]
10:01 A.M.: LOCAL PILOT SAW FLIGHT 93 ROCKING BACK AND FORTH [Notes. Remote Hijacking Was Trying To Get Back Control from Pilot]
10:03 A.M.: FLIGHT 93 IS SHOT DOWN BY MILITARY JET OVER PENNSYLVANIA [Notes. Per Presidential and Vice-Presidential Order with Defense Secretary Donald Rumsfeld's knowledge which he acknowledged during speech in Iraq on Dec. 24, 2004]

WHY THEY (Military) SHOT DOWN FLIGHT UA 93?
The most scholarly analysis would suggest that the remote hijackers chose Airports and Flights very wisely so that the actual crash times were within an early hour window 8:45 a.m. to 9:45 a.m. on a Monday morning before Government works effectively yet to inflict massive casualty dubbed spectacular by then US intelligence and counter terrorism Czars! They also chose sets of two adjacent prominent-popular public structures separated by hundreds of miles to divert public focus and attention. Thus Flight 11 and Flight 175, both Boeing 767, were delayed approximately 14 minutes so that they could hit the programmed targets WTC around 8:45 a.m. and 9 a.m. (actual 8:46 a.m. and 9:02 a.m.). Flight 77 and Flight 93, both Boeing 757, were also

delayed conveniently so that they could hit programmed targets Pentagon and White House around 9:30 a.m. and 9:45 a.m. The most wise speculation would be that Explosives were also timed in those building programmed around the intended crash timings.

But the remote hijacking started losing control with UA 93 on and off Beginning at 9:10 a.m. which led to ATC early rumours of losing UA 93! False threats to pertinent ATC also led to evacuation of ATC leaving emergency Transponder codes on the ATC screens from desperate pilots unattended and unanswered. **Since the planned bomb(s) went off in Pentagon around 9:32 a.m.** and remote hijackers experienced trouble with UA 93 they needed new strategy to reprogram Flight 77 hit Pentagon as quickly as possible passing over White House and taking a miraculous 270 degree turn at 500+ mph without rocking. Around 9:36 a.m., remote hijackers got back control of UA 93 over west of Cleveland, Ohio, and most likely reprogrammed for new destination as White House! **"At 9.45 the Secret Service ordered the complete evacuation of the White House - United Flight 93 was still airborne and heading towards Washington. Agents ran from office to office screaming: "Get out! Get out now! This is real!" [William Langley, Telegraph, Dec 16, 2001]**

They had to shoot down UA 93 to conceal remote military hijacking because if escorted by Fighters to nearby Military Base or Airport it would have revealed that there were no physical hijackers.

Thus, 9/11 was nothing but a high-tech military coup in broad day light which forced Mr. Bush to fly to the military bases (Barksdale, Louisiana & Offutt, Omaha) to be baptised with the next procedures to help the coup blaming Bin Laden. That could also explain why newly upgraded most sophisticated Naval Command Center (NCC) had to be destroyed along with all key personnel guaranteeing NSA-Air Force dominance!

So, let us try to find some meaning why a Super Power President and Vice President sitting at the top of the technology and military deterrent suffered from indecisiveness which caused so many deaths and so much destruction....

The reason will be obvious from the statements of ex-FBI Translator Sibel Edmonds regarding **MOSSAD agents within US Military and FBI.** Edmonds wrote to the inspector general's office in March 2002 when a U.S. military officer and his wife another FBI translator tried to persuade her to work for Mossad - **"Investigations are being compromised, Incorrect or misleading translations are being sent to agents in the field. Translations are being blocked and circumvented."** [Washington post, 6/19/2002]
[http://www.fpp.co.uk/BoD/Mossad/Target_group.html]

Let us again hear from the American God Father David Rockefeller justifying secretive Bilderberg private plan for one world:
"It would have been impossible for us to develop our plan for the world if we had been subjected to the lights of publicity during those (last 40) years. But, the world is more sophisticated and prepared to march towards a world government. The supranational sovereignty of an intellectual elite and world bankers is surely preferable to the national autodetermination practiced in past centuries."
  -- David Rockefeller, Speaking at the June, 1991 Bilderberger meeting in Baden, Germany (a meeting also attended by then-Governor Bill Clinton and by Dan Quayle

Thus FBI and many US top level law enforcement personnel are no longer working for the American Interests, rather they are compromising American well being and security for the benefit of a greater alliance of a few! 9/11 wasn't an isolated incident. British and US troops were already exercising with massive number of armies along with unprecedented troops manoeuvring around the world since World War II and Nordic Cross was preparing for realizing prophesised world supremacy from Israel using Holy See.

Let us hear what FBI counterterrorism expert **John O'Neill** had to say about Bin Laden and Al-Qaeda! In July 2001 O'Neill said, **"The main obstacles to investigate Islamic terrorism were US oil corporate interests and the role played by Saudi Arabia in it."** He added, "All the answers, everything needed to dismantle Osama bin Laden's organization, could be found in Saudi Arabia." **O'Neill also believed the White House was obstructing his investigation of bin Laden because they were still keeping the idea of a pipeline deal with the Taliban open** [IRISH TIMES, 11/19/2001; BRISARD AND DASQUIE, 2002, PP. XXIX; CNN, 1/8/2002; CNN, 1/9/2002] He died during World Trade Center demolition on 9/11 while working as the new security chief under the new private owner Silverstein Properties and Westfield America which mysteriously acquired 99 year lease on WTC on July 24, 2001, eventually harvesting 4.55 billion US in profit from the insurers of WTC!

Summarization:

The above discussion relating facts and testimonies from the horses' mouths regarding the September 11, 2001, destructive event, rather Neocons anticipated New Pearl Harbour, never could happen on US soil if normal procedures were simply followed by the President, the Vice-President, Congress, Senate, Military, CIA, FBI, NSA, FAA, and NORAD performing their duty to safeguard America and the Americans.

But on 9/11 normal US airline procedures were deliberately changed and/or violated while the Bush Administration, CIA, FBI, FAA, NSA, NORAD, and Military ensured nothing could help those flights until they hit programmed targets hijacked remotely during preponed nationwide US Military Exercises including Global Guardian and Practice Armageddon running war games from Pentagon and NRO, while watching their success status on big screen establishing FAA security line with White House before the first crash at 8.45am. Since Media and responsible politicians became part of the cover up afterwards, accepting justification of US/NATO Alliance Military Supremacy and/or **fear of retribution from the subsequent Anthrax attack**, general population had difficulty to even think of the possibility that US Military-CIA-FBI-FAA-NSA-NORAD-President and Vice President could hurt their own people and infrastructures! But the evidences logically suggest that they did and still doing using **900,000 secret federal employees** violating all democratic rights of open Government since 1816.

The cover-up was possible mainly because of the very FBI, who failed the Americans to begin with blocking search of **Zakarias Moussaoui's** laptop and belongings, letting suspected militants enter USA illegally and then guarding them from the local and national law enforcements, became in charge of all the crime scenes, rescue operations, investigations, evidence collections, United and American Airlines Emergency Centre operations as well as guardian of related Air Traffic Terminals confiscating all recorded materials and black boxes; while CIA ensured Mainstream Media remain mostly silent about trivial anomalies while bombarding citizens with massive disinformation and propaganda against the alleged dead hijackers with box cutters, Bin Laden, and Islam.

In his farewell address in Iraq outgoing President George W. Bush said, 'Iraq War was hard', killing and displacing millions, 'but needed to protect U.S. and for peace'! Well Mr. President, **you didn't protect U.S. on 9/11 letting military coup** kill 3000 Americans in cold blood! That must have been even harder especially uttering incredible lies afterwards in order to protect the Alliance of the few. While you installed antiaircraft gun at the roof of the resort in Florida on the night of 9/10, no anti-aircraft gun was fired to save pentagon and NCC, no fighter planes were dispatched to go after the hijacked airplanes on 9/11 betraying victims who had absolute faith in their government and sense of security under you as their commander-in-chief.

References:

- **Real Path To Well Planned Precisely Enacted 9/11 Disaster In US Soil:**
  http://www.kolki.com/peace/Real-Path-To-9-11.htm
- **So, What Is Al-Qaeda?** http://www.kolki.com/peace/What-Is-Al-Qaeda.htm
- **Remote Hijacking of Passenger Jets:** http://www.kolki.com/peace/Home-Run.htm
- **Sibel Edmonds Interview:**
  http://www.kolki.com/peace/FBI-Translator-Sibel-Edmonds-Interview.htm
- **Patriots Question 9/11:** http://patriotsquestion911.com/
- http://911research.wtc7.net/index.html
- **Center for Research on Globalization:** http://www.globalresearch.ca
- **Air Marshals Can't Stop Remote Hijacking:** How Air Marshals, Border & Airport Security, can stop Remote Control Hijacking and flight termination?
- **PNAC:** Rebuilding Americas Defences', Page 51,
  http://www.kolki.com/peace/RebuildingAmericasDefenses.pdf
- **Operation Northwoods,** http://www.kolki.com/peace/US-NSA-Face.htm
- **Mossad Within FBI and Military:** http://www.fpp.co.uk/BoD/Mossad/Target_group.html
- **CIA Destroyed Torture Videos:** http://www.consortiumnews.com/2009/030209a.html
- **Remember the Main:** http://www.smplanet.com/imperialism/remember.html

- **Bush's Missing Hours Revealed:**
http://www.telegraph.co.uk/news/worldnews/northamerica/usa/1365455/Revealed-what-really-went-on-during-Bush%27s-%27missing-hours%27.html
- **Bomb In Pentagon at 9:32am:** http://physics911.net/pdf/honegger.pdf
- **Systematic Disinformation:** http://911research.wtc7.net/talks/noplane/distraction.html
- **9-11 Timeline:** http://www.historycommons.org/project.jsp?project=911_project
- **9-11 Commission Report:** http://www.9-11commission.gov/report/911Report.pdf
- **Thirst For Justice**: http://www.prolognet.qc.ca/clyde/cfr.html

End Note: What was wrong with 9/11 Commission?

The two co-chairs of the Commission, Thomas Kean and Lee Hamilton, believed that the government established the Commission in a way that ensured that it would fail. In their book **"Without Precedent: The Inside Story of the 9/11 Commission"** describing their experience serving, Hamilton listed a number of reasons for reaching this conclusion, including:

1. the late establishment of the Commission and the very short deadline imposed on its work;
2. the insufficient funds (3 million dollars), initially allocated for conducting such an extensive investigation (later the Commission requested additional funds but received only a fraction of the funds requested and the chairs still felt hamstrung);
3. the many politicians who opposed the establishment of the Commission;
4. the continuing resistance and opposition to the work of the Commission by many politicians, particularly those who did not wish to be blamed for any of what happened;
5. the deception of the Commission by various key government agencies, including the Department of Defense, NORAD and the FAA;
6. and, the denial of access by various agencies to documents and witnesses.

"So there were all kinds of reasons we thought we were set up to fail."

Let us address the trivial anomalies Media, Administration, Military, Intelligence, Senate and Congress never addressed Poem "9/11 Hijacking"

In April of 2002, FBI director Robert Mueller - who admitted that several hijacker identities were in doubt due to identity thefts - made this stunning announcement:

"In our investigation, we have not uncovered a single piece of paper - either here or in the treasure trove of information that has turned up in Afghanistan and elsewhere - that mentioned any aspect of the September 11 plot."

How Western Media and Politicians Betraying Citizens without addressing trivial 9-11 anomalies!

9/11 Hijacking (Bin Laden or Military?)
(Dedicated to all who have been suffering for well coordinated 9/11 disaster)
[NEADS – North Eastern Air Defense, FAA – Federal Aviation Authority]

[If George Bush were to be judged by the standards of the Nuremberg Tribunals[1], he'd be hanged – American linguist Noam Chomsky]

If Bin Laden had to mastermind 9/11 operation
First he had to change normal US-hijacking protocol!
Overriding NEADS sector commander's power
Of scrambling fighter jets after the hijackers!

If Bin Laden had to execute 9/11 disaster
He had to authorize Mike Canavan, as FAA hijack coordinator,
The sole contact for the National Military Command Center
And making sure he hides in Puerto Rico without answer!

If Bin Laden had to coordinate 9/11 as commander
He had to order **General Montague Winfield Brigadier Entrust** Charles Leidig, the deputy for Command Center
In charge overseeing the period during disaster!

If Bin Laden disciples were the hijackers
They would have been listed as passengers!
With their Islamic names on ticket and computer
Validated by passport and licence having picture!

If Cessna trained hijackers somehow could hijack

Pilot or crew had ample time to activate transponder!
Located at multiple points throughout jet airliners
Informing ground control 'I have been hijacked'!

If box cutters armed hijackers could over power
All captains and crew members, taller and stronger!
The takeover saga would have been there
In cockpit voice recorder for half an hour!

If Cessna trained hijackers could fly Boeing jetliners
Flight turns would be at the mercy of Boeing flight software
Having built in restriction maximum 1.5g manoeuvre
Could never collide with WTC overriding anti-collision feature!

If Bin Laden and hijackers with box cutters
Could undertake such mission of precision mass murder
President Bush must have ordered 'Global Guardian'
Bring those drones down locking on transponders!

Reference:
1. Noam Chomsky, Noam Chomsky Interview, BBC 05/20/04

Let us define Al-Qaeda - not based on hearsay but based on statements from FBI, CIA, Politicians, Administration and operations around the world

(So what is Al-Qaeda?)

So, what is Al-Qaeda? Irrespective of the Origin it became covert wing of US/NATO/Israeli Intelligence using private mercenaries like Black Water!

[CIA-Central Intelligence Agency, FBI-Federal Bureau of Investigation, Mossad–Israeli Intelligence Agency, MI6-UK Intelligence Agencies, NSC–National Security Council, NORAD–North American Aerospace Defense Command, ISI–Inter-Services Intelligence, RFU–FBI Radical Fundamentalist Unit]

[**Abstract:** While the US-British-Australian-Canadian intelligence, US Federal Bureau of Investigation, Key Politicians, and Main Stream Media ignored and/or helped breed Al-Qaeda in US-British-Canadian soil before 9/11, they were equivocally prompt to convict Al-Qaeda moments after 9/11 implementation bypassing/shutting all standard intellectual investigation towards the truth of 9/11. Since then the World has been terrorized, countries have been invaded/destroyed, Airport/Airline securities have been heightened costing world Governments dear tax dollars, US/NATO leaders obtained authoritarian power, Islam Bashing fulfilled Evangelical dreams deifying virtual Bin Laden, all in the name of fighting terrorism while NATO expansion has been continuing conveniently! But the only survived suspected hijacker mastermind in US custody Zakarias Moussaoui didn't have the Bin Laden's phone number in his diary rather the phone number of US Private mercenary company Black Water! Since 9/11, Al-Qaeda inflicted more damages to the Islamic world than the NATO countries helping evangelical's control on Vatican and the world. Based on the quotes from US leaders, politicians, then CIA director, FBI counter terrorism expert & translator and actions of high ranking CIA-FBI officials it can be concluded that Al-Qaeda has become the covert wing of US/NATO/Israeli military/intelligence using US/British/Australian/New Zealand/Israeli private mercenaries including Black Water. Kolki]

(Between February 24-August 16, 2001): Moussaoui Writes Blackwater Phone Number in Notebook

A page of Zacarias Moussaoui's notebook with a phone number for the security contractor Blackwater. *[Source: US District Court for the Eastern District of Virginia, Alexandria Division]*Zacarias Moussaoui writes the phone number for the private security contractor Blackwater in his notebook. [US DISTRICT COURT FOR THE EASTERN DISTRICT OF VIRGINIA, ALEXANDRIA DISTRICT, 7/31/2006]

As the U.S. District Judge Robertson speaks for the military (the main suspect of 9/11 disaster) and against open democracy by leaving the fate of the Guantanamo Bay detainees to military tribunal burying the truth forever it is time to spell out what Al-Qaeda has become exactly to ensure US/NATO/Israeli global security for supremacy! World citizens must not forget that based on the 9/11 anomalies US military, Intelligence, and FBI are the major suspects for the 9/11 disaster on US soil! Thus trying Al-Qaeda detainees under military tribunal is like making the murderer also the Judge of a trial!

Let us start the revelation with statement from Sibel Edmonds, former FBI translator, **"If they were to do real investigations we would see several significant high level criminal prosecutions in this country. And that is something that they are not going to let out. And, believe me; they will do everything to cover this up."**

Let us also hear from the Director Col. Robert Bowman of the U.S. "Star Wars" space defense program in both Republican and Democratic administrations, who was a senior Air Force colonel who flew 101 combat missions. He stated that 9/11 was an inside job. He also said: "If our government had merely done nothing, and I say that as an old interceptor pilot—I know the drill, I know what it takes, I know how long it takes, I know what the procedures are, I know what they were, and I know what they've changed them to—if our government had merely done nothing, and allowed normal procedures to happen on that morning of 9/11, the Twin Towers would still be standing and thousands of dead Americans would still be alive. That is treason!"

I am fully confident that upon reading this article fellow Americans and world citizens would vehemently protest against the Military Tribunal and world politicians would think twice before signing any major deal with the current shadow US administration where all major foreign policy decisions are being made in secret disrespecting transparency of democratic Government! Just imagine, how cold blooded 9/11 perpetrators were that they formed a Secret Government without any knowledge of the elected Senate and Congress that would be effectively running USA as the 9/11 planes were hitting World Trade Centre (WTC) and Pentagon without any Military-CIA-FBI-NORAD interceptions!

The only survivor of the alleged 9/11 plot masterminds Zakarias Moussaoui didn't have Bin Laden's phone number in his diary rather he had the phone number of the private US mercenary company Blackwater [Source: *US District Court for the Eastern District of Virginia, Alexandria Division*]. Blackwater supplies private mercenaries throughout the world including Kosovo/Bosnia, Afghanistan, and Iraq as private security contractors recruiting ex-military personnel and previously trained international militias, highly skilled with explosives and covert assassinations!

It is to be noted that all unproven charges of CIA/FBI/MI6/MOSSAD against Bin Laden and Al-Qaeda always helped the US/NATO/Israeli military agenda tangibly or intangibly including 9/11 and all other attacks around the globe before and after 9/11. This article would prove beyond reasonable doubt that prior to 9/11 Al-Qaeda has been totally converted to US/NATO/Israeli covert wing of intelligence operations using their training facilities and private mercenaries like Black Water! This interpretation is the best educated assumption not just based on hearsay or scholarly work but focusing on the words from horse's mouth and their actions!

When FBI Radical Fundamentalist Unit Headquarter vehemently opposed search warrant from the FBI Minneapolis field office for the suspected terrorist mastermind Zacarias Moussaoui's belongings Minneapolis division chief Coleen Rowley said, "I feel that certain facts... have, up to now, been omitted, downplayed, glossed over and/or mischaracterized in an effort to avoid or minimize personal and/or institutional embarrassment on the part of the FBI and/or perhaps even for improper political reasons." She asked, "Why would an FBI agent deliberately sabotage a case? The superiors acted so strangely that some agents in the Minneapolis office openly joked that those higher-ups 'had to be spies or moles... working for Osama bin Laden.'

Thus, everyone must wait for the final judgement and urge their governments to press United Nations to take the lead for an honest, open, and thorough public investigation for exposing Al-Qaeda and the culprits of 9/11 disaster, so that world can live happily ever after!

Let us hear what FBI counterterrorism expert John O'Neill had to say about Bin Laden and Al-Qaeda! In July 2001 O'Neill said, **"The main obstacles to investigate Islamic terrorism were US oil corporate interests and the role played by Saudi Arabia in it."** He added, "All the answers, everything needed to dismantle Osama bin Laden's organization, could be found in Saudi Arabia." **O'Neill also believed the White House was obstructing his investigation of bin Laden because they were still keeping the idea of a pipeline deal with the Taliban open** [IRISH TIMES, 11/19/2001; BRISARD AND DASQUIE, 2002, PP. XXIX; CNN, 1/8/2002; CNN, 1/9/2002] He died during World Trade Center demolition on 9/11 while working as the new security chief under the new private owner Silverstein Properties and Westfield America which mysteriously acquired 99 year lease on WTC on July 24, 2001, eventually harvesting 4.55 billion US in profit from the insurers of WTC!

Yet in May 2001 the US introduced the "Visa Express" program in Saudi Arabia, which allowed any Saudi Arabian to obtain a visa through his or her travel agent instead of appearing at a consulate in person - "The issuing officer had no idea whether the person applying for the visa was actually the person in the documents and application." [US

NEWS AND WORLD REPORT, 12/12/2001; US CONGRESS, 9/20/2002] An ideal disguise for fabrication of covert operation by the authoritarian intelligences like CIA, MI6, and MOSSAD!

At the same time, warnings of an attack against the US led by the Saudi Osama bin Laden were higher than they had ever been before— "off the charts" as one senator later put it. [LOS ANGELES TIMES, 5/18/2002; US CONGRESS, 9/18/2002] The CIA warned the interagency Counterterrorism Security Group (CSG) that al-Qaeda members "believed the upcoming attack would be 'spectacular,' qualitatively different from anything they had done till date." [9/11 COMMISSION, 3/24/2004; 9/11 COMMISSION, 7/24/2004, PP. 259]

Incidentally, Defense Secretary Donald Rumsfeld predicted "New Pearl Harbour" during his inaugural speech in January 2001 who was also one of the signatories of the 'Project For The New American Century (PNAC)' where they argued about the requirement for a "New Pearl Harbour" to maintain American supremacy throughout the world. Rich B. of CIA Alec Station who was Vice President Richard B. Cheney, another signatory, also predicted it a week before 9/11/2001. Yet CIA moved all its airplanes and helicopters to Monterey, California, for training and the North Eastern Air force fighters were sent to Turkey for training exercise leaving Capital and North East region unprotected - even lowered the threat level prior to 9/11 so that the perpetrators could setup the remote hijacking and demolition requirements with precision needed to ensure success!

CIA Director George Tenet later claimed in his 2007 book, "a group of assets from a Middle Eastern service was unknowingly working for the CIA by that time. Out of the more than twenty people in that group, one third was working against al-Qaeda. By September 2001, two assets had successfully penetrated al-Qaeda training camps in Afghanistan." [TENET, 2007, PP. 145]

Here is a brief recollection of partitioning of India in 1947. For the enlightenment of the reader, it is being re-iterated that it was the British Military who formed ISI of Pakistan while CIA was officially formed in USA (1948) with zero accountability and congressional license of covert global hostile activities. The newly formed intelligence ISI of a nascent tiny country like Pakistan had an extensive covert wing for international espionage! **Now just imagine why newly formed Pakistani intelligence would need international covert operations just after separating from India?**

Well, the only logical answer is that ISI became the hub of British covert intelligence outside Britain to pursue shadow Monarchial activities which would be illegal in Britain against existing laws and accountabilities built in the British Parliamentary System! During the same time in 1948 CIA was officially granted international covert activities around the globe by US Congress! And we all know CIA, FBI, and MI6 are just allies of NATO expansion since WW II even overtly claiming victory in many James Bond movies!

It is to be noted that it was then ISI Director Lt. Gen. Mahmood Ahmed who transferred 100,000+ to alleged Muhammad Atta's Florida account irrespective of who this Atta was who couldn't speak German (not certainly the framed Atta who had been studying in Germany)! The same ISI Director Lt. Gen. Mahmood Ahmed visited Washington, DC, from September 4-13, 2001, for mysterious meetings at the Pentagon and National Security Council as well as meetings with CIA Director Tenet, unspecified officials at the White House and the Pentagon, and his "most important meeting" with Marc Grossman, US Under Secretary of State for Political Affairs. On the very morning of 9/11, Ahmad was at a breakfast meeting on Capitol Hill hosted by Senator Bob Graham and Rep. Porter Goss, the chairmen of the Senate and House Intelligence committees.

Ever wonder why Pakistan could never sustain democratic Government which can live in peace with its ex-better half democratic India? When then ISI director was visiting Washington in October 12, 1999, Musharaf came to military power dismantling democratic government of Pakistan. It is to be noted that all Pakistani leaders were assassinated whoever dared to make peace with India. That is because peace with India will make ISI transparent to Pakistani citizens and the world that they don't belong to Pakistan rather an international covert intelligence force which later became Al-Qaeda to protect and expand US/NATO/Israeli and Vatican's worldwide interest!

Here is a short list of events that led to the official success of 9/11 disaster on US soil with complete knowledge of most responsible top officials and their deliberate efforts to block information flow through normal proper channel keeping citizens in darkness while keeping Al Qaeda attack theme alive spreading rumours using most sophisticated US/NATO/Israeli propaganda dissemination methods and methodology:

> **September 2000:** *Rebuilding America's Defences: Strategies, Forces And Resources For A New Century*, was written by the Project for the New American Century. It called for unprecedented hikes in military spending, American military bases in Central Asia and Middle East, toppling of non-complying regimes, abrogation of international treaties, control of the world's energy sources, militarization of outer space, total control of cyberspace, and the willingness to use nuclear weapons to achieve "American" goals. (Source)
> The plan emphasized in Page 51, **"The process of transformation is likely to be a long one, absent some catastrophic and catalyzing event - like a new Pearl Harbor."** American Free Press asked Christopher Maletz, asst. director of the PNAC about what was meant by the "need for a new Pearl Harbor": "They needed more

money to up the defense budget for raises, new arms, and future capabilities," Maletz said. "Without some disaster or catastrophic event," neither the politicians nor the military would have approved.

• January 2001: Bush Installed as US President by the Supreme Court
Bush was appointed to the US Presidency undemocratically and in turn appointed leadership of PNAC to highest levels of Executive branch and Pentagon including Richard B. Cheney, Donald Rumsfeld, Paul Wolfowitz, and Lewis Libby. Jeb Bush, a PNAC member, helped his brother to win the disputed Florida State as Governor. Bush started executing PNAC plan proposing trillion dollar tax cuts and trillion dollar increase in defense budget which would eventually bankrupt USA! PNAC leadership in the White House and Pentagon started implementing New Pearl Harbour immediately coordinating with CIA, FBI, NSA, FAA, Media, and Military.

• 2000-2001: The military conducted exercises simulating hijacked airliners used as weapons to crash into targets causing mass casualties. One target is the World Trade Center (WTC), another the Pentagon. Yet after 9/11, over and over the White House and security officials said they're shocked that terrorists hijacked airliners and crashed them into landmark buildings. [USA Today, 4/19/04, Military District of Washington, 11/3/00, New York Times, 10/3/01, WantToKnow.info]

• February 13, 2001: The existing system of Interagency Working Groups was abolished
President Bush issued a little-noticed directive that dramatically changed the way information flowed among top Bush administration officials ending all National Security accountabilities. The directive also stated, "The existing system of Interagency Working Groups is abolished." Instead, Rice would coordinate a series of eleven new interagency coordination committees within the NSC. Professor Margie Burns will later ask rhetorically, "How could the White House ever have thought that abolishing the interagency work groups was a good idea, if security was the objective? Why was so much responsibility placed on the shoulders of one person, Condoleezza Rice, whose [only] previous experience had been at Stanford University and Chevron?" [US PRESIDENT, 2/13/2001; CHRONICLES MAGAZINE, 1/2004]

• February 2001-March 2001: Withdrawal Of DIA Support Contributed To End Of Able Danger Program
Able Danger was an 18-month highly classified operation tasked, according to Army reserve Lieutenant-Colonel Anthony Shaffer, with "developing targeting information for al-Qaeda on a global scale", and used data-mining techniques to look for "patterns, associations, and linkages". He said that he himself had first encountered the names of the four alleged hijackers in mid-2000.

• **February 26, 2001: Paul Bremer: Bush Administration Paying No Attention to Terrorism**

Paul Bremer, who was appointed the US administrator of Iraq in 2003, said in a pre-9/11 speech that the Bush administration was "paying no attention" to terrorism. "What they will do is stagger along until there's a major incident and then suddenly say, 'Oh my God, shouldn't we be organized to deal with this.'" Bremer spoke shortly after chairing the National Commission on Terrorism, a bipartisan body formed during the Clinton administration. [ASSOCIATED PRESS, 4/29/2004] Iraq didn't have Al-Qaeda before US-British-Australian invasion which flooded Iraq with more private security forces (mercenaries) than ethically trained patriotic military forces. Ironically it was Paul Bremer who issued Order 17 before leaving Iraq that insured **"all International Consultants shall be immune from Iraqi legal process."**

• **January-March 2001: FBI Told Agent Wright 'Let Sleeping Dogs Lie'**
[They wanted the framing up of patsy's to go on as they prepare for the remote controlled execution on 9/11, the New Pearl Harbour]
Kathleen McChesney. *[Source: FBI]* FBI agent Robert Wright was continuing to protest and fight the cancellation of the Vulgar Betrayal, the most significant US government investigation into terrorist financing. In January 2001, he claimed that his supervisor told him, "I think it's just better to let sleeping dogs lie." FBI agent John Vincent backed up the allegation. [ABC NEWS, 12/19/2002]

• **March 2001: Regional Expert Saw Continuing Close Ties Between the CIA and ISI**
Selig Harrison, a long-term regional expert working at the Woodrow Wilson International Centre for Scholars, said, "the CIA still has close links with the ISI." Harrison is said to have "extensive contact with the CIA and political leaders in South Asia." He also claimed that the US worked with Pakistan to create the Taliban. [Times of India, 3/7/2001]

• **In April 2001, NORAD ran a war game in which the Pentagon was to become incapacitated**; a NORAD planner proposed the simulated crash of a hijacked foreign commercial airliner into the Pentagon but the Joints Chiefs of Staff rejected that scenario as "too unrealistic".

• **APRIL 30, 2001: ANNUAL TERRORISM REPORT SAID FOCUSING ON BIN LADEN WAS MISTAKE**

The US State Department issued its annual report on terrorism. The report cited the role of the Taliban in Afghanistan, and noted the Taliban "continued to provide safe haven for international terrorists, particularly Saudi exile Osama bin Laden and his network." However, as CNN described it, **"Unlike last year's report, bin Laden's al-Qaeda organization is mentioned, but the 2001 report does not contain a photograph of bin Laden or a lengthy description of him and the group."** [CNN, 4/30/2001]

• APRIL 30, 2001: WOLFOWITZ IN DEPUTY SECRETARY MEETING: WHO CARES ABOUT [BIN LADEN]?
The Bush administration finally has its first Deputy Secretary-level meeting on terrorism. [TIME, 8/4/2002] Deputy Defense Secretary Paul Wolfowitz said the focus on al-Qaeda was wrong. He stated, **"I just don't understand why we are beginning by talking about this one man bin Laden,"** and **"Who cares about a little terrorist in Afghanistan?"** [CLARKE, 2004, PP. 30, 231; NEWSWEEK, 3/22/2004]

• **Spring 2001:** A series of military and governmental policy documents is released that seek to legitimize the use of US military force in the pursuit of oil and gas. One advocates presidential subterfuge and hiding the reasons for warfare "as a necessity for mobilizing public support." [Sydney Morning Herald, 12/26/02]

• **May 2001: Bush administration hired Dov Zakheim as the Comptroller of the Pentagon** [http://judicial-inc.biz/Dov_zakheim.htm]
He was the Corporate Vice President of Systems Planning Corporation which specialized in Remote Control Flight Termination from the ground. He also brought with him extensive knowledge of WTC building structures and security.

• **May 8, 2001: Vice President Richard B. Cheney was** placed in charge **of anti-terrorism training and military preparedness exercises by Bush.** This gave him command authority during the 9/11 attacks because as many as nine war game exercises involving military and intelligence agencies were occurring simultaneously.

• MAY 2001: MEDICS TRAINED FOR AIRPLANE BOEING 757 HITTING PENTAGON (9/11 Rehearsal?)
The Army's DiLorenzo Tricare Health Clinic (DTHC) and the Air Force Flight Medicine Clinic, both housed within the Pentagon, held a tabletop exercise along with Arlington County Emergency Medical Services. The scenario practiced for was of an airplane crashing into the Pentagon's west side—the same side as was impacted in the attack on 9/11. [US DEPARTMENT OF HEALTH AND HUMAN SERVICES, 7/2002,

PP. B17; GOLDBERG ET AL., 2007, PP. 23 AND 107] Reportedly, the purpose of the exercise was "to fine-tune their emergency preparedness." [US MEDICINE, 10/2001] According to US Medicine newspaper, the plane in the scenario was a hijacked Boeing 757. [US MEDICINE, 1/2002] (Flight 77, that targeted the Pentagon on 9/11, was a 757. [NEW YORK TIMES, 9/13/2001]

• MAY 2001: TENET SECRETLY VISITS PAKISTAN, HAD LONG MEETING WITH ISI DIRECTOR [who eventually sent 100,000+ to alleged Atta's account in Florida before his week long trip (Sep 4-13) to Washington DC]

Richard Armitage, US Deputy Secretary of State, a former covert operative and Navy Seal, traveled to India on a publicized tour while CIA Director Tenet made a quiet visit to Pakistan to meet with President Pervez Musharraf. Armitage had long and deep Pakistani intelligence (ISI) connections (as well as a role in the Iran-Contra affair). While in Pakistan, Tenet, in what was described as "an unusually long meeting," also secretly met his Pakistani counterpart, ISI Director Lt. Gen. Mahmood Ahmed. [SAPRA (NEW DELHI), 5/22/2001]

• May 23-24, 2001: Rumsfeld, Himself A PNAC Member And Proposer For The Need Of New Pearl Harbour, Warned Of Inevitability Of Strategic Surprise; Referring To Pearl Harbor

During a meeting with the House Armed Services Committee, Secretary of Defense Donald Rumsfeld said that the inevitability of surprise was a guiding principle of the Bush administration's national security strategy. [US DEPARTMENT OF DEFENSE, 5/23/2001; ASSOCIATED PRESS, 5/24/2001]

• June 2001: PNAC Dominated Bush Administration Set Up Belgium Based Secret SWIFT Money Tracking System worldwide

With all possibilities this system had been in use not only to track but also to launder money to Al-Qaeda in disguise throughout the world including USA and Britain using 2.3 trillion missing Pentagon Fund supporting Shadow Government agenda of worldwide domination with disruption of normal life and financial system which is obvious in the current worldwide financial turmoil. The question is with all these covert intelligence operations, shadow governments, secret wire tapping, money tracking and laundering where is open free Democracy? Aren't lawmakers who are quietly voting to keep the illegal secretive system of few alive performing criminal acts in a society of rule-of-law and accountability?

• JULY 11, 2001: ASSISTANT FBI DIRECTOR PREDICTS TERRORIST ATTACK IN THE US [Source FBI]

At a <u>conference held</u> in Washington, DC, Assistant FBI Director Dale Watson, the head of the Counterterrorism Division, warned that a significant terrorist attack was likely on US soil. He said, "I'm not a gloom-and-doom-type person. But I will tell you this. [We are] headed for an incident inside the United States." [NATIONAL GOVERNORS ASSOCIATION, 7/10/2001 🔖; REUTERS, 7/12/2001; NEWSDAY, 4/10/2004]

• MID-JULY 2001: PENTAGON OFFICIAL SUGGESTS TO CIA DIRECTOR THAT AL-QAEDA IS JUST 'PHANTOM ENEMY'

Shortly after a pivotal al-Qaeda warning given by the CIA to top officials (JULY 10, 2001 HistoryCommons.org), Undersecretary of Defense for Intelligence Steve Cambone expressed doubts. He spoke to CIA Director George Tenet, and, as Tenet later recalled, **"he asked if I had considered the possibility that al-Qaeda threats were just a grand deception, a clever ploy to tie up our resources and expend our energies on a phantom enemy that lacked both the power and the will to carry the battle to us."** Tenet claimed he replied, **"No, this is not a deception, and, no, I do not need a second opinion.... We are going to get hit. It's only a matter of time."** [TENET, 2007, PP. 154] [The question is if Tenet was so sure why he didn't go public and to media the way he predicted many Al-Qaeda attacks around the world!]

• JULY 19, 2001: FBI DIRECTOR TOLD FIELD OFFICES TO BE READY TO RESPOND TO NEW ATTACK BUT NOT TO PREVENT IT

Acting FBI Director Thomas Pickard held a periodic conference call with the heads of all FBI field offices. This was to bring to light of all the increased threat reporting. However, he did not task the field offices to look into whether any plots were being considered within the US; nor did he tell them to take any action to disrupt any such plots. [9/11 COMMISSION, 7/24/2004, PP. 259]

• (BEFORE JULY 24, 2001): RISK ASSESSMENT IDENTIFIED AIRCRAFT STRIKING WTC AS ONE OF THE 'MAXIMUM FORESEEABLE LOSSES'

A property risk assessment report was prepared for Silverstein Properties before it acquired the lease for the World Trade Center (HistoryCommons.Org). It identified the scenario of an aircraft hitting one of the WTC towers as one of the "maximum foreseeable losses." The report said, "This scenario is within the realm of the possible, but highly unlikely." [NATIONAL INSTITUTE OF STANDARDS AND TECHNOLOGY, 5/2003, PP. 16]

• July 24, 2001: World Trade Center Ownership Changed Hands For The First Time

[The deal was brokered by Banker-Developer David Rockefeller (who used to get CIA briefings from source) and mainly funded JP Morgan Chase tied to his family interests]

Real estate development and investment firm Silverstein Properties and real estate investment trust Westfield America finalized a deal worth $3.2 billion to purchase a 99-year lease on the World Trade Center. The agreement covered the Twin Towers, World Trade Center Buildings 4 and 5 (two nine-story office buildings), and about 425,000 square feet of retail space. [NEW YORK TIMES, 4/27/2001PORT AUTHORITY OF NEW YORK AND NEW JERSEY, 7/24/2001; IREIZINE, 7/26/2001]

• July 26, 2001: Ashcroft Stopped Flying Commercial Airlines; Refused To Explain Why except 'not for Al-Qaeda';

CBS News reported that Attorney General Ashcroft had stopped flying commercial airlines due to a threat assessment, but "neither the FBI nor the Justice Department... would identify [to CBS] what the threat was, when it was detected or who made it." [CBS NEWS, 7/26/2001]

• AUGUST 6, 2001: Bush Told Cia Regarding Bin Laden Warning, 'You've Covered Your Ass, Now'

A CIA briefer went to Bush's Crawford ranch to read the president a briefing called, "Bin Laden Determined to Strike in US" (2 redacted pages out of 11 reported). After the briefing, Bush told the CIA man, "All right. You've covered your ass, now." Bush then went fishing. [They don't like anymore warnings as they prepare for the big event; also Bush knew CIA's propaganda against Bin Laden as the military prepared for New Pearl Harbour]

• EARLY AUGUST 2001: Mass Casualty Exercise At The Pentagon Includes A Plane Hitting The Building [Again, ironically, they are not guarding Pentagon but want a plane to hit]

A mass casualty exercise, involving a practice evacuation, is held at the Pentagon. General Lance Lord of US Air Force Space Command, one of the participants in the exercises, later recalled: "[It was] purely a coincidence, the scenario for that exercise included a plane hitting the building." [AIR FORCE SPACE COMMAND NEWS SERVICE, 9/5/2002]

• August 15, 2001: CIA Counterterrorism Head Cofer Black: "We Are Going To Be Struck Soon"

[He didn't say, 'we are hitting US soon'; all top officials knew by now what's going on, many cooperating others silenced by fear for life and livelihood; They all accepted this small American sacrifice for big Alliance interests]

• **August 16, 2001: Ins Agent Pressed For Moussaoui Warrant** But Blocked by FBI RFU Unit

Immigration and Naturalization Service agent Steve Nordmann, one of the officers who arrested Zacarias Moussaoui [HISTORYCOMMONS.ORG], pressed for a warrant so that law enforcement bodies could search Moussaoui's computer files. He would later write of his regret that they were not allowed to access Moussaoui's laptop. More details were not known as Nordmann died in a motorcycle accident in 2003 and would not testify at Moussaoui's trial. [STAR-TRIBUNE (MINNEAPOLIS), 6/28/2003; ST. CLOUD TIMES, 9/7/2003] [The search would have exposed Blackwater – Al-Qaeda – CIA link]

• **August 16-September 10, 2001: Fbi Failed To Inform Own Director Of Moussaoui Case**

The FBI failed to inform its own head of the arrest of Zacarias Moussaoui. It was unclear how this failure occurred. The highest FBI official to be informed of Moussaoui's arrest was apparently Michael Rolince, head of the FBI's International Terrorism Operations Section [HISTORYCOMMONS.ORG], but he seemed to have failed to pass the information on. [9/11 COMMISSION, 7/24/2004, PP. 275]

• **August 21, 2001: FBI Headquarters Blocked Criminal Investigation into Moussaoui**

Dave Frasca of the FBI's Radical Fundamentalist Unit (RFU) denied a request from the Minneapolis FBI field office to seek a criminal warrant to search the belongings of Zacarias Moussaoui, who was arrested on August 15 as part of an intelligence investigation [US DISTRICT COURT FOR THE EASTERN DISTRICT OF VIRGINIA, ALEXANDRIA DIVISION, 3/9/2006]. A criminal warrant to search Moussaoui's belongings would be granted only after the 9/11 attacks [HISTORYCOMMONS.ORG]. [The question arises naturally, why? Well, the investigation would have exposed FBI, Black Water, CIA, Al-Qaeda, MI6 and Mossad links that were active for the success of 9/11 and subsequent cover ups;]

• **August 22, 2001: Top FBI Al-Qaeda Expert Left Fbi In Frustration; Misses Important Warnings**

Counterterrorism expert John O'Neill retired from the FBI. He said that it was partly because of the recent power play against him, but also because of repeated obstruction of his investigations into al-Qaeda. [NEW YORKER, 1/14/2002]

• **August 31, 2001: Transportation Department Held Plane Hijacking Exercise**

[This was the rehearsal to test the final script for the actors and players to support the hijacking theory while planes would be remotely hijacked from Pentagon and CIA centres]

According to Ellen Engleman, the administrator of the DOT's Research and Special Programs Administration, *"this was actually much more than a tabletop exercise"*, recounting, *"During that exercise, part of the scenario, interestingly enough, involved a potentially hijacked plane and someone calling on a cell phone, among other aspects of the scenario that were very strange when twelve days later, as you know, we had the actual event [of 9/11]."* [MINETA TRANSPORTATION INSTITUTE, 10/30/2001, PP. 108]

• Mid-August-September 11, 2001: New York Air National Guard Unit In Saudi Arabia As Part Of Operation Southern Watch [Military ensured New York sky was safe for remote hijacking and hitting WTC without threat of NORAD and its own patriotic military pilots re-scheduling October 2001 exercises on 9/11]

About 100 members of the 174th Fighter Wing, part of the New York Air National Guard, were deployed to Sultan Air Base, Saudi Arabia, to patrol the no-fly zone over southern Iraq, as part of the ongoing Operation Southern Watch. This was the unit's second deployment there, its first having been in March 2001. [POST-STANDARD (SYRACUSE), 9/11/2001; POST-STANDARD (SYRACUSE), 9/12/2001; US CONGRESS, 3/1/2005; 174TH FIGHTER WING, 12/9/2005] The unit was due to arrive back at Hancock Field at around 3 p.m. on 9/11 [POST-STANDARD (SYRACUSE), 9/14/2001]

• Late August-Early December 2001: Fighters From Langley Air Force Base Deployed To Iceland For Operation Northern Guardian [As Americans were guarding Iceland and Turkey, no one was there to defend Americans, even Pentagon, from its own Frankenstein mastermind of 9/11]

In late August 2001, two-thirds of the 27th Fighter Squadron was sent overseas. Six of the squadron's fighters and 115 people went to Turkey to enforce the no-fly zone over northern Iraq as part of Operation Northern Watch. Another six fighters and 70 people were sent to Iceland to participate in "Operation Northern Guardian." The fighter groups would not return to Langley until early December. [FLYER, 7/1/2003]

• September 2, 2001: Bush Administration Enthusiastic To 'Take Down Saddam Once And For All' [HISTORYCOMMONS.ORG] [One can see why they were quiet about the warnings because they needed New Pearl Harbour to justify invasion of Iraq]

• Early September 2001: Suspicious Trading in Reinsurance Companies
[HISTORYCOMMONS.ORG] [Masterminders cashing in harvesting fruits of would be 9/11]
It would later be speculated that, around that time, people with foreknowledge of the 9/11 attacks short sold reinsurance company stocks that were insuring either or

both the airplanes and the buildings involved in the attacks. [AGENCE FRANCE-PRESSE, 9/17/2001]

• **Early September 2001: NYSE Saw Unusually Heavy Trading in Airline and Related Stocks** [Again, Masterminders cashing in harvesting fruits of would be 9/11]

The Securities and Exchange Commission (SEC) later announced that they were investigating the trading of shares of 38 companies in the days just before 9/11. [ASSOCIATED PRESS, 10/2/2001; SAN FRANCISCO CHRONICLE, 10/3/2001]

• **Early September 2001: Sharp Increase In Short Selling Of American And United Airlines Stocks**

There was a sharp increase in the short selling of American and United Airlines stocks on the New York Stock Exchange prior to 9/11. [REUTERS, 9/20/2001; SAN FRANCISCO CHRONICLE, 9/22/2001]

• **September 4-11, 2001: ISI Director Visited Washington For Mysterious Meetings** [ISI is offshore Mi6 and CIA formed by British general]

ISI Director Lt. Gen. Mahmood Ahmed visited Washington for the second time. On September 10, a Pakistani newspaper reported on his trip so far. It said his visit had "triggered speculation about the agenda of his mysterious meetings at the Pentagon and National Security Council" as well as meetings with CIA Director Tenet [HISTORYCOMMONS.ORG], unspecified officials at the White House and the Pentagon, and his "most important meeting" with Marc Grossman, US Under Secretary of State for Political Affairs. [NEWS (ISLAMABAD), 9/10/2001]

• <u>**Shortly Before September 6, 2001: CIA Secretly Warned Faa About Imminent, Spectacular Attack From Muslim Fundamentalists**</u> [Why secretly? Why not went public so that the country could prepare for it? Well, then the covert plan for New Pearl Harbour enacting remote military hijacking couldn't be executed!]

On the morning of 9/11, David Welna, National Public Radio's Congressional correspondent, said, *"I spoke with Congressman Ike Skelton—a Democrat from Missouri and a member of the Armed Services Committee"*—who said, *"just recently the Director of the CIA [George Tenet] warned that there could be an attack—an imminent attack—on the United States of this nature. So this was not entirely unexpected."* [NPR, 9/11/2001]

• **September 5-8, 2001: Raid On Arab Web Hosting Company Preceded 9/11 Spectacular Event**

Terrorism Task Force conducted a three-day raid of the offices of InfoCom Corporation, a Texas-based company that hosted about 500 mostly Arab websites, including Al Jazeera, the Arab world's most popular news channel. [GUARDIAN, 9/10/2001; WEB HOST INDUSTRY REVIEW, 9/10/2001] Three days after the initial raid, the task force was "still busy inside the building, reportedly copying every hard disc they could find. It was not clear how long these websites remained shut down." [GUARDIAN, 9/10/2001]

[Just imagine that Top FBI and CIA officials were preventing searching **Zakarias Moussaoui** Laptop in US custody without search warrant yet were performing this big search operation copying InfoComCorp databases to aid post 9/11 cover up and propaganda against Islam]

[http://www.peacethrujustice.org/moussaoui1.htm]

• **Before September 11, 2001: Tenet Said To Warn Congress (**Congressman Ike Skelton—a Democrat from Missouri and a member of the Armed Services Committee) **People About Imminent Attack On The Us** [Again why not tell the media, why Congress was silent? They all wanted New Pearl Harbour and were waiting for it to happen at the cost of American and International lives and destruction! That was why while warning Congress CIA moved all of its planes and helicopters to California, military emptied Air force bases in New York and Maryland to Saudi Arabia, Turkey and Iceland and president changed NORAD protocol as well as lowered security threat so that FBI Special Forces and Al-Qaeda as mercenaries (Blackwater) could work freely inside USA for the success of the spectacular event]

• **Just Before September 11, 2001: CIA, FBI, Lacked Counterterrorism Resources, And Focus** [Imagine when CIA director had been preaching imminent attack for six months and Defence Secretary was expecting New Pearl Harbour and Counter Terrorism Tsar was expecting Spectacular event which they all know of] [If they added more people they would have known Al-Qaeda was living within CIA and FBI who they wanted to guard for the cover up to protect real masterminds of the New Pearl Harbour]

• **On the morning of September 11, 2001,** the National Reconnaissance Office, who were responsible for operating U.S. reconnaissance satellites, had scheduled an exercise simulating the crashing of an aircraft into their building, four miles (6 km) from Washington Dulles International Airport.

• **September 11, 2001: Dick Cheney Warned Bush Hijackers Knew Transponder of Air force One**
[This is a direct evidence that virtual hijackers were hijacking 9/11 planes locking on the transponders since Vice President Cheney called President Bush in Florida asking him not to

come to the White House warning that the hijackers might know the Transponder code for Air force One.]

• **September 28, 2001: Bin Laden Denied Accusation for 9/11 Blaming Jews and US Secret Service**
"I have already said that I am not involved in the 11 September attacks in the United States. As a Muslim, I try my best to avoid telling a lie. I had no knowledge of these attacks, nor do I consider the killing of innocent women, children and other humans as an appreciable act. Islam strictly forbids causing harm to innocent women, children and other people. Such a practice is forbidden even in the course of a battle." – Bin Laden [Ummat Karachi, 9/28/2001].
Now let us hear again from ex-FBI Translator Sibel Edmonds regarding MOSSAD agents within US Military and FBI: **Edmonds wrote to the inspector general's office in March 2002 when a U.S. military officer and his wife another FBI translator tried to persuade her to work for Mossad** - "Investigations are being compromised," "Incorrect or misleading translations are being sent to agents in the field. Translations are being blocked and circumvented." [WASHINGTON POST, 6/19/2002] [http://www.fpp.co.uk/BoD/Mossad/Target_group.html]

• Up to 200 Israeli agents were arrested and detained in relation to 9/11 including five Mossad agents who were celebrating the World Trade Center job with "cries of joy and mockery." The Justice Department (sic) released all of the Israelis, and the entire matter was made "classified."

• **Everyone was rewarded after the success of 9/11 New Pearl Harbour** including all PNAC members in Bush team! No one was punished for the disaster that killed 3000 Americans, destroyed WTC and Pentagon due to inaction and/or covert actions of all responsible earning decent salary from tax dollars yet were idle and/or inactive to prevent such attack in broad daylight.

Let us end this article with excerpts from the 2007 book written by then CIA Director George Tenet where he would say, **"As a result of the intelligence community's efforts, in concert with our foreign partners, by September 11, Afghanistan was covered in human and technical operations."**

In the book "At The Center of the Storm, USA, 2007" Tenet also claimed by September 11, 2001:

" The CIA is working with eight separate Afghan tribal networks
- The CIA has more than 100 recruited sources inside Afghanistan
- Satellites are repositioned over Afghanistan
- Al-Qaeda training camps are systematically mapped
- Efforts are stepped up to closely monitor news about al-Qaeda in the media around the world
- Major collection facilities" are placed on the borders of Afghanistan
- Other "conventional and innovative collection methods" are used to penetrate al-Qaeda worldwide
- Leadership of the FBI given full transparency into the CIA's efforts." [Tenet, 2007, pp. 120-121]

Now imagine why a Government with so much knowledge of and cosiness with Al-Qaeda wouldn't be prepared for a terrorist attack like the September 11, 2001, that would change our way of life forever! Isn't the answer quite clear that Al-Qaeda has become the covert wing of NATO/Israeli military intelligence using private mercenaries like Blackwater? There are enormous data out there to support this case. I was very selective to ensure briefness of this article so that it could retain reader's interests while not getting lost in the vastness!

[http://london-bombs.blogspot.com/2005/08/christophe-chaboud.html]
Now let us consider the July 7, 2005, London Subway bombing which had many similarities with 9/11 terrorist attack including presence of Al-Qaeda suspect with MI6's knowledge, lowering security threat level during G8 summit, and use of military grade explosives for the explosions as confirmed by France's then new anti-terrorism coordinator Christophe Chaboud. In an interview with Le Monde, he announced to the world that he knew "the nature of the explosives" used in the London bombings. It "appears to be military, which is very worrisome," he said, adding: "...How did they get them? Either by trafficking, for example, in the Balkans, or they had someone on the inside who enabled them to get them out of a military base."

Bush-Cheney administration vehemently opposed any public inquiry into unthinkable 9/11 mistry attack on USA that happened with full knowledge of high ranking government, military, intelligence, FAA, and NORAD offcials! Following the foot step former Prime Minister Tony Blair said, "An independent inquiry would undermine support for the security service". Just imagine how government prosecutors spent enormous amount of time and public money to prosecute citizens sometime for minor felonies based on hearsay yet the same governments were unwilling to diagnose the source of the Al-Qaeda virus bringing it under people's microscope!

US/NATO/Israeli intelligence now spreading the rumour again that Al-Qaeda is regrouping and getting stronger than ever! Of course, without open public investigation of 9/11 this new alliance of covert intelligences has been gaining steam every day encouraging every intelligence on Earth in joining this shadow power and run Government from outside making politicians robots who could only talk about tax cuts, service cuts, tough on crime, and need for more military for war mongering and prisons to silence dissents!

The new Al-Qaeda is equipped with Echelon which can listen to and record/modify all phone conversations, see/modify all text messaging, can break into any internet firewall to eavesdrop/doctor data for framing up opponents as convenient! It is well funded by Belgium based SWIFT money laundering secret Bank [SourceWatch] and well guarded by NATO. This Al-Qaeda openly meets for covert brainstorming as Bilderberg [BBC], Head Quartered in Switzerland, attended by major media owners (e.g., Graham, Donald E. - Chairman and CEO, The Washington Post Company), Publishing monopoly like Canadian Chapter-Cole-Indigo (e.g., Reisman, Heather M. Chair and CEO, Indigo Books & Music Inc.), Key US Senators and would be leaders, key business executives, lawyers, most members of Council of Foreign Relations (CFR) and academic think tanks chaired by one of the worst war criminals in history Henry Kissinger [ZPUB.COM]. The Bilderberg Conference 2001 - May 24-27 - Gothenburg, Sweden [BILDERGBERG.ORG], was attended by Senator Christopher Dodd (Democrat), Chuck Hagen (Republican), and John Kerry along with most CFR members. Senator Obama's Vice President Selector ("Johnson, James A." "Vice Chairman, Perseus, LLC) also attended the 2008 Bilderberg covert conference! Thus it is obvious Obama has to speak for the military and support Bilderberg's covert agenda for overt war-on-terror irrespective of the will of the voters, rather against citizen's voice and democracy!

It is to be noted that Senator Obama's running mate Senator Joseph Biden met then Pakistani ISI Chief General Mahmoud Ahmad on September 13, 2001, in Washington DC, two days after the attack on WTC and the Pentagon. It is well known that General Mahmoud instructed Omar Saeed Sheikh, the alleged assassin of Daniel Pearl, to wire $100,000 to alleged lead hijacker Mohammed Atta prior to 9/11.

The ISI Chief arrived in Washington exactly one week before 9/11 to have meeting with Pentagon, White House National Security Council and CIA officials, including George Tenet, and Marc Grossman, then U.S. Under-Secretary of State for Political Affairs.

Why mainstream media is silent or deceptive about investigating this Al-Qaeda?
Let us hear from David Rockefeller [WIKIPEDIA], former Chairman of Chase Manhattan Bank and Council of Foreign Relation (CFR), member of covert Bilderberg Steering Committee, and founder of covert Trilateral Commission [WIKIPEDIA] who also

orchestrated the deal to transfer WTC ownership from Port Authority to Silverstein Properties and Westfield America prior to 9/11: "We are grateful to the Washington Post, the New York Times, Time Magazine and other great publications whose directors have attended our meetings and respected their promises of discretion for almost forty years."

In other words, most mainstream US media became aristocratic CIA operatives [LA TIMES] as **"Operation MOCKINGBIRD** [HUPPI.COM] — The CIA begins recruiting American news organizations and journalists to become spies and disseminators of propaganda. The effort is headed by Frank Wisner, Allan Dulles, Richard Helms and Philip Graham. Graham is publisher of *The Washington Post,* which becomes a major CIA player. Eventually, the CIA's media assets will include ABC, NBC, CBS, *Time, Newsweek,* Associated Press, United Press International, Reuters, Hearst Newspapers, Scripps-Howard, Copley News Service and more. By the CIA's own admission, at least 25 organizations and 400 journalists will become CIA assets."

Thus the media subscribed to Winston Churchill's dictum [WIKIPEDIA] that, **"In wartime, truth is so precious that she should always be attended by a bodyguard of lies."** And for the CIA, all time is wartime.

What this Al-Qaeda wants? Let us hear from horse's mouth again: "It would have been impossible for us to develop our plan for the world if we had been subjected to the lights of publicity during those years. But, the world is more sophisticated and prepared to march towards a world government. The supranational sovereignty of an intellectual elite and world bankers is surely preferable to the national auto determination practiced in past centuries."
-- David Rockefeller, Speaking at the June, 1991 Bilderberg meeting in Baden, Germany (a meeting also attended by then-Governor Bill Clinton as well as PNAC signatory Dan Quayle)

A special note about David Rockefeller: it was in Room 3603 in Rockefeller Center [WIKIPEDIA] that Allen Dulles [WIKIPEDIA], then head of CIA, had set up his WWII operational center after Pearl Harbor [WIKIPEDIA], liaising closely with MI6 [WIKIPEDIA] which also had their principal U.S. operation in the Center! Moreover, in *Cary Reich's* biography of his brother Nelson, a former CIA agent states that David was extensively briefed on covert intelligence operations by himself and other Agency division chiefs, under the direction of David's "friend and confidant", CIA Director Allen Dulles! Thus it is obvious that David Rockefeller had full knowledge of all CIA and MI6 warnings about imminent spectacular "New Pearl Harbour" when he orchestrated the WTC ownership transfer from public Port Authority to private Silverstein Properties and Westfield America funded by JP Morgan Chase tied with Rockefeller family interests!

Fellow Americans, Canadians, and world citizens are not gaining anything out of this shadow alliance among aristocratic private covert Bilderberg [BBC], covert union of NATO/Israeli military intelligence wings as Al-Qaeda, private mercenaries recruiting ex-military/ex-CIA militias from around the world and media monopoly meticulously glorifying military, evangelism, and monarchy. It only helps NATO Constitutional Monarchs [KOLKI.COM] expand NATO and monarchy around the world dismantling true participatory democracy of **"We the people, by the people, for The People"** [Abraham Lincoln, Gettysburg, Pennsylvania, November 19, 1863].

Reference: (Overall)
i. 9/11 Timeline from official 9/11 commission documents and interviews
ii. Newspapers articles from around the globe
iii. George Tenet (Ex-CIA Director), "At The Center of the Storm, USA, 2007"
iv. Interview with Ex-FBI translator Sibel Edmonds (Appendix)
v. http://oldamericancentury.org/pnac_timeline.htm
vi. www.historycommons.org
vii. Scholars For 9/11 Truth & Justice, http://stj911.org/
viii. Don Paul, Facing Our Fascist State, www.questionnquestion.net
ix. Steve Kangus, A Timeline of CIA Atrocities, www.huppi.net

Let us now summarize Al-Qaeda in poem 'Guantanamo Bay'

Guantanamo Bay

(Dedicated to all victims who have been silenced depriving them from <u>Rule of Law</u> and <u>Proof of Conviction</u> around the world)

[Ever wonder why Al-Qaeda suspects aren't allowed to speak for themselves before States build their cases? Why covert CIA destroyed 100s of interrogation tapes as obstructions to justice? Because Guantanamo Bay is a camp to baptize innocent/kidnapped world citizens as Al-Qaeda with harsh treatments and false promises to use them for Aristocrative Evangelical military success around the world! Let's not forget the first question in Democracy – 'What if they are not militant'? We must not live under criminal military and intelligence hiding under National Security and secrecy! Kolki]

Welcome to Guantanamo Bay Cuba!
We specialize in converting innocent people to Al-Qaeda!
Headquartered in the Indian Ocean, Island of Diego Garcia!
The management brain is in Washington DC/Virginia!
Our main North American branch is in Indiana,
Branch offices recruiting all over including Britain and Australia!
Middle Eastern branches are in Kuwait and Saudi Arabia!
The newest branch is in Mississauga, Ontario, Canada!

If you cooperate we will make an offer you can't refuse!
If you don't, you are in for endless torture and abuse!
We make sure no one can hear you but everyone only hears us!
So whatever we tell media is the final words!

We trained for years detained Palestinians as suicide bombers!
Methodology starts by putting you in solitary cell lighted 24 hours!
Ensuring sleep deprivation waking you up every half an hour!
Interrogations and tortures follow until you surrender –
And prepared to say what we want you to say and follow orders!

You will be chained in hands and legs, looking at the floor all day!

Yet have to finish your meal within five minutes permitted!
Natures call will be rationed prohibited if you ever protest!
You won't be allowed to talk to anyone not even yourself!
No religious practice or bowing to anybody except ourselves!
Until you are baptized as Al-Qaeda wholly committed!

We will train you in all sophisticated bombs and weapons!
You will learn to behead forgetting all superstition -
How to bring a tower down by creative demolition!
When you pass flight termination, we will send you for mission -
Using private charter flights flying towards worldwide destinations
Based on demands from allies or to silence countries in oppositions!
Occasionally you will be part of a unique secret mission -
As programmable deep water divers inside ocean faults
Stimulating Earthquakes and Tsunami detonating Neutron Bombs!

People think we only transfer prisoners for outsourcing torture!
Our intelligent media keep the gossip alive with Islamic Posture!
You will be part of our valued team of 900,000 plus soldiers -
Running worldwide shadow Governments without UN backlash!
Our political wing keeps politics groovy with 'tough on crime' and 'tax cuts'!
Our voting machines are paperless sensitive to remote touch!
World Health Organization resonates with our pandemic cause!
Our NGOs are busy converting UN to private charter!
But all these goodness come with only one minor catch!
We will use your video in media for Al-Qaeda broadcast!

[CIA interrogators **threatened to kill the children of one detainee** at the height of the Bush administration's war on terror and implied that **another's mother would be sexually assaulted**, newly declassified documents revealed Monday, August 24, 2009 as the government launched a criminal investigation into the spy agency's "unauthorized, improvised, inhumane" practices.

... suspect Abd al-Nashiri, the alleged mastermind of the 2000 USS Cole bombing, **was hooded, handcuffed and threatened with an unloaded gun and a power drill.** The unidentified interrogator **also threatened Nashiri's mother and family, implying that they would be sexually abused in front of him,** ... other interrogators told Sept. 11 mastermind Khalid Sheikh Mohammed that "if anything else happens in the United States, **'We're going to kill your children,'"** ... Death threats violate anti-torture laws...
in another instance, an interrogator pinched the carotid artery of a detainee until he started to pass out, then shook him awake. He did this three times. **The interrogator said he had never been taught how to conduct detainee questioning....** By STEVEN R. HURST and DEVLIN BARRETT, Associated Press Writers, August 24, 2009.]

Too much power & money in few like minded group of private hands led to 9/11, related chaos and injustice, insecurity everywhere, failure of the banking & justice systems, almost no accountability, and biased polling by their media to support all that making citizens fight and gossip against each other worldwide. It is time to take back governments from private agencies and outsourcing to live freely **as we the people, by the people and for the people** – enjoying true bliss of Participatory Democracy. **Kolki**

How Feasible Was

Remote Hijacking of Passenger Jets

Inside USA on/before 9/11?

"Home Run"- Electronically Hijacking of Passenger Jet Aircrafts By Military/Intelligence

What is 'Home Run'? America faced a new crisis in the mid-seventies where US commercial jets were being hijacked for geopolitical purposes. Determined to gain the upper hand in this new form of aerial warfare, two American multinationals collaborated with the Defense Advanced Projects Agency (DARPA) on a project designed to facilitate the remote recovery of hijacked American aircraft. It was a brilliant concept, "Home Run" [not its real code name], which allowed specialist ground controllers to listen to cockpit conversations on the target aircrafts, eventually taking absolute control of the computerized flight control system by remote means. Until recently Swedish 'Telia' used Boeing's 'Home Run' to allow passengers to **surf free of charge on-board airplanes.**

Transponder and 'Home Run': Technically a transponder is a combined radio transmitter and receiver which operates automatically, in reference to 9/11 relaying data between the four aircrafts and air traffic controls on the ground. The communication protocols provide a unique "identity" for each aircraft, which are essential to avoid mid-air collisions in crowded airspace, and equally essential for 'Home Run' controllers lock onto the intended aircrafts for remote control manoeuvrings. Once the correct aircraft has been located, Home Run "piggy backs" a data transmission onto the transponder channel and takes direct control from the ground. Per 9-11 commission time line, all 9/11 planes had transponders turned off during hijacking! This explains why none of the 9/11 aircraft sent a special "I have been hijacked" transponder code, despite multiple activation points on all four aircrafts. Because once the transponder frequency had already been piggy backed by Home Run, transmission of the special hijack code was rendered impossible. This was the first hard proof that the 9/11 target aircrafts had been hijacked electronically from the ground.

Helpless Pilots: Once control has been taken away from the ground using top secret computer codes (known only to top secret military and Boeing specialists), regardless of the wishes of the hijackers or flight deck crew, the hijacked aircraft could be recovered remotely forcing it to land at an airport of choice or programmed destination, with no more difficulty than flying radio-controlled model planes or military drones like Global Hawk. With reference to 9/11, the orchestrators selected World Trade Centre (WTC) and Pentagon as well as, probably Capitol/White House (aborted Flight 93) as the targeted destinations. All flights were delayed for convenience of remote hijacking! Unfortunately, Flight 93 encountered additional delay due to unpredictable traffic situation disrupting the rather precision plan. Donald Rumsfeld admitted it was shot down by the same people who hijacked the other planes.

How a pilot operates an aircraft? In order to control an aircraft in three-dimensional space, the pilot uses the control yoke (joystick) in front of him, rudder pedals under his feet, and a bank of engine throttles located at his side. Without engine thrust the aircraft would not fly at all, so for more speed or altitude the pilot increases throttle, and for less speed or altitude the pilot decreases throttle.

In order to raise or lower the nose of the aircraft, the pilot pulls or pushes on the control yoke, which in turn raises or lowers the elevators on the horizontal tail plane. To bank the aircraft left or right, the pilot moves the control yoke to the left or right, which in turn operates the ailerons on the outer wings. Lastly, to turn left or right at low speed or "balance" turns at high speed, the pilot presses the left or right rudder pedals as required, which in turn move the rudder on the vertical stabilizer.

Automated Boeing 757 and 767: Most modern jet air planes have automated flight management system which can be programmed to do everything a pilot would do and even more. On top of it Boeing 757 and 767 have "Home Run" option integrated with the Transponder to take that control from the ground, if and when necessary. That was probably the reasons why 757-200 had been Military's choice as C-32A since June 1998 and 767 as KC-767 since March 2001. The 9/11 perpetrators knew all of these very well sitting at the top of technology and intelligence shrouded in secrecy and utilized it to justify 870 Billion dollars military spending implementing much anticipated "New Pearl Harbour" required for continuing US/NATO military domination of the world in peace time.

Now let us hear from Transportation Secretary Norman Mineta testifying before 9/11 commissions "during the time that the airplane was coming into the Pentagon, there was a young man who would come in and said to the Vice President, 'the plane is 50 miles out, the plane is 30 miles out.' And when it got to 'the plane is 10 miles out," the young man also said to the Vice President, 'Do the orders still stand?' And the Vice President...said, 'Of course the orders still stand. Have you heard anything to the contrary?"

Since the airplane was not intercepted and destroyed, even though the vice president knew of it, "the orders" may have been to allow the plane to hit the Pentagon.

To confirm remote control hijacking from Pentagon on 9/11 imagine what novice Cessna trained box cutter armed alleged Al-Qaeda hijacker Hani Hanjour had to do to manoeuvre American Airlines Flight 77 that struck the Pentagon. It would require not only outfoxing military radar for over an hour but the quite miraculous performance of descending 7,000 feet in two minutes while executing a 270-degree banked turn and bashing into the Pentagon without touching or damaging the lawn, a feat of aeronautical magic.

Now let us hear former Defense Secretary Rumsfeld's recollection at 8am on 9/11 when Deputy Defense Secretary Paul Wolfowitz, and Representative Christopher Cox (R) were meeting in Rumsfeld's private Pentagon dining room, discussing missile Defense. Rumsfeld told CNN's Larry King Live, "I had said at an eight o'clock breakfast that sometime in the next two, four, six, eight, ten, twelve months there would be an event that would occur in the world that would be sufficiently shocking that it would remind people again how important it is to have a strong healthy Defense Department that contributes to—that underpins peace and stability in our world." [CNN, 12/5/01.

"Lt. Colonel Steven Butler has been suspended for writing a letter in which he called President Bush 'a joke' and accused Bush of knowing about the Sept. 11 attacks."
— The Monterey County Herald, 3 June 2002

In fact, then Defense secretary Donald Rumsfeld gave many hints (predicting New Pearl Harbour during inauguration, disclosing 2.3 trillion missing Pentagon Fund (to be used to run shadow government following 9/11) and telling the world shooting down of Flight 93 by hijackers(?)) which media, analysts, scholars, and politicians chose to ignore for economic, geopolitical, Monarchial, and evangelical reasons – bringing otherwise peace loving world to the brink of World War III. May God (Universal loving expression) bless our world and guide all peace loving people stand tall for revealing much needed truth for an eternal co-existence!

A Secret Service page at 10:32 a.m. warned: "ANONYMOUS CALL TO JOC REPORTING ANGEL IS TARGET." Angel is the Secret Service codeword for Air Force One; JOC means Joint Operations Center.[Wikileaks.org] By that time Air Force One was in the air suggesting warning was about "Remote Hijacking" locking on the Transponder using secret code only known to military.

Reference:
• "Home Run" Electronically *Hijacking the World Trade Center Attack Aircraft,* Joe Vialls October 2001
• March/April issue of "Tikkun" magazine, "a bimonthly Jewish critique of Politics, Culture & Society, Article by Dr. Griffin."
• 9-11 Timeline per Commission Report
• http://www.homerun.telia.com/eng/news/
• http://wikileaks.org/wiki/Egads%21_Confidential_9/11_Pager_Messages_Disclosed

GPS-Guided Autopilot Systems on B757 and B767

Despite careful avoidance of the sensitive Remote Hijacking issue by the 9/11 Commission, US Politicians, and Media alike the information collected after the terrorist attacks of September 11, 2001 has raised questions about the alleged ability and motivation of the people accused of piloting four Boeing 757 and 767 planes into the World Trade Center, the Pentagon building and a field in Shanksville, Pennsylvania; speculations have since lingered regarding the covert use of Flight Termination Technology to hijack and precisely navigate the four airliners to the intended targets that day disabling onboard pilot control.

The development and implementation of pre-9/11 state-of-the-art systems capable of facilitating precise automated navigation of the Boeing 757 and 767 aircraft is well documented by the U.S. federal government and civil aviation industry publications. The Global Positioning System (GPS) is a space-based radio-navigation system that generates accurate positioning (providing 100-meter accuracy in raw form), navigation, and timing information for civil use at no cost. The information signal can be obtained through the use of <u>GPS signal receiving equipment</u>[1].

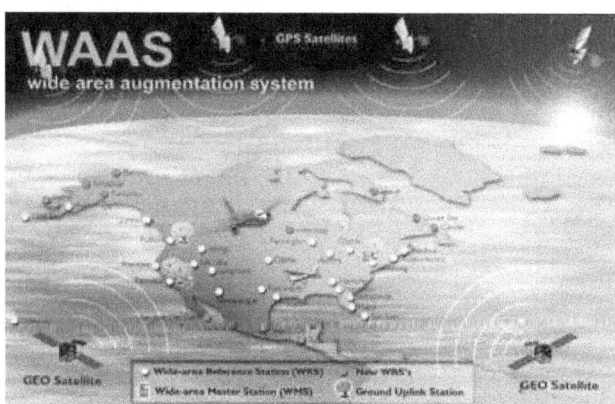

Augmented GPS signal service was developed during the mid-to-late 1990s by the Federal Aviation Administration (FAA) and Raytheon.

Wide Area Augmentation System or 'WAAS', is basically a continental DGPS system, 'D' stands for differential. It precisely surveys ground-based Wide-area Reference Stations that monitor and collect GPS satellite signal errors. Grounds based Wide-area Master Stations then transmit corrected GPS signal information to ground-based Ground Uplink Stations which then transmit the corrected GPS signal information to Geostationary Satellites. These satellites then broadcast the corrected positional information back to Earth for use within a GPS-like signal.

The FAA announced[2] on August 24, 2000 - just 13 months prior to the September 11, 2001 attacks - that the WAAS signal was available pending final approval by the FAA. Horizontal and vertical positional data **accurate to between one to three meters** was now available throughout the contiguous United States. The WAAS signal provides positional accuracy[3] sufficient for Category I precision aircraft runway approaches. Raytheon's director of satellite navigation systems even reported[4] that rescue personnel utilized the newly activated WAAS signal, in order to precisely survey the Ground Zero site following the September 11, 2001, alleged terrorist attacks.

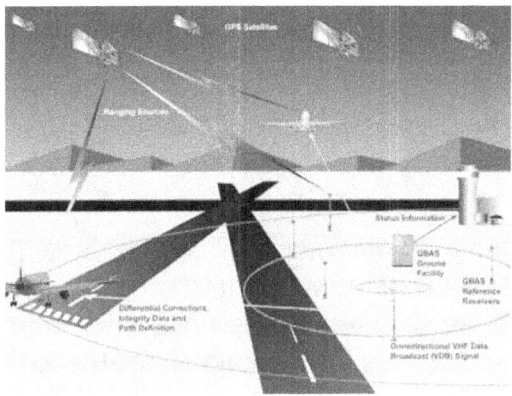

GPS navigation for aviation requires waypoints which are three dimensional locations within the US National Air Space - comprised of longitude, latitude and altitude coordinates. An aircraft flight[5] path may include a series of waypoints[6,] e.g., the (late) World Trade Center towers, Washington Monument in Washington DC, and the Space Needle in Seattle, Washington. Study revealed the FAA needed about 24 reference receivers scattered across the U.S. to gather pretty good correction data for most of the country. That data would make GPS accurate enough for "Category 1" landings (i.e. very close to the runway but not zero visibility).

To complete the system the FAA needed Local Area Augmentation Systems (LAAS) near runways.
These would work like the WAAS but on a smaller scale. The reference receivers would be near the runways and so would be able to give much more accurate correction data to the incoming planes. With a LAAS aircraft would be able to use GPS to make Category 3 landings (zero visibility).

Utilizing WAAS and LAAS and related technologies FAA and National Aeronautics and Space Administration (NASA) sponsored auto landing runway approach and touchdown test flights during the mid-to-late 1990s using Boeing 700 series aircrafts including Boeing 757, 767 obtaining horizontal and vertical positional accuracies of just several meters or less.

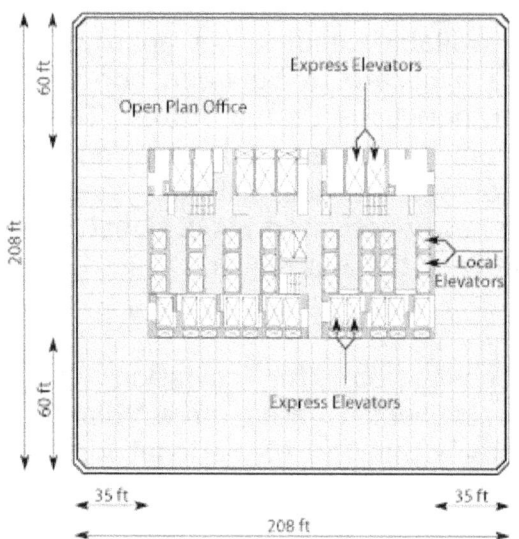

The four aircrafts used to carry out the September 11, 2001, attacks inside USA were also Boeing 757-200 and 767-200 model aircrafts. Runways of major U.S. airports like JFK International, Chicago-O'Hare International and Los Angeles International are between 150 and 200 feet wide. The World Trade Center towers were each 208 feet wide.

Founded by alumni of the Stanford University Department of Aeronautics and Astronautics, IntegriNautics of Palo Alto, California commercialized a precision landing system. The work had been assisted by Langley Research Center's Small Business Technology Transfer (STTR) Program. The research sparked new thinking on a precision touchdown concept called the Integrity Beacon Landing System.

Fig. Boeing 737 conducts series of automatic aircraft touchdowns relying on a new precision navigation system.

During a four-day period in October 1994, the idea was put to the test on Runway 35 at NASA's Crows Landing Flight Facility in California. These tests proved the validity of using what IntegriNautics terms integrity beacon "pseudolites." Compact in size, the ground-based low-power transmitters each fit entirely on a circuit board the size of a credit card. Capable of running on a 9-volt battery for over 12 hours, the inexpensive devices transmit just a few microwatts of power, emulating a GPS satellite. The beacons were situated in pairs on either side of the approach path to the runway. Power of the broadcast signals from the pseudolites was set low, measurable only inside a "bubble" emanating from the transmitter.

Using signals from orbiting GPS satellites and the ground-generated pseudolite signals, 110 autopilot-in-the-loop landings of a United Airlines Boeing 737 were completed. The integrity beacons provided consistent accuracies on the order of a few centimeters during each of the autopiloted runway touchdowns. The successful series was sponsored by the Federal Aviation Administration (FAA) as part of that agency's satellite navigation program.

Evaluation of test results provides confidence that the level of integrity yielded by satellite positioning and the ground-based monitors would improve passenger safety. High integrity of the beacon landing system translates to just one failure in a billion approaches.

IntegriNautics developed technology and products for a range of FAA, NASA, and Defense Department requirements, as well as commercial and international customers since 1997. Now it is known as Novariant [http://www.novariant.com/]. During July and August of 1995, Honeywell, Boeing and NASA sponsored tests using NASA's Boeing 757-200 test aircraft and performed 75 autopilot approaches and touchdowns. The predicted augmented GPS system accuracy of 1-2 meters[9] was successfully achieved[10].

During December, 1998, augmented GPS signal flight tests sponsored by the FAA in cooperation with Ohio University were conducted. 50 autopilot approaches and touchdowns were successfully performed[11] by a donated United Parcel Service Boeing 757-200 series aircraft. The augmented GPS positional signal was integrated into the aircraft Flight Management System (FMS).

During August of 1999, multiple augmented GPS signal autopilot approach and touchdown tests were performed using a donated United Parcel Service 767 aircraft. These tests were sponsored by the FAA and were centered on the prototype GPS-based Local Area Augmentation System (LAAS), which is intended to compliment the FAA's WAAS signal. The LAAS signal can provide positional accuracy of less than one meter [FAA] vertically and laterally. Several years prior to 9/11 GPS based avionics systems were installed in the Boeing 757 and 767 model military and passenger aircrafts, similar to those involved in the September 11, 2001, alleged terrorist attacks.

On September 6, 1996 Rockwell-Collins Commercial Avionics announced [High Beam Research, http://www.highbeam.com/doc/1G1-18652301.html] plans by Boeing and major commercial airlines, to install Rockwell-Collins Multi-Mode Receiver (MMR) landing systems within their Boeing 757 and 767 aircraft. The MMR system can utilize [FAA, GNSS Library] the WAAS signal as well as the basic GPS signal, the VHF, UHF, VOR navigation signals and eventually the LAAS navigation signal.

On September 7, 1998 Honeywell International announced [Aviation Week, September 7, 1998] plans by American Airlines [WARISCRIME.COM] and United Airlines, to install the GPS capable Pegasus Flight Management System (FMS) within their Boeing 757 and 767 aircraft, with 150 waypoint route capacity. An aircraft FMS is comprised of three major systems including an aircraft's Auto-Flight System. Aircraft Auto-Flight Systems were utilized during the afore mentioned GPS signal test flight approaches and touchdowns. By 1999, Boeing 757 and 767 aircraft contained digital flight control systems that can "automatically fly the airplanes on pre-selected routes, headings, speed or altitude manoeuvres [http://www.highbeam.com/doc/1G1-55993162.html]."

On October 9, 2001, Cubic Defense Systems, Inc. applied for a U.S. patent that removes control of an aircraft from its pilot and utilizes an aircraft's auto-pilot system to implement an uninterruptible pre-programmed autopilot flight plan in order to navigate an aircraft to a given destination during an emergency. This would be accomplished through the use of an electronic or mechanical relay or relays that become activated by pilot operation of an aircraft hijack notification system. Surprisingly to some, none of the four aircraft destroyed on September 11, 2001 are known to have entered unique transponder hijack notification codes, suggesting either modified function or insufficient activation time. One optional feature of the Cubic system is termination of an aircraft's ability to communicate. In two cases, hijacker communications aimed at passengers on-board American Airlines flight 11 [WarisCrime.com] and United Airlines flight 93 on September 11, 2001 were heard instead by air traffic controllers, suggesting modified communication functions. The Cubic patent also references Honeywell's 1995 augmented GPS flight navigation research and development, presumably as a signal navigation aid. The system also envisions the use of new aircraft flight instructions transmitted by a remote sender, that would override aircraft functions [USPTO, Anti-Hijacking System] already underway and direct an aircraft auto-pilot system to navigate an aircraft to a predetermined landing destination. A data link interface between an aircraft Flight Management System (FMS) and the Management Unit for the Aircraft Communication Addressing and Reporting System (ACARS), was developed during the early 1990s. This communication system allows for the update an aircraft FMS in mid-flight [WIKIPEDIA, http://en.wikipedia.org/wiki/ACARS]. An aircraft auto-pilot system is part of the FMS.

Because the Flight Data Recorders (FDRs) for American Airlines flight 11 and United Airlines flight 175 were not recovered, details regarding the operation of each aircraft are not known. The FDRs for American Airlines flight 77 and United Airlines flight 93 were recovered and indicate pilot control of each aircraft. However, the FDR readout file for American Airlines flight 77 was completed four hours and fifteen minutes [911Blogger.com] before the said FDR was recovered, suggesting false or altered FDR information. And the FDRs for American Airlines flight 77 and United Airlines flight 93 are virtually the only ones during the previous 20 years of major National Transportation Safety Board (NTSB) U.S. aviation mishap investigations, for which unique inventory control serial numbers were not published. Such serial numbers are required [NTSB, http://www.ntsb.gov/Aviation/Manuals/FDR_Handbook.pdf]   to facilitate FDR data readouts. In fact the NTSB possesses no records pertaining to the positive identification of the FDRs for American Airlines flight 77 and United Airlines flight 93.

References:
1. http://www.gps.gov/
2. Wide Area Augmentation System Signal Now Available, http://www.faa.gov/news/press_releases/news_story.cfm?newsId=5249
3. WAAS Fact Sheet, http://www.faa.gov/about/office_org/headquarters_offices/ato/service_units/techops/navservices/gnss/library/factsheets/
4. WAAS, Back in Step, http://www.aviationtoday.com/av/categories/commercial/12571.html
5. 9/11 Attacks Generated by GPS-Guided US Made Autopilot System, http://www.wariscrime.com/2008/10/05/articles/911-attacks-generated-by-gps-guided-autopilot-systems/
6. Waypoints, http://www.waypoint.org/
7. Augmented GPS, http://www.trimble.com/gps/dgps-advanced5.shtml
8. GETTING TO THE POINT IN PINPOINT LANDING, SPINOFF 1998, NASA-STI, http://www.sti.nasa.gov/tto/spinoff1998/t2.htm
9. Honeywell's Differential GPS Satellite Landing System, http://www.bluecoat.org/reports/Lewison_96_DGPS.pdf
10. NASA Facts, Dec 1999, http://oea.larc.nasa.gov/PAIS/757.html
11. FAA, http://www.tc.faa.gov/logistics/grants/success/OU.pdf

Can US Military and Intelligence

Hurt Own Citizens

Including Soldiers?

'Operation Northwoods' - Terrorist Side of US Military Even Hurting Americans and GIs

Before 9/11/2001, world didn't know much about virtual Al-Qaeda; attacking countries at peace were meant to be War Crimes. Before US-Led illegal invasion and destruction of peaceful Iraq, entire land was Green Zone void of Al-Qaeda, suicide bombings, sectarian violence and friendly fires! But under massive US-British-Australian brutal occupying forces – the only Green Zone became new US Embassy Fortress (Late Saddam Hussein's Palace) and virtual Al-Qaeda seems to be omnipresent dividing Iraqis while prolonging oppressive occupation as justification of military might! How and why?

Recently declassified Pentagon documents, after more than 40 years, highlight a set of terrorist proposals on Cuba by the US military Joint Chiefs of Staff codenamed OPERATION NORTHWOODS.

Details of Operation Northwoods can be found in ABC News and US National Archives (ARC Identifier: 305036, Title: Northwoods, U.S. Military Intervention in Cuba, 1962), as well as the book on US National Security Agency 'Body of Secrets' from Doubleday by author James Bamford.

The document, titled "**Justification for U.S. Military Intervention in Cuba**" was provided by the then American Joint Chiefs of Staff, President Eisenhower appointee Army Gen. Lyman L. Lemnitzer, to Secretary of Defense Robert McNamara on March 13, 1962, outlining the key components of Operation Northwoods.

The top secret document was written in response to a request from then Chief of the Cuba Project, Col. Edward Lansdale describing U.S. military plans to covertly engineer various terrorist pretexts leading to justification of invading Cuba.

The proposals -- **part of a secret anti-Castro program known as Operation Mongoose** – included:
• Staging the assassinations of Cubans living in the United States,
• Developing a fake "Communist Cuban terror campaign in the Miami and other cities of Florida, as well as Washington DC,"
• Sinking a boatload of Cuban refugees (real or simulated),"

- Faking **remote controlled** Cuban air force attack on a civilian jetliner, and
- Concocting a "**Remember the Maine**" incident by blowing up a U.S. ship in Cuban waters and then blaming the incident as Cuban sabotage.

Details of the plans described in 'Body of Secrets' suggest deliberate U.S. military casualties as obvious from quote: "We could blow up a U.S. ship in Guantanamo Bay and blame Cuba," and, "casualty lists in U.S. newspapers would cause a helpful wave of national indignation." **It is now obvious how 9/11 US media coverage helped destroy Afghanistan and Iraq, without investigation.**

President Kennedy rebuked the idea and Gen. Lemnitzer was transferred to another job after a month. President Kennedy was assassinated on November 22nd, 1963, Friday, in Dallas, Texas, in broad day light.

Operation Northwoods is an ideal example that US military can 'plan & execute' 9/11 style precision well coordinated terrorism blaming on prefabricated Islamic militants and their leader Osama Bin Laden.

"The Association for Responsible Dissent estimates that by 1987, 6 million people had died as a result of CIA covert operations. Former State Department official William Blum correctly calls this an "American Holocaust"[1]. The question is why American Intelligence needs to kill people, destroy democracies, and destabilize other nations for American business and national interests with utmost secrecy and a black budget without congressional accountability that eventually demonizes true freedom loving Americans and enriches the Monarchial alliance?

A Chronology of Worldwide CIA Atrocities
Coordinating with MI6, ISI, and Mossad

 World citizens wonder how and why American Military and intelligence became so brutal since WWII despite apparent goodwill gestures towards a peaceful global village among most world leaders and politicians. USA fought more wars since WWII and having dominating troops installed in many countries around the world including Germany, Korea, Japan, Kuwait, Iraq, and Afghanistan despite the existence of the United Nations and illusory International Court of Justice.

To understand one needs to revisit history of CIA, MI6(SIS), ISI and Mossad – all share the common goal of creating a new world order under the modern United Kingdom of Israel (Church[2]).

SIS SECRET INTELLIGENCE SERVICE, UK
[Actual logo cab be found at: http://www.sis.gov.uk/output/sis-home-welcome.html]

 As Britain's secret service, SIS (MI6) provides the British Government with a global covert capability to promote and defend the national security and economic well-being of the United Kingdom.
SIS operates world-wide to collect secret foreign intelligence in support of the British Government's policies and objectives. To do this effectively SIS must protect the secrets of its sources and methods. The last statement itself safeguards abuses, lies and war crimes.

"CIA operations follow the same recurring script. First, American business interests abroad are threatened by a popular or democratically elected leader. The people support their leader because he intends to conduct land reform, strengthen unions, redistribute wealth, nationalize foreign-owned industry, and regulate business to protect workers, consumers and the environment. So, on behalf of American business, and often with their help, the CIA mobilizes the opposition. First it identifies right-wing groups within the country (usually the military), and offers them a deal: "We'll put you in power if you maintain a favourable business climate for us." The Agency then hires, trains and works with them to overthrow the existing government (usually a democracy). It uses every trick in the book: propaganda, stuffed ballot boxes, purchased elections, extortion, blackmail, sexual intrigue, false stories about opponents in the local media, infiltration and disruption of opposing political parties, kidnapping, beating, torture, intimidation, economic sabotage, death squads and even assassination. These efforts culminate in a military *coup*, which installs a right-wing dictator. The CIA trains the dictator's security apparatus to crack down on the traditional enemies of big business, using interrogation, torture and murder. The victims are said to be "communists," but almost always they are just peasants, liberals, moderates, labour union leaders, political opponents and advocates of free speech and democracy. Widespread human rights abuses follow.

This scenario has been repeated so many times that the CIA actually teaches it in a special school, the notorious 'School of the Americas'. It opened in Panama but later moved to Fort Benning, Georgia. Critics have nicknamed it the 'School of the Dictators' and 'School of the Assassins'. Here, the CIA trains Latin American military officers how to conduct coups, including the use of interrogation, torture, and murder.

The Association for Responsible Dissent estimates that by 1987, 6 million people had died as a result of CIA covert operations. (2) Former State Department official William Blum correctly calls this an 'American Holocaust'.

The CIA justifies these actions as part of its war against communism. But most *coups* do not involve a communist threat. Unlucky nations are targeted for a wide variety of reasons: not only threats to American business interests abroad, but also liberal or even moderate social reforms, political instability, the unwillingness of a leader to carry out Washington's dictates, and declarations of neutrality in the Cold War. Indeed, nothing has infuriated CIA Directors quite like a nation's desire to stay out of the Cold War.

The ironic thing about all this intervention is that it frequently fails to achieve American objectives. Often the newly installed dictator grows comfortable with the security apparatus the CIA has built for him. He becomes an expert at running a police state. And because the dictator knows he cannot be overthrown, he becomes independent and defiant of Washington's will. The CIA then finds it cannot overthrow him, because the police and military are under the dictator's control, afraid to cooperate with American spies for fear of torture and execution. The only two options for the U.S at this point are impotence or war. Examples of this "boomerang effect" include the Shah of Iran, General Noriega and Saddam Hussein. The boomerang effect also explains why the CIA has proven highly successful at overthrowing democracies, but a wretched failure at overthrowing dictatorships".

The following timeline[1] describes just a few of the hundreds of atrocities and crimes committed by the CIA throughout post WWII world which are more than enough to justify why the covert CIA along with its covert cousins including MI6, Mossad, and ISI must be abolished and replaced by true information-gathering and analysis organizations needed for a civilized peace loving world. The covert intelligences like CIA cannot be reformed — because they are institutionally, politically, and culturally corrupt.

1929

The culture we lost — Secretary of State Henry Stimson refuses to endorse a code-breaking operation, saying, "Gentlemen do not read each other's mail."

1941

COI created — In preparation for World War II, President Roosevelt creates the Office of Coordinator of Information (COI). General William "Wild Bill" Donovan heads the new intelligence service.

1942

OSS created — Roosevelt restructures COI into something more suitable for covert action, the Office of Strategic Services (OSS). Donovan recruits so many of the nation's rich and powerful that eventually people joke that "OSS" stands for "Oh, so social!" or "Oh, such snobs!"

1943

Italy — Donovan recruits the Catholic Church in Rome to be the center of Anglo-American spy operations in Fascist Italy. This would prove to be one of America's most enduring intelligence alliances in the Cold War.

1945

OSS is abolished — The remaining American information agencies cease covert actions and return to harmless information gathering and analysis.

Operation PAPERCLIP - While other American agencies are hunting down Nazi war criminals for arrest, the U.S. intelligence community is smuggling them into America, unpunished, for their use against the Soviets. The most important of these is Reinhard Gehlen, Hitler's master spy who had built up an intelligence network in the Soviet Union. With full U.S. blessing, he creates the "Gehlen Organization," a band of refugee Nazi spies who reactivate their networks in Russia. These include SS intelligence officers Alfred Six and Emil Augsburg (who massacred Jews in the Holocaust), Klaus Barbie (the "Butcher of Lyon"), Otto von Bolschwing (the Holocaust mastermind who worked with Eichmann) and SS Colonel Otto Skorzeny (a personal friend of Hitler's). The Gehlen Organization supplies the U.S. with its only intelligence on the Soviet Union for the next ten years, serving as a bridge between the abolishment of the OSS and the creation of the CIA. However, much of the "intelligence" the former Nazis provide is bogus. Gehlen inflates Soviet military capabilities at a time when Russia is still rebuilding its devastated society, in order to inflate his own importance to the Americans (who might otherwise punish him). In 1948, Gehlen almost convinces the Americans that war is imminent, and the West should make a pre-emptive strike. In the 50s he produces a fictitious "missile gap." To make matters worse, the Russians have thoroughly penetrated the Gehlen Organization with double agents, undermining the very American security that Gehlen was supposed to protect.

1947

Greece — President Truman requests military aid to Greece to support right-wing forces fighting communist rebels. For the rest of the Cold War, Washington and the CIA will back notorious Greek leaders with deplorable human rights records.

CIA created — President Truman signs the National Security Act of 1947, creating the Central Intelligence Agency and National Security Council. The CIA is accountable to the president through the NSC — there is no democratic or congressional oversight. Its charter allows the CIA to "perform such other functions and duties... as the National Security Council may from time to time direct." This loophole opens the door to covert action and dirty tricks.

1948

Covert-action wing created — The CIA recreates a covert action wing, innocuously called the Office of Policy Coordination, led by Wall Street lawyer Frank Wisner. According to its secret charter, its responsibilities include "propaganda, economic warfare, preventive direct action, including sabotage, antisabotage, demolition and evacuation procedures; subversion against hostile states, including assistance to underground resistance groups, and support of indigenous anti-communist elements in threatened countries of the free world."

Italy — The CIA corrupts democratic elections in Italy, where Italian communists threaten to win the elections. The CIA buys votes, broadcasts propaganda, threatens and beats up opposition leaders, and infiltrates and disrupts their organizations. It works -- the communists are defeated.

1949

Radio Free Europe — The CIA creates its first major propaganda outlet, Radio Free Europe. Over the next several decades, its broadcasts are so blatantly false that for a time it is considered illegal to publish transcripts of them in the U.S.

Late 40s

Operation MOCKINGBIRD — The CIA begins recruiting American news organizations and journalists to become spies and disseminators of propaganda. The effort is headed by Frank Wisner, Allan Dulles, Richard Helms and Philip Graham. Graham is publisher of *The Washington Post*, which becomes a major CIA player. Eventually, the CIA's media assets will include ABC, NBC, CBS, *Time*, *Newsweek*, Associated Press, United Press International, Reuters, Hearst Newspapers, Scripps-Howard, Copley News Service and more. By the CIA's own admission, at least 25 organizations and 400 journalists will become CIA assets.

1953

Iran – CIA overthrows the democratically elected Mohammed Mossadegh in a military coup, after he threatened to nationalize British oil. The CIA replaces him with a dictator, the Shah of Iran, whose secret police, SAVAK, is as brutal as the Gestapo.

Operation MK-ULTRA — Inspired by North Korea's brainwashing program, the CIA begins experiments on mind control. The most notorious part of this project involves giving LSD and other drugs to American subjects without their knowledge or against their will, causing several to commit suicide. However, the operation involves far more than this. Funded in part by the Rockefeller and Ford foundations, research includes propaganda, brainwashing, public relations, advertising, hypnosis, and other forms of suggestion.

1954

Guatemala CIA overthrows the democratically elected Jacob Arbenz in a military coup. Arbenz has threatened to nationalize the Rockefeller-owned United Fruit Company, in which CIA Director Allen Dulles also owns stock. Arbenz is replaced with a series of right-wing dictators whose bloodthirsty policies will kill over 100,000 Guatemalans in the next 40 years.

1954-1958

North Vietnam — CIA officer Edward Lansdale spends four years trying to overthrow the communist government of North Vietnam, using all the usual dirty tricks. The CIA also attempts to legitimize a tyrannical puppet regime in South Vietnam, headed by Ngo Dinh Diem. These efforts fail to win the hearts and minds of the South Vietnamese because the Diem government is opposed to true democracy, land reform and poverty reduction measures. The CIA's continuing failure results in escalating American intervention, culminating in the Vietnam War.

1956

Hungary — Radio Free Europe incites Hungary to revolt by broadcasting Khruschev's Secret Speech, in which he denounced Stalin. It also hints that American aid will help the Hungarians fight. This aid fails to materialize as Hungarians launch a doomed armed revolt, which only invites a major Soviet invasion. The conflict kills 7,000 Soviets and 30,000 Hungarians.

1957-1973

Laos — The CIA carries out approximately one coup per year trying to nullify Laos' democratic elections. The problem is the Pathet Lao, a leftist group with enough popular support to be a member of any coalition government. In the late 50s, the CIA even creates an "Armee Clandestine" of Asian mercenaries to attack the Pathet Lao. After the CIA's army suffers numerous defeats, the U.S. starts bombing, dropping more bombs on Laos than all the U.S. bombs dropped in World War II. A quarter of all Laotians will eventually become refugees, many living in caves.

1959

Haiti — The U.S. military helps "Papa Doc" Duvalier become dictator of Haiti. He creates his own private police force, the "Tonton Macoutes," who terrorize the population with machetes. They will kill over 100,000 during the Duvalier family reign. The U.S. does not protest their dismal human rights record.

1961

The Bay of Pigs — The CIA sends 1,500 Cuban exiles to invade Castro's Cuba. But "Operation Mongoose" fails, due to poor planning, security and backing. The planners had imagined that the invasion will spark a popular uprising against Castro -- which never happens. A promised American air strike also never occurs. This is the CIA's first public setback, causing President Kennedy to fire CIA Director Allen Dulles.

Dominican Republic — The CIA assassinates Rafael Trujillo, a murderous dictator Washington has supported since 1930. Trujillo's business interests have grown so large (about 60 percent of the economy) that they have begun competing with American business interests.

Ecuador — The CIA-backed military forces the democratically elected President Jose Velasco to resign. Vice President Carlos Arosemana replaces him; the CIA fills the now vacant vice presidency with its own man.

Congo (Zaire) — The CIA assassinates the democratically elected Patrice Lumumba. However, public support for Lumumba's politics runs so high that the CIA cannot clearly install his opponents in power. Four years of political turmoil follow.

1963

Dominican Republic — The CIA overthrows the democratically elected Juan Bosch in a military coup. The CIA installs a repressive, right-wing junta.

Ecuador — A CIA-backed military coup overthrows President Arosemana, whose independent (not socialist) policies have become unacceptable to Washington. A military junta assumes command, cancels the 1964 elections, and begins abusing human rights.

1964

Brazil — A CIA-backed military coup overthrows the democratically elected government of Joao Goulart. The junta that replaces it will, in the next two decades, become one of the most bloodthirsty in history. General Castelo Branco will create Latin America's first death squads, or bands of secret police who hunt down "communists" for torture, interrogation and murder. Often these "communists" are no more than Branco's political opponents. Later it is revealed that the CIA trains the death squads.

1965

Indonesia — The CIA overthrows the democratically elected Sukarno with a military coup. The CIA has been trying to eliminate Sukarno since 1957, using everything from attempted assassination to sexual intrigue, for nothing more than his declaring neutrality in the Cold War. His successor, General Suharto, will massacre between 500,000 to 1 million civilians accused of being "communist." The CIA supplies the names of countless suspects.

Dominican Republic — A popular rebellion breaks out, promising to reinstall Juan Bosch as the country's elected leader. The revolution is crushed when U.S. Marines land to uphold the military regime by force. The CIA directs everything behind the scenes.

Greece — With the CIA's backing, the king removes George Papandreous as prime minister. Papandreous has failed to vigorously support U.S. interests in Greece.

Congo (Zaire) — A CIA-backed military coup installs Mobutu Sese Seko as dictator. The hated and repressive Mobutu exploits his desperately poor country for billions.

1966

The *Ramparts* Affair — The radical magazine *Ramparts* begins a series of unprecedented anti-CIA articles. Among their scoops: the CIA has paid the University of Michigan $25 million dollars to hire "professors" to train South Vietnamese students in covert police methods. MIT and other universities have received similar payments. *Ramparts* also reveals that the National Students' Association is a CIA front. Students are sometimes recruited through blackmail and bribery, including draft deferments.

1967

Greece — A CIA-backed military coup overthrows the government two days before the elections. The favourite to win was George Papandreous, the liberal candidate. During the next six years, the "reign of the colonels" — backed by the CIA — will usher in the widespread use of torture and murder against political opponents. When a Greek ambassador objects to President Johnson about U.S. plans for Cypress, Johnson tells him: "Fuck your parliament and your constitution."

Operation PHEONIX — The CIA helps South Vietnamese agents identify and then murder alleged Viet Cong leaders operating in South Vietnamese villages. According to a 1971 congressional report, this operation killed about 20,000 "Viet Cong."

1968

Operation CHAOS — The CIA has been illegally spying on American citizens since 1959, but with Operation CHAOS, President Johnson dramatically boosts the effort. CIA agents go undercover as student radicals to spy on and disrupt campus organizations protesting the Vietnam War. They are searching for Russian instigators, which they never find. CHAOS will eventually spy on 7,000 individuals and 1,000 organizations.

Bolivia — A CIA-organized military operation captures legendary guerrilla Che Guevara. The CIA wants to keep him alive for interrogation, but the Bolivian government executes him to prevent worldwide calls for clemency.

1969

Uruguay — The notorious CIA torturer Dan Mitrione arrives in Uruguay, a country torn with political strife. Whereas right-wing forces previously used torture only as a last resort, Mitrione convinces them to use it as a routine, widespread practice. "The precise pain, in the precise place, in the precise amount, for the desired effect," is his motto. The torture techniques he teaches to the death squads rival the Nazis'. He eventually becomes so feared that revolutionaries will kidnap and murder him a year later.

1970

Cambodia — The CIA overthrows Prince Sahounek, who is highly popular among Cambodians for keeping them out of the Vietnam War. He is replaced by CIA puppet Lon Nol, who immediately throws Cambodian troops into battle. This unpopular move strengthens once minor opposition parties like the Khmer Rouge, which achieves power in 1975 and massacres millions of its own people.

1971

Bolivia — After half a decade of CIA-inspired political turmoil, a CIA-backed military coup overthrows the leftist President Juan Torres. In the next two years, dictator Hugo Banzer will have over 2,000 political opponents arrested without trial, then tortured, raped and executed.

Haiti — "Papa Doc" Duvalier dies, leaving his 19-year old son "Baby Doc" Duvalier the dictator of Haiti. His son continues his bloody reign with full knowledge of the CIA.

1972

The Case-Zablocki Act — Congress passes an act requiring congressional review of executive agreements. In theory, this should make CIA operations more accountable. In fact, it is only marginally effective.

Cambodia — Congress votes to cut off CIA funds for its secret war in Cambodia.

Watergate Break-in — President Nixon sends in a team of burglars to wiretap Democratic offices at Watergate. The team members have extensive CIA histories, including James McCord, E. Howard Hunt and five of the Cuban burglars. They work for the Committee to Re-elect the President (CREEP), which does dirty work like disrupting Democratic campaigns and laundering Nixon's illegal campaign contributions. CREEP's activities are funded and organized by another CIA front, the Mullen Company.

1973

Chile — The CIA overthrows and assassinates Salvador Allende, Latin America's first democratically elected socialist leader. The problems begin when Allende nationalizes American-owned firms in Chile. ITT offers the CIA $1 million for a coup (reportedly refused). The CIA replaces Allende with General Augusto Pinochet, who will torture and murder thousands of his own countrymen in a crackdown on labour leaders and the political left.

CIA begins internal investigations — William Colby, the Deputy Director for Operations, orders all CIA personnel to report any and all illegal activities they know about. This information is later reported to Congress.

Watergate Scandal — The CIA's main collaborating newspaper in America, *The Washington Post*, reports Nixon's crimes long before any other newspaper takes up the subject. The two reporters, Woodward and Bernstein, make almost no mention of the CIA's many fingerprints all over the scandal. It is later revealed that Woodward was a Naval intelligence briefer to the White House, and knows many important intelligence figures, including General Alexander Haig. His main source, "Deep Throat," is probably one of those.

CIA Director Helms Fired — President Nixon fires CIA Director Richard Helms for failing to help cover up the Watergate scandal. Helms and Nixon have always disliked each other. The new CIA director is William Colby, who is relatively more open to CIA reform.

1974

CHAOS exposed — Pulitzer prize winning journalist Seymour Hersh publishes a story about Operation CHAOS, the domestic surveillance and infiltration of anti-war and civil rights groups in the U.S. The story sparks national outrage.

Angleton fired — Congress holds hearings on the illegal domestic spying efforts of James Jesus Angleton, the CIA's chief of counterintelligence. His efforts included mail-opening campaigns and secret surveillance of war protesters. The hearings result in his dismissal from the CIA.

House clears CIA in Watergate — The House of Representatives clears the CIA of any complicity in Nixon's Watergate break-in.

The Hughes Ryan Act — Congress passes an amendment requiring the president to report nonintelligence CIA operations to the relevant congressional committees in a timely fashion.

1975

Australia — The CIA helps topple the democratically elected, left-leaning government of Prime Minister Edward Whitlam. The CIA does this by giving an ultimatum to its Governor-General, John Kerr. Kerr, a long-time CIA collaborator, exercises his constitutional right to dissolve the Whitlam government. The Governor-General is a largely ceremonial position appointed by the Queen; the Prime Minister is democratically elected. The use of this archaic and never-used law stuns the nation.

Angola — Eager to demonstrate American military resolve after its defeat in Vietnam, Henry Kissinger launches a CIA-backed war in Angola. Contrary to Kissinger's assertions, Angola is a country of little strategic importance and not seriously threatened by communism. The CIA backs the brutal leader of UNITAS, Jonas Savimbi. This polarizes Angolan politics and drives his opponents into the arms of Cuba and the Soviet Union for survival. Congress will cut off funds in 1976, but the CIA is able to run the war off the books until 1984, when funding is legalized again. This entirely pointless war kills over 300,000 Angolans.

"The CIA and the Cult of Intelligence" — Victor Marchetti and John Marks publish this whistle-blowing history of CIA crimes and abuses. Marchetti has spent 14 years in the CIA, eventually becoming an executive assistant to the Deputy Director of Intelligence. Marks has spent five years as an intelligence official in the State Department.

"Inside the Company" — Philip Agee publishes a diary of his life inside the CIA. Agee has worked in covert operations in Latin America during the 60s, and details the crimes in which he took part.

Congress investigates CIA wrong-doing — Public outrage compels Congress to hold hearings on CIA crimes. Senator Frank Church heads the Senate investigation ("The Church Committee"), and Representative Otis Pike heads the House investigation. (Despite a 98 percent incumbency re-election rate, both Church and Pike are defeated in the next elections.) The investigations lead to a number of reforms intended to increase the CIA's accountability to Congress, including the creation of a standing Senate committee on intelligence. However, the reforms prove ineffective, as the Iran/Contra scandal will show. It turns out the CIA can control, deal with or sidestep Congress with ease.

The Rockefeller Commission — In an attempt to reduce the damage done by the Church Committee, President Ford creates the "Rockefeller Commission" to whitewash CIA history and propose toothless reforms. The commission's namesake, Vice President Nelson Rockefeller, is himself a major CIA figure. Five of the commission's eight members are also members of the Council on Foreign Relations, a CIA-dominated organization.

1979

Iran — The CIA fails to predict the fall of the Shah of Iran, a long-time CIA puppet, and the rise of Muslim fundamentalists who are furious at the CIA's backing of SAVAK, the Shah's bloodthirsty secret police. In revenge, the Muslims take 52 Americans hostage in the U.S. embassy in Tehran.

Afghanistan — The Soviets invade Afghanistan. The CIA immediately begins supplying arms to any faction willing to fight the occupying Soviets. Such indiscriminate arming means that when the Soviets leave Afghanistan, civil war will erupt. Also, fanatical Muslim extremists now possess state-of-the-art weaponry. One of these is Sheik Abdel Rahman, who will become involved in the World Trade Center bombing in New York.

El Salvador — An idealistic group of young military officers, repulsed by the massacre of the poor, overthrows the right-wing government. However, the U.S. compels the inexperienced officers to include many of the old guard in key positions in their new government. Soon, things are back to "normal" — the military government is repressing and killing poor civilian protesters. Many of the young military and civilian reformers, finding themselves powerless, resign in disgust.

Nicaragua — Anastasios Samoza II, the CIA-backed dictator, falls. The Marxist Sandinistas take over government, and they are initially popular because of their commitment to land and anti-poverty reform. Samoza had a murderous and hated personal army called the National Guard. Remnants of the Guard will become the Contras, who fight a CIA-backed guerrilla war against the Sandinista government throughout the 1980s.

1980

El Salvador — The Archbishop of San Salvador, Oscar Romero, pleads with President Carter "Christian to Christian" to stop aiding the military government slaughtering his people. Carter refuses. Shortly afterwards, right-wing leader Roberto D'Aubuisson has Romero shot through the heart while saying Mass. The country soon dissolves into civil war, with the peasants in the hills fighting against the military government. The CIA and U.S. Armed Forces supply the government with overwhelming military and intelligence superiority. CIA-trained death squads roam the countryside, committing atrocities like that of El Mazote in 1982, where they massacre between 700 and 1000 men, women and children. By 1992, some 63,000 Salvadorans will be killed.

1981

Iran/Contra Begins — The CIA begins selling arms to Iran at high prices, using the profits to arm the Contras fighting the Sandinista government in Nicaragua. President Reagan vows that the Sandinistas will be "pressured" until "they say 'uncle.'" The CIA's *Freedom Fighter's Manual* disbursed to the Contras includes instruction on economic sabotage, propaganda, extortion, bribery, blackmail, interrogation, torture, murder and political assassination.

1983

Honduras — The CIA gives Honduran military officers the *Human Resource Exploitation Training Manual - 1983*, which teaches how to torture people. Honduras' notorious "Battalion 316" then uses these techniques, with the CIA's full knowledge, on thousands of leftist dissidents. At least 184 are murdered.

1984

The Boland Amendment — The last of a series of Boland Amendments is passed. These amendments have reduced CIA aid to the Contras; the last one cuts it off completely. However, CIA Director William Casey is already prepared to "hand off" the operation to Colonel Oliver North, who illegally continues supplying the Contras through the CIA's informal, secret, and self-financing network. This includes "humanitarian aid" donated by Adolph Coors and William Simon, and military aid funded by Iranian arms sales.

1986

Eugene Hasenfus — Nicaragua shoots down a C-123 transport plane carrying military supplies to the Contras. The lone survivor, Eugene Hasenfus, turns out to be a CIA employee, as are the two dead pilots. The airplane belongs to Southern Air Transport, a CIA front. The incident makes a mockery of President Reagan's claims that the CIA is not illegally arming the Contras.

Iran/Contra Scandal — Although the details have long been known, the Iran/Contra scandal finally captures the media's attention in 1986. Congress holds hearings, and several key figures (like Oliver North) lie under oath to protect the intelligence community. CIA Director William Casey dies of brain cancer before Congress can question him. All reforms enacted by Congress after the scandal are purely cosmetic.

Haiti — Rising popular revolt in Haiti means that "Baby Doc" Duvalier will remain "President for Life" only if he has a short one. The U.S., which hates instability in a puppet country, flies the despotic Duvalier to the South of France for a comfortable retirement. The CIA then rigs the upcoming elections in favor of another right-wing military strongman. However, violence keeps the country in political turmoil for another four years. The CIA tries to strengthen the military by creating the National Intelligence Service (SIN), which suppresses popular revolt through torture and assassination.

1989

Panama — The U.S. invades Panama to overthrow a dictator of its own making, General Manuel Noriega. Noriega has been on the CIA's payroll since 1966, and has been transporting drugs with the CIA's knowledge since 1972. By the late 80s, Noriega's growing independence and intransigence have angered Washington... so out he goes.

1990

Haiti — Competing against 10 comparatively wealthy candidates, leftist priest Jean-Bertrand Aristide captures 68 percent of the vote. After only eight months in power, however, the CIA-backed military deposes him. More military dictators brutalize the country, as thousands of Haitian refugees escape the turmoil in barely seaworthy boats. As popular opinion calls for Aristide's return, the CIA begins a disinformation campaign painting the courageous priest as mentally unstable.

1991

The Gulf War — The U.S. liberates Kuwait from Iraq. But Iraq's dictator, Saddam Hussein, is another creature of the CIA. With U.S. encouragement, Hussein invaded Iran in 1980. During this costly eight-year war, the CIA built up Hussein's forces with sophisticated arms, intelligence, training and financial backing. This cemented Hussein's power at home, allowing him to crush the many internal rebellions that erupted from time to time, sometimes with poison gas. It also gave him all the military might he needed to conduct further adventurism — in Kuwait, for example.

The Fall of the Soviet Union — The CIA fails to predict this most important event of the Cold War. This suggests that it has been so busy undermining governments that it hasn't been doing its primary job: gathering and analyzing information. The fall of the Soviet Union also robs the CIA of its reason for existence: fighting communism. This leads some to accuse the CIA of intentionally failing to predict the downfall of the Soviet Union. Curiously, the intelligence community's budget is not significantly reduced after the demise of communism.

1992

Economic Espionage — In the years following the end of the Cold War, the CIA is increasingly used for economic espionage. This involves stealing the technological secrets of competing foreign companies and giving them to American ones. Given the CIA's clear preference for dirty tricks over mere information gathering, the possibility of serious criminal behaviour is very great indeed.

1993

Haiti — The chaos in Haiti grows so bad that President Clinton has no choice but to remove the Haitian military dictator, Raoul Cedras, on threat of U.S. invasion. The U.S. occupiers do not arrest Haiti's military leaders for crimes against humanity, but instead ensure their safety and rich retirements. Aristide is returned to power only after being forced to accept an agenda favourable to the country's ruling class".

References:
1. Steve Kangas , A Timeline of CIA Atrocities,
   http://www.huppi.com/kangaroo/CIAtimeline.html
2. Dr. Thomas McCall, Israel and the Church,
   http://www.levitt.com/essays/israel- church.html

9/11 Fatalities

Fatalities (excluding alleged hijackers)

New York City:
New York

World Trade Center (WTC)
2,604 people died and another **23** remain listed as missing

88 people (Passenger plus Crew) died when American Airlines Flight 11 from Boston to Los Angeles crashed into WTC North Tower

59 people (Passenger plus Crew) died when United Airlines Flight 175 from Boston to Los Angeles crashed into WTC South Tower

Washington DC

125 people (Military plus Civilian) died from the explosion and destruction from AA 77 collision in Pentagon

59 people (Passenger plus Crew) died when American Airlines Flight 77 from Washington Dulles International Airport to Los Angeles International Airport crashed into Pentagon

Shanksville

40 people (Passenger plus Crew) died when United Airlines Flight 93 from Newark to San Francisco was shot down by military jets over Shanksville Pennsylvania

Total

2,975 died and another 23 remain listed as missing.

There were 2,975 (official) fatalities, **not including the 19 alleged hijackers** whose names were not in the original Airliners list: 246 on the four planes (no one on board any of the hijacked aircraft survived), 2,603 in New York City in the towers and on the ground, and 125 at the Pentagon.

Lieutenant General Timothy Maude, alumni of Golden Gate University was the highest ranking person killed at the Pentagon on 9/11. He was serving as the U.S. Army's Deputy Chief of Staff for Personnel and was at a meeting when allegedly bombs exploded around 9:32am followed by the crash around 9:37am of American Airlines Flight 77 into the west side of the Pentagon. **His offices had recently been moved to the most recently renovated section of the well guarded Pentagon.** Maude began the 'Army of One' campaign using television and internet advertising and on September 4, 2001 it was reported that the Army had met its goals early for active duty soldiers and that the Army Reserve and National Guard would meet theirs by the end of the month with transparency.

Timothy Maude

John P. O'Neill

John P. O'Neill was a former assistant director of the FBI who assisted in the capture of Ramzi Yousef and was the head of security at the World Trade Center when he was killed trying to rescue people from the South Tower. An additional 24 people remain listed as missing.

"The main obstacles to investigate Islamic terrorism were US oil corporate interests and the role played by Saudi Arabia in it. All the answers, everything needed to dismantle Osama bin Laden's organization, could be found in Saudi Arabia. White House was obstructing my investigation of bin Laden because they were still keeping the idea of a pipeline deal with the Taliban open."

Frank De Martini, an architect who works as the World Trade Center's construction manager, was interviewed for a History Channel documentary about the WTC towers.

Frank De Martini

He said, "I believe the building probably could sustain multiple impacts of jetliners because this structure is like the mosquito netting on your screen door, this intense grid, and the jet plane is just a pencil puncturing the screen netting. It really does nothing to the screen netting." [Dwyer and Flynn, 2005, pp. 149] De Martini would be in his office on the 88th floor of the North Tower when it was hit on 9/11. He apparently died when the tower collapsed, after helping more than 50 people escape. [Associated Press, 8/29/2003; New York Times]

1366 people died who were at or above the floors of impact in the North Tower (1 WTC). According to the Commission Report, hundreds were killed instantly by the impact while the rest were trapped and died after the tower collapsed. As many as 600 people were killed instantly or were trapped at or above the floors of impact in the South Tower (2 WTC). Only about 18 managed to escape in time from above the impact zone and out of the South Tower before it collapsed. At least 200 people jumped to their deaths from the burning towers since the rooftop door was securedly closed, landing on the streets and rooftops of adjacent buildings hundreds of feet below. To witnesses watching, a few of the people falling from the towers seemed to have stumbled out of broken windows. Some of the occupants of each tower above its point of impact made their way upward toward the roof in hope of helicopter rescue, but no rescue plan existed for such an eventuality. The roof access doors were locked and thick smoke and intense heat would have prevented rescue helicopters from landing.

Cantor Fitzgerald L.P.[1], an investment bank on the 101st–105th floors of One World Trade Center, lost 658 employees, considerably more than any other employer. Cantor Fitzgerald L.P. is a global financial services firm specializing in bond trading, as well as investment banking, asset management, market data and brokerage services. It was founded in 1945 by Bernard Gerald Cantor and John Fitzgerald as a limited partnership and remains so today. Cantor Fitzgerald is one of seventeen primary dealers who trade U.S. government securities directly with the Federal Reserve Bank of New York.

Marsh Inc.[2], located immediately below Cantor Fitzgerald on floors 93-100 (the location of Flight 11's impact), lost 295 employees, Prior to the September 11 Attacks, the corporation held offices on 8 floors of the North Tower of the World Trade Center, between floors 93 and 100. When American Airlines Flight 11 crashed into the building as part of the attacks, their offices composed the entire impact zone, which was between floors 93 and 99. No one present in the offices at the time survived the attack and the firm lost 295 employees.

175 employees of Aon Corp.[3] were also killed. The New York City Fire Department (FDNY)[4] lost 341 firefighters and 2 paramedics, while 23 New York Police Department (NYPD)[5], 37 Port Authority Police Department[6] officers, and 8 private ambulance personnel were killed. The dead included 8 children: 5 on American 77 ranging in age from 3 to 11, 3 on United 175 ages 2, 3, and 4. The youngest victim was a 2 year-old child on Flight 175, the oldest an 82 year-old passenger on Flight 11. In the buildings, the youngest victim was 17 and the oldest was 79. After New York, New Jersey was the hardest hit State, with the town of Hoboken[7] sustaining the most fatalities. All of the fatalities were civilians except for some of the 125 victims in the Pentagon[8].

According to the Associated Press, the city identified over 1,600 bodies but was unable to identify the rest (about 1,100 people). They report that the city has "about 10,000 unidentified bone and tissue fragments that cannot be matched to the list of the dead." Bone fragments were still being found in 2006 as workers prepared the damaged Deutsche Bank Building for demolition. The average age of all the dead in New York City was 40.

American Airlines Flight 77 Captain Charles Burlingame

His plane flew into Pentagon after spending almost an hour in the air flying without transponder avoiding military intercept/escort or warning shots fired from NORAD fighter planes per hijacking procedure.

Burlingame was a military man who'd flown Navy jets for eight years, served several tours at the Navy's elite Top Gun school, and been in the Naval Reserve for 17 years. [Associated Press, 12/6/2001]

Pentagon: "The Navy Command Center was the Target of the Attack; "The US Authorities have tried to make believe that the damage caused to the Pentagon, on September 11, 2001 was caused by the crash of a hijacked Boeing airliner on the building. This lie was meant to hide the fact that a bombing attack was in fact carried out by a group of people who had authorized access to the Pentagon and that the target was not the Department of Defense in general but the new Navy Command Center." ... Why might someone want to target the Naval Command Center (NCC)? Most people know of the NORAD "all seeing" defensive network, with radar and satellite capabilities. But in their shadow, the NCC also was a very formidable command and control facility, with some overlapping capacities. The site of the attack occurred on the first floor at the Naval Command Center portion of the Pentagon. The facility was a powerhouse of information gathering, command and control, and systems for monitoring "all warfare mission areas." ... Starting in 1996 the Navy was implementing an upgrade; The Tactical Command System (TCS) upgrades the Navy's Command Control, Computer and Intelligence (C3I) systems and processes C3I information for all warfare mission areas including planning, direction and reconstruction of missions for peacetime, wartime and times of crises. Included among these C3I systems were: the unified command centers of Commander in Chief, Pacific Command (CINCPAC) and Commander in Chief, Atlantic Command (CINCLANT), the Navy Command Center...[i] ... The only U.S. Navy Command Center survivor, Lieutenant Kevin Shaeffer, claimed: "Had the Command Center not been destroyed it surely would have been able to provide the

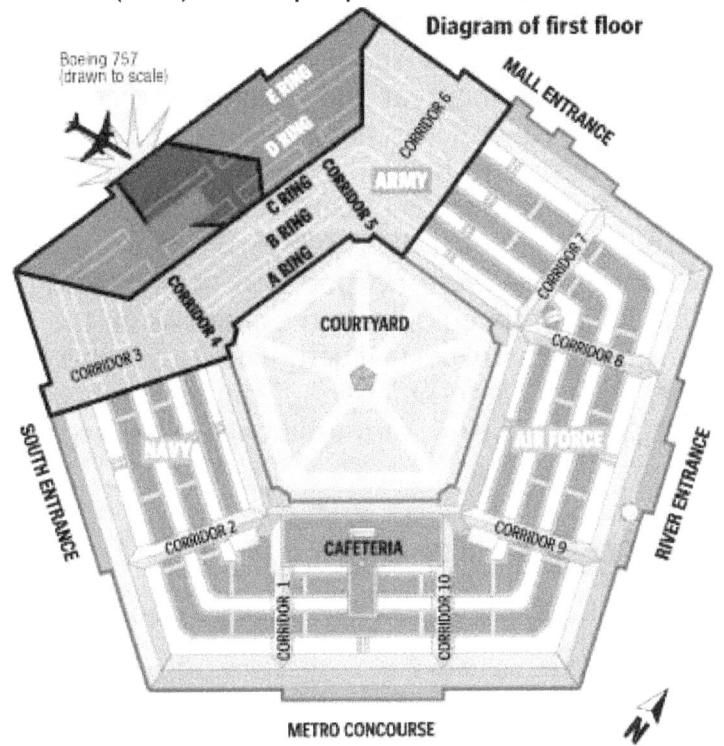

Diagram of first floor

highest levels of our Navy leadership with updates as to exactly what was occurring", including 9/11 saga.

Rhett Flater, Executive Director of the American Helicopter Society who personally knew and communicated regularly with the highest-ranking first responders at the WTC on 9/11, commented that the New York City Fire Department (FDNY) - presumably its **Fire Chief who reported to then mayor Rudolph Giuliani - ordered the doors to the roofs of the WTC towers be locked, which blocked the only avenue of escape for victims above the Airplanes impact floors, ensuring their horrific deaths.** At least one of the two New York Police Department (NYPD) helicopters seen on television footage hovering near the burning towers on 9/11 morning, and probably both were equipped with winches and jump seats designed for the rescue of victims. Ironically the same helicopter and crew had rescued victims from the burning WTC Tower One during 1993 bombing attack, but on 9/11 the NYPD helicopters were ordered by the Fire Department not to try to rescue victims from the towers, even though there were heliports on the roofs and the winches and jump seats could have been dropped outside the windows on the sides of the towers where victims were waiting to be rescued. The Fire Department (FDNY) also explicitly refused the help of large numbers of military helicopters, whose pilots spontaneously converged on the New York area only to be ordered to wait at a nearby base.

Pentagon Casualty List

Name	Age	Town	State
Spc. Craig Amundson	28	Fort Belvoir	Va.
Melissa Rose Barnes	27	Redlands	Calif.
(Retired) Master Sgt. Max Beilke	69	Laurel	Md.
Kris Romeo Bishundat	23	Waldorf	Md.
Carrie Blagburn	48	Temple Hills	Md.
Lt. Col. Canfield D. Boone	54	Clifton	Va.
Donna Bowen	42	Waldorf	Md.
Allen Boyle	30	Fredericksburg	Va.

Christopher Lee Burford	23	Hubert	N.C.
Daniel Martin Caballero	21	Houston	Texas
Sgt. 1st Class Jose Orlando Calderon-Olmedo	44	Annandale	Va.
Angelene C. Carter	51	Forestville	Md.
Sharon Carver	38	Waldorf	Md.
John J. Chada	55	Manassas	Va.
Rosa Maria (Rosemary) Chapa	64	Springfield	Va.
Julian Cooper	39	Springdale	Md.
Lt. Cmdr. Eric Allen Cranford	32	Drexel	N.C.
Ada M. Davis	57	Camp Springs	Md.
Capt. Gerald Francis Deconto	44	Sandwich	Mass.
Lt. Col. Jerry Don Dickerson	41	Durant	Miss.
Johnnie Doctor	32	Jacksonville	Fla.
Capt. Robert Edward Dolan	43	Alexandria	Va.
Cmdr. William Howard Donovan	37	Nunda	N.Y.
Cmdr. Patrick S. Dunn	39	Springfield	Va.
Edward Thomas Earhart	26	Salt Lick	Ky.
Lt. Cmdr. Robert Randolph Elseth	37	Vestal	N.Y.
Jamie Lynn Fallon	23	Woodbridge	Va.
Amelia V. Fields	36	Dumfries	Va.
Gerald P. Fisher	57	Potomac	Md.
Matthew Michael Flocco	21	Newark	Del.
Sandra N. Foster	41	Clinton	Md.

Capt. Lawrence Daniel Getzfred	57	Elgin	Neb.
Cortz Ghee	54	Reisterstown	Md.
Brenda C. Gibson	59	Falls Church	Va.
Ron Golinski	60	Columbia	Md.
Diane M. Hale-McKinzy	38	Alexandria	Va.
Carolyn B. Halmon	49	Washington	D.C.
Sheila Hein	51	University Park	Md.
Ronald John Hemenway	37	Shawnee	Kan.
Maj. Wallace Cole Hogan	40	Fla.	
Jimmie Ira Holley	54	Lanham	Md.
Angela Houtz	27	La Plata	Md.
Brady K. Howell	26	Arlington	Va.
Peggie Hurt	36	Crewe	Va.
Lt. Col. Stephen Neil Hyland	45	Burke	Va.
Robert J. Hymel	55	Woodbridge	Va.
Sgt. Maj. Lacey B. Ivory	43	Woodbridge	Va.
Lt. Col. Dennis M. Johnson	48	Port Edwards	Wis.
Judith Jones	53	Woodbridge	Va.
Brenda Kegler	49	Washington	D.C.
Lt. Michael Scott Lamana	31	Baton Rouge	La.
David W. Laychak	40	Manassas	Va.
Samantha Lightbourn-Allen	36	Hillside	Md.
Maj. Steve Long	39	Ga.	
James Lynch	55	Manassas	Va.
Terence M. Lynch	49	Alexandria	Va.
Nehamon Lyons	30	Mobile	Ala.
Shelley A. Marshall	37	Marbury	Md.

Teresa Martin	45	Stafford	Va.
Ada L. Mason	50	Springfield	Va.
Lt. Col. Dean E. Mattson	57	Calif.	
Lt. Gen. Timothy J. Maude	53	Fort Myer	Va.
Robert J. Maxwell	53	Manassas	Va.
Molly McKenzie	38	Dale City	Va.
Patricia E. (Patti) Mickley	41	Springfield	Va.
Maj. Ronald D. Milam	33	Washington	D.C.
Gerard (Jerry) P. Moran	39	Upper Marlboro	Md.
Odessa V. Morris	54	Upper Marlboro	Md.
Brian Anthony Moss	34	Sperry	Okla.
Ted Moy	48	Silver Spring	Md.
Lt. Cmdr. Patrick Jude Murphy	38	Flossmoor	Ill.
Khang Nguyen	41	Fairfax	Va.
Michael Allen Noeth	30	New York	N.Y.
Diana Borrero de Padro	55	Woodbridge	Va.
Spc. Chin Sun Pak	25	Lawton	Okla.
Lt. Jonas Martin Panik	26	Mingoville	Pa.
Maj. Clifford L. Patterson	33	Alexandria	Va.
Lt. J.G. Darin Howard Pontell	26	Columbia	Md.
Scott Powell	35	Silver Spring	Md.
(Retired) Capt. Jack Punches	51	Clifton	Va.
Joseph John Pycior	39	Carlstadt	N.J.
Deborah Ramsaur	45	Annandale	Va.
Rhonda Rasmussen	44	Woodbridge	Va.
Marsha Dianah	34	Prichard	Ala.

Ratchford			
Martha Reszke	36	Stafford	Va.
Cecelia E. Richard	41	Fort Washington	Md.
Edward V. Rowenhorst	32	Lake Ridge	Va.
Judy Rowlett	44	Woodbridge	Va.
Robert E. Russell	52	Oxon Hill	Md.
William R. Ruth	57	Mount Airy	Md.
Charles E. Sabin	54	Burke	Va.
Marjorie C. Salamone	53	Springfield	Va.
Lt. Col. David M. Scales	44	Cleveland	Ohio
Cmdr. Robert Allan Schlegel	38	Alexandria	Va.
Janice Scott	46	Springfield	Va.
Michael L. Selves	53	Fairfax	Va.
Marian Serva	47	Stafford	Va.
Cmdr. Dan Frederic Shanower	40	Naperville	Ill.
Antoinette Sherman	35	Forest Heights	Md.
Don Simmons	58	Dumfries	Va.
Cheryle D. Sincock	53	Dale City	Va.
Gregg Harold Smallwood	44	Overland Park	Kan.
(Retired) Lt. Col. Gary F. Smith	55	Alexandria	Va.
Patricia J. Statz	41	Takoma Park	Md.
Edna L. Stephens	53	Washington	D.C.
Sgt. Maj. Larry Strickland	52	Woodbridge	Va.
Maj. Kip P. Taylor	38	McLean	Va.
Sandra C. Taylor	50	Alexandria	Va.
Karl W. Teepe	57	Centreville	Va.
Sgt. Tamara Thurman	25	Brewton	Ala.

Lt. Cmdr. Otis Vincent Tolbert	38	Lemoore	Calif.
Willie Q. Troy	51	Aberdeen	Md.
Lt. Cmdr. Ronald James Vauk	37	Nampa	Idaho
Lt. Col. Karen Wagner	40	Houston	Texas
Meta L. Waller	60	Alexandria	Va.
Staff Sgt. Maudlyn A. White	38	St. Croix	Virgin Islands
Sandra L. White	44	Dumfries	Va.
Ernest M. Willcher	62	North Potomac	Md.
Lt. Cmdr. David Lucian Williams	32	Newport	Ore.
Maj. Dwayne Williams	40	Jacksonville	Ala.
Marvin R. Woods	57	Great Mills	Md.
Kevin Wayne Yokum	27	Lake Charles	La.
Donald McArthur Young	41	Roanoke	Va.
Lisa L. Young	36	Germantown	Md.
Edmond Young	22	Owings	Md.

For a list of all the WTC victim, please refer to :
World Trade Center Casualty List, Genelogy Trains, History Group,
http://genealogytrails.com/main/sept11_wtcdead.html

Some Statistics Around 9/11 Fatalities

- Number of firefighters and paramedics killed: 343
- Number of New York Police Department (NYPD) officers: 23
- Number of Port Authority police officers: 37
- Number of WTC companies that lost people: 60
- Number of employees who died in Tower One: 1,402
- Number of employees who died in Tower Two: 614

- Number of employees lost at Cantor Fitzgerald: 658
- Number of U.S. troops killed in Operation Enduring Freedom: 22
- Number of nations whose citizens were killed in attacks: 115
- Ratio of men to women who died: 3:1
- Age of the greatest number who died: between 35 and 39
- Bodies found "intact": 289
- Body parts found: 19,858
- Number of families who got no remains: 1,717
- Estimated units of blood donated to the New York Blood Center: 36,000
- Total units of donated blood actually used: 258
- Number of people who lost a spouse or partner in the attacks: 1,609
- Estimated number of children who lost a parent: 3,051
- Percentage of Americans who knew someone hurt or killed in the attacks: 20
- Fire Department City of New York (FDNY) retirements, January–July 2001: 274
- FDNY retirements, January–July 2002: 661
- Number of firefighters on leave for respiratory problems by January 2002: 300
- Number of funerals attended by Rudy Giuliani in 2001: 200
- Number of FDNY vehicles destroyed: 98
- Tons of debris removed from site: 1,506,124
- Days fires continued to burn after the attack: 99
- Jobs lost in New York owing to the attacks: 146,100
- Days the New York Stock Exchange was closed: 6
- Point drop in the Dow Jones industrial average when the New York Stock Exchange (NYSE) reopened: 684.81
- Days after 9/11 that the U.S. began bombing Afghanistan: 26
- Total number of hate crimes reported to the Council on American-Islamic Relations nationwide since 9/11: 1,714
- Economic loss to New York in month following the attacks: $105 Billion
- Estimated cost of cleanup: $600 Million
- Total FEMA money spent on the emergency: $970 Million
- Estimated amount donated to 9/11 charities: $1.4 Billion
- Estimated amount of insurance paid worldwide related to 9/11: $40.2 Billion
- Estimated amount of money needed to overhaul lower-Manhattan

subways: $7.5 Billion
- Amount of money recently granted by U.S. government to overhaul lower-Manhattan subways: $4.55 Billion
- Estimated amount of money raised for funds dedicated to NYPD and FDNY families: $500 Million
- Percentage of total charity money raised going to FDNY and NYPD families: 25
- Average benefit already received by each FDNY and NYPD widow: $1 Million
- Percentage increase in law-school applications from 2001 to 2002: 17.9
- Percentage increase in Peace Corps applications from 2001 to 2002: 40
- Percentage increase in CIA applications from 2001 to 2002: 50
- Number of songs considered "**inappropriate**" by Clear Channel Radio to play after 9/11: 150
- Number of mentions of 9/11 at the Oscars: 26
- Apartments in lower Manhattan eligible for asbestos cleanup: 30,000
- Number of apartments whose residents have requested cleanup and testing: 4,110
- Number of Americans who changed their 2001 holiday-travel plans from plane to train or car: 1.4 Million
- Estimated number of New Yorkers suffering from post-traumatic-stress disorder as a result of 9/11: 422,000

End Notes:
1. **Cantor Fitzgerald L.P.** is a global financial services firm specializing in bond trading, as well as investment banking, asset management, market data and brokerage services. It was founded in 1945 by Bernard Gerald Cantor and John Fitzgerald as a limited partnership and remains so today. Cantor Fitzgerald is one of seventeen primary dealers who trade U.S. government securities directly with the Federal Reserve Bank of New York.
2. **Marsh & McLennan Companies, Inc. (MMC)** is a US-based global professional services and insurance brokerage firm. In 2007, it had over 57,000 employees and annual revenues of $12.069 billion. Marsh & McLennan Companies was ranked the 207th largest corporation in the United States by the 2007 Fortune 500 list, and the 5th largest U.S. company in the diversified financial industry. It was formed by Henry W. Marsh and Donald R. McLennan in Chicago in 1905. Prior to the September 11 Attacks, the corporation held offices on 8 floors of the North Tower of the World Trade

Center, between floors 93 and 100. When American Airlines Flight 11 crashed into the building as part of the attacks, their offices composed the entire impact zone, which was between floors 93 and 99. No one present in the offices at the time survived the attack and the firm lost 295 employees.

3. **Aon Corporation** (NYSE: AOC) is a provider of risk management services, insurance and reinsurance brokerage, human capital and management consulting, and specialty insurance underwriting. Aon was created in 1982, when the Ryan Insurance Group (founded by Pat Ryan in the 1960s) merged with the Combined Insurance Company of America (founded by W. Clement Stone in 1919).

4. The FDNY, the largest municipal fire department in the United States, has approximately 11,600 uniformed officers and firefighters and over 3,200 uniformed EMTs and paramedics.

5. The **New York City Police Department** (NYPD), established in 1845, is currently the largest police force in the United States, with primary responsibilities in law enforcement and investigation within the five boroughs of New York City. The NYPD was the first police department established in the United States.

6. The **Port Authority of New York and New Jersey Police Department**, or **Port Authority Police Department** (PAPD), is a law enforcement agency in New York and New Jersey, the duties of which are to protect all facilities owned by the Port Authority of New York and New Jersey, and to enforce state and city laws at all the facilities.

7. **Hoboken** is a city in Hudson County, New Jersey, United States. As of the 2000 United States Census, the city's population was 38,577. The city is part of the New York metropolitan area and contains Hoboken Terminal, a major transportation hub for the region.

8. **The Pentagon** is the headquarters of the United States Department of Defense, located in Arlington, Virginia. As a symbol of the U.S. military, "the Pentagon" is often used metonymically to refer to the Department of Defense rather than the building itself which was dedicated on January 15, 1943, after ground was broken for construction on September 11, 1941. The Pentagon is the world's largest office building by floor area. The Pentagon houses approximately 23,000 military and civilian employees and about 3,000 non-defense support personnel. It has five sides, five floors above ground (plus two basement levels), and five ring corridors per floor with a total of 17.5 miles (28.2 km) of corridors.

Anthrax Attack: Was it a backup military option just in case the coordinated remote hijackings and demolitions plan failed?

"Judicial Watch Wants to Know Why White House Went on Cipro Beginning September 11th: What Was Known and When?" - June 7, 2002, Judicial Watch Press Release, Chairman and General Counsel Larry Klayman.

Any one who doubts about the pre-knowledge of 9/11 among competent

authorities inside US Administration, Department of Transportation, FEMA, CIA, FBI, FAA, Pentagon as well as key personnel in Senate and Congress must know that the **Anthrax deterrent CIPRO was delivered[1] to the White House on September 10, 2001,** one day prior to 9/11 – in anticipation of a massive biological attack on the New York City and the Washington DC area. And FEMA along with New York City Emergency response team were all ready on September 10, 2001, for that anticipated massive attack in the guise of emergency drill scheduled on September 12, 2001.

The question remains who can send the letters containing US military grade Anthrax Spores to then Senate Majority Leader Tom Daschle and Senate Judiciary

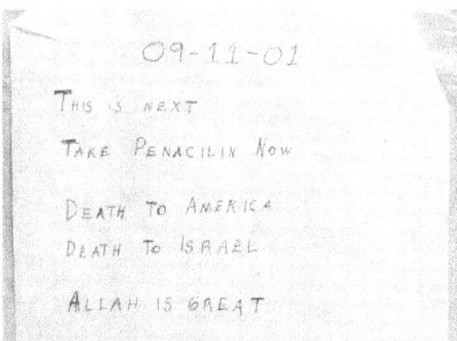

Committee Chairman Patrick Leahy after 9/11, especially considering that the Senators would be the custodians of the 9/11 investigation which both then President Bush and Vice President Cheney were dead against. And why and how the attackers would use US Military grade Anthrax Spores? **"We believe that the White House knew or had reason to know that an anthrax attack was imminent or underway."** - Larry Klayman.

Anyone with self interest can send a letter faking as Islamic militant as a convenient scapegoat!

"Material that is readily airborne is weapons-grade. Only someone with a connection to an existing or a former bioweapons program could produce aerosolized anthrax." - Richard Spertzel, former head of the United Nations biological inspection team in Iraq.

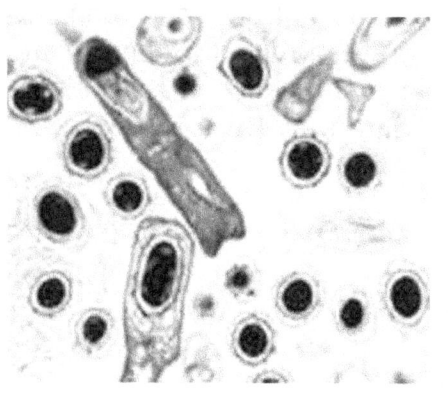
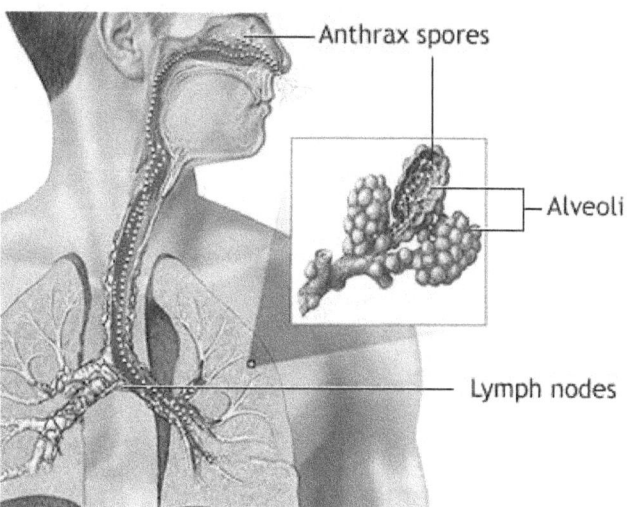

9/11 destroyed the NY City Emergency Command Center housed on WTC 7 and the Bio Terror drill preparation ended up with real emergency rescue operation after the WTC airlines crashes and subsequent demolitions of the towers. But the Bio Terror never happened in USA as anticipated instead of selective mails containing the US military anthrax spores to responsible people in the Government and Media as warnings to derail 9/11 fact finding investigations while creating an atmosphere of fear around the nation!

Furthermore FBI (by now the main suspect of 9/11 masterminding) took charges of all Anthrax related sites including postal stations depriving Center for Disease Control (CDC) from testing the affected sorting machines. Thus the clearance by FBI of a sorting machine still affected with deadly spores led to many more infections among postal employees who were attending the machine as well as the mail receivers generating more anthrax fear around USA and the world.

Jake Wagman of the *Philadelphia Inquirer* reported, "a CDC industrial hygienist testified that he and his group were not allowed in the building while the FBI conducted its tests. **And it was later revealed that the wrong mail sorter had been decontaminated, leaving equipment identified as carrying anthrax in operation for three days.** Dozens of employees used it to sort millions of pieces of mail."

Ironically, while staffers from the Supreme Court and Congress were evacuated from their buildings, postal officials, against union protests, insisted that mail facilities remain open.

 **"'The American people deserve a full accounting from the Bush administration, the FBI and other agencies concerning the anthrax attacks. The FBI's investigation seems to have dead-ended, and frankly, that is not very reassuring given their performance with the September 11th hijackers. One doesn't simply start taking a powerful antibiotic for no good reason. The American people are entitled to know what the White House staffers knew nine months ago.'"**- Judicial Watch Chairman and General Counsel Larry Klayman.

Thus, void of an honest open Government investigation into 9/11 and the follow up Anthrax terror inside USA, it can be speculated that the united perpetrators of the New Pearl Harbour had a backup plan of terrorizing US citizens just in case the remote controlled flight terminations into WTC and Pentagon failed while the demolitions bombs already damaged WTC and part of Pentagon.

The disturbing question keeps on bothering; **can a Government intentionally harm its own subjects/citizens? Well, the answer is yes when national security means well guarded secrecy under military and covert intelligence operatives running black budget without transparent accountabilities.**

Here is a British example: **The *BBC Online* reported on August 24, 2001 that Porton Down scientists at the defense center exposed 20,000 volunteers to nerve gas and other chemical and biological agents. Some volunteers believed they were helping find a cure for the common cold. .... The police had discovered an unusually high death rate among the volunteers** (rather British subjects).

"**The optimal US weaponization process is secret— it involves a combination of chemicals. There is no evidence that any other country possesses the formula.**" - Bill Patrick, inventor who holds five secret patents on the process.

Then what is the origin of the Anthrax spores? Dr. Rosenberg seems to have the answer, "**a genetic analysis conducted at Northern Arizona University excluded three academic institutions and two foreign defense laboratories, placing "the focus on USAMRID [Ft. Detrick], Dugway and Battelle as the source of the Ames strain for the letters.**"

In a speech at the Woodrow Wilson School of Public and International Affairs at Princeton University, Dr. Rosenberg said, "**We can draw a likely portrait of the perpetrator as a former Fort Detrick scientist who is now working for a contractor in the Washington, D.C. area. He had reason for travel to Florida, New Jersey and the United Kingdom.**"

Who gain from this kind of secretive attacks?

Well the direct benefit of WTC demolitions went to the Silverstein Properties and Westfield America who harvested $4.55 Billions as insurance money compared to less than a billion they paid for the private lease of 99 years! Also the short sellers of stocks on 9/11 targets and related companies, Pentagon and their Private defense contractors along with the evangelical NATO power that gaining more security around the world from the war on terror.

Similarly, "**The perpetrator must have realized in advance that the anthrax attack would result in the strengthening of US Defense and response capabilities. This is not likely to have been a goal of anti-American terrorists, who would also be unlikely to warn the victims in advance. Perhaps the** perpetrator stood to gain in some way from increased funding and recognition for biodefense programs. Financial beneficiaries would include the BioPort Corp., the source of the US anthrax vaccine, and other potential vaccine contractors."

In July 2000, Germany's Bayer AG had negotiated an unprecedented sole endorsement by the Federal Drug Administration of Cipro for anthrax, despite Cipro's high price and largely untested status (one animal study for anthrax treatment in 1993). Cipro sales rose by 1000% since the Anthrax attack and the Bush administration awarded an exclusive Health and Human Services contract to the pharmaceutical giant. A controversial anthrax vaccine was already being produced by BioPort Corporation.

BioPort, as well as Battelle (which first reported a false negative for its test of the Daschle letter), works closely with American intelligence and defense officials on classified programs. Both firms have connections with the U.S. Army Dugway Proving Ground, which admitted in December 2001 that the Army facility in the Utah desert has produced weapons-grade anthrax, although the government had supposedly ended the offensive biological weapons program in 1969.

Dr. Rosenberg maintains, "The FBI knows that the anthrax attack was an inside job". The attack also helped FBI to disrupt US mailing system for 9/11 censorship.

Some Victims of US Anthrax Attack:

• October 5, 2001, Bob Stevens of American Media died of anthrax inhalation
• Six postal workers contracted inhalation anthrax; two of them died, and four recovered. Three others recovered from skin anthrax.
• On October 21, 2001, postal officials shut down the Brentwood Road Mail Processing Center in northeast Washington after two Brentwood workers died of anthrax inhalation.
• On November 21, 2001, a 94-year-old woman in Connecticut died of anthrax inhalation.
• Centers for Disease Control and Prevention reported that 32,000 Americans were on a Cipro regimen.
• Eight more postal workers from Brentwood postal facility have died.

• Corbin Jr., a healthy 58--year-old Brentwood employee, had worked on the infamous sorting machine number 17 that had processed the anthrax-laden letter sent to Senator Daschle. Fully a week after congressional offices were decontaminated and the staff medicated, health officials remembered to look into the problem at Brentwood.

• During October 2001, letters containing powdered anthrax arrived in New York at the headquarters of ABC News, CBS News, and *The New York Post*. Six employees and one employee's infant all tested positive for skin anthrax and were treated.

• Around 10:15 on October 15, a member of Senate Majority Leader Tom Daschle's staff opened an envelope containing a suspicious substance. The Daschle sample became airborne when the envelope was opened, and within 24 hours thirty people had tested positive.

• On October 16, twelve senate offices closed and hundreds of staffers got anthrax tests. Within days, the House, the Senate, and the Supreme Court shut down.

• On October 25, a mailroom worker in an offsite State Department facility in Virginia was hospitalized with inhalation anthrax. The facility was shut down and all mailroom employees were medicated.

• On October 18, Norma Wallace, the first postal worker in New Jersey to contract inhalation anthrax, was hospitalized. Overall six postal workers contracted inhalation anthrax; two of them died, and four recovered. Three others recovered from skin anthrax, a less serious form of the disease.

• On November 9, 2001, Postal Service officials announced that four more facilities in New Jersey tested positive for anthrax. All four of them were linked to a regional facility outside Trenton in Hamilton Township. The Hamilton facility had handled anthrax-laced letters sent to Senator Daschle, Tom Brokaw, and the *New York Post*. Two more facilities in Pennsylvania harboured anthrax spores, one facility in West Windsor and a second regional processing and distribution center in Bellmawr, and these, too, were linked with the Hamilton facility.

Reference:
1. Michelle Mairesse , 'Did the Government Okay The Anthrax Attacks', http://www.hermes-press.com/anthrax_atrocities2.htm
2. Barbara Hatch Rosenberg, "Analysis of the Anthrax Attacks" posted on the Federation of American Scientists website in January and early February of 2002.

World Trade Center Demolitions Plan

Videotaped testimony of William ("Willy") Rodriguez, former World Trade Center janitor and the last person to leave the WTC alive on September 11, in the 9/11 documentary "Loose Change," second edition", text in parentheses added: "All of a sudden we hear 'Boom!' in the basement. I thought it was a generator that blew up, and I said to myself, 'Oh, my God, I think it was a generator. And I was going to verbalize it, and when I finished saying that in my mind I heard (another, second) 'Boom!' right on the top (above), pretty far away. And so it was a difference (in space and time) between coming from the basement and coming from the top...and a person comes running into the office (in the first basement level, from a deeper basement level) saying 'Explosion!'...and he said '(it was from) The elevators!' And there were many (deep basement WTC1) explosions."

Frank De Martini. *[Source: New York Times]* Frank De Martini, an architect who works as the World Trade Center's construction manager, was interviewed for a History Channel documentary about the WTC towers. He said, "**I believe the building probably could sustain multiple impacts of jetliners because this structure is like the mosquito netting on your screen door, this intense grid, and the jet plane is just a pencil puncturing the screen netting. It really does nothing to the screen netting.**" [DWYER AND FLYNN, 2005, PP. 149] De Martini would be in his office on the 88th floor of the North Tower when it was hit on 9/11. He apparently died when the tower collapsed, after helping more than 50 people escape. [ASSOCIATED PRESS, 8/29/2003; NEW YORK TIMES]

(BEFORE JULY 24, 2001): RISK ASSESSMENT IDENTIFIES AIRCRAFT STRIKING WTC AS ONE OF THE 'MAXIMUM FORESEEABLE LOSSES'

A property risk assessment report is prepared for Silverstein Properties before it acquires the lease for the World Trade Center (see JULY 24, 2001). **It identifies the scenario of an aircraft hitting one of the WTC towers as one of the "maximum foreseeable losses."** The report says, "This scenario is within the realm of the possible, but highly unlikely." Further details of the assessment, such as who prepared it, are unreported. [NATIONAL INSTITUTE OF STANDARDS AND TECHNOLOGY, 5/2003, PP. 16; BARRETT AND COLLINS, 2006, PP. 189; AMERICAN PROSPECT, 9/1/2006]

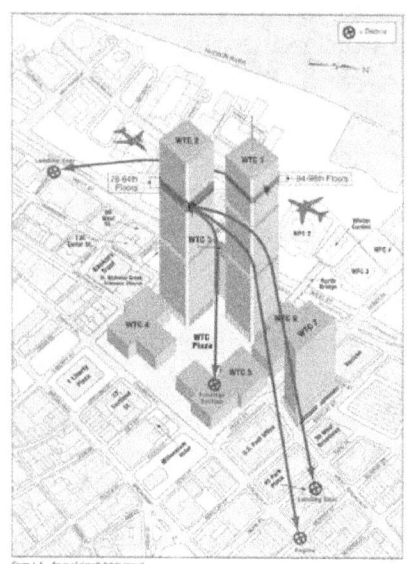

Figure 1-4 Area of aircraft debris impact

Ever wondered why people trapped above the crash affected WTC floors were not rescued from the roofs by NYPD and FEMA helicopters?

"These 110th floor stairway doors were labelled inside the stairway as "NO Re-entry," with the closest re-entry floor indicated on a sign. Physical access to the roof was through a set of two doors, essentially a mantrap. A small group of individuals had access card privileges, which would open the first door to the roof; and they then would present their ID card and themselves via CCTV and the second door was **electronically unlocked open by the Operations Control Center.**" – Testimony of Alan Reiss, Deputy Director of Aviation at The Port Authority of New York and New Jersey, to 9/11 Commission, May 18, 2004.

[Note: **The question is why NYPD, FDNY, and FEMA didn't ask the 'The Operations Control Center' to unlock the doors electronically knowing thousands trapped above the crashed floors? WHY?**
Because the New Pearl Harbour script warranted maximum casualty to sway public opinion towards unquestionable military spending needed for their illegal wars on Afghanistan and Iraq. This is the same reason why people were asked to stay in the building by some WTC guards persuading personally as well as using the public address system. The normal procedure is mandatory evacuation of the building in case of considerable fire.]

On September 11th 2001, BBC World reported at 4:57pm Eastern Time that the Salomon Brothers Building (more commonly known as WTC7 or World Trade Building 7) had collapsed. This even made the 5pm EST Headlines! **But what was bizarre was that the building did not actually collapse until 5:20pm EST suggesting strongly BBC was also part of the New Pearl Harbour implementation script.**

WTC complex owner Larry Silverstein rushed immediately calling his people over cell phone to "pull it down", which he admitted on a September 2002 PBS documentary, 'America Rebuilds' that **he and the** NYFD **decided to 'pull' WTC 7 on the day of the attack.** The word 'pull' is industry jargon for taking a building down with explosives.

JULY 24, 2001: WORLD TRADE CENTER OWNERSHIP CHANGED HANDS FOR THE FIRST TIME

Larry Silverstein. *[Source: Silverstein Properties publicity photo]*

Real estate development and investment firm Silverstein Properties and real estate investment trust Westfield America finalize a deal worth $3.2 billion to purchase a 99-year lease on the World Trade Center. The agreement covers the Twin Towers, World Trade Center Buildings 4 and 5 (two nine-story office buildings), and about 425,000 square feet of retail space. [NEW YORK TIMES, 4/27/2001; PORT AUTHORITY OF NEW YORK AND NEW JERSEY, 7/24/2001; IREIZINE, 7/26/2001] Westfield America will be responsible for the retail space, known as the Mall. Silverstein Properties' lease will cover the roughly 10 million square feet of office space of the Twin Towers and Buildings 4 and 5. Silverstein Properties already owns Building 7 of the WTC, which it built in 1987. This is the only time the WTC has ever changed hands since it was opened in 1973. [INTERNATIONAL COUNCIL OF SHOPPING CENTERS, 4/27/2001; WESTFIELD GROUP, 7/24/2001; DAILY TELEGRAPH, 9/11/2001; NEW YORK TIMES, 11/29/2001; CNN, 8/31/2002] It was previously controlled by the New York Port Authority, a bi-state government agency. [WALL STREET JOURNAL, 5/12/2007] Larry Silverstein, the president of Silverstein Properties, only uses $14 million of his own money for the deal. His partners put up a further $111 million, and banks provide $563 million in loans. [BRILL, 2003, PP. 156] The Port Authority had carried only $1.5 billion in insurance coverage on all its buildings, including the WTC, but Silverstein's lenders insist on more, eventually demanding $3.55 billion in cover. [AMERICAN LAWYER, 9/3/2002] After 9/11, Larry Silverstein will claim the attacks on the World Trade Center constituted two separate events, thereby entitling him to a double payout totalling over $7 billion. [DAILY TELEGRAPH, 10/9/2001; GUARDIAN, 8/18/2002] Eventually, after several years of legal wrangling, a total of $4.55 billion of insurance money will be paid out for the destruction of the WTC (see MAY 23, 2007). Most of this appears to go to Silverstein Properties. How much goes to Westfield America is unclear. [NEW YORK POST, 5/24/2007]

AUGUST 6, 2001: SUSPICIOUS TRADING OF COMPANIES AFFECTED BY 9/11 MIGHT HAVE BEGUN BY THIS DATE

[*All top officials in CIA, FBI, NSA, Military, FAA, FEMA and Administration knew by now that New Pearl Harbour was all set for implementation and trying to reap the harvest as much as they can without fear of repercussion knowing world would be busy fighting terrorism and self declared American wars*]

Insider trading based on advanced knowledge of the 9/11 attacks may have begun on this date, if not earlier. Investigators later discover a large number of put option purchases (a speculation that the stock will go down) that expire on September 30 at the Chicago Board Options Exchange are bought on this date. If exercised, these options would have led to large profits. One analyst later says, "From what I'm hearing, it's more than coincidence." [REUTERS, 9/20/2001]

AUGUST 23, 2001: FORMER FBI AL-QAEDA EXPERT BEGINS JOB AS HEAD OF SECURITY AT THE WTC

John O'Neill begins his new job as head of security at the WTC. O'Neill had been the special agent in charge of the FBI's National Security Division in New York, and was the bureau's top expert on al-Qaeda and Osama bin Laden. [NEW YORK MAGAZINE, 12/17/2001; NEW YORKER, 1/14/2002] He'd left his job with the FBI just the day before (see AUGUST 22, 2001). His friend Jerome Hauer, who is the former head of New York's Office of Emergency Management, had found him the job at the World Trade Center. Developer Larry Silverstein, who recently took over the lease of the WTC (see JULY 24, 2001), had been highly impressed with O'Neill but insisted he start in the post no later than the first week of September, when his firm Silverstein Properties is set to assume control of the buildings. O'Neill had agreed to this. [WEISS, 2003, PP. 336-338, 345-346 AND 349-351] **After hearing that O'Neill has got this job, Chris Isham, a senior producer at ABC News who is a close friend, says to him, "Well, that will be an easy job. They're not going to bomb that place again." O'Neill replies, "Well actually they've always wanted to finish that job. I think**

they're going to try again." [PBS FRONTLINE, 5/31/2002] After a few days as the WTC security director, O'Neill will move into his new office on the 34th floor of the South Tower. [WEISS, 2003, PP. 353-354 AND 366]

LATE AUGUST-SEPTEMBER 10, 2001: WTC SECURITY RAISED, THEN SCALED BACK, IN WEEKS BEFORE 9/11 ATTACK

The Independent reports that in late August, "security [is] abruptly heightened at the World Trade Center with the introduction of sniffer dogs and systematic checks on trucks bringing in deliveries. No explanation has been given for this measure." [INDEPENDENT, 9/17/2001] Newsday claims that around the same time, security personnel at the WTC begin working extra-long shifts because of numerous phone threats. However, on September 6, bomb-sniffing dogs are abruptly removed. Security further drops right before 9/11. WTC guard Daria Coard says in an interview later on the day of 9/11: "Today was the first day there was not the extra security." [NEWSDAY, 9/12/2001]

EARLY SEPTEMBER 2001: SUSPICIOUS TRADING IN REINSURANCE COMPANIES

[Were the *Masterminders cashing in harvesting fruits of 9/11?* Imagine, how easy it could have been for CIA-FBI to identify these gainers because these were computer transactions with full log of those accounts leading to identify the real 9/11 terrorists who only benefited every which way at the cost of so many lives and sufferings around the world]

It will later be speculated that, around this time, people with foreknowledge of the 9/11 attacks short sell reinsurance company stocks that are insuring either or both the airplanes and the buildings involved in the attacks. Munich Re, the largest European reinsurance company, loses 22 percent of its value in the two month before 9/11, with about half of that taking place in the week before the attacks. German authorities will later alert the Securities and Exchange Commission of "suspect movements" with Munich Re. [AGENCE FRANCE-PRESSE, 9/17/2001] Suspicious inquiries into the short selling of millions of company shares are made in France days before the attacks. [REUTERS, 9/20/2001; SAN FRANCISCO CHRONICLE, 9/22/2001] Munich Re stock will plummet after the attacks, as they claim the attacks will cost them $2 billion. [DOW JONES BUSINESS NEWS, 9/20/2001] There is also suspicious trading activity involving reinsurers Swiss Reinsurance and AXA. These trades are especially curious because the insurance sector "is one of the brightest spots in a very difficult market" at this time. [LOS ANGELES TIMES, 9/19/2001] A source within AXA will later say,

"There are indications that the shorting has been going on for some time. People inside the company could not understand why" there had been so much shorting of the stock in recent weeks. "This could give some explanation why the stocks were going down so much when there seemed to be no apparent reason." AXA shares drop almost 10 percent in the week before 9/11, and will plummet afterwards. The attacks will cost the company up to $400 million because of its coverage of both airplanes and buildings. [LOS ANGELES TIMES, 9/18/2001]

BETWEEN SEPTEMBER 1 AND SEPTEMBER 7, 2001: SILVERSTEIN PROPERTIES TAKES OVER CONTROL OF THE WORLD TRADE CENTER

In the first week of September 2001, the real estate development and investment firm Silverstein Properties assumes control of the World Trade Center. The company had acquired the lease to operate the Twin Towers from the New York Port Authority in late July (see JULY 24, 2001). It has already begun managing the facility with its own executives. *Selected Port Authority employees, including Alan Reiss, the director of the World Trade Center, have been assisting the firm during a three-month transition period.* **But in the weeks prior to 9/11, according to the New York Times, "Silverstein Properties asked Mr. Reiss to let it more fully operate everything from safety systems to tenant relations."** [NEW YORK TIMES, 9/13/2001; WEISS, 2003, PP. 338; 9/11 COMMISSION, 5/18/2004]

BETWEEN SEPTEMBER 3, 2001 AND SEPTEMBER 7, 2001: WTC STRUCTURAL ENGINEER SAYS TRADE CENTER DESIGNED FOR 707 CRASHING INTO IT

Leslie Robertson. *[Source: Publicity photo]*Leslie Robertson, one of the two original structural engineers for the World Trade Center, is asked at a conference in Frankfurt, Germany what he had done to protect the Twin Towers from terrorist attacks. He replies, "I designed it for a 707 to smash into it," though does not elaborate further. [CHICAGO TRIBUNE, 9/12/2001; KNIGHT RIDDER, 9/12/2001] The Twin Towers were in fact the first structures outside the military and nuclear industries designed to resist the impact of a jet airplane. [ROBERTSON, 3/2002; FEDERAL EMERGENCY MANAGEMENT AGENCY, 5/1/2002, PP. 1-17] The Boeing 707 was the largest in use when the towers were designed. Robertson conducted a study in late 1964, to calculate the effect of a 707 weighing 263,000 pounds and traveling at 180 mph crashing into one of the towers. He concluded that the tower would remain standing. A previous analysis, carried out early in 1964, calculated that the towers would handle the impact of a 707 traveling at 600 mph without collapsing (see FEBRUARY 27, 1993). The planes that hit the WTC on 9/11 are 767s, which are almost 20 percent heavier than 707s. [SCIENTIFIC AMERICAN, 10/9/2001; NEW YORKER, 11/19/2001]

SEPTEMBER 4, 2001: ISRAELI COMPANY MOVES OUT OF WTC
[Israeli intelligence could save Israelis but American Intelligence wanted maximum casualty for the success of New Pearl Harbour]

The Zim-American Israeli Shipping Co. moves their North American headquarters from the 16th floor of the WTC to Norfolk, Virginia, one week before the 9/11 attacks. The Israeli government owns 49 percent of the company. [VIRGINIAN-PILOT, 9/4/2001] Zim announced the move and its date six months earlier. [VIRGINIAN-PILOT, 4/3/2001] More than 200 workers had just been moved out; about ten are still in the building making final moving arrangements on 9/11, but escape. [JERUSALEM POST, 9/13/2001; JOURNAL OF COMMERCE, 10/18/2001] The move leaves only one Israeli company, ClearForest, with 18 employees, in the WTC on 9/11. The four or five employees in the building at the time manage to escape. [JERUSALEM POST, 9/13/2001] One year later, a Zim ship is impounded while attempting to ship Israeli military equipment to Iran; it is speculated that this is done with the knowledge of Israel. [AGENCE FRANCE-PRESSE, 3/29/2002]

SEPTEMBER 6-10, 2001: SUSPICIOUS TRADING ON STOCKS OF TWO LARGE WTC TENANTS

The Chicago Board Options Exchange sees suspicious trading on Merrill Lynch and Morgan Stanley, two of the largest WTC tenants. In the first week of September, an average of 27 put option contracts in its shares are bought each day. Then the total for the three days before the attacks is 2,157. Merrill Lynch, another WTC tenant, see 12,215 put options bought between September 7-10, when the previous days had seen averages of 252 contracts a day. [INDEPENDENT, 10/14/2001] Dylan Ratigan of Bloomberg Business News, speaking of the trading on Morgan Stanley and other companies, says, "This would be one of the most extraordinary coincidences in the history of mankind if it was a coincidence." [ABC NEWS, 9/20/2001]

John Kerry Confirms WTC7 Demolition:

2004 Democratic Presidential candidate John Kerry directly contradicted the official story about WTC7 when questioned by members of 'Austin 9/11 Truth Now': "I do know that that wall, I remember, was in danger and I think they made the decision based on the danger that it had in destroying other things, that they did it in a controlled fashion."

Pulling down WTC7 is another smoking gun because wiring a massive 47 storied building like WTC7 would require weeks of expert preparations suggesting all three buildings were wired for controlled demolitions synchronizing with the remotely hijacked GPS controlled precisely programmed crash of Flight 11 and Flight 175 (Boeing 767).

Fig. Reichstag Fire, Germany
February 27, 1933 (WikiPedia)

Fig. World Trade Center demolition on 9/11
September 11, 2001

The Reichstag Fire in Germany gave Hitler and his Nazi regime authoritarian power preparing for the World War II blaming the fire on a communist patsy. 9/11 destructions and demolitions along with Anthrax attack gave the Bush-Cheney Neoconian regime the authoritarian power starting worldwide self declared War on Terror blaming virtual patsies.

Finally, an insider speaks out about 911

(Excerpts from Kurt Sonnenfeld, 9/11 FEMA videographer at Ground Zero)

As official videographer for the U.S. government, Kurt Sonnenfeld was detailed to Ground Zero on September 11, 2001, where he spent one month filming 29 tapes and said, "What I saw at certain moments and in certain places ... is very disturbing!" He never handed them over to the authorities and has been persecuted ever since. Kurt Sonnenfeld lives in exile in Argentina, where he wrote "El Perseguido" (the persecuted). Below is an excerpt from his exclusive interview by *The Voltaire Network*.

On September 11, 2001, the area known as "Ground Zero" was sealed from the public eye. Sonnenfeld, however, was given unrestricted access enabling him to document for the investigation (that never took place) and provide some "sanitized" pool video to virtually every news network in the world. The tapes that reveal some of the anomalies which he discovered at Ground Zero are still in his possession. [Fig. source FEMA]

Voltaire Network: *You have suggested that you observed things at Ground Zero that did not tally with the official account. Did you do or say anything to arouse suspicion in this respect?*

Kurt Sonnenfeld: In that same telephone call I said that I would "go public", not only with my suspicions about the events surrounding September 11, 2001, but about several contracts I had worked on in the past.

Fig. WTC remains & rescue, OSHA

Voltaire Network: *What are your suspicions based on?*

Kurt Sonnenfeld: There were many things, in hindsight, that were disturbing at Ground Zero. It was odd to me that I was dispatched to go to New York even before the second plane hit the South Tower, while the media was still reporting only that a "small plane" had collided with the North Tower — far too small of a catastrophe at that point to involve FEMA . FEMA was mobilized within minutes, whereas it took ten days for it to deploy to New Orleans to respond to Hurricane Katrina, even with abundant advance warning! It was odd to me that all cameras were so fiercely prohibited within the secured perimeter of Ground Zero, that the entire area was declared a crime scene and yet the "evidence" within that crime scene was so rapidly removed and destroyed. And then it was very odd to me when I learned that FEMA and several other federal agencies had already moved into position at their command center at Pier 92 on September 10th, one day before the attacks!

Rubber landing-gear tyres visible in evidence container marked "FBI Plane Parts Only." We are asked to believe that all four of the "indestructible" black boxes of the two jets that struck the twin towers were never found because they were completely vaporized, yet I have footage of the rubber wheels of the landing gear nearly undamaged, as well as the seats, parts of the fuselage and a jet turbine that were absolutely not vaporized.

What happened with Building 7 is incredibly suspicious. I have video that shows how curiously small the rubble pile was, and how the buildings to either side were untouched by Building Seven when it collapsed. It had not been hit by an airplane; it had suffered only minor injuries when the Twin Towers collapsed, and there were only small fires on a couple of floors. There's no way that building could have imploded the way it did without controlled demolition. Yet the collapse of Building 7 was hardly mentioned by the mainstream media and suspiciously ignored by the 911 Commission.

Voltaire Network: *Reportedly, the underground levels of WTC7 contained sensitive and undoubtedly compromising archival material. Did you come across any of it?*
Kurt Sonnenfeld: The Secret Service, the Department of Defense, the Federal Bureau of Investigation, the Internal Revenue Service, the Securities and Exchange

Commission and the Office of Emergency Management's "Crisis Center" occupied huge amounts of space there, spanning several floors of the building. Other federal agencies had offices there as well. After September 11, it was discovered that concealed within Building Seven was the largest clandestine domestic station of the Central Intelligence Agency outside of Washington DC, a base of operations from which to spy on diplomats of the United Nations and to conduct counterterrorism and counterintelligence missions.

Approaching the entrance to the sub-level areas of Building 6

There was no underground parking level at Seven World Trade Center. And there was no underground vault. Instead, the federal agencies at Building Seven stored their vehicles, documents and evidence in the building of their associates across the street. Beneath the plaza level of US Customs House (Building 6) was a large underground garage, separated off from the rest of the complex's underground area and guarded under tight security. This was where the various government services parked their bomb-proofed cars and armoured limousines, counterfeit taxi cabs and telephone company trucks used for undercover surveillance and covert operations, specialized vans and other vehicles. Also within that secured parking area was access to the sub-level vault of Building 6.

When the North Tower fell, the US Customs House (Building 6) was crushed and totally incinerated. Much of the underground levels beneath it were also destroyed. But there were voids. And it was into one of those voids, recently uncovered, that I descended with a special Task Force to investigate. It was there we found the security antechamber to the vault, badly damaged. At the far end of the security office was the wide steel door to the vault, a combination code keypad in the cinderblock wall beside it. But the wall was cracked and partially crumbled, and the door was sprung partially open. So we checked inside with our flashlights. Except for several rows of empty shelves, there was nothing in the vault but dust and debris. It had been emptied. Why was it empty? And when could it have been emptied?

Voltaire Network: Is this what set alarm bells ringing for you?
Kurt Sonnenfeld: Yes, but not immediately. With so much chaos, it was difficult to think. It was only after digesting everything that the "alarm bells" went off.

Building Six was evacuated within twelve minutes after the first airplane struck the North Tower. The streets were immediately clogged with fire trucks, police cars and blocked traffic, and the vault was large enough, 15 meters by 15 meters by my estimate, to necessitate at least a big truck to carry out its contents. And after the towers fell and destroyed most of the parking level, a mission to recover the contents of the vault would have been impossible. The vault had to have been emptied before the attack.

I've described all of this extensively in my book, and it's apparent that things of importance were taken out of harm's way before the attacks. For example, the CIA didn't seem too concerned about their losses. After the existence of their clandestine office in Building Seven was discovered, an agency spokesman told the newspapers that a special team had been dispatched to scour the rubble in search of secret documents and intelligence reports, though there were millions,

if not billions of pages floating in the streets. Nevertheless, the spokesman was confident. "There shouldn't be too much paper around," he said.

The bizarre hollowed-out vestiges of The US Customs House (Building Six) And Customs at first claimed that everything was destroyed. That the heat was so intense that everything in the evidence safe had been baked to ash. But some months later, they announced that they had broken up a huge Colombian narco-trafficking and money-laundering ring after miraculously recovering crucial evidence from the safe, including surveillance photos and heat-sensitive cassette tapes of monitored calls. And when they moved in to their new building at 1 Penn Plaza in Manhattan, they proudly hung on the lobby wall their Commissioner's Citation Plaque and their big round US Customs Service ensign, also miraculously recovered, in pristine condition, from their crushed and cremated former office building at the World Trade Center.

Voltaire Network: With the publication of your book, you have become a "whistleblower" – yet another step on which there is no going back! There must be many people with inside knowledge about what really happened or did not happen on that fateful day. Yet, hardly any have stepped up to the plate and certainly no one who was directly involved in an official capacity. This is what makes your case so compelling. Judging from your ordeal, it is not difficult to imagine what is holding such people back.

Kurt Sonnenfeld: Actually, there are several other very smart and credible people blowing whistles, too. And they are being discredited and ignored. Some are being harassed and persecuted, as I am.

People are gripped by fear. Everybody knows that if you question US authority you will have problems in some way or another. At minimum you will be discredited and dehumanized. Most likely you'll find yourself indicted for something completely unrelated, like tax evasion — or something even worse, as in my case. Look at what happened to Secret Service whistle-blower Abraham Bolden, for example, or to chess master Bobby Fischer after he showed his disdain for the US. There are countless other examples. In the past I asked friends and associates to speak out for me to counter all the lies being planted in the media, and all of them were terrified as to the ramifications to themselves and their families.

Voltaire Network: To what degree would your discoveries at Ground Zero expose the government's involvement in those events? Are you familiar with the investigations that have been carried out by numerous scientists and qualified professionals which not only corroborate your own findings but, in some instances, far exceed them? Do you regard such people as "conspiracy nuts"?

Kurt Sonnenfeld: At the highest levels in Washington, DC, someone knew what was going to happen. They wanted a war so badly that they at least let it happen and most likely even helped it happen.

Sometimes it seems to me that the "nuts" are those who hold to what they've been told with an almost religious fervour despite all of the evidence to the contrary — the ones who won't even consider that there was a conspiracy. There are so many anomalies to the "official" investigation that you can't blame it on oversight or incompetence. I am familiar with the scientists and qualified professionals to whom you refer, and their findings are convincing, credible, and presented according to scientific protocol — in stark contrast to the findings of the "official" investigation. In addition, numerous intelligence agents and government officials have now come forward with their very informed opinions that the 911 Commission was a farce at best or a cover-up at worst. My experience at Ground Zero is but one more piece of the puzzle.

Voltaire Network: Those events are nearly 8 years behind us. Do you consider that uncovering the truth about 9/11 continues to be an important objective? Why?
Kurt Sonnenfeld: It is of absolute importance. And it will be equally as important in 10 years, or even 50 years if the truth still has not been exposed. It is an important objective because, at this point in history, many people are too credulous to whatever "authority" tells them and too willing to follow. People in a state of shock seek guidance. People who are afraid are manipulable. And being able to manipulate the masses results in unimaginable benefits to a lot of very rich and very powerful people. War is incredibly expensive, but the money has to go somewhere. War is very profitable for the very few. And somehow their sons always end up in Washington DC, making the decisions and writing the budgets, while the sons of the poor and the poorly-connected always end up on the enemy lines, taking their orders and fighting their battles. The enormous black-budget of the US Department of Defense represents an unlimited money machine for the military-industrial complex, figuring in the multi-trillions of dollars, and it will continue to be so until the masses wake up, recuperate their skepticism and demand accountability. Wars (and false pretexts for war) will not cease until the people realize the true motive of war and stop believing "official" explanations.

Voltaire Network: What is referred to as the 9/11 Truth Movement, has been asking for a new, independent investigation into those events. Do you think that the Obama Administration holds out some hope in this respect?

Kurt Sonnenfeld: I really hope so, but I'm skeptical. Why would the leadership of any established government willingly undertake any action that would result in a serious compromise to their authority? They will prefer to maintain the status quo and leave the things the way they are. The conductor of the train has been changed, but has the train changed its course? I doubt it. The push has to come from the public, not only domestically, but internationally, like your group is doing.

....

Voltaire Network: As we said, deciding to write this book and to go public was a huge step. What pushed you to do it?

Kurt Sonnenfeld: To save my family. And to let the world know that things are not what they seem.

Voltaire Network: Last but not least: what will you do with your tapes?

Kurt Sonnenfeld: I am convinced that my tapes reveal many more anomalies than I am capable of recognizing given my limited qualifications. I will therefore cooperate in any way that I can with serious and reliable experts in a common endeavour to expose the truth.

Voltaire Network: Thank you very much!

Why Mainstream Media Is Silent and/or Deceiving?

The dishonesty of the media

John Swinton, the former Chief of Staff at the New York Times, made this candid confession when asked to give a toast before the prestigious New York Press Club [it's worth noting that Swinton was called "The Dean of His Profession" by other newsmen, who admired him greatly]:

"There is no such thing, at this date of the world's history, as an independent press. You know it and I know it. There is not one of you who dares to write your honest opinions, and if you did, you know beforehand that it would never appear in print. I am paid weekly for keeping my honest opinions out of the paper I am connected with. Others of you are paid similar salaries for similar things, and any of you who would be so foolish as to write honest opinions would be out on the streets looking for another job.

If I allowed my honest opinions to appear in one issue of my paper, before twenty-four hours my occupation would be gone. The business of the journalist is to destroy the truth; to lie outright; to pervert; to vilify; to fawn at the feet of mammon, and to sell the country for his daily bread. You know it and I know it and what folly is this toasting an independent press. We are the tools and vassals of the rich men behind the scenes. We are the jumping jacks, they pull the strings and we dance. Our talents, our possibilities and our lives are all the property of other men. **We are intellectual prostitutes. "**

Propagandist media ignoring the most intriguing true issues

Recently Ex-President Bill Clinton was asked during his speech in Toronto, Canada, August 29, 2009 on "Embracing Our Common Humanity" where Clinton tried to explain "why his country is so reluctant to change the way it delivers health care". He said that in the U.S., there were **"incentives to keep people misinformed and full of fear."** - Sunny Freeman, The Canadian Press

Since the time of Spanish War, US media re-invented and embraced Yellow Journalism when Randolph Hearst and Joseph Pulitzer sold the non-existent Spanish War to the American people in support of hegemony assuring on site reporters "**... You furnish the pictures, I'll furnish the war**". Since then Pulitzer Prize winners mainly advanced Yellow Journalism in USA and around the world with utmost deception disrespecting journalistic oaths.

The group of people who historically wanted the whole world as their promise land managed to hold key monarchy, military, evangelic, mining, business, political, legal, strategist, analyst, scientific, and media 'anchorship & ownership' positions and have been working coherently towards re-establishing '**new world order**' of nobles and aristocrats at the cost of the old world even sacrificing own people as collateral damages!

It may sound like biased propaganda but it's a reality as the monarchist alliances regrouped themselves through 'World War I & II' gaining steam for the final episode of world war III to occupy the promise world nullifying all revolutions towards democratic governments and society! The massive Evangelic propaganda of '**Second coming of violent Christ**' and '**End of the World**', which resemble more like Alexander the Conqueror or Caesar - weeding out 2/3rd of world population, are all part of a systematic manipulations of world opinions towards the acceptance of population control that perpetuate Monarchial Supremacy supported by few Bankers and Elites using United Nations (UN), World Bank and World Health Organization (WHO).

It's all started with Hellenism in Greek destroying ancient Grecian participatory democracy installing aristocratic nobility! Gained steam looting rich Persia and conquering Rome contributing to Greco-Roman empire. The Monarchs and Elites became Jews and Christians for convenient cover while working meticulously towards the goal of absolute power maintaining intelligence and communications with each other. As Jews they persecuted Hebrews! As Christians they orchestrated crusades against Christians, Muslims, Hindus and Hebrew Jews!

Ever wonder who funds these wars! Who funded Alexander the conqueror for massive invasions, occupations and dominations around the ancient world creating Dorian Greek Empire? Who funded Caesar's long barbaric campaign against the civilized Romans which eventually created Greco-Roman Hellenistic Empire? Who funded Hitler's military and war machinery when Germany was choking from cruel allied sanctions and contributions spelt in the Versailles treaty? Who is funding American war on terror when Bush Administration bankrupted the Government with 500 plus billion deficits and 2.3 trillion missing Pentagon funds? Who is gaining out of all these wars and religious evangelic campaign while most humans suffer physically or psychologically?

We are already familiar from 'Simple Proof' with Reporter (Ex-AP, Newsweek) Robert Parry's conviction, **"The people who succeeded and did well were those who didn't stand up, who didn't write the big stories, who looked the other way when history was happening in front of them, and went along either consciously or just by cowardice with the deception of the American people."**

We have also seen US media obedience to secretive One World Thinkers Bilderberg that has been keeping people in dark void of honest investigative reporting: **"We are grateful to the Washington Post, the New York Times, Time Magazine and other great publications whose directors have attended our meetings and respected their promises of discretion for almost forty years."** - Chairman David Rockefeller, 1991 meeting at Baden, Germany.

We are beginning to realize that the success of 9/11 operations and subsequent rapid cover ups were not possible without massive cooperative participation of the higher ups in CIA and FBI. This is only possible in ever vigilant continental USA by **CIA's covert subversion of the media.**

Final Proof

*Let us make the closing statement with details towards proof
addressing anomalies
of 9-11 terror act
supported by facts, figures, tables, and opinions.*

Real Path To Well Planned Precisely Enacted 9/11 Destruction In US Soil

[CIA-Central Intelligence Agency, FBI-Federal Bureau of Investigation, Mossad-Israeli Intelligence Agency, MI6-UK Intelligence Agencies, NSC–National Security Council, NORAD-North American Aerospace Defense Command, ISI–Inter-Services Intelligence, NEADS- North Eastern Air Defense System, FAA-Federal Aviation Agency, WTC-World Trade Center]

Abstract: Since the only investigative US journalist Daniel Pearl was beheaded in Pakistan by ISI, CIA's main link to Al-Qaeda, an ordinary world citizen had to establish an integrated theory about what really happened on 9/11 and who were responsible for that unthinkable precisely delivered disaster, behind all the rhetoric and fear of apprehension, and why! This is a simple theory put together so that every world citizen (juror) can extend a verdict saying 9/11 is a plot master minded from the White House and Executed by the Pentagon along with high level FBI/FAA/NORAD operatives collaborating with high level CIA/MI6/ISI/Mossad officials.

Gist: 9/11 never happened the way it happened without President George Bush's authorization changing existing NORAD protocol inactivating NORAD's authority to scramble fighter jets against any suspicious airplanes, especially flying without transponder, in the North American Airspace! The newly authorized Federal Aviation Authority (FAA) Hijack Coordinator, Mike Canavan, was sent to Puerto Rico without backup where he was out of contact throughout 9/11 operation enabling the success of the well coordinated precision Remote Control Military Plan, like Operation Northwoods!

The signatories of the 'Project of the New American Century (PNAC)', including Vice President Cheney and defense secretary Donald Rumsfeld, masterminded 'The New Pearl Harbor' on 9/11 using Air Force to remotely hijack well known military/commercial jets, Boeing 757 and 767, locking on the transponders from Pentagon running airplane crash simulation from the National Reconnaissance Office (NRO), in Chantilly Virginia, making the patriotic pilots watch helpless destructions!

There were no physical hijackers! The fake calls and rumors were part of the planned implementation as originally envisioned in Operation Northwoods against Cuba! All hijackers name were given to CIA by the Israeli Authority long before September 11, 2001 for investigation! They used the names to frame and blame Islamic militants who never took any of those flights as confirmed by all 9/11 flight's passenger lists!

Well choreographed and timed mysterious Bin Laden video may help International Republican Party re-elect Republican type administrations fooling Americans and the world but none of them can ever address the 9/11 anomalies illustrated as conclusion in this thesis!

Before we present our case, let us hear from physical Bin Laden regarding the 9/11 accusation:

Here is an excerpt from an interview with Osama bin Laden that was published in a Karachi-based Pakistani daily newspaper, Ummat, on September 28, 2001 -

"I have already said that I am not involved in the 11 September attacks in the United States. As a Muslim, I try my best to avoid telling a lie. I had no knowledge of these attacks, nor do I consider the killing of innocent women, children and other humans as an appreciable act. Islam strictly forbids causing harm to innocent women, children and other people. Such a practice is forbidden even in the course of a battle. It is the United States, which is perpetrating every maltreatment on women, children and common people . . .".

Profoundly patriotic aristocrative Western Media managed to suppress this Ummat interview while indulging in mysterious manufactured video obtained from garbage cans in support of the official fiction-like theory.

Key Points of Prosecution:

If Bin Laden could have done 9/11/2001 style precision well coordinated military operation on the US soil in broad day light evading US Military, NORAD, CIA, FBI, NSA, FAA, and pre-emptive media like CNN, then world would have seen **Kyoto ratified**, **Landmines banned**, **a rational International Court**, and **a stronger united UN** pre-emptively addressing world issues for universal well being in the 21st century while containing terrorism with Rule-of-Law & Proof-of-Conviction! Thus, let us examine the real motives and means of accomplishing 9/11 type operation justifying once for all the need for an open public investigation analyzing facts and accountabilities logically to establish truth – the very basis of peaceful coexisting just world.

Motives:

1.   All signatories of the Project For the New American Century were either member of the Bush/Cheney Administration or Pentagon who asked for New Pearl Harbor in their ambition of Rebuilding America's Defense (Page 51) "Creating Tomorrow's Dominant Force - the process of transformation, even if it brings revolutionary change, is likely to be a long one, absent some catastrophic and catalyzing event like a New Pearl Harbor". Coincidentally, then Defense secretary Rumsfeld predicted New Pearl Harbour during his inaugural speech.

Thus, 9/11 was a requirement for re-establishing American Supremacy throughout the world, as viewed by this group of people.

2.   **David Rockefeller, Speaking at the June, 1991, secret Bilderberger meeting in Baden, Germany** (also attended by Bill Clinton & Dan Quayle) "We are grateful to the Washington Post, the New York Times, Time Magazine and other great publications whose directors have attended our meetings and respected their promises of discretion for almost forty years.

It would have been impossible for us to develop our plan for the world if we had been subjected to the lights of publicity during those years. But, the world is more sophisticated and prepared to march towards a world government. The supranational sovereignty of an intellectual elite and world bankers is surely preferable to the national autodetermination practiced in past centuries."

[Note: with his God like influence in New York City, he negotiated for the transfer of WTC to private hands of Silverstein Properties and Westfield America on July 24, 2001, 6 weeks before 9/11. With CIA briefings privilege like ex-presidents, he was well informed of the upcoming "Spectacular Event" like New Pearl Harbour which enriched Rockefeller private empire with billions including bailout of CITIGROUP]

3.   Bush Administration was putting the final touches on a Middle East initiative, which included recognition of a Palestinian State, endorsement of the Mitchell Plan, and position statements about Palestinian refugees and the status of Jerusalem. This initiative was to be shared with the Saudi Ambassador to the United Nations on Sept. 13, 2001, with a formal presentation to the U.N. General Assembly by the Secretary of State Colin Powell on September 23.

But, 70 million Zion's Christian soldiers in USA were against any deal with the Palestinian!

4. Excerpt from Donald Rumsfeld's interview on Larry King Live regarding his 9/11 morning meeting with a congressional delegation including Deputy Defense Secretary Paul Wolfowitz, and Representative Christopher Cox (R) – "I had said at an 8:00 o'clock breakfast that sometime in the next two, four, six, eight, ten, twelve months there would be an event that would occur in the world that would be sufficiently shocking that it would remind people again how important it is to have a strong healthy Defense department that contributes to – That underpins peace and stability in our world".

5. (CBS) On Sept. 10, 2001, Secretary of Defense Donald Rumsfeld declared war on Pentagon bureaucracy. He said, "Money wasted by the military poses a serious threat, in fact, it could be said it's a matter of life and death,". "According to some estimates we cannot track $2.3 trillion in transactions," Rumsfeld admitted.

9/11 Disaster brought all humane peace and international initiatives to a grinding halt, as per requirements in the document 'Project of the New American Century'!

Main Arguments:

Once the motives of ideological evangelic supremacy infected the like-minded authorities, all they needed revive "Operation Northwoods" in a broader scale using High-Tech military remote hijacking while framing and blaming Islamic Hijackers from data collected by the CIA and NSA as Operation Able-Danger since 1999. But NORAD was on their way with its capabilities of seeing any domestic flight without transponder on their screens and scrambling authority of fighter jets after suspected aircraft(s).

♦ On 9/11/2001, normal US routines and procedures were violated by few Government officials including President and Vice President, inactivating the Airline procedures of hijacked airliner and follow up responses from FAA, NORAD, Pentagon and the White House for about two hours.

♦ The most important point is the NORAD hijacking protocol before 9/11: Per 1st Air Force's own book about 9/11, the "sector commander [at NEADS] would have authority to scramble the airplanes.".

But, the Protocol in place on 9/11 stated, "the escort service will be requested by the FAA hijack coordinator, Mike Canavan, by direct contact with the National Military Command Center (NMCC)." Ironically Mike Canavan was sent to Puerto Rico that morning without backup.

♦ The second most important point is the US Military and NORAD readiness: They were at the highest state of alert performing "Global Guardian" military training exercise when the planes with Transponders off were flying without interruption to programmed targets. Generally NORAD could see any plane (Hubbub) and act immediately the moment the Transponder stopped responding.

♦ The third most important point is the apparent silence from the helpless pilots: The very fact that during the entire hijacking drama none of the crew members could contact the ground control suggested that the controls had been taken from ground piggybacking Primary Channel and disabling cockpit voice recorder while keying on the cockpit microphone produced blank voice recorders.

♦ Whoever sent US Military grade Anthrax to Capitol Hill to kill mainly Democratic Senators and media critical of Bush Administration are directly linked with the Remote Control Hijacking of all 9/11 flights which were Boeing 757 and 767 built for both military and commercial use equipped with Home Run remote control capability that Lufthansa had to de-install.

♦ Since 9/11 flights were fully automated Boeing military and passenger drones, NORAD didn't have to scramble fighter planes, they could have just brought them down to nearest US Air force Base using secret codes only known to key NORAD and US military officials.

♦ Thus, **there were no physical hijackers**. Helpless pilots watched their Airplanes being flown as drones ending in irrecoverable disasters.

♦ The plan was conceived starting 2000 when Able/Danger project was dissolved and implemented with the hiring of Dr. Dov Zakheim as the Comptroller of the Pentagon in May 2001. He was the Corporate Vice President of Systems Planning Corporation (SPC) which specialized in Remote Control Flight Termination from the ground. Also, Dr. Zakheim was very familiar with WTC structures, infrastructures, and security arrangements from his involvement with SPC Subsidiary TRIDATA CORPORATION that oversaw 1993 WTC explosion related investigation and auditing.

Able/Danger project was tracking alleged Mohamed Atta and three of the 19 hijackers since 1999 inside USA. The file was destroyed by Pentagon after 9/11 which became a subject of Congressional investigation.

♦ One and half months before 9/11, WTC ownership and security were transferred to David Rockefeller (financed by his empire Citigroups, JP Morgan/Chase) brokered Private hands Silverstein Properties and Westfield America to facilitate wiring of the engineering wonders for controlled demolition on 9/11 following the programmed crashes per New Pearl Harbour implementation script.

Rather coincidentally, Marvin Bush's Securacom's contract with WTC was to expire after 9/11. That seems to be the reason why US military and NORAD preponed their yearly vigorous military exercises (Practice

Armageddon, Global Guardian, Vigilant Warrior, Amalgam Warrior and Vigilant Guardian) from October 22-31, 2001, to the week of September 11, 2001. Global Guardian started at 8:30am from Barksdale Airforce Base, Louisiana, launching three (3) E-4B National Airborne Operations Center (NAOC) planes including one over Pentagon witnessing Flight 77 hit unguarded Pentagon with miraculous manoeuvring around 9:37am.

Silverstein Properties and Westfield America which mysteriously acquired 99 year lease on WTC from Port Authority of New York and New Jersey on July 24, 2001, eventually harvested 4.55 billion US in profit from the insurers of WTC including officially demolished WTC7.

♦ With full knowledge of CIA/FBI/Homeland Security/Key Senators-Representatives of the upcoming "Spectacular Event" all CIA/FBI emergency and rescue planes/helicopters were moved to Monterey, California, as well as North-Eastern Air Defense fighters were sent to Saudi Arabia, Iceland, and Turkey prior to 9/11 endangering USA.

♦ Whoever wanted journalist Daniel Pearl beheaded for pursuing Indian lead linking ISI, Richard Armitage (US Deputy Secretary of State) and $100,000 wire transfer from Pakistan's Army General Mahmoud Ahmad to alleged Mahammed Atta's Florida Account must be investigated as the real perpetrators.

Additional Arguments:

1. Failure of Normal Air Traffic Controller (ATC), FAA, and NORAD procedures.

   It is a normal FAA procedure that NORAD fighter planes must scramble within minutes of a confirmed hijacking! This was even true for a small aircraft Learjet 35 of Golfer Stewart Payne before 9/11! But on 9/11 NORAD stayed inactive awaiting for missing FAA hijacking coordinator's coordination!

2. None of the passenger lists of the 9/11 flights were complete, rather out of sync with the FBI doctored list of names. It is a standard practice that each person boarding a flight must show a photo Id with the name that is on the ticket making the airlines passenger lists as the final. Interestingly, the FBI

edited list couldn't even tally the passenger total-count with the list of passengers.

3.

One must wonder how the FBI named all supposedly dead 9/11 hijackers on 9/12. Surprisingly FBI even found a clean passport lying by ground zero! Per 9/11 Commission Report, Israel warned USA in August 2001 of possible Al-Qaeda attack delivering a list of 19 Arab terrorist names to FBI collected by Mossad agents inside USA acting as Art Students!

4. The securities of all 9/11 related Airports were contracted to just one private security company called ICTS-International, owned by an Israeli, Ezra Harel, and registered in the Netherlands!

3. Hours before the House version of the first Patriot Act went to a vote in October 2001, "technical corrections" were inserted into the body of the legislation whereby foreign security companies such as ICTS-International would be immune from lawsuits related to the events of 9/11.

Vice President Dick Cheney warned Democrats "to not seek political advantage by making incendiary suggestions ... that the White House had advance information that would have prevented the tragic attacks of 9-11". President Bush also warned media and democrats 'not to indulge in outrageous Conspiracy Theories'!

4. Destruction of the World Trade Center and all evidences for future analysis and investigation:

[On September 11th 2001, BBC World reported at 4:57pm Eastern Time that the Salomon Brothers Building (more commonly known as WTC7 or World Trade Building 7) had collapsed. But the building actually collapsed at 5:20pm! Larry Silverstein, the owner of the WTC complex, admitted on a September 2002 PBS documentary, 'America Rebuilds' that he and the NYFD decided to 'pull' *WTC 7* on the day of the attack. The word 'pull' is industry jargon for taking a building down with explosives.

Let us also hear from the 2004 US Presidential Candidate John Kerry when questioned on WTC 7 by members of Austin 9/11 Truth Now at a Book

People event in Austin Texas, he responded, "I do know that that wall, I remember, was in danger and I think they made the decision based on the danger that it had in destroying other things, that they did it in a controlled fashion."

This statement of John Kerry and Larry Silverstein is a smoking gun Because controlled demolition of 47-story WTC 7 would normally require about a week for preparation by experts! Which suggests WTC 7 was wired for controlled demolition before 9/11 along with South and North Tower!

Dr. Steven Jones of 'Scholars for 9/11 Truth' tested samples of steel from the Twin towers as well as recovered dust, which have both tested positive for the chemical signature of Thermate used to cut support beams in localized reactions during a controlled demolition.

Controlled demolitions expert Danny Jowenko was shown footage and building schematics of Building 7 by Dutch television who immediately concluded that the collapse was a result of deliberately placed explosives.]

a. All recovered steel frames were sold to scrap dealers as soon as possible and were kept away from all private engineering investigators.
b. Surveillance tapes and logs had been missing from a distant Bank's Vault.
c. Security threats were lowered just before 9/11 abruptly removing the bomb-sniffing dogs.
d. Marvin P. Bush, the president's younger brother, was a principal in a company called Securacom that provided security for the World Trade Center, United Airlines, and Dulles International Airport on 9/11. It was very unusual that a Kuwait-American owned foreign company would be given so much authority over high level security establishments.
e. WTC was powered down from 9/8-9/9 for 36 hours disabling cameras and security locks.
f. Destruction of Evidence from Ground Zero at the World Trade Center
g. Timed Demolition of World Trade Center depriving Victims to be rescued by Fire Fighters, military, and National Guards!

h. Bush Administration and Environmental Protection Agency (EPA) had been shying away from WTC Ground Zero Radiation Testing infuriating New York Senator Clinton.

5. Absence of rescue efforts by military or national guards before the collapse of the World Trade Center:

If 9/11 was a foreign terrorist act world would have seen a rescue effort using choppers and military technology Hollywood could never dream of. The very slow pace of rescue using hands and plastic mugs in human chains only ensured death of any survivors beneath the apparently demolished WTC debris.

6. Obstruction of justice and stone walling by the Bush Administration:

A doctor never hides a patient's condition or health data from the family! Then the question should be asked why every effort from Bush Administration was exerted to hide information, mislead public with misinformation and obstruct/delay a public inquiry of the disaster as long as possible instead of being prompt and voluntary!

7. Lowering Security Level despite World wide pre-9/11Warnings: All US friends even apparent foes tried their best to inform American Government and Intelligence about the upcoming disaster without realizing that those threats were propaganda by CIA/MI6/Mossad to deviate all thoughts of Remote Control hijacking of airplanes as drones!

8. List of detainees never disclosed:

For trust and accountability citizens must know the suspects arrested after 9/11 incident and the nature of their crimes irrespective of nationality and religion. Hiding detainees away from justice and public only helping towards mistrust of a Government which lacked credibility right from the beginning of 9/11 disaster.

9. No Airport Security video showing Hijackers boarding not even from one of the four flights from four Airports: The only photo showing alleged Atta passing through Portland was rather irrelevant.

10. The World Trade Center Collapse without bending or buckling despite visibly undisturbed towers after the initial collisions: per Firemen testimony they were trying to put off small fires that were still burning before they were ordered to leave the building.

11. Shutting down the WTC elevators when firemen were waiting with rescued victims and trapped employees:

12. Concealing and censoring Flight Recorders: Flight Recorders had been known to withstand inland crash and always found intact. FBI and CIA concealed WTC flight recorders and censored Pentagon and Pennsylvania recorders in an effort to support the Government version of illogical fabrication.

Let us quote few relevant high level testimonies from US officials before conclusion:

> • <u>Sibel Edmonds</u>, **former FBI translator** - "If they were to do real investigations we would see several significant high level criminal prosecutions in this country. And that is something that they are not going to let out. And, believe me; they will do everything to cover this up."

> • Director Col. Robert Bowman of the U.S. "Star Wars" space defense program - "<u>9/11 was an inside job</u>. If our government had merely done nothing, and I say that as an old interceptor pilot—I know the drill, I know what it takes, I know how long it takes, I know what the procedures are, I know what they were, and I know what they've changed them to   if our government had merely done nothing, and allowed normal procedures to happen on that morning of 9/11, the Twin Towers would still be standing and thousands of dead Americans would still be alive. That is treason!"

> • FBI Minneapolis division Chief Coleen Rowley - "I feel that certain facts... have, up to now, been omitted, downplayed, glossed over and/or mischaracterized in an effort to avoid or minimize personal and/or institutional embarrassment on the part of the FBI and/or perhaps even for

improper political reasons." She wondered, "Why would an FBI agent deliberately sabotage a case **(Zacarias Moussaoui's)**? The superiors acted so strangely that some   agents in the Minneapolis office openly joked that those higher-ups 'had to be spies or moles... working for Osama bin Laden.'

▪ Ex-FBI counterterrorism expert John O'Neill - "The main obstacles to investigate Islamic terrorism were US oil corporate interests and the role played by Saudi Arabia in it. All the answers, everything needed to dismantle Osama bin Laden's organization, could be found in Saudi Arabia. White House was obstructing my investigation of bin Laden because they were still keeping the idea of a pipeline deal with the Taliban open."

▪ Lt. Colonel Guy S. Razer, U.S. Air Force fighter pilot, former instructor at the USAF Fighter Weapons School and NATO's Tactical Leadership Program – "I am 100% convinced that the attacks of September 11, 2001 were planned, organized, and committed by treasonous perpetrators that have infiltrated the highest levels of our government .... Those of us in the military took an oath to support and defend the Constitution of the United States against all enemies, foreign and domestic. Just because we have retired does not make that oath invalid, so it is not just our responsibility, it is our duty to expose the real perpetrators of 9/11 and bring them to justice, no matter how hard it is, how long it takes, or how much we have to suffer to do it."

▪ Lt. Colonel Shelton F. Lankford –

"9/11 was an inside job. This isn't about party, it isn't about Bush Bashing. It's about our country, our constitution, and our future.

...

Your countrymen have been murdered and the more you delve into it the more it looks as though they were murdered by our government, who used it as an excuse to murder other people thousands of miles away."

Reference:

•Project of the New American Century (PNAC);
•Complete 9-11 Time Line; 9-11 Commission Report;
•History Commons: http://www.historycommons.org
•"Home Run" Electronically *Hijacking the World Trade Center Attack Aircraft,* Joe Vialls October 2001
•http://en.wikipedia.org/wiki/9/11_Truth_Movement containing links to many 9/11 truth related sites.

Related Links:
• So, What Is Al-Qaeda: www.kolki.com/peace/What-Is-Al-Qaeda.htm
• "Home Run"- Electronically Hijacking of Passenger Jet Aircrafts By Military/Intelligence:
  www.kolki.com/peace/Home-Run.htm
• "Operation Northwoods":
  www.kolki.com/peace/US-NSA-Face.htm

Closing Statements

If 9/11 was the work of the Cave Dweller Diabetic Patient Bin Laden and his 19 Cessna trained Box cutters armed disciples and President George Bush didn't authorize change in normal NORAD hijacking procedures, then –

- Crew (Pilot/Captain) would have pressed the transponder signalling hijacking and Ground Control would have followed normal hijacking procedures immediately.

- NORAD would have acted promptly scrambling fighter planes after the hijacked Airplanes, eventually grounding or destroying them as per normal procedures.

- Since all 9/11 flights were Boeing 757 & 767 NORAD would have brought them down to nearby US Air force Base terminating flights using Remote Control option available to key US Military & NORAD personnel piggybacking primary channel of the Flight Management System.

- Even if the hijackers could hit buildings, world would have seen a rescue operation from WTC using Helicopters and US military stunt Hollywood could never produce!

- Passenger lists of all Airlines would have shown hijackers names consistent with their Passports and Photo-Ids. No one could fly in US without ID as on the Ticket!

- Lists of all detainees by nationality would have been published immediately for open justice satisfying public interests and trusts!

- Anthrax would have been sent to The White House and Pentagon, NOT the Democratic Senators and media critical to Bush Administration creating post 9/11 'Psychological Warfare'.

- President Bush would have flown to White house directly as the Commander-In-Chief instead of getting briefed for four hours in Offutt Air Force Base,

A barrier to peace, good environment and universal well being

Home of the U.S. Strategic Command Headquarters, Omaha, Nebraska!

[Imagine a father consulting with a physician when a child was drowning! President is the Commander-in-Chief and those dying children of 9/11 needed immediate help and attention in WTC and Pentagon but were betrayed]

- World would have seen the fastest high-tech recoveries of the victims from the World Trade Center debris, NOT the slowest recovery using hands and plastic tubs.

- No one would steal World Trade Center Security Videos from distant secured Bank's Vault!

- All scrap metal from World Trade center would have been saved for Engineering Analysis to determine the reason for such an unconventional Structural Failure!

- Bush Administration would not have been planning to attack Iraq when WTC and Pentagon victims were probably still suffering underneath the fiery debris.

- FBI could never know the real names of the dead Hijackers and their links.

- FBI and National Transportation Safety Board (NTSB) must have found all cockpit voice recorders and data recorders proudly presenting them to the Americans to build their honest case.

- President Bush would never block, delay, and disrupt investigation and ignore recommendations from the 9/11 inquiry panel regarding future homeland security.

- There would have been considerable Jewish American victims among the dead in WTC instead of one out of 4000+ employees confirming prior knowledge from warning by the Wall Street Israeli company Odigo two hours before the attack.

- Wall Street Journal reporter Daniel Pearl would be still alive, rewarded by the US Government for his courage to establish truth and justice!

- US Prosecutors, Politicians, and Media would have been after
  2.3 trillion missing Pentagon Fund as well as mysterious post
  9/11 Anthrax perpetrators before prosecuting Enron scandal and hearsay
  Martha Steward felony!

Finally, Can Bin Laden Execute Massive 9/11 Operation Even If He Was Planning Similar Event, Hiding in Tora Bora**? Let us re-iterate it poetically:**

If Bin Laden had to mastermind 9/11 operation
First he had to change normal US-hijacking protocol!
Overriding NEADS sector commander's power
Of scrambling fighter jets after the hijackers!

If Bin Laden had to execute 9/11 disaster
He had to authorize Mike Canavan, as FAA hijack coordinator,
The sole contact for the National Military Command Center
And making sure he hides in Puerto Rico without answer!

If Bin Laden had to coordinate 9/11 as commander
He had to order **General Montague Winfield Brigadier
Entrust** Charles Leidig, the deputy for Command Center
In charge overseeing the period during disaster!

If Bin Laden disciples were the hijackers
They would have been listed as passengers!
With their Islamic names on ticket and computer
Validated by passport and licence having picture!

If Cessna trained hijackers somehow could hijack
Pilot or crew had ample time to activate transponder!
Pressing buttons located at multiple points throughout jet airliners
Informing ground control '**I have been hijacked**'!

If box cutters armed hijackers could somehow over power

All captains and crew members, taller and stronger!
The takeover saga would have been there
In cockpit voice recorder for half an hour!

If Cessna trained hijackers could fly Boeing jetliners
Flight turns would be at the mercy of Boeing flight software
Having built in restriction maximum 1.5g manoeuvre
Could never collide with WTC overriding anti-collision feature!

If Bin Laden and hijackers with box cutters
Could undertake such mission of precision mass murder
President Bush must have ordered 'Global Guardian'
Bring those drones down locking on transponders!

Here's what Defense Secretary Rumsfeld said to U.S. Troops in Iraq on Friday, December 24, 2004 (CNN) - during the Christmas Eve Speech regarding shooting down of Flight 93 over Pennsylvania by the hijackers?

"I think all of us have a sense if we imagine the kind of world we would face if the people who bombed the mess hall in Mosul, or the people who did the bombing in Spain, or the people who attacked the United States in New York, shot down the plane over Pennsylvania and attacked the Pentagon, the people who cut off peoples' heads on television to intimidate, to frighten - indeed the word 'terrorized' is just that. Its purpose is to terrorize, to alter behaviour, to make people be something other than that which they want to be."

Flight 93 Shot Down Confirmed by Vice President Dick Cheney:
"Well, I discussed it with the president. Are we prepared to order our aircraft to shoot down these airliners that have been hijacked? He said yes... I--it was my advice. It was his decision."(Vice President Dick Cheney, September 11, 2001, source CBS News Archives)

Flight 93 Shooting Down Order Confirmed by President Bush:
"That's a sobering moment, to order your own combat aircraft to shoot down your own civilian aircraft. But it was an easy decision to make, given the--given the fact that we had learned that a commercial aircraft was being used as a weapon. I say easy decision. It was--I didn't hesitate; let me put it to you that way. I knew what

had to be done."(President George W. Bush, September 11, 2001, source CBS News Archives)

These testimonies of shooting down Flight 93 would make US Military, CIA, FBI, NSA, FAA, NORAD and NTSB liars for equivocally declaring that Flight 93 crashed over Pennsylvania despite the debris were scattered miles apart. This would also make the military and NORAD the real hijackers with full knowledge of top level CIA-FBI-NSA officials as proposed by then Defense Secretary Donald's Rumsfeld (even if the truth came out as slip of tongue!).

Thus the only outrageous Conspiracy Theory seems to be that real Bin Laden could physically accomplish 9/11 type well coordinated multi-tasking precision operation, subsequent Anthrax attack on Democrats and media critical to Supreme Court installed Presidency, related killings & destruction of evidence −numbing US/NATO Intelligence, military, NORAD, FBI, NSA, Homeland Security and United States Government's accountabilities!

Let us summarize

Real Path to 9/11

as a poem "New Pearl Harbour"

New Pearl Harbour

[Throughout history someone had to rise to the occasion to address things important for corrective measures to ensure humane developments towards a better world. 9/11 brought down a mystic spell on academics, journalists, politicians, lawyers and scholars throughout North America and NATO lands that is allowing the monster have it all against the will of the masses. I am writing and campaigning to make them awake exposing the true nature of this historic monster. Scholarly world used to be free exchanges of ideas before the same invisible force invented virus, spam, firewalls as the ultimate censorship for profit. When wise act ignorant or indifferent world becomes a dangerous place, of course many want it that way to maintain supremacy or status quo diplomatic hypocrisy! Kolki]

NEOCONS in the United States of America had fantasy!
To rule the world in peace time with hostile vision of Supremacy!
Where, as minority, they govern US and the world with secrecy;
Maintaining parallel military Government hijacking democracy;
Installing NEOCON ambassadors in UN and Embassies!
Indulging citizens in gossips and rumours of private ideology!
Spreading Al-virus in the cyberspace exploiting technology;
Occupy promise world fulfilling Biblical Prophecy!

So, they wrote in peace-time the dossier of world supremacy
'PNAC', The Project of the New American Century!
Reviving century old imperial tools of divide and rule policy
Dismantling all peace initiatives, poisoning global intimacy
Financing NGOs as crusaders for the International Republican Party
Asked then President Clinton to sign and implement it!

Rebuffed from a man of passion and extreme humanity
They trapped his vulnerability using Jewish American Monica Lewinsky!
Ruined the possibility of Al Gore Presidency with constant publicity
Marred 2000 election with deceptions and fraudulent activities
Patronized cunning George Bush for presidential candidacy
Encouraged Supreme Court for undemocratic Republican victory!

With firm grip on NSA, CIA, FBI, NASA, FED and Military –

They fooled Clinton Administration with false Al-Qaeda activities
Framing Islamic militants with tips from allied Intelligence Agencies!
Revived idea of Military Coup rebuffed by President Kennedy in sixties
Started implementing 'New Pearl Harbour' under George Bush's presidency!

The military plan of hijacking Passenger Jet came to life from infancy
Hiring Dov Zakheim, the Guru in Flight termination technology!
With knowledge of 'Home-Run' locking Boeing 757/767 as drones remotely
All they needed to change existing NORAD fighter scrambling methodology
Making Mike Canavan (FAA) the sole contact using presidential authority
Transferring WTC ownership to private from Port Authority
Implementing demolition plan under well guarded FBI and Mayoral authority
Rescheduled 'Global Guardian' before Colin Powel's UN diplomacy!
9/11, **a bolt from the blue**, empowered NECONS with dream publicity -
For unleashing 'Shock & Awe', the ultimate terror, destruction and hostility!

[Every time the Airport securities ask us to remove shoes, confiscate intimate essential personal belongings including toothpaste, water, and feeding bottle; treat us like animals in the ropeways making travelling often humiliating & strenuous; only to hide the possibilities of remote hijacking by covert military intelligence technology, rather popular US-Israeli Flight Termination Methodologies! All modern jets, ships, ferries which are equipped with GPS guiding systems are susceptible to remote control hijacking, manoeuvring, and termination without trivial traceability – for political and evangelical gain! Kolki]

Similarity Between "Pearl Harbour" and "New Pearl Harbour":

Several writers, including journalist Robert Stinnett and former United States Navy Rear Admiral Robert A. Theobald, have argued that various parties high in the U.S. and British governments knew of the Pearl Harbour attack in advance and may even have let it happen or encouraged it in order to force America into war via the "back door." Evidences supporting this view were taken from quotations and source documents including the release of newer materials.

Let us examine who really gained from 9/11

In an unprecedented move the pontiff (Pope) met Mr Bush for their final encounter not in the papal library, as is usual under normally strict Vatican protocol, but at

St John's Tower, a restored medieval tower in the Vatican walls used to house the Vatican's VIP guests. [Times Online, June 13, 2008]

"I see a commitment to a powerful and purposeful Europe that advances the values of liberty within its borders and beyond, ... the relationship between the United States and Europe is the broadest and most vibrant it has ever been." Mr Bush said in a speech in Paris.

9/11 helped Monarchial Evangelic NATO expansion blaming and demonizing Islam bypassing rule of law and proof of convictions. The massive dropping of Christian fliers from US and allied War planes suggest the Evangelic (crusadic) nature of the self declared 'war on terror' killing and wounding millions as well as destroying ancient cultures and civilizations.

Netanyahu said 9/11 terror attacks good for Israel

"The Israeli newspaper Ma'ariv on Wednesday reported that Likud leader Benjamin Netanyahu told an audience at Bar Ilan University that the September 11, 2001 terror attacks had been beneficial for Israel". (Haaretz - 2008-04-16)

US Military – Pentagon as well as Covert and Mercenary wings obtained everything they asked for from Congress including 870+ Billion Tax Payer's Money, funding for illegal War in Afghanistan and Iraq - using Guns having Biblical Quotations.

"I am 100% convinced that the attacks of September 11, 2001 were planned, organized, and committed by treasonous perpetrators that have infiltrated the highest levels of our government....

Those of us in the military took an oath to "support and defend the Constitution of the United States against all enemies, foreign and domestic". Just because we have retired does not make that oath invalid, so it is not just our responsibility, it is our duty to expose the real perpetrators of 9/11 and bring them to justice, no matter how hard it is, how long it takes, or how much we have to suffer to do it. - **Lt. Colonel Guy S. Razer**

"This isn't about party, it isn't about Bush Bashing. It's about our country, our constitution, and our future....

Your countrymen have been murdered and the more you delve into it the more it looks as though they were murdered by our government, who used it as an excuse to murder other people thousands of miles away" - **Lt. Colonel Shelton F. Lankford**

"Fascism will come to this country and it will come disguised as Americanism." - **Governor Huey Long**

"No one man can terrorize a whole nation unless we are all his accomplices." - **Edward R Murrow**

"If tyranny and oppression come to this land, it will be in the guise of fighting a foreign enemy." - **James Madison**

The real menace of our Republic is the invisible government which like a giant octopus sprawls its slimy legs over our cities, states and nation. At the head is a small group of banking houses... This little coterie...run our government for their own selfish ends. It operates under cover of a self-created screen...seizes...our executive officers...legislative bodies...schools...courts...newspapers and every agency created for the public protection." - **N.Y. Mayor, John Hylan**

Let us celebrate 9/11 as Day of Consciousness triggering events towards a peaceful loving world

Day of Consciousness
(Dedicated to all victims of 9/11 and unilateral illegal invasive 'War on Terror')

["If they were to do real investigations we would see several significant high level criminal prosecutions in this country. And that is something that they are not going to let out. And, believe me; they will do everything to cover this up." -Sibel Edmonds, former FBI translator]

Let us make September the Eleven -
A day of global Consciousness!
Where rule of law, accountability and openness
Are the themes of true participatory democratic Governments!

Where scholars seeking truth as the seed for peaceful living!
Academics are vocal beyond journals and networking!
Corporations evolving for the benefit of all being!
Media wait for news before speculating!
Economists are not analysts for fear breeding!
Inquiry Commissions can't shut immediate public hearing!
Militaristic Leaders not using propaganda video for 'war of supremacy'!
Intelligence can't hide felons behind national security!

Where scientists educate mass against destructive technology!
Politicians serve the people before succumbing to lobbying!
Doctors advise patients against products intoxicating
Lawyers don't prey on victims for profit making!
Judges ensure innocence till proven guilty!

Where tax revenue are spent mostly for general well being!
Military can never grow out of control as bullies -
Rather help nations during national emergencies -
Fight, against abuse , - for peace, freedom, and justice!

Teachers teach students about world wide fellow feelings!
Religious leaders embrace truth before preaching
Enlightening people in the light of mercy and giving
Knowing God is universal, omnipresent and all encompassing!

[Must we ask ourselves, can a student without prior record of violence kill 33 academics of Virginia Tech? Where was 40 billion dollar homeland security to prevent Virginia Tech massacre especially after 2 shots fired earlier in the morning? What the creative writing class was writing to deserve this in the supposedly 'Land of the free and home of the brave'? Why DC sniper killed FBI cyber-analyst Linda Franklin? Why US Congress-Senate-Media-Military-CIA-FBI-Administration holding Al-Qaeda report by FBI Translator Sibel Edmonds?

How 4 RCMP officers in Canada were gunned down by a man with no prior gun record whose vehicle was parked 24 kilometres away from the scene? Where were pre-emptive CSIS & RCMP that spent millions of dollars to detain internet fanatics without criminality? Why CSIS-RCMP would destroy most important Air India terrorism tapes and documents and delay/postpone public inquiry into nationwide killings of fellow officers or citizens under custody?

Can a homemade bomb packed in knap-sack gut few London Subway Cars? How Scotland Yard identified those knap-sackers from such elaborate underground videos immediately after the disaster? Why the unarmed casually dressed Brazilian was shot to death inside subway car after following him all the way from his apartment, walking and on the bus? Was that he knew the truth about the kidnapped accused under custody being baptized as Al-Qaeda?

Aren't they enough food for civilized thought?]

Appendix

9/11 Securities
Courtesy of Marvin Bush

Ref: What Really Happened

Marvin P. Bush, the president's younger brother, was a principal in a company called Securacom that provided security for the World Trade Center, United Airlines, and Dulles International Airport. The company, Burns noted, was backed by KuwAm, a Kuwaiti-American investment firm on whose board Marvin Burns also served. [Utne]

According to its present CEO, Barry McDaniel, **the company had an ongoing contract to handle security at the World Trade Center "up to the day the buildings fell down."**

The company lists as government clients "the U.S. Army, U.S. Navy, U.S Air force, and the Department of Justice," in projects that "often require state-of-the-art security solutions for classified or high-risk government sites."

Stratesec (Securacom) differs from other security companies which separate the function of consultant from that of service provider. **The company defines itself as a "single-source" provider of "end-to-end" security services, including everything from diagnosis of existing systems to hiring subcontractors to installing video and electronic equipment. It also provides armoured vehicles and security guards.**

The Dulles International contract is another matter. Dulles is regarded as "absolutely a sensitive airport," according to security consultant Wayne Black, head of a Florida-based security firm, due to its location, size, and the number of international carriers it serves.

Black has not heard of Stratesec, but responds that for one company to handle security for both airports and airlines is somewhat unusual. It is also delicate for a security firm serving international facilities to be so interlinked with a foreign-owned company: "Somebody knew somebody," he suggested, or the contract would have been more closely scrutinized.

As Black points out, **"when you [a company] have a security contract, you know the inner workings of everything." And if another company is linked with the security company, then "What's on your computer is on their computer."** [American Reporter]

A heightened WTC security alert was lifted on 9/6/2001...

> The World Trade Center was destroyed just days after a heightened security alert was lifted at the landmark 110-story towers, security personnel said yesterday [September 11]. Daria Coard, 37, a guard at Tower One, said the security detail had been working 12-hour shifts for the past two weeks because of numerous phone threats. **But on Thursday [September 6], bomb-sniffing dogs were abruptly removed.** [NY Newsday]

...there was a power down in WTC 2 the weekend before 9/11...

> On the weekend of 9/8, 9/9 there was a 'power down' condition in WTC tower 2, the south tower. This power down condition meant there was no electrical supply for approx 36 hrs from floor 50 up... **"Of course without power there were no security cameras, no security locks on doors and many, many 'engineers' coming in and out of the tower."** [WingTV]

9/11 Related pictures

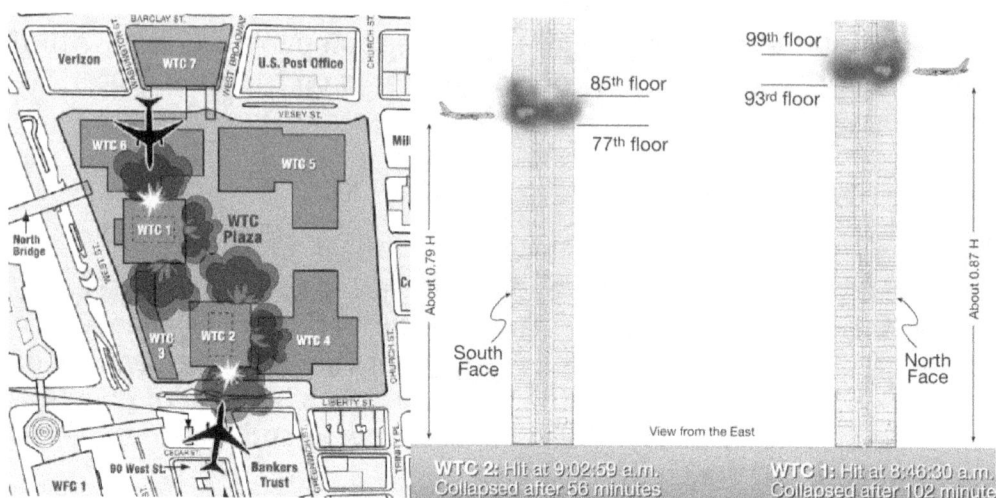

9/11 Flights Impact – FEMA   WTC Towers – Vertical Impact Locations

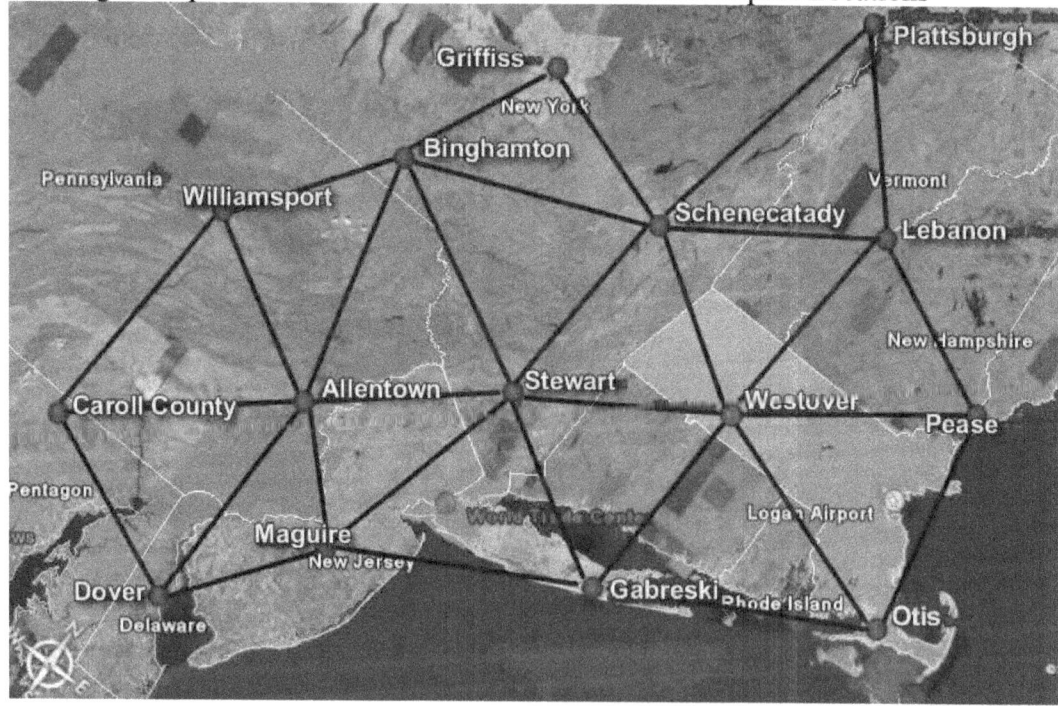

Grid connecting US Army bases over which 9/11 flights passed through

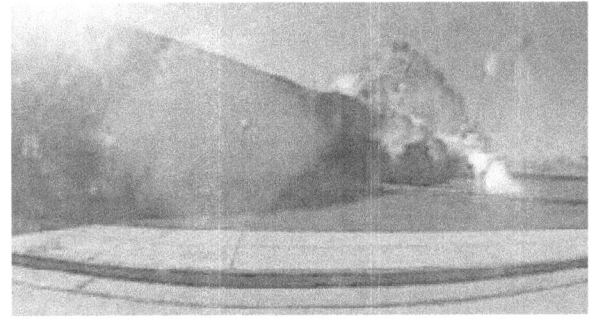

Pentagon Blast

Pentagon Airline Wreckage

Hole in an inner wall of the Pentagon

OSHA at WTC Demolition Site

WTC Explosion – North Tower (EPA)

View from EPA offices – South Tower

Related Tables

All 9/11 Flights Were Delayed For Remote Hijacking Convenience

Flight	Schedule Departure	Actual Departure	Delay	Transponder Off	Crashed/Shot Down
AA 11 767-223ER	7.45am	7.59am	14 min	8:20am	8.46.26am Crashed WTC
UA 175 767-222	7.58am	8.14am	16 min	8.46am	9.02.54am Crashed WTC
AA 77 757-223 Reportedly passed overhead the White House and entered a tight 270 deg turn, heading for the US Department of Defense building (the Pentagon).	8.10am	8.20am	10 min	8:52-8.56am(NYT)	9.37am Crashed Pentagon; Most probably originally programmed to hit White House before 9:45am! Had to be reprogrammed for Pentagon due to loss of UA 93 remote control!
UA 93 757-200 **Gregory Callahan, 41, Newark International Airport tower controller**	8.01am At about 8:40 a.m., he cleared United Airlines Flight 93 for departure.	8.42am Should have taken off around 8:06am, that will make the departure times 6-7 minutes apart	41 min About 39 min Reasons for this delay is still unknown but convenient for remote programming strategy	9.10-9.20am The jet was hijacked about 45 minutes later. 9:36 abrupt turn West of Cleveland	10.03am Shot Down* Most likely was programmed to hit Pentagon before 9:32 am when Bombs exploded reportedly)

(Ref: 9-11-Timeline and Media Reports; compiled by Deepak Sarkar)

*[(AFTER 9:56 A.M.): BUSH AND CHENEY CONFER ON ACTIONS TO BE TAKEN; SHOT DOWN ORDER HAS BEEN CONFIRMED
10:00 A.M.: FLIGHT 93 TRANSPONDER GIVES BRIEF SIGNAL
10:01 A.M.: LOCAL PILOT SEES FLIGHT 93 ROCKING BACK AND FORTH
10:03 A.M. : Flight 93 Was Shot Down by Military Jet]

AA – American Airlines
UA – United Airlines

FBI's lack of interest in collecting real evidence: so far we have seen FBI's indifference and sometimes direct interventions towards the success of 9/11. Thus, it is obvious that FBI would have conflict of interest in saving and protecting evidences – in Pentagon, WTC, and the Pennsylvania site.

(12:15 P.M.) SEPTEMBER 11, 2001: FBI LIMITS WHAT EVIDENCE NEEDS TO BE PHOTOGRAPHED AT PENTAGON

FBI Special Agent Garrett McKenzie, who is coordinating the effort to photograph evidence at the Pentagon, pulls together a dozen photographers for a briefing. He instructs them: "We don't need to photograph all the plane parts, only unique airplane parts or something specific. Like the pilot's yoke, or anything with part of a serial number on it. If we have to prove what kind of plane this was, the serial numbers will be what we need." [CREED AND NEWMAN, 2008, PP. 181-183]

Garrett McKenzie. *[Source: Rudi Williams]*

Pre-9/11 Silence In America, Why?

There was a united silence in Media, among Politicians, Analysts and Strategists despite massive warnings and speculations towards the up coming disaster.

They were all waiting for the great even to occur as New Pearl Harbour to unleash their wrath as global power **hurting own people and national monuments for the sake of allied** Military, Intelligence and Business interests overpowering true national interests and justifying inhumane collateral damages.

Throughout history it's always killing and assassinating citizens and leaders and blaming on patsy either individual or a formidable holistic external source since the time of Dorian Greek Alexander's Father.

Rumsfeld and fellow NEOCONS re-invented that politics of fear and smear to silence people for the advancements of hegemonistic causes and programs.

Rewarding the Perpetrators

All Government and military officials and private agencies were rewarded for their united failures that led to the success of spectacular 9/11 killing nearly 3000 individuals and destructing national pride and faith in government. Imagine US government as a corporation and the board of directors and top level management were rewarded for the failure of the corporation. Now we can see why USA has been what it is now, most debt ridden country on Earth, and where it is going rewarding dishonest treasoners.

US military, Defence contractors, and Silverstein became the direct winners of 9/11 disaster Related fortunes. Many got promoted to better positions within CIA, FBI, Homeland Security, Military and NSA. Mercenary firms like Blackwater and CACI got hugely benefited from war related contracts.

While honest citizens and true patriots for 9/11 truth had been harassed and abused as conspiracy theorists and non-patriotic, the facilitators towards the success of 9/11 were rewarded with promotions and bonuses as well as massive authority to destroy and abuse own kind!

PNAC-supporter Eliot Cohen became member of the Pentagon's Defense Policy Board (DPB) under Richard Perle.
Douglas Feith, appointed the members of the DPB. Fred C. Ikle, member of DPB, Bruce P. Jackson (ex-Lockheed, former Military Intelligence Officer, President of the U.S. Committee on NATO) and many more.

DPF members include prominent firms and current war profiteers like Boeing, TRW, Northrop Grumman, Lockheed Martin and Booz Allen Hamilton (ex-CIA James Woolsey) or smaller players like Symantec Corp., Technology Strategies, Alliance Corp., and Polycom Inc.

Corporate Affiliations: Ronald R. Fogleman (DERCO Aerospace, The Mitre Corp.), David Jeremiah (Northrop Grumman, Wackenhut Services), James Schlesinger (MITRE), Jack Sheehan (Bechtel) or Chris Williams (TRW, merged in 2002 with Blackstone, which obtained a mortgage of WTC 7 in October 2000)

Former FBI Translator Sibel Edmonds Calls Current 9/11 Investigation Inadequate
Interviewed by Jim Hogue

INTRODUCTION: Sibel Edmonds and Behrooz Sarshar, beginning in December of 2001, began filing reports to their superiors at the FBI. These reports could lead to the collapse of a corrupt power structure that has a stranglehold on the very institutions that are obligated to control it. We cannot excuse these institutions, for while they fiddle, they pass death sentences on their own troops, and on the people of Afghanistan and Iraq.

"If they were to do real investigations we would see several significant high level criminal prosecutions in this country. And that is something that they are not going to let out. And, believe me; they will do everything to cover this up."

-Sibel Edmonds, former FBI translator

On April 30th, Sibel Edmonds was my guest for 50 minutes on WGDR radio. What follows is an edited transcript of the interview. The editing is for the sake of a more readable piece.

Sibel Edmonds is a former FBI translator. She blew the whistle on the cover-up of intelligence that names some of the culprits who orchestrated the 9/11 attacks. These culprits are protected by the Justice Department, the State Department, the FBI, the White House and the Senate Judiciary Committee. They are foreign nationals and Americans. Ms. Edmonds is under two gag orders that forbid her to testify in court or mention the names of the people or the countries involved.

THE INTERVIEW

JH: The people who have so far been interviewed on this program have all been authors and researchers, and here we have someone who, for the most part, has first-hand information. Ladies and Gentlemen, your guest is Sibel Edmonds, formerly of the FBI, a translator who joined the FBI shortly after 9/11.

Ms. Edmonds, what I'll do is invite you to tell us whatever you would like--your stint with the FBI-- and what the brouhaha with Ashcroft and company is all about.

SE: I started working for the Bureau immediately after 9/11 and I was performing translations for several languages: Farsi, Turkish, and Azerbaijani. And I do have top-secret clearance. And after I started working for the Bureau, most of my translation duties included translations of documents and investigations that actually started way before 9/11. And certain documents were being sent that needed to be re-translated for various reasons, and of course certain documents had to be translated for the first time due to the backlog.

During my work there I came across some very significant issues that I started reporting in December of 2001 to the mid-level management within the FBI. They said to basically leave it alone, because if they were to get into those issues it would end up being a can of worms. And after I didn't see any response from this mid-level bureaucratic management I took it to higher levels all the way up to [assistant director] Dale Watson and Director Mueller. And, again, I was asked not to take this any further and just let it be. And if I didn't do that they would retaliate against me.

At that point, which would be around February 2002, they came and they confiscated my computer, because, they said, they were suspecting that I was communicating with certain Senate members and taking this issue outside the Bureau. And, at that point, I was not. They did not find anything in my computer after they confiscated it. And they asked me to take a polygraph as to the allegations and reports I'd made. I volunteered and I took the polygraph and passed it without a glitch. They have already confirmed this publicly.

In March 2002 I took this issue to the Senate Judiciary Committee and also I filed it with the Department of Justice Inspector General's office. And as per the Senate Judiciary Committee's request the IG started an expedited investigation on these serious issues; and they promised the Senate Judiciary Committee that their report for these investigations would be out by fall 2002 latest. And here we are in April 2004 and this report is not being made public, and they are citing "state privilege" and "national security" for not making this report public.

Three weeks after I went to the Senate Judiciary Committee the Bureau terminated my contract, and they cited "government's convenience." I started working with the Senate Judiciary Committee that was investigating this case, and I appeared before the Inspector General's office for their investigation several times, and I also requested documents regarding these reports under the Freedom of Information Act; and they blocked this by citing again the "state secret privilege" and "national security" refusing to make these documents public.

On October 18th 2002 Attorney General Ashcroft came out personally, in public, asserted this rare "state secret privilege" on everything that had to do with my case. And they cited "diplomatic relations" and certain "foreign relations" that would be "at stake" if I were to take this issue and make it public. And, since then, this has been acting as a gag on my case.

I testified before the [9/11] commission on February 11th 2004, and as I said, I have been waiting for this report that they [the Attorney General's office] have been blocking for a year and a half from becoming public. The information I requested under the Freedom of Information Act has been blocked for two years. And I have been campaigning for the past three months trying to get the Senate Judiciary Committee that has the oversight authority and responsibility to start its own public hearings. However, this request is again being blocked. Now they [AG] are citing this upcoming election as reason. And here I am.

JH: And it is the Attorney General who is blocking your testimony.

SE: Senator Leahy, on April 8, 2004, sent a very strong letter to Attorney General Ashcroft, citing my case stating that he, Senator Leahy, has been asking questions, and has a lot of issues that have not been addressed, and asking AG Ashcroft to come and provide answers. And AG Ashcroft for the past two years has refused. So he [Leahy] is calling for a public hearing. However, Senator Hatch, who is the Republican Chairman of the Senate, has been a road block. And Senator Grassley [a Republican member of the Senate Judiciary Committee] went on the record with New York Observer's Gail Sheehy and said that Senator Hatch is blocking this investigation from taking place and for this public hearing to be held by the Senate Judiciary Committee.

JH: So Hatch has the power to keep Leahy and Grassley....

SE: Correct. And now it is becoming a partisan issue. However, I keep reminding them that this issue is not a new issue that has come out for this election. This issue has been in the courts for two years and two months now.

JH: I've watched Hatch perform since the Contra Hearings in the mid 1980s, and I can assure you that for Hatch, everything is a partisan issue. You have a tough one.

SE: We have to remind the people: Congress has the constitutional obligation and public responsibility to oversee these issues and the Department of Justice's operations. That's why they are elected. That's why they are there. That's what they are getting paid for.

JH: Do you think that Leahy and Grassley are going to try to plow ahead with this, or do you think that there is a back door deal with Hatch?

SE: Well....as far as I see, Senator Leahy has been trying, and it's a strong letter that he issued a few weeks ago. [Ms. Edmonds refers here to the GPO's PDF (Senate--April 8, 2004; pages s4012-4014) regarding Ashcroft's appearance before the Senate Judiciary Committee in 2003. Senator Leahy describes the inaction of Attorney General Ashcroft since their first meeting on September 19th 2001 as a "flagrant avoidance of accountability."]

However, I'm very disappointed with Senator Grassley's office and his staff members. They initially were very supportive. But what I am getting from their office every time I call is, "Well this issue is under the Inspector General," and that their hands are tied. And then I press further and ask, "Well, what do you mean, 'our hands are tied'? Who's tying your hands? Untie it. Let's get it untied." They don't have any response. They say, "Well, this issue is very complex, and as you know, it is being investigated." And I'm not seeing any issue being investigated. What I'm seeing is that this issue is being covered up, and relentlessly being covered up, in consideration of "state privilege," which people are calling "the neutron bomb of all privilege."

JH: I can assure you that there are probably thirty issues just like yours that are being covered up. And they are allowing reporters, writers, internet contributors, and journalists from around the world to do these investigations, because they know that most Americans will never hear any of that. But as soon as someone like yourself gets too close to actually finding out who did anything, "state privilege" or something....

SE: "National security" as a classification.

JH: Why that makes us more secure, to let the people guilty of 9/11 run around free is, of course, the question that no one is willing to deal with.

I have a question having to do with "mid-level" management at the FBI. Why do you think that mid-level FBI management would care enough to stop you from doing your job?

SE: This was mainly for the reason of accountability. As you know, and as the chairman for the 9/11 Commission [Thomas Kean] answered during Tim Russert's show: to this day, not a single person has been held accountable. And certain issues, yes, they were due to a certain level of incompetence. But there were certain other issues--you know they keep talking about this "wall," and not having communication. I beg to differ on that, because there are certain instances where the Bureau is being asked by the State Department not to pursue certain investigations or certain people or certain targets of an investigation--simply citing "diplomatic relations." And what happens is, instead of targeting those people who are directly related to these illegal terrorist activities, they just let them walk free.

JH: And they interrogate people who are trying to make voting safe.

SE: And that is hypocritical. I see people detained for simple INS violations. On the other hand I have seen several, several top targets for these investigations of these terrorist activities that were allowed to leave the country--I'm not talking about weeks, I'm talking about months after 9/11.

JH: And there were four major FBI investigations, not counting yours, that were squelched in Phoenix, Minneapolis, Chicago and New York.

SE: Correct.

JH: And yours was even outside of that.

SE: Correct.

JH: So, obviously, we have mid-level FBI people who have been told something. It was the mid-level FBI people who knew enough to squelch many of these investigations before they went further. So how did they know to do that? Can all of them have been incompetent?

SE: No. Absolutely not.

JH: So they got the word down from Mueller, probably.

SE: I cannot confirm that for sure, but I can tell you that there is so much involvement, that if they did let this information out, and if they were to hold real investigations--I'm not talking about this semi-investigation they're holding under this "Joint Inquiry"--the pure show of the 9/11 Commission that has been getting the mass media's attention. If they were to do real investigations we would see several significant high level criminal prosecutions in this country. And that is something that they are not going to let out. And, believe me; they will do everything to cover this up. And I am appalled. I am really surprised. I'm taken back by seeing the mass media's reaction to this. They are the window to our government's operation and what are they doing?

JH: We've been screaming about it for a long time. And it goes on.

SE: And you see many people just turning away from these channels of mass media, and they're just turning in to alternative providers, because they just see what's happening.

JH: I have another question: when the gag order was written, it had to do with "diplomatic relations." Right?

SE: That is what Attorney General Ashcroft cited.

JH: Are you allowed to say that it's the Saudis?

SE: I cannot name any country. And I would emphasize that it's plural. I understand the Saudis have been named because fifteen of the nineteen hijackers were from Saudi Arabia. However, the names of people from other countries, and semi-legit organizations from other countries, to this day, have not been made public.

JH: And the information that you have been gagged on has to do with that specifically.

SE: Correct. And specifically with that and their ties to people here in this country today.

JH: I understand why you can't say anything about this, but there are several books out about the Bush ties to the Saudis and the bin Ladens in particular. And in David Griffin's book, *The New Pearl*

Harbor, there is a very good synopsis of the ISI, which is the Pakistani intelligence service. He shows the direct connections between the CIA, the ISI, and Mohamed Atta. He makes a very convincing case that the Pakistani ISI had been helping to plan 9/11 for a long time.

I don't imagine that you are allowed to say much about that.

SE: You are correct. But I can tell you that the issue, on one side, boils down to money--a lot of money. And it boils down to people and their connections with this money, and that's the portion that, even with this book, has not been mentioned to this day. Because then it starts touching some people in high places.

JH: Can you explain more about what money you are talking about?

SE: The most significant information that we were receiving did not come from counter-terrorism investigations, and I want to emphasize this. It came from counter-intelligence, and certain criminal investigations, and issues that have to do with money laundering operations.

> **"The most significant information that we were receiving did not come from counter-terrorism investigations, and I want to emphasize this. It came from counter-intelligence, and certain criminal investigations, and issues that have to do with money laundering operations."**
>
> **--Sibel Edmonds, former FBI translator**

You get to a point where it gets very complex, where you have money laundering activities, drug related activities, and terrorist support activities converging at certain points and becoming one. In certain points - and they [the intelligence community] are separating those portions from just the terrorist activities. And, as I said, they are citing "foreign relations" which is not the case, because we are not talking about only governmental levels. And I keep underlining semi-legit organizations and following the money. When you do that the picture gets grim. It gets really ugly.

....**JH:** Let me read you a short quote from Dr. Griffin's book, quoting from War and Globalization: The Truth Behind September 11 by Michel Chossudovsky and ask you to comment on it. "...The transfer of money to Atta [$325,000], in conjunction with the presence of the ISI chief in Washington during the week, [is] the missing link behind 9/11....The evidence confirms that al-Qaeda is supported by Pakistan's ISI (and it is amply documented that) the ISI owes its existence to the CIA."

SE: I cannot comment on that. But I can tell that once, and if, and when this issue gets to be, under real terms, investigated, you will be seeing certain people that we know from this country standing trial; and they will be prosecuted criminally.

JH: Here's a question that you might be able to answer: What is al-Qaeda?

SE: This is a very interesting and complex question. When you think of al-Qaeda, you are not thinking of al-Qaeda in terms of one particular country, or one particular organization. You are looking at this massive movement that stretches to tens and tens of countries. And it involves a lot of sub-organizations and sub-sub-organizations and branches and it's extremely complicated. So to just narrow it down and say al-Qaeda and the Saudis, or to say it's what they had at the camp in Afghanistan, is extremely misleading. And we don't hear the extent of the penetration that this organization and the sub-organizations have throughout the world, throughout their networks and throughout their various activities. It's extremely sophisticated. And then you involve a significant amount of money into this equation. Then things start getting a lot of overlap-- money laundering, and drugs and terrorist activities and their support networks converging in several points. That's what I'm trying to convey without being too specific. And this money travels. And you start trying to go to the root of it and it's getting into somebody's political campaign, and somebody's lobbying. And people don't want to be traced back to this money.

JH: [Laughter] I guess not. This leads me to think of a beef I have with Seymour Hersh that I'd like to bring up with you? Do you know who he is?

SE: Yes.

JH: He seems to presume that the U.S. Intelligence Services want to collect the kind of intelligence that you have been gagged from repeating. I have suggested to him in a letter that there is an alternative to incompetence as to why intelligence doesn't get through to where it is supposed to go. But he's not interested. He doesn't seem to want to take that step.

SE: Not many people are willing to do that.

JH: But there are a lot of people who have laid out the road map.

SE: But people and your listeners have to go further than that. I understand this administration and their anti-transparency, anti-accountability and their corrupt attitudes. But that aside, we are not made of only one branch of government. We are supposed to have a system of checks and balances. And I am saying, how about the other two branches? And putting the pressure on our representatives in the Senate and the Congress, and the court system. They should be counter-acting this corruption, but they are sitting there silent. And they are just an audience, just watching it happen. Senators Leahy and Grassley and Hatch have the obligation to do that. It's not that they can choose not to do it. They don't have that luxury. This needs to be demanded of them. People need to pick up their phones. They need to write to these people and say, "You'd better fulfill your responsibilities."

JH: And you know what Senator Leahy is going to do? He's going to forward his letter, his Senate testimony, on to us to prove how hard he is working.

SE: I saw a reporter the other day who had just spoken to Senator Leahy. And Senator Leahy said that, well...he doesn't know what the next step will be. And it came to the issue of the hearing, and investigating this case, and he basically ended the conversation. And I think that with a little more pressure from us, from you and from your listeners, we can change that.

JH: Some folks up here think of him as Saint Patrick, I'm afraid. Be that as it may, are you aware of the on-line news service, TRUTHOUT?

SE: I've heard of it.

JH: There is an article in the April sixth TRUTHOUT by Paul Sperry from WorldNet Daily about you and one of your colleagues...

SE: Mr. Sarshar?

JH: Behrooz Sarshar.

SE: He is another translator who worked in the same department as I did. Mr. Sarshar wanted to make this information public, however he just wanted to go to the Senate Judiciary Committee and receive their support and protection under the whistleblower protection act. And I facilitated this meeting, and several 9/11 family members and I took Mr. Sarshar to the Senate Judiciary Committee meeting in Senator Grassley's office. Mr. Sarshar provided them with detailed information, however, to this day Senator Grassley has not acted upon that, and he passed the buck to the 9/11 Commission. Next we arranged for a briefing between the 9/11 Commission and Mr. Sarshar, and he went there on February 12th, 2004 and he provided the investigators for the 9/11 Commission, for almost three hours with all the details of the investigation that had to do with the 9/11 terrorist attack. He gave them the names of certain assets used by the Bureau for at least twelve years. He gave them contact information for certain agents who were aware of these issues. And they, themselves, wanted to come and talk about it, but they needed certain protection. Mr. Sarshar provided them with all this information and where to look for these documents etc. and, to this day, the Senate Judiciary Committee and the 9/11 Commission have been passing this buck back and forth.

So, all this information has been sitting in front of them. They have not called any of those witnesses introduced by Mr. Sarshar to them. And during the 9/11 Commission hearing with [FBI] Director Mueller, none of these questions were asked. In fact they did not have any questions for Director Mueller, and they left it at that [except for the remark by Mr. Ben-Veniste that they should be addressing the translation issues behind closed doors.] And "behind closed doors" has become a black hole for me because I have been in these closed door sessions so many times within the Senate, within the Inspector General's office, within the 9/11 Commission. And whatever information you are providing them behind these closed doors, you know for sure that that information will stay there and will never get out.

That is why we are demanding to have public hearings with the Senate Judiciary Committee on the Senate floor and open to the public.

JH: Do you think the Ellen Mariani case will help any of this? [Ellen Mariani is a 9/11 widow whose attorney, Philip Berg, is suing the United States under the RICO statute for the death of Mr. Mariani at the WTC.]

SE: I have read about her case. But there is another lawsuit: the Motley Rice legal firm that is representing over a thousand family members. They sent me a subpoena to provide them with a deposition. And one day before that deposition took place, the government attorneys intervened and asked the court for a hearing and they quashed this subpoena request. They sent eight heavyweight attorneys from the Department of Justice, and Mr. Ashcroft's right hand. And basically put on this show in front of the judge, saying, "Sibel Edmonds, if you were to provide this information, our national security and our state secret privilege and our foreign relations will be destroyed. Therefore, Your Honor, we want you to quash this subpoena." Motley Rice told the judge that they wanted to ask for information that has already been made public. The government maintained that even though the information was public, it was still classified. And Judge Walton granted their request.

JH: There is some hope coming from statements made by former FBI counterintelligence agent I.C.Smith who thinks that 9/11 would have been stopped, had the FBI been allowed to do its job. He is strongly critical of FBI assistant director Dale Watson.

Do you believe that 9/11 could have been stopped if information like yours had been properly handled?

SE: At the very least, as early as May/June 2001, we could have issued a red code alert to the public, and we would have issued this very urgent warning system, which would, in return, have increased our Airport and INS security. Could we have prevented in 100% certainty? I don't think anything is that certain. However, we would have had a very, very good chance for preventing it. And agent Smith and I, we crossed the same person, because my case has to do with Dale Watson too.

JH: The trouble is: once you make this information public, you mess up the plan. And if one of the investigations from Phoenix, Chicago, New York, or Minneapolis had been followed through, let alone all four, it would have burst the bubble.

SE: Look, Jim, they had those four pieces you mentioned, and far more than that, believe me, far more than that. And that has not been made public. And for them to say that we did not have any specific information is just outrageous. Because what were they waiting for? An affidavit signed by bin Laden?

JH: "Hey Dumb Ass! Coming 9/11!" So their statement that they didn't have the information is outrageous.

SE: And they have been backing off from that. About two weeks before Condoleezza Rice appeared before the 9/11 Commission she made the statement, "We had no specific information." And I told the press that that was an outrageous lie. That was printed on the front page of *The Independent* [UK] and several other papers here. And what she did during the hearing was very interesting. She corrected herself saying, "Well, I made a mistake. I should not have said 'we.' I should say that I personally did not have specific information." And that is exactly what I stated. "We" includes the FBI, and therefore I can tell you with 100% certainty that that is an outrageous lie.

Yet the Commission didn't ask, "Well, who is the rest of this 'we'?"

JH: They don't want to know.

SE: No, they don't want to know. This is the heart of it. The attitude of the Senate members has been "See no evil. Hear no evil. Just let it go." And you can't let that happen. The only people I have seen who have been truly pushing for the truth are the family members. All they have asked for are three things. They want the truth, the facts, the real facts, the straightforward truth. They want accountability. And they want us to improve our security. That's it. They have no other agenda. And now they're smearing their names.

JH: They'll never run out of people to smear. Everybody who talks gets smeared.

SE: I have been given a warning that my turn is coming. I have been waiting for this for two years and two months, Jim. And they have not done it to this day, and they have not even denied anything. But I have been told to expect something to occur soon.

JH: Well, they have to figure out the angle.

[At this point we opened the lines for callers, as the scheduled time for the interview was drawing to a close.]

CALLER: But, of course, you are trying to spoil our American Dream. We want to dream in peace! What are you doing? [Laughter] Let us sleep!

JH: That's it. That's what they're up to.

CALLER: The depth of that psychology is incredible. It goes from A to Z through our life cycle. It's so disempowering. It's so depressing. Well, thank you for being lunatics out there who are trying to get yourselves shot. [Laughter]

JH: That's okay. Anytime. Just for you. Bye bye.

SE: Even from people from whom I've been receiving support, so many times you run across people who say, "Yeah, it's terrible. I understand. And it's very courageous what you are doing." But you know how this thing is. It's a boat you can't rock. And that is what is allowing these people to take everything this far. We need to stop saying we can't rock this boat when it needs to be rocked. Listen, we pay for this boat. We elect this boat. It's our money that maintains this boat. And we are the ultimate boss here. If this boat or some section of it needs rocking, you bet we have the right and we have the power to do it. And we have the power to demand it. Otherwise we are making ourselves powerless.

JH: And if we don't do it, we don't deserve it.

SE: Correct.

2nd CALLER: [Question re 9/11 stand down of the air defense system]

SE: I don't have direct knowledge of it. And I have been trying to stay within what exactly I know-- the exact truth--not the conspiracy theories--no exaggerations--everything that I know, that I came across that is well documented where I can say, "Pull out this document; pull out this evidence. Make this document public; make that document public."

However, I have been working with other people who have been trying to address other aspects of this issue.

2nd CALLER: The issue of whether or not they new it was going to happen becomes somewhat moot when you look at the air force stand down. They new it was going to happen. Well, who did it then? There was a show on TUC [Time of Useful Consciousness] radio with....

JH: Michael Ruppert.

2nd CALLER: Yes. He went step-by-step of what actually happened with the Air Force stand-down. It's so obvious that we're in some sort of farcical dream, and what [the previous caller] said was quite relevant, that most people don't want to wake up from this. So I was just curious. I appreciate your work very much. And those are the two things that stand out to me--the Pentagon and the air force stand down. But what else can you really do at this point than just make a little noise? Anyway, thank you for doing what you are doing.

SE: He has a point there. There are so many questions that they don't want answered. And they remain unanswered. And I'm afraid they will not be answered unless we have a real investigation. And to this day there has been no real investigation. Without this, people cannot just let them wrap it up and say, "OK this is the report from the 9/11 Commission," where anything that has any value is redacted because it is top secret classified information.

JH: And pretty much all the shoes have dropped. The evidence at this point is overwhelming, and still nobody seems to be doing anything about it.

2nd CALLER: Right, but if you look at the Warren Commission--you look at the magic bullet theory--you know that's official! But who buys it? What can we do? This is going to happen. They're going to pull it off because the press won't report the truth.

SE: That goes to the heart of the matter: The media, as I said is the window to the government, and that window has turned into a wall.

JH: We can have a little more faith in the average person despite what [the two callers] say. I just did an informal survey in southern Virginia in a factory of over a hundred people, and I asked, "Would you be surprised to learn that the Bush Administration was complicit in the 9/11 attacks?" 100% responded, "No." So it's not like people are afraid to find out information. They go through life struggling, working eight hours a day at least. They don't believe anything the media or the government tells them any more. They are able to except the fact that Bush & Co was responsible for 9/11; and they don't care. They almost expect it.

2nd CALLER: I would have suspected the opposite. These are emotional issues where people don't want their bubble burst. They say, "Well, the government would never kill their own people." Psychopaths go oversees and kill people with war machines. They're over the notion of patriotism. And I think that for most people it's hard to make that step.

JH: I'm not saying they made or didn't make a step. I'm just saying that, for these workers, the machinations of government are beyond their concern. But Ms. Edmonds has to leave shortly....

2nd CALLER: OK I'll let you go. I appreciate very much what both of you have done, and thank you very much.

JH: Ms. Edmonds, thanks for being our guest.

SE: Thank you very much. I'm honored to be on your show and I hope I'll be on again. And I hope you will able to get Senator Leahy. I'd like to be able to have a chat with him. [Laughter]

JH: Fat chance. He withers at the thought.

SE: We're going to still be pounding. I'm preparing this petition, and it's going to be signed by many, many people and I'm going to be wheeling it in personally to both Senators Leahy and Grassley. And it will have some level of coverage. And once they see the cameras and the people, suddenly their personalities change. It's like Dr. Jekyll and Mr. Hyde. They become very sweet.

JH: If you see either one of those two [Leahy or Grassley], I'd be more than happy to have either one them on - with you. Let's see what we can do.

SE: Okay, let's hope. Thank you, Jim. Bye.

EDITOR'S NOTE: Jim Hogue provided the following conclusion to this interview: "The facts reported by Sibel Edmonds and Behrooz Sarshar are incontrovertible. Result: Silence. And you must agree to be a part of this silence. The gag order permeates the White House, the Senate Judiciary Committee, all levels of the FBI, the CIA, the 9/11 Commission, the NSC, the Pentagon, the Republican Party, the Democratic Party, and the mass media. The media and the White House will next assassinate Miss Edmond's character, as they have done to others who haven't rolled over and played dead. Never in the course of human events has so great a story been covered up by so many on the orders of so few.

The likes of Seymour Hersh, Bob Woodard and Judith Miller should put their tails between their legs and slink away, while the obscure academic, Dr. David Ray Griffin, while candidate John Buchanan, citizen Eric Hufschmid, author Gore Vidal, independent journalists Michael Ruppert and Christopher Bollyn, and the 9/11 families are recognized among those who kept open the window to Democracy.

Miss Edmonds has challenged us to do our jobs as citizens. It isn't often that a phone call could change the course of history. Now is such a time."

Jim Hogue, a retired high school teacher and professional actor, has been doing a Vermont-based listener-sponsored radio show each week for over 10 years. Prior to 9/11, the show was literary in nature, but since then Hogue's coverage has greatly expanded.

Able Danger adds twist to 9/11
Alleged 9/11 Ringleader connected to secret Pentagon operation

Courtesy of Dr. Daniele Ganser, Senior Researcher at the Center for Security Studies
Global Research, August 27, 2005,

Four years after the 11 September 2001 attacks on the US, the revelation of a top secret Pentagon operation adds a new twist to a story about which we still know very little.

For the past four years, we have been told by the administration of George Bush and by the official 9/11 Commission report of Chairman Thomas Kean and Executive Director Philip Zelikow that alleged Egyptian extremist Mohammed Atta was the key player in the 11 September 2001 terrorist attacks. Atta, according to the Kean report, was the "tactical leader of the 9/11 plot". He was the alleged pilot who on that dreadful morning flew the first plane, American Airlines 11, into the North Tower of the World Trade Center in New York. It was Atta's face, on television and in newspapers across the world, that became the symbol of Islamic terrorism. And it was Atta's name - not the names of any of the 18 other hijackers allegedly lead by Atta on that day - that was cited by international security researchers. Atta was, as the Kean report stresses, "the tactical commander of the operation in the United States". According to both the Bush administration and the official 9/11 Commission report, he was working on the orders of Osama Bin Laden who, from remote Afghanistan, controlled the entire operation.

Now, almost exactly four years after 9/11, the facts appear to have been turned upside down. We now learn that alleged Atta was also connected to a top secret operation of the Pentagon's Special Operations Command (SOCOM) in the US. According to Army reserve Lieutenant-Colonel Anthony Shaffer, a top secret Pentagon project code-named Able Danger had identified the name Atta and three other 9/11 hijackers as members of an al-Qaeda cell more than a year before the attacks.

Able Danger was an 18-month highly classified operation tasked, according to Shaffer, with "developing targeting information for al-Qaeda on a global scale", and used data-mining techniques to look for "patterns, associations, and linkages". He said he himself had first encountered the names of the four hijackers in mid-2000.

Schaffer himself was fully aware of the delicacy of his revelations. As such, he chose to first speak to US lawmaker and Speaker of the House Dennis Hastert (Republican, Illinois) and House Intelligence Committee Chairman Peter Hoekstra (Republican, Michigan). Schaffer said the two had assured him that exposing the secret "was the right thing to do". "I was given assurances we would not suffer any adverse consequences for bringing this to the attention of the public," he said.

The conversations with Hastert and Hoekstra took place before Schaffer anonymously leaked the information to the media on 8 August in the offices of Republican Curt Weldon of Pennsylvania, the vice chairman of the House Armed Services and Homeland Security committees who also supported the exposure of this secret.

Schaffer's decision to expose Operation Able Danger has given rise to some difficult questions, not the least of which concerns the role of alleged Atta in the top secret operation. It also raises the question of whether anyone in the Pentagon knew in advance what Atta was planning on 9/11.

For now, though, the questions are likely to go unanswered, as the Pentagon claims there is no evidence to support allegations that it had had military intelligence on a 9/11 bomber a year before the attack. The Pentagon has acknowledged the existence of Operation Able Danger, but denies claims that it had identified Atta and three others as early as 1999.

When the "official" facts are turned upside down, we need to go back to the sources and ask: What do we really know about 9/11? Our most important source, Atta himself, is dead. So for now, there is only Schaffer, a 42-year-old native of Kansas City, who worked for the Defense Intelligence Agency (DIA) in Washington at the time of the 9/11 attacks and had insights into the Pentagon's top secret operation. **According to Schaffer, when he informed the FBI and urged them to arrest Atta, the Pentagon's lawyers intervened and protected Atta for reasons that remain unclear.**

The official 9/11 Commission report, which according to its own declaration aimed "to provide the fullest possible account of the events surrounding 9/11" in its 567-page report, fails to mention Operation Able Danger or any other US-based SOCOM operations. On the contrary, in its recommendations as to how the US could be better protected from "terrorists" in the future, *the Kean report on page 415 suggests that SOCOM be given larger powers to carry out covert action operations, previously a domain controlled by the CIA.*

The Kean commission also recommended better oversight in order *"to combat the secrecy and complexity"*. Yet, at the same time, we learn from Schaffer that the Kean commission did not provide the full story on 9/11, and specifically on Able Danger. Schaffer, according to his own testimony, had personally informed Zelikow about Able Danger. Yet Zelikow covered up this piece of the puzzle and, to Schaffer's frustration and disbelief, decided not to include this data on the pretext that it was "not historically relevant".

If it is true that Zelikow declined to include the information on Able Danger in the Kean report, and if it is true, as Zelikow wrote, that Atta was the "tactical leader of the 9/11 plot", and if it is furthermore true, as Schaffer publicly explained, that SOCOM protected Atta prior to his deadly attack on the US, which claimed 3,000 lives, then the account as provided by the official 9/11 report is discredited, and we are faced with a sea of lies and cover-ups.

Four years after 9/11, we are presented with facts that are diametrically opposed to the official narrative. While the biggest questions remain unanswered and there is a possibility that they will never be answered, the media would do well by the public to be diligent enough to keep the issue alive and not allow it to be swept under the rug in the face of confusion and complexity.

MAY 2001: EFFORT TO KEEP ABLE DANGER ALIVE IS UNSUCCESSFUL [Military and Administration unitedly obstructed to justice .....]

According to a later account by Lt. Col. Anthony Shaffer, Capt. Scott Phillpott calls him "in desperation" around this time. Able Danger has been effectively shut down, but Phillpott wants to know if he can bring the Able Danger options that had been presented to higher officials in early 2001 (see EARLY 2001, JANUARY-MARCH 2001 and MARCH 2001) and use one of Shaffer's Stratus Ivy facilities to continue to work. Shaffer claims that he replies, "I tell him with all candor that I would love nothing better than to loan him my facility and work the options with him (to exploit them for both [intelligence] potential and for actual offensive operations) but tell him that my DIA chain of command has directed me to stop all support to him and the project. In good faith, I ask my boss, Col. Mary Moffitt if I can help Scott and exploit the options—and that there would be a DIA quid pro quo of obtaining new 'lead' information from the project. She takes offense at me even mentioning Able Danger in this conversation, tells me that I am being insubordinate, and begins the process of removing me from my position as chief of Stratus Ivy. As a direct result of this conversation, she directs that I be 'moved' to a desk officer position to oversee Defense [human intelligence] operations in Latin America." [US CONGRESS, 2/15/2006]

9/11

A Barrier to World Peace

Without 9/11
(Dedicated to truthful resolution of 9/11 mystery with open public investigation)

[Without 9/11 truth all efforts of peace and green movement becoming moot point as felon leaders, politicians, military, and intelligence officials along with self censored media leading the world towards catastrophe sooner than many want to believe! This revelation would be the greatest turning point in history of mankind in re-establishing the much waited 'Heaven on Earth' celebrating everything good people on Earth can offer with cultural diversity for the betterment of all sentient being! Kolki]

Without 9/11 -
Thousands of Americans still be alive on Earth with vigour!
Hundreds of fire fighters would be rescuing with honour!
World trade center would be standing tall in New York!
US taxpayers would enjoy trillion dollars for homeland care!
Defence industry would starve from 40 billion terrorism fear!
Kyoto will be ratified and implemented with cheers!
Land mines would be banned as true evil in civilized world!
US administration won't be nightmare of Founding Fathers!

Without 9/11 -
Al-Qaeda would never exist virtually!
Taliban would run Afghanistan as citizens lawfully!
Bin Laden would be seen preaching physically!
Iraqis would still be enjoying sovereignty peacefully!
Airport security won't harass people with delays and worries!
US/NATO/Israeli war crimes couldn't hide under insurgency!
Terrorism wouldn't seize most national agenda in 21st century!

Without 9/11 -
Suicide bombing won't be an industry of the military!
Anthrax perpetrators would be in jail not running country!
World won't be scratching heads for endless anomalies -
Why Holocaust survivors so united for war with secrecy!
Neo-Conservatism couldn't hijack main stream Conservatives!
Most media won't be plagued with patriotic nationalism!

Without 9/11 (Cont.)

Without 9/11 – there is no 'War on Terror'!
World would have redefined war as the vehicle of Terror!
Earth would have been better with message to share and care!
Establishing unity with equity, ensuring freedom beyond borders!

It is unfortunate, RAW became part of CIA and MI6, just like ISI; what else can world have except anarchy?

"In the councils of government, we must guard against the acquisition of unwarranted influence, whether sought or unsought, by the military-industrial complex. The potential for the disastrous rise of misplaced power exists and will persist."
Dwight D. Eisenhower,
Farewell Address to the Nation, January 17, 1961

Terrorism is a good business for the US & Israeli Private Defense Industries which targeted Indian Market using emerging Indian Private Defense Industries including Tata Advanced Systems (TAS) owned by Ratan Tata, who is also the owner of Taj Mahal Hotel in Mumbai! Indians must not give in to this fear mongering aristocratic evil doers who have been recruiting youths around the world as Al-Qaeda foot soldiers for cover ups; rather help recognize these few multinationals like United Technologies, Lockheed Martin, Sikorsky, Boeing, who have invested 40 billion USD in Terrorism Industry since 9/11 and now justifying market spreading terror with their private mercenaries like Blackwater and MPRI using bullets and ammunition banned even for international ware fare!

Here is Ratan Tata on CNN: "The restaurant where the firefight took place is riddled with bullet marks, and the walls are scarred with grenade blasts. And it looks like it's been hit by a bomb.... We had people who died being shot through bullet-proof vests.... I knew several of the staff members ... Some of them were gone just in cold blood, I understand, just shot in the head or shot at point-blank range."

Ratan Tata is often described as India's David Rockefeller! Well, David Rockefeller was one of the chief architects of 9/11 terror in USA transferring World Trade Center 6-weeks prior to controlled demolitions as would be obvious in 'Real Path To 9/11', he was also Ex-Chairman of the secretive world power Bilderberg and the current chairman of another secretive aristocratic power Trilateral Commision as well as a permanent steering committee member of Bilderberg - a strong proponent of "supranational sovereignty of an intellectual elite and world bankers".

The recent Mumbai incident has all the signatures of 9/11 and UK subway bombing – they had warnings, they increased security, they lowered security prior to the event, and the event was well planned – professionally executed. Let us hear Ratan Tata on CNN again: "There seems to be no doubt that they knew their way around the hotel, that they seemed to know it in the night or in the daytime. They seemed to have planned their moves quite well. And there seemed to have been a lot of pre-planning in terms of what they did, and how they managed to carry on for three days and sustain themselves during that time".

The question is who are they for whom security can be lowered despite threat for successful terror implementation? The answer can be found only analyzing who evetually benefit from this economically and politically! The obvious gainers of 9/11 were the Private Defense contractors, Mercenaries, Silverstein Properties & Westfield America, Rochefeller empire including Citigroup and Zion's Evangelic Christian Soldiers who have been counting days for genocidal Armageddon (Biblical end of the world)!

The cozy relation among Indian multinationals like TATA (TAS) and Wipro with US and Israeli Defense & Security Industry Giants have started importing terror and related economy to India at the cost of , of course, expendable innocent lives and destruction as colateral damages!

And here is what Ratan Tata suggests on CNN what Indian should do; "if we need to get expertise from outside, we should not stand on ceremony to hold back. We should go to the best place possible to get expertise, and have that installed with us in terms of hardware, in terms of training, in terms of strategy". Now imagine the economic gain for TATA if TAS is the main interface in India of arming governments, institutions, and corporations with helicopters and technologies in all cities and provinces throughout India to pre-emptively guard them from virtual Al-Virus terrorism!

Now let us hear from Sikorsky president Jeffrey P. Pino: "India represents an expansive rotorcraft market with enormous potential and opportunity. I am most excited at the possibility of working with the well-known and admired Tata Group, and tapping into India's skilled aerospace industry and capability".

Finally, President Bush's call to Prime minister, Manmohan Singh: "out of this tragedy can come an opportunity to hold these extremists accountable and demonstrate the world's shared commitment to combat terrorism", White House spokesman Gordon Johndroe said in a statement.

No amount of Hi-Tech security can secure the world when Intelligence works in secrecy without accountabilities for aristocrative private gains. **Only truth can overcome fear!**

No country must allow FBI agents inside the country for investigation. They will either try to destroy/implant evidence to support their counterpart within law enforcements in framing up the theory that most suites US/NATO alliance for evangelic aristocratic supremacy along with gathering success status of the covert operation!

It is unfortunate that India gave up sovereignty to US/NATO alliance under the current inefficient minority Government where RAW became part of CIA just like ISI, dealing with criminal Bush administration which murdered their own American citizens for world supremacy on 9/11!

Now they are together enjoying the success of 9/11 in USA, converting minority governments to military Junta leading India to US like financial melt-down because the Zionists can't compete with the old world under fair game; so they are rewriting their barbaric Hellenistic history including new monetary policy - because world already know their techniques which they can't play anymore.

Local citizens have always been fooled by events and related rumours since the time of Alexander the conqueror helping Hellenistic history repeat again and again as most wise act ignorant.

What has been going on in India can't happen without the help of RAW and top level Police and Military Brass, just like in USA, UK, and elsewhere.

Unfortunately, it's all about shadow government that started from USA in 1980 under Ronald Regan, now spreading the world as Al-Virus with the help of

Bilderberg (the Aristocrative Mafia), covert Intelligence wings including CIA, MI6, Mossad, and ISI, the Queen and the Vatican (Holy See).

It's all about taking world back to monarchy in the name of democratic oligarchy, uniting them under the cross (void of love of Buddha, Jesus and Muhammad).

God helps world citizens to rise unitedly against this destructive power, starting with banning all foreign NGOs following Russia's lead that will end the violent advancement of the CROSS giving commoners much needed relief and peace in normal way of life!

When religions coexist, leaders communicate, media respect neutrality, laws not blinded by immunity, and citizens' needs take precedence over profitability - peace becomes reality, world lives in harmony - Kolki

When Nobel Peace Prize Goes To Environment and discriminatory[1] Human Rights, Peace Becomes Illusive Ignoring Ongoing US/NATO/Israeli War Crimes[2]!

[**Abstract:** Among many peace prizes around the world Nobel Peace Prize[3] is recognized as the most prestigious one. But we often forget as media deifies the winner(s) that prestige is a synonym of aristocracy and royalty which also sustains wars and Monarchies. This article will review the original intention of the peace prize as envisioned by Alfred Nobel[4] in 1895 and its historical implications since then as world embraced WW I, WW II, wars in (Korea, Vietnam, Laos & Cambodia), Iraq-Iran war, NATO bombing in Yugoslavia as well as illegal US-Led invasions of Iraq and Afghanistan - killing, wounding, and displacing millions. It seems the peace prize has been used often to promote evangelical Christianism and feudal colonial Capitalism around the world by the Norwegian Monarchy established in 1905 which is an extension of Danish-British Monarchy with pride in Nordic Superiority[5]. It will also be evident that in some instances the prize even instigated violence in a country like Indonesia (East Timor[6]) and Tibet[7] while ignoring true Arms Control effort like Strategic Arms Limitation Treaty as well as strong Monarchial support for Arming Israel with Nuclear capability. It can also be concluded that the conversion of Democratic United States of America to Constitutional Monarchy started with awarding the prize to bullyish president Theodore Roosevelt in 1906, prior to WW I, and ended with 9/11/2001 making New York Mayor Rudolf Giuliani the Knight[8], Vice-President Cheney the Monarch and demoting Presidency as a puppet domestic Prime Minister following military command. Finally, the prize honoured many for humanitarian reasons but ignored/punished system/people who eradicated hunger and homelessness with egalitarian vision.]

{Note: One should read this article keeping in mind that behind all rhetoric of Democracy most NATO countries are Constitutional Monarchs[9], Vatican is Absolute[10] Monarchy, and USA is without a Central Election Commission with administrative authority guaranteeing fair election throughout the country enforcing standard election techniques, practices, and verification process! Thus, like 'war on terror', if USA declares martial law[11] NATO will probably follow through endangering true democracies and human rights around the world!}

We must always cheer the goodwill toward good environment, but the 2007 Nobel Peace Award is a direct slap for the true peace activists and peace loving leaders around the world who have been working fervently for achieving lasting world peace in a lawful and truthful global society! It once again ignored that aggressive military activities around the world are the main causes of global warming and pollution besides destruction of Earth and killings of sentient being. In fact, leaders who fought vehemently against all odds to stop US-led illegal Iraqi invasion must have been ideal candidates to respect peace and truth.

Very few people probably know that **Alfred Nobel made his fortune through Explosives** (Dynamite & Ballistite) Making Defense Industry and selling them to then Norwegian-Swedish military union, as well as countries including Germany, France, Belgium, Russia, and USA. But the intention to invest his vast financial empire for humanitarian causes is obvious from his will "The prize for peace was to be awarded to the person who **"shall have done the most or the best work for fraternity between nations, for the abolition or reduction of standing armies and for the holding of peace congresses."** The prize was to be awarded "by a committee of five persons to be elected by the Norwegian Storting."

Thus it is obvious that Nobel Peace Award as envisioned by Nobel was a true noble effort with good intention to demilitarize the world. But many times it was awarded to people or organizations which were unrelated to peace making the award counterproductive, even rewarding real war criminals in few occasions while cleverly ignoring military occupations, dominations, and war crimes of allied nations (an extension of Norway - now NATO) since its inception. It may even have been contributing to the advancement of Swiss-English-Nordic Cross which was obvious when allied victory tried to change German flag resembling Cross twice in 1919 and 1948. The very first prize was given to the founder of Red Cross (Flag of England) and proponent of the Jewish State in Palestine supported by then Monarchial Union. Thus behind all humanitarian gestures Red Cross (The English Flag) can be seen as the allied military hospital in war zones to minimize allied casualty! In other words formation of International Red Cross prepared the world for endless wars for allied victory while establishing the symbol of crusades (Red Cross) in otherwise non-violent regions of the planet.

The most important incident that happened since Nobel's death in 1896 was that Norway became Monarchy tied to Demark and England in 1905 severing union with Sweden. The 2nd most important thing happened was that Dee Beer, the largest diamond factory, originally founded in South Africa by British Colonialist Ceceil Rhodes, also became the largest dynamite factory in the world beginning 1903. The 3rd most important thing happened was that The United States of America ended its isolationism and joined imperialism under Theodore Roosevelt. The British Empire that ended with American Independence needed a sophisticated way to rebuild worldwide empire! Thus it can be seen that Norwegian King envisioned spread of British colonialism annexing the world under The United Kingdom of Israel carefully manipulating the Nobel peace prize along with Red Cross (Flag of England), related missionary NGOs and right groups supervised from Vatican.

The very discriminative nature of the committee got exposed when they voted down Mohandas Gandhi who was nominated five times and the name made to the committee's short list three times. In 1948 the committee awarded no prize; it indicated that it had found "no suitable living candidate", a reference to Gandhi. It thus seems likely that he would have been awarded the prize if he had not been assassinated in January 1948. Still, the committee had had earlier opportunities to honour the man who, in hindsight, is generally seen as the leading spokesperson of non-violence in the 20th century. Under the statutes then in force, Gandhi could have been awarded even the 1948 prize, as seen by the posthumous prize awarded to Hammarskjöld in 1961. Even the 1963 prize could have been awarded to Gandhi instead of Red Cross (The English Flag) celebrating 100 years since inception in Switzerland (The main crusading flag).

Henry Kissinger, who orchestrated the worst chemical weapon attacks in the villages of Vietnam, Laos, and Cambodia is an ideal example of the political side of the award.

In 1973 the Nobel Peace Prize was awarded to US National Security Adviser and Secretary of State Henry A. Kissinger and North Vietnamese leader and negotiator Le Duc Tho for the 1973 Paris agreement intended to bring about a cease-fire in the Vietnam War and a withdrawal of the American forces. This award is definitely the most controversial one in the history of the Nobel Peace Prize. Le Duc Tho declined the Peace Prize, the only person to have done so, since there was still no peace agreement. Kissinger did not come to Oslo to receive the prize in person and soon indicated he wanted to return it, but was told the statutes did not permit this; two of the committee members resigned after it had become known that there had been disagreement and that they had in fact been against the award. (They supported Brazilian archbishop Helder Camara, who received a Norwegian people's prize instead.) Public reaction to the prize, both in Norway and internationally, was largely negative.

In 1978, Egyptian President Mohamed Anwar al-Sadat and Israeli Prime Minister Menachem Begin were honoured for the Camp David Agreement, which brought about a negotiated peace between Egypt and Israel. This agreement too, proved controversial. Only Begin came to Oslo to receive the award. A technicality prevented the American president, Jimmy Carter, from being the third Laureate; the committee actually wanted to include him, but he had not been nominated when the deadline expired on February 1 of that year.

In 1983, Lech Walesa, a polish trade unionist, a devout Roman Catholic, was awarded the Nobel peace prize which cannot be equated to contributions that foster fraternity between nations and disarmament. It was a political prize sending a clear blow to communism which eventually dismantled the Soviet Block systems and helped NATO rise as a major military power reinvigorating the arms race and new pre-emptive wars in the world.

In 1987 OSCAR ARIAS SÁNCHEZ, Costa Rica's president, was honored for his leadership in having the five presidents of Central America sign a peace agreement for the area. This and 1978 awards could be seen as the intervention of the Norwegian Nobel Committee in conflicts where progress toward peace had definitely been made, but conflicts had been far from resolved. Although Arias promoted the idea of Central American Parliament he managed to keep Costa Rica out of it. Also his coming back to presidency in 2007 voiding constitutional amendment that forbade presidential reelection meant not so Noble!

Shimon Pares
In 1994, the Peace Prize was awarded to Palestinian leader Yasser Arafat, Israeli Prime Minister Yitzhak Rabin and Israeli Foreign Minister Shimon Peres for the Oslo Agreement, which brought about a mutual recognition and a framework for peace between the Palestine Liberation Organization (PLO) and Israel. The three politicians had accomplished much, but they were still far from establishing a final peace between Israelis and Palestinians. The award resulted in one member leaving the committee, the leading spokesman in Norway for the Likud party in Israel. This was the third resignation in the history of the Norwegian Nobel Committee. To world citizens surprise peace prize winner Peres joined indicted war criminal Ariel Sharon for endless violence against the Palestinians disrespecting the Oslo agreement!

Thus it is obvious that the committee is a good example of partisan politics to advance evangelical (non-Semite Zionist) monarchial causes other than peace sometimes to divert attention from real peace related global issues. This was most obvious when the peace award went to reverred Mother Teresa for her evangelical humanitarian work diverting US military actions against South Korean Democracy! As the world was celebrating Mother Teresa Carter administration approved South

Korean plans to use military troops against pro-democracy demonstrations ten days before former General Chun Doo Hwan seized control of the country in a May 17, 1980, military coup, according to newly released U.S. government documents, to solidify US occupation of South Korea. Now imagine that ex-president Jimmy Carter was awarded the 2002 peace prize for humanitarian reason to divert attention from 9/11 destruction, unknown detainees, and US invasion and destruction of Afghanistan without proof of conviction enacting many war crimes per Geneva Convention. The list can go on.

Nobel Peace Prize and Vatican's Evangelical Ambition:

With Swiss-Cross, English-Cross, Nordic-Cross, Red-Cross playing important role in the Nobel peace prize it won't be out of context to analyze whether Papal Cross could gain grounds from the awarding of the peace prize, at least in few occasions! Ironically for the secular world it would be seen that many of the peace prizes were awarded to Catholic Bishops who were not directly related with any peace activities but helped bringing in existing or newly formed countries under Papal Constituency, e.g., Poland, East Timor…..or avoid mass revolution and/or conversion to Islam of non-Christian countries around the world. The peace prize award to Roman Catholic Bishop of East Timor, Carlos Belo, can be seen as direct intervention from Vatican since he was a product and member of the Salesian Society who **was appointed as the head of the East Timor Church against the choice of the Timorese priests.** Within months of his consecration as Bishop which made him directly responsible to Pope he started campaigning for Independence leading to violence which eventually facilitated presence of massive evangelical Monarchial Australian Forces on the Island! To add more Papal spices the Salesian Society in agreement with Holy See chose him to be the new crusader in Mozambique – a former British colony as Rhodesia!

1946 prize to John R. Mott of Young Men's Christian Association (YMCA), 1947 prize to "Religious Society of Friends", 1952 prize to Albert Schweitzer for "Reverence for Life" depicting a Jesus who expected the imminent end of the world, 1958 prize to George Pire a Monk from Pontifical International College Angelicum in Rome of Holy See, are notable mention. Even the 1964 prize to Southern Baptist Christian minister Dr. Martin Luther King, Jr. for American Civil Rights movement could be seen as evangelical since the movement would be a moot point without Euro-American Slavery Network; the prize definitely helped in suppressing the rise of Islamic black leader MalcolmX as African American Uniter! The prize venerated many Gandhian Christian activists including Bishop Desmond Tutu, Baptist Minister

Dr. King, Nelson Mandela, yet managed to ignore the father of non-violence, Gandhi a Hindu!

Thus it is obvious that in a world full of heroes from all sects and religions Christian mission and missionaries were always preferred by the Norwegian Nobel committee even when the prize was awarded to few in the non-Christian parts of the world.

Inter-Parliamentary Union (IPU): At the beginning, the peace prizes were mostly shared among European allied nations awarding leading personalities of the IPU eight Nobel Peace Prizes confirming local nature of the fraternity and disarmament:

- 1901: Frédéric Passy (France)
- 1902: Albert Gobat (Switzerland)
- 1903: William Randal Cremer (United Kingdom)
- 1908: Fredrik Bajer (Denmark)
- 1909: August Marie Francois Beernaert (Belgium)
- 1913: Henri La Fontaine (Belgium)
- 1921: Christian Lange (Norway)
- 1927: Ferdinand Buisson (France)

To summarize, Nobel Peace Committee is entirely Norwegian, under a government which is Constitutional Monarch and part of expansionist NATO, an increasingly rich Northern state firmly attached to the West and with strong sympathies for Israel! That is why many peace prizes seemed to be an effort to divert US/NATO military atrocities after WWII defying their own War Crime laws set up via Geneva Convention and Nuremberg Trial. Thus while the committee selected people for fighting hunger and homeless ignored the countries and leaders who eradicated hunger and homelessness like in Soviet Union, China and Cuba! Not to mention most of the prizes were initially shared among the League of Nations and its extension United Nations and NATO war helping hand Red Cross (Flag of England)! The 1990 peace prize went to Mikhail Gorbachev for dismantling guaranteed food, shelter, and education for Soviet Block citizens bringing back chaos, uncertainty, discriminations, and homelessness. Similarly 1989 peace prize went to Dalai Lama who has no known contribution to any peace effort in any part of the world except being a Western Spokesperson for the Tibetans who have been enjoying much egalitarian life under the Chinese system. The 2006 peace prize went to Mohammad Yunus of Bangladesh for his contribution in economics in forming 'Gramin Bank – A Credit Source for the poor without collateral' who should have been given the 2006 economics prize. But surprizingly the 2006 prize in economics went to Edmund Phelps of Columbia University, a guardian for the beholder of Capitalism that requires unemployments to sustain low inflation.

Thus if we analyze the sequence of events surrounding the peace prize:

1. In 1863 Jean Henry Dunant founded Red Cross (The Flag of England) in Switzerland mainly to minimize Austrian military casualty; He also established the Palestine Colonial Company to assist Jews in making Aliyah (settling in Palestine). This is equivalent to forming slave trading company to send Africans to work in the newly colonized land.
2. In the same year, 1863, Alfred Nobel obtains the first patent on nitroglycerin (dynamite) an industrial explosive
3. 1896 – Nobel signs will for Nobel Prize in Physics, Chemistry, Biology, Economics and Peace.
4. Theodor Herzl, Founder of **Zionism** in **1897,** an Austrian Jew born to a prosperous, emancipated Budapest family, laid down foundation for Anti-Semite (against Semites – the old world) Activities:
"It is essential that the sufferings of Jews. . . become worse. . . this will assist in realization of our plans. . . I have an excellent idea. . . I shall induce anti-Semites to liquidate Jewish wealth. . . The anti-Semites will assist us thereby in that they will strengthen the persecution and oppression of Jews. The anti-Semites shall be our best friends". -- From Herzl's Diary
[Note: Whenever Zionists mention "sufferings of the Jews" they mean everyone else as ancient diasporic Hebrews (the old world) except themselves. Ancient Hebrew was a culture, not a race, which can be traced back to Harappan civilization]
5. 1898 - Birth of Yellow Journalism in America that supports state terrorism to justify wars for global invasions
6. 1898 – America became imperialist embracing Internationalism ending founding fathers vision of Isolationism. 1906 peace prize to Spanish-American War General Theodore Roosevelt was an indirect invitation to America to join then imperial alliance which would be called later 'League of nations'!

No one knows exactly what was going through Alfred Nobel's mind when he was signing his will in Swedish-Norwegian Club in Paris especially giving the Peace Prize responsibilty to the Norwegian and not Sweden. But it certainly helped in spreading colonialism and evangelism (zionist) illuding disarmament while bringing world in firm grips of military industrial complex supervised by the Constitutional Monrachs promoting their shadow foreign policies implemnted through secretive-nonaccountable powerful intelligence branches! The British-Nordic unconditional monarchial support to US-Led 'war on terror' ignoring Rule-of-Law and Proof-of-Conviction probably would have been the worst nightmare for Alfred Nobel considering his vision of 'Fraternity among nations and rewards for disarmaments'!

Even in science awarding prizes to practical Physics, Chemistry and Biology led researchers more towards military needs of advanced warefare eventually leading to the Atomic Bombs and Biological Waepons. People still wonder why there were no Nobel Prizes in Mathematics and Theoretical Sciences! The answer may be that none of them help military activities directly although enlightening for universal vision.

Now to top everything with some more colonial spices, Switzerland has the same medieval crusading flag of England only inverted and its National Anthem still sung in British tune 'God saves the Queen'! It is the major country in the world for secret bank deposits as well as house of most international institutes like World Health Organization, United Nations, Red Cross. The International Court of Justice is in Monarchial Hague, Netehrlands. And all Nordic countries share the same crusading flag only in different colours as Nordic Cross. Thus it can be concluded that the peace prize along with all the monarchial organizations established from Developed Monarchies are very well coordinated sophisticated efforts to perpetuate monarchy expanding zionist colonialism in its modern form promoting evangelism and anti-Semitism.

The best way to end this article is to quote Nobel Laureate Poet Rabindra Nath Tagore during his speech in USA in 1920, "It was easier for us to speak out against the British Empire in England than in America."! Now imagine that George Washington fought to end British colonialism in 1781 and Tagore's speech was just after World War I when 2.5 million new Zionists joined America's existing one million who already thought America was Zion. While George Washington's farewell address was a stern warning against involvement in foreign wars, awarding of the 1906 peace prize to <u>bullyish president Theodore Roosevelt</u> dragged USA into WW I satisfying <u>Royalist agenda</u> and beginning American colonialism & imperialism. Most people on earth love peace which is the very basis of displaying everything best of human being through social and cultural evolution. But prestigious Nobel peace prize often became the victim or tool of monarchial ambition which is against egalitarian coexistence valuing universal <u>basic human rights</u>!

Tagore <u>rejected knighthood</u>, a <u>crusading title</u>, which the New York Mayor Rudolf Giliani proudly embraced as the forebearer for the success of the <u>9/11</u> domestic disaster <u>transfering World Trade Center (WTC) ownership</u> to Silverstein Properties and Westfield America, Making <u>New York City Emercency Command</u> Center on 23rd floor of 7 World Trade Center, assigning <u>Securacom</u> (Stratesec)(KuwAm Corporation) operated by Bush family in charge of <u>WTC</u> security until <u>9/11</u>, and overseeing the slowest recovery process in the most advanced country.

Finally, to pay our best tribute of respect to the visionary will of Alfred Nobel for "<u>fraternity</u> between nations and <u>disarmament</u> " the peace prize should be administered from a country which is truly <u>democratic</u> voted by a world body conatining <u>peace activists</u> and leaders who are also truly dedicated to brokering peace among nations using only diplomacy and universal vision.

References:
1. RIGHTS-US: U.N. Panel Finds Two-Tier Society, IPS, http://ipsnews.net/news.asp?idnews=41556
2. NATO/US Warcrimes in KOSOVO, http://www.iraqwar.org/natowarcrimes.htm
3. Nobel Prize, http://nobelprize.org/nobel_prizes/peace/laureates/
4. Alfred Nobel, http://en.wikipedia.org/wiki/Alfred_Nobel
5. Nordic Race, http://en.wikipedia.org/wiki/Nordic_theory
6. Carlos Filipe Ximenes Belo, East Timor,
   http://en.wikipedia.org/wiki/Carlos_Filipe_Ximenes_Belo
7. Why is the Dalai Lama suppressing religious freedom?,
   http://wisdombuddhadorjeshugden.org/
8. Papal Orders of Chivalry, http://en.wikipedia.org/wiki/Papal_Orders_of_Chivalry
9. Developed Nations Constitutional Monarchy,
   http://www.kolki.com/peace/Developed-Constitutional-Monarchies.htm
10. Vatican State and Government, http://www.vaticanstate.va/EN/State_and_Government/
11. Martial Law Threat Is Real, http://www.commondreams.org/archive/2007/07/27/2813
12. **100 years of Nobel Peace Prize History** (Overall Reference)

Peace Is A Threat To Worldwide Military And Oil Based Economy!

USA and NATO members including Great Britain need a live testing ground in some parts of the world every few years! New weapons need to be tested. Old weapons need to be used to replenish stocks with new private defense contracts creating new jobs. That is why they will create/ keep the term 'devil'/'evil'/'terror' in this world and would create some pretext to use their military might disguising as the authority of democracy and freedom around the world. They will bomb and destroy world civilization following their path of past wraths including **Vietnam, Korea, IRAQ, Yugoslavia, Somalia, Panama, Folk Land Island and Afghanistan – killing millions as well as destroying our already fragile environment.**

The world would be democratic and peaceful without NATO US and British military might who need wars or conflicts to divert their internal problems of poverty, homelessness, crimes and inadequate health care, while deifying Constitutional Monarchs as well as empowering Holy See (Vatican). Their co-lateral damages cause severe human and environmental destruction around the world. They hurt and eradicate innocent-helpless people and their culture with unparalleled media censorship in the name of National/Allied Security.

Ironically, US and British citizens are not part of their national security. They are one of the most overworked people on earth with endless responsibilities and little or no vacation. **Good US and British Politicians lose their battle for humanity and social justice to constant self-proclaimed conservative military propaganda labeling peace-loving politicians as 'Soft On Crimes and/or National Security'.**

The best national security the politicians can guarantee for their country is by converting apparent enemies to friends, through communication and understanding. Faith and friendship is the best security for the world citizens. From Jesus to Gandhi, imperialists always labeled reformer/freedom fighter as terrorists. Let us stop that process in the light of 21st century making the world united sharing technology, communication and culture, thereby breaking the barriers, mistrusts and ignorance!

Its time that a deficit ridden Superpower like USA and allied power like NATO stop bullying and disrupting young democracies around the world strengthening cunning Monarchist Alliance in the process. Its time that true participatory democracies prevail throughout the world ending all Constitutional Monarchies including United Kingdom (UK), Netherlands, Belgium, Denmark, Norway, Sweden, Japan, and Canada. Its time that USA and some NATO members stop assassinating democratically elected Presidents or Prime Ministers replacing them with military dictatorships. Its time that USA and some NATO members stop testing their new military technology and equipment attacking and destroying sovereign countries in some pretext, making United Nations (UN) an invalid mere spectator of real War Crimes! USA and NATO hold the key to world peace! Unfortunately, peace is an apparent threat to their Military and Oil based economy as well as Evangelic ideology for world supremacy! God bless our beloved living planet protecting her from all EVIL military powers and their destructive alliance!

55 Million Died During World War II Besides Human Sufferings, Pollution, and Debris!

As Israel, Evangelical Christians, and most North American as well as some European Media are provoking US to take unilateral action against Iran following the self-proclaimed hegemonic success with illegal invasion of Iraq, against the will of world citizens, we must not ignore that this unjust 21st Century wars in the name of virtual war on terror may soon lead us all to World War III. We also must not forget that every country must respect UN resolutions including Israel which is the worst violator of UN resolutions since 1967 and USA who has vetoed most resolutions for peace citing Israel's security concern while arming them to be one of the best Air Forces in the world!

The immense military and civilian loss, during and after World War II, often gets buried under the constant reference to Non-Semite European Jewish Holocaust and search for Nazis around the world. At least 55 million people died, 25 million of those military and 30 million civilians, during World War II, along with 5 million plus Jews (mostly ancient Semite Hebrews) who made Europe home following 70 AD persecution in and evictions from Israel!

Former Soviet Union, **USSR, suffered the most** with more than 13,000,000 military and 7,000,000 civilian deaths. **China was the second** who suffered 3,500,000 military and 10,000,000 civilian deaths. **Germany was the third** with 3,500,000 military and 3,800,000 civilian deaths. Poland lost 120,000 military and 5,300,000 civilian. Japan lost 1,700,000 military and 380,000 civilian. Yugoslavia lost 300,000 military and 1,300,000 civilian. Romania lost 200,000 military and 465,000 civilian. France lost 250,000 military and 360,000 civilians. British Empire and Commonwealth lost 452,000 military and 60,000 civilian. Italy lost 330,000 military and 80,000 civilian. Hungary lost 120,000 military and 280,000 civilian. Czechoslovakia lost 10,000 military and 330,000 civilian.

Of the 405,399 Americans that lost their lives during World War II, there were 78,976 missing in Action. It was the **Americans who suffered the least** number of civilian deaths.

A rough consensus has been reached on the total cost of the World War II. In terms of money spent, it has been put at more than $1 trillion! Just imagine what a better place the world could have been if that money was spent for overall human welfare instead of enriching the Monarchist supremacist desires! The true cost of the war is still unknown. The Soviet government calculated that the USSR lost 30 percent of its national wealth, while Nazi/Zionist executions and looting were of incalculable amounts in the occupied countries. The full cost to Japan has been estimated at $562 billion. **In Germany, allied bombing and shelling had produced 4 billion cu m (5 billion cu yd) of rubble.** Of course, this does not include the pollution and associated long-term harm done to the world atmosphere and weather. Also, this does not include the overall loss of animals, birds, forests, and plants.

Iraq was invaded illegally despite it obeyed most UN resolutions as well as accepted independent UN inspectors from countries including Britain and US. knowing well some of them were covert CIA/British/Mossad agents whose only aims were to destroy Iraq and its ancient culture – even manufacturing and spreading lies.

Finally, we must not ignore that Israel, not Iraq /Iran/ North Korea, is the most UN resolutions violator – even denying UN inspectors during Jenine massacre and overall destruction of the UN supervised land of democratic Palestine. Israel violated UN resolutions since 1967 challenging its authority and ignoring all international call for peace. The worst is that Israel is now provoking non-democratically installed NEOCONS dominated George Bush administration to attack Iran unilaterally based on speculated fear from Iran's much needed domestic Nuclear Power Generation.

World has lost a lot since 9/11 without an open public investigation! Ironically the European Union is now joining hands with the new axis alliance to sanction against Iran while disrespecting the democratically elected government of Palestine and ignoring daily atrocities and ongoing genocide by the Israeli military! This kind of crusadic alliance only takes world closer and closer to the ultimate nuclear war, Armageddon, as envisioned by most Evangelical Christians!

Religion evolves from evolved culture maintaining harmony among economics, politics, and celebrations! Unfortunately all talk about separation of Church and

State in USA only helped Evangelical (Zion's Christian Soldiers) takeover of US administration and most government decision making, incapacitating the voice of true Jesus (Peace) loving Christians, leading to world domination for military supremacy!

The most worrying part of this Necons/ Zionists/ Evangelists alliance which started with Norwegian-Swedish Alliance and mutated through World Wars as the NATO alliance is that it doesn't have any obedience or patriotism to a country/nation but the alliance whose ultimate goal is to galvanize aristocratic rule of few over the masses of the world with extreme secrecy and democratic hypocrisy!

There is every cause for celebrating united efforts towards one world but world citizens must stand tall to ensure that world is not ruled from the underworld with mafia like covert intelligence agencies, Bilderberg like secret aristocratic constitutional monarchy and Vatican like intruding evangelical supremacy – whose only aim is to continue Oligarchy!

Democracy

(Dedicated to a true participatory open democratic majority ruled free world)

[It is time to end Constitutional Monarchy to secure true democracies around the world!
Ever wonder how & why countries form ally and send troops for illegal invasion or sign
private pacts bypassing votes and rule-of-law, ignoring majority opinion! Kolki]

World has been governed by many custodianships!
Aristocracy, Autocracy, Despotism, Democracy!
Dictatorship, Meritocracy, Oligarchy, Plutocracy!
Republic, Islamic republic, Monarchy, Constitutional Monarchy!
Absolute monarchy, Single-party state, Theocracy and Tyranny!

Each worked with its pros and cons and legitimacy!
As divided world tried its best for stability!
But time and technology have brought us to proximity –
Giving us a wonderful chance to live as one community!
Reuniting people of all sects with elections participatory!

But as we talk about participatory democracy -
Its time to end all constitutional monarchy!
Where idle Monarchs have a history of turning fascists!
Silently working from behind for military supremacy!
Uniting kings and dictators to re-establish Feudalistic Oligarchy!

[Developed Nations Constitutional Monarchy: United Kingdom, Australia,
Spain, Norway, Denmark, Belgium, Sweden, Netherlands,
Japan, Canada, New Zealand – where non-elected Monarchs are the
military commander-in-chiefs who are silently working towards prophesized
supremacy guarded by non-accountable intelligence and nobility! That is why
democracies have been toppled or disrupted throughout the world since World
War II. Since 9/11 US Vice President Dick Cheney has been acting as Monarch
beyond rule-of-law and accountabilities! Kolki]

Like Most NATO Countries Bhutan Silently Became Constitutional Monarch Guaranteeing Monarchy and Eluding Democracy Forever

Like most NATO countries Bhutan silently became Constitutional Monarch guaranteeing monarchy and eluding democracy forever. Bhutan's Oxford educated prince now is the unconditional head of state resembling Constitutional Monarch of England. Here is the list of major Constitutional Monarchs running North Atlantic Treaty Organization (NATO) and its world domination mission from the Head Quarter in Brussels, Belgium: **United Kingdom, Belgium, Denmark, Netherlands, Norway, Sweden, Australia, Canada, New Zealand, Spain, and Japan**. USA became quasi Constitutional Monarch since introducing electorate college which is the ultimate authority of electing president disregarding long election campaign and popular vote. US Presidential candidate Al Gore is an ideal example as victim who won the 2000 election in popular vote despite illegal stopping of Florida vote counts but George W. Bush, Jr., became the president ignoring the definition of democracy. Since 9/11 US Vice Presidency rose to a new authority without congressional accountabilities making major military and intelligence initiatives bypassing votes and citizens voice!

World wonders why neoconservative politicians in Netherlands, Denmark would go so many extra miles to defame Islam and other religion creating cartoons and video on the internet without realizing the mode of Monarchial propaganda machine! Well, all these efforts including 9/11 sophisticated mass murders, Madrid & London subway bombing, ongoing war on terror, are to re-establish monarchy throughout the world in disguise of democracy which is a threat to their supremacist hold on the power!

Now, let us see how many NATO countries with license to kill people calling them militants, insurgents, Al-Qaeda, terrorist, are really true democratic! It is surprising to discover that the beholders of democracy which is trying to implement democratic methodology in the world themselves are constitutional Monarchs! Once again the short list is: **United Kingdom, Belgium, Denmark, Netherlands, Norway, Sweden, Australia, Canada, New Zealand, Spain, and Japan**. It is easy to identify democratic countries within NATO like Germany and France who stood against the allied illegal invasion of IRAQ.

What is wrong with Constitutional Monarch? It divides people forever as opponents depriving mass from united celebration of life. It guarantees Monarchy whose main focus is stronger military and evasive intelligence for domination behind the parliamentary process making people's voice inert and inactive against the non-elected head of the state! In absolute Monarchy Monarch has to deal with day to day events of the country, general well being of the subjects, and can rise and fall accordingly sharing blames. But Constitutional Monarchy will always find a patsy, a willing or unwilling victim, in parliament to withstand all storms of dissents while Monarchial administration enjoys absolute immunity furthering the cause of stronger unconditional Monarchy!

These Monarchs are not religious because they know that they are the religion and GOD as king why they use religion as a tool to divide people and world keeping voters busy with infighting and gossiping while emperors unite as allied power. They create League of Nations, United Nations (UN), North Atlantic Treaty Organization (NATO), World Health Organization (WHO), International Monetary Fund (IMF), World Bank (IFC), for just one mission, running the world with Monarchial vision. That is why world has seen more wars and devastation since the foundation of UN, more hunger and refugees since foundation of World Bank and IMF, more deadly diseases spread the world since formation of WHO. These are all political organizations, the Monarchs support them as long as they work for their causes to guarantee worldwide supremacy otherwise they form new alliance and new institutions keeping citizens in chaos and disarray! They write laws (like **Nuremberg Tribunals)** for the War Criminals only to disrespect them as convenience for promoting illegal wars!

Throughout history this process continued dividing people introducing fear whenever nations tried to be united for permanent peace and harmony! They embraced Mahayana Buddhism replacing Buddha's universal teachings, they imposed Judaism on ancient Hebrew secularism, they replaced loving Jesus with Cross to become God, divided Islam inflicting pain to Muhammad's united vision. That is why the Monarchial NATO countries can send troops beyond border or execute bombing campaigns without declaring war and disclosing mission despite opposition from majority citizens. With massive possessions of Nuclear, Biological and conventional weapons deadlier than ever the race for the Monarchial supremacy only leading us towards the evangelic end of the world which even the chosen won't survive to live as the only race.

Thus it is time that every country on earth embraces true participatory democracy and vote unitedly for the abolition of all forms of Constitutional Monarchs giving world much needed true democratic voice leading to long lasting peace on earth.

Intelligence
(Dedicated to an honest open neighbourly society)

[Isn't Intelligence shrouded in secrecy leading to military within military,
country within a country, state within a state, city within a city, community
within a community, with special immunity? Kolki]

Our fight is with enemies who reside in virtual heaven!
What we do to save nations is absolute secret!
Tax payers must feed us billions without checks and balances!
We will rid the world from old weeds as evil suspects!
Our covert operations are prescriptions for democratic causes!

We cannot tell who when how and why -
But terrorists are working against us day and night!
Why threat level cycles in red orange yellow and red light!
Everyone must look around for suspects in disguise!
Back yard, front yard, under bed and hat, wherever they may hide!

Senators cannot see our minutes its secret!
Congress can't view them its top secret!
Judiciary committee can't review its secretively secret!
Only officials who sympathise with our causes
Will praise our good work in media and speeches!
Glorifying the need to re-classify all declassified secrets!
Lest someone has idle-time to analyze our achievements!

Our mission is defined in Biblical events!
Our agents are licensed to kill for self defence!
Democratic laws for citizens work against our commitments!
We are intelligence - modern faith based guardian angels!

[9/11 cover-ups (with destruction of evidence, stone walling, and obstruction to open
justice) and trivial anomalies made CIA, FBI, NSA, US Military, suspected criminals
that is why all confessions of detainees under their custody are assumed invalid! Kolki]

Who Will Free Korea, Japan, and Germany From US Occupations After Half A Century (50+ Years)

Whoever dreams about USA freeing Iraqi people must be day dreaming without knowledge that Japan (with **35,307**, US army), Germany (**69,395** US, army) and Korea (**32,744** US, Army) are still occupied by US military after 50+ years! USA also maintains large number of military personnel in Kuwait (15,000), Italy (**12,258**) and United Kingdom (**11,093**) apart from 130,000 soldiers plus 180,000 contractors in Iraq! **It is obvious that presence of foreign military in someway affect the country's sovereign decision making process always safeguarding and enlightening the chosen few while maintaining the status quo!**

Currently there are **702+ US military bases** stationed in **132+ different countries** across the globe to maintain US/NATO strategic interests, rather military and economic Supremacy! In other words, since World War II, US/NATO have been ensuring that indigenous nations can never rise to show the alternative living methodologies they once evolved with and exercised for a peaceful coexisting world, before the slave prescription of 'Ten Commandments' overpowered them! Mysterious 9/11 gave US military an excuse to deploy 900,000 more secret military personnel around the world dedicated in executing secret missions with funds channelized using Belgium based SWIFT money tracking system as secret CIA/FBI money laundering! Thus it seems obvious that late Hitler's dream of conquering the world became US/NATO reality since WW II!

What's wrong with Domination? It blocks indigenous natural growth enforcing endless slavery encouraging internal conflicts! To illustrate it further, **let us consider India** which was under British occupation for more or less 200 years! Dominating British left India with 16% literacy, a fragile-volatile cash crop based economy, Ireland like deadly famine, while Britons in India and Great Britain enjoyed 98% literacy, secured and pampered life! We all know how Israel has been treating Palestinians in the occupied land inflicting most brutal and humiliating experience ever extended to mankind by fellow human being!

Since independence in 1947, Indians currently enjoy 66+ % literacy, a vibrant economy, a strong defensive military and sufficient food to feed 1.2 billion people, all within 58 years! Palestine was thriving within a year after signing the Oslo peace treaty before Israeli terrorists assassinated their own peace loving Prime Minister Yitzhak Rabin re-establishing endless military aggressions, death and destructions!

We can easily extrapolate the ill effects of foreign occupations and domination by few chosen reviewing present dominated lands including Iraq, Afghanistan, Palestine, Lebanon, Ireland, Haiti, South Korea, Panama, Hawaii, Falkland Island, Columbia, Guantanamo Bay, Diego Garcia, just to name a few!

The world has seen how natives and aboriginals in Asia, North America, Australia, South America, New Zealand have been treated with hostility and abuse leading to almost annihilation, in some cases, by few chosen invaders (guests) who once enjoyed utmost hospitality in a foreign land!

It was the foreign domination and exploitation of natural resources for rapid profit making motives in the newly found lands which enslaved millions from Africa causing the African Holocaust! Natives and aboriginals who once lived in small communities without endless digging and logging of our lonely living planet now forced to live in unhealthy intoxicated segregated reservations in many parts of the world!

In summary, domination deprives the world from the very art of creative evolutions much needed to maintain sustainable eco-friendly development guaranteeing peaceful, sharing and caring coexistence! Thus it is time World and UN remind USA/NATO forces to respect freedom around the world ending all military occupations!

Bush/Blair/Rumsfeld Responsible For All Beheading, Killings and Abuses In IRAQ, Afghanistan

Bush/Blair/Rumsfeld are directly responsible for all beheading, killings, bombing and abuses in Iraq and Afghanistan! World must accuse them as war criminal because it is their unjust and unilateral military invasions and occupations which have been creating genocide in Iraq and Afghanistan! **Saddam Hussein built modern Iraq which they destroyed killing more than 100,000 Iraqis, destroying all infrastructures and polluting environment with depleted uranium worst in human history!**

Muslims must not be fooled by car/suicide bombings, which are destroying deferent sects of Islam! US Special forces along with their trained militia are doing it to divide Iraqis and the Muslim world. **This is the only way US/Britain can justify prolonging brutal occupations killing all possible opponents of their long-term mission.** This is the 21st Century crusade against Islam and the world **to maintain US/British military supremacy as evident from the Zionist Dossier "**The New American Century**" and "**Rebuilding America's Defenses**"!**

If we try to see the pattern of who they are beheading, displaying bodies hanging from the trees or killing journalists, Red Cross and UN personnel, it is obvious everything is happening in Iraq and Afghanistan is a direct planning from the Pentagon, the White House and 10 Downing Street!

Let us remember what Bush said in his speech after 9/11, 'You are with us or you are with them'! So, any US or foreign personnel who are observing daily systematic killings and abuses in Iraq or Afghanistan and showing their dissatisfaction or disapproval of the process are terrorists to Bush/Blair Administration!

If we analyze the pattern of beheadings, killings or abductions, it is obvious most of the victims are not US or British military personnel! They are beheading, killing or abducting US or foreign citizens working in Iraq or Afghanistan who CIA or FBI thought may be linked with the terrorists and were under investigation!

Let us take the example from one of the latest beheading **and why CIA and FBI along with US led Iraqi Militia must have done it blaming and framing virtual Al-**

Qaeda! According to Reuters 'The FBI saw Nick Berg, the American civilian beheaded in Iraq, three times while he was being detained by Iraqi police, the U.S.-led occupation authority said Wednesday, May 12, 2004'. US led Iraqi police arrested Mr. Nick Berg before his execution!

British imperial forces performed these atrocities before in all occupied lands including India! Israeli military have been doing this to the Palestinian people for half a century! But the irony is that the Bush/Blair/Rumsfeld committing these heinous crimes in brought day light using 21st century minority owned private military media!

Earth

(Dedicated to Mother's Day appreciating everything motherly including beloved Planet Earth)

Oh Mother Earth!
Bestow upon us the energy of fire!
Help us rise above shyness, greed, and fear!
Warm our hearts as we breathe truth so dear -
Make our mind logical, thoughtful, and clear!

Oh Loving Power! Reveal your messages for co-existence!
Alas! We fight wars and destroy delicate Eco system –
Despite you made us creative and intelligent!
Enlighten us to feel heavenly bliss in non-violence!

Oh dearest Living Planet!
Energize us with your evolving secrets -
Of overcoming poverty, supremacy, and global hazards -
A simple methodology of selfless love and care!

Let our united minds spread Mother's Day messages
That civilization excels with joyous selflessness!
Ensuring a World Court unbiased towards all races,
A United Nations vocal against all violence,
World Health Organization free from pandemic alliance,
Religions enjoy separation of Church and State,
Intelligence means open enlightenment!
Recognizing War is destruction of life irrespective of label,
Power becomes Super embracing Total Excellence!

Any list of countries harboring terrorism excluding US, Britain, and Israel is incomplete and will only help terrorism to succeed with a different face

We must understand the problem to solve it correctly whether it is mathematical, economical, political or international. Thus, the definition of terrorism and terrorists need to be established clearly for the sake of a long lasting world peace. If we consider Newton's Third Law Of Motion - 'Every action has an equal and opposite reaction'. This is equally true for all US actions including Vietnam, Korea, Philippines, Indonesia, throughout South America, Middle East and Africa, and former Yugoslavia. For ideological war or economic interests, most terrorists have been either trained in US or trained by US in some way, including many notorious world dictators!

It is once again unfortunate that President (Non-Democratically Elected) George Bush has started labelling countries with ancient civilization and heritage as terrorist. This is being done at a time when the world was so close to be united against the evils of arms race, global warming, mines, guns as well as weapons of mass destruction including chemical, biological and nuclear weapons.

Our beautiful World had a wonderful chance after World War II for a long lasting peace! Unfortunately, imprudent partitioning and redrawing of many Asian, African and European countries were done to satisfy long term American and British strategic interests. The very interests of the local people, cultures, values and securities, were sacrificed for the sake of the American and British economic and military interests.

There is still time to begin 21st Century in a good note ensuring peace and good environment while maintaining a sustainable worldwide economy considering mutual interests of all countries. We must not miss this wonderful opportunity by separating countries and dividing the world, in the name of a virtual enemy 'terrorism'.

Since its inception, Israel has been terrorizing Palestinians and Arabs armed with latest US weapons including nuclear bombs and missiles. They even destroyed USS Liberty killing 34 and wounding 171 American marines in 1967. Prime Minister

Sharon himself has been charged as a war criminal who helped kill and massacre 20,000+ Lebanese and butchered thousands of Palestinians refugees including women and children. Israeli intelligence regularly conducts assassinations throughout the world.

Most people in the world including US and Israel are for peace and common good of mankind. It is the self-censored commercial media which diverts world opinion labeling death and destruction as collateral damage.

This is a time when our beloved world leaders must use their power and intelligence toward uniting the world and not dividing it further in the name of terrorism!

9/11
A Barrier to Good Environment

Pollution
(Dedicated to a pristine co-existing world)

[Ratifying KYOTO[1] is not an option, rather a rare chance to be part of Global Solidarity of humankind. Peace and Good Environment are threats[2] to Military Domination[3] and Private[4] Defense Industries – Kolki]

Humans end up polluting a part of the Earth!
Whatever we do to make our life easier or better!
Even as we make fire we pollute the air -
But that is something natural world can bear!

We feel so good planting a tree but pollute with fertilizer!
We care for dear plants but spray insecticides or bug killers!
That end up polluting soil, insects, bacteria and earthworms[5]!
Logging to mining, speed boating to Space Shuttle mission -
It's all about creating additional pollution!

Riding bicycle for short commute is a wonderful idea!
While driving gasoline car releases carbon dioxide in atmosphere!
Often adding carbon monoxide from vehicles without mufflers!
Not to mention the sound pollution that comes as a bonus!
Buildings and shopping malls expose living things under!
That equates to polluting when pesticides kill them over!

From fuelled bus to ship to train to airplanes to military jets -
We need energy constantly to run civilized brains!
Burning Coal, Gasoline, or Nuclear power
Forgetting resources are limited but enough to share!

Nothing pollutes jet streams[6] like allied military sorties over
Or football field size battleships[7] bullying around the world!

That is why Kyoto[8] is a threat to military power
Although good for everything else we care –
Including economy, good jobs, and life[9] on Earth!

Reference:

1. 'United Nations Framework For Climate Change', http://unfccc.int/2860.php
2. 'Peace Is A Threat', http://www.kolki.com/peace/Peace-A-Threat.htm
3. 'Domination Is Terrorism', http://www.kolki.com/peace/domination.htm
4. 'Evil Thought', *Poems by Kolki – Absolutely Humane*, Trafford Publishing, Victoria, Canada
5. 'Worm Watch',
   http://www.naturewatch.ca/english/wormwatch/about/ecology.html
6. 'Jet Stream', http://en.wikipedia.org/wiki/Jet_stream
7. USS South Dakota, http://www.kolki.com/peace/BattleShip.doc
8. 'The Kyoto Protocol', http://ec.europa.eu/environment/climat/kyoto.htm
9. 'Life Is Simple', *Poems by Kolki – Absolutely Humane*, Trafford Publishing, Victoria, Canada

US Bombs Destroying Delicate/Fragile Himalayan Eco System Apart From Alleged Al-Qaeda and Taliban

Using world's sympathy for the September 11th , 2001, mysterious disaster and self censored US WAR media including CNN and Fox, US has been using weapons of mass destruction including 15,000 pounds FAE (Fuel Air Explosive, BLU-82), Cluster Bombs (Depleted Uranium) and Bunker Busting Nuclear Weapons (.2 ktons and up), throughout Afghanistan and bordering Pakistan!

US has been also probably testing their small Nuclear bombs underneath Hindu Kush mountain causing various unusual earthquakes resulting in enormous death and destruction and clearing the path of the much anticipated Kazakhstan oil pipeline.

Those bombs, explosions, and related radiations definitely killing suspected Al-Qaeda or Taliban avoiding Rule-of-Law and Proof-of-Conviction as well as simultaneously destroying delicate/fragile yet wonderful Eco system and heavenly landscapes of the Himalayas, polluting the pristine lakes and downstream rivers, killing rare birds, animals, trees, and plants.

The Hindu Kush Himalayan region, stretching 3,500 km over eight countries, from Afghanistan in the west to Myanmar in the east, is home to more than 140 million people and affects the lives of three times as many in the plains and river basins below. The region is not only the world's highest mountain region, but also its most populous.

Considering the location and the altitude (7000+ feet from see level) of Afghanistan, the dust and radiation from Massive US Bombing will spread throughout the world causing more disease and unpredictable weather. The effect will be many folds of the dust from the Desert Storm, which was conducted almost at the sea level yet the dust and radiation traveled to North America.

While the present imprudent US president labels some countries as terrorists or axis of evils, it is US which possess and use weapons of Mass Destruction to show its Military Might without any respect for human rights and environment.

US love to use its weapons of mass destruction in wars including Hiroshima, Nagasaki, Korea, Vietnam, Iraq, Kosovo and Afghanistan, killing millions of people and animals, destroying ancient civilization and culture.

Hope good sense would prevail to world leaders and US citizens could read better to understand their own leaders and military who are depriving the world from a good environment and peaceful coexistence, in the name of national security and interests. It is time that the US national interest be also part of the World interest.

From Cave to White House, Leaders Always Hide When Our Young Fight Wars Destructing Own Kind and Environment

President Bush was correct in his speech on the Pearl Harbour Day and before invasion of Iraq in 2003 that **leaders**, whether the commander of chief of the most powerful nation or the spoke person of a fragile extremist group or the President of a weaker sovereign nation, **always hide in shelters when young soldiers fight on the front in the middle of death and destruction.**

Wars, irrespective of labels, **cause destruction of innocent lives and civilization**, confusing and terrifying all living animals in the affected part of this beautiful world. It is the race for military supremacy which has been contributing to additional Green House Gases making USA the worst polluter on planet Earth. Aggressive Military actions that lead to massive global pollution can certainly be equated to environmental terrorism. Ironically, 9/11 gave USA-Britain-Israel unconditional and unlimited military build ups authority and pre-emptive actions worldwide without a simple honest truth bearing investigation – insulting the very notion of rule-of-law and proof-of-conviction.

We can give our **soldiers** all kinds of technology, make them the ultimate killing machines in the front lines, but they **are still frightened about the uncertainty, death and destruction around their dug holes, or sorties above.**

Most people on this planet just want to go ahead with their daily life in peace and harmony maintaining rich culture and diversity. They believe that most conflict can be resolved with honest and sincere diplomacy. Military strategic interests and security only leading us to live in racist hegemonistic world dominated my supremacists.

It is easy to demonize someone for political gain and spend **billions of dollars to divert world attention in justifying use of military might.** But **wars**, in any form, **beget future war keeping hatred and vengeance alive** in the mind of the surviving friend and family of the victims.

Thus, it is time that world leaders work through the United Nations and the International Court of Justice to resolve conflicts punishing all violators of peace and human rights, as appropriate, without bias.

Let love, mercy and mutual understanding be the tool for the 21st century world diplomacy. Let us believe that international conflicts minus super power strategic interest results in peaceful coexistence!

The universal equation of peace is:
International conflicts - Super power strategic interests = Lasting peaceful coexistence!

Planet Earth
(Dedicated to sustainable healthy planet Earth)

In this vast universe
Among seemingly infinite space and distant stars
I am the living Planet Earth
Revolving merrily as family around my star, the Sun!

I have been living for ages caring for millions
Mineral, oil, gas deposits act like my organs!
My soil is fertile to satisfy being of all forms
Plants, insects, birds, and animals!
My oceans are mechanisms for atmospheric balance
Ensuring a predictable life support system immortal!

While most sentient being respect my natural order
Humans need mining, drilling, and logging, for life and culture!
But the entrepreneurial ambitions for material gains of lust
Resembling my existence as decapitated body parts!

So it is time for humans to ask -
Is it alright to siphon last drop of oil sheltered by the rock?
Is it alright to clear cut and uproot old growth to log?
Is it alright to extract metallic ores creating miles of holes?
Don't they unitedly constitute their living abode?

It is time for humans to understand -
Thousands of years prepared my body for genetic evolution
Soon to be hostile place to live for generations!
That time may be running out to fix my scars from self healing
Making me slip/wobble during daily spin
Producing unpredictable day, night, and seasons!

Planet Earth (Cont.)

If humans continue drilling, logging, mining for greed
Transferring earth around for quick profit
Induced imbalance may soon affect axial inclination
Causing enormous calamities leading to global devastations!
Depriving world from solstices, equinoxes, and celebrations
Resulting in permanent summer or winter in many regions
Triggering endless migrations, wars, and annihilations!

Hope 'Earth Day' becomes a day of global consciousness
Respecting unison with the spirit of peaceful coexistence!

9/11
A Barrier to Universal Well Being
And
Our Way of Life

Giving
(Dedicated to egalitarian distribution of resources throughout the world)

[Most world problems are direct or indirect effects of colonialism beginning with Dorian Greek Alexander the conqueror inflicting divisions, fear of persecutions among peaceful nations, slavery, and triggering diasporic migrations of people to uninhabitable parts of Earth especially true in Africa! World as a whole is a complete resource base which need to be shared and distributed equally among world citizens to achieve true democracy, human rights, and everlasting peace! Kolki]

'There is no free lunch', it's a modern saying -
Confirming to feudal beginning
When universal lands and resources became limited as private
Leading humans to slavery of conditional evangelism
Ending evolutionary wisdom of sharing and giving!

But lunch has been free in temples and gatherings
To celebrate life together with blessings!
Roadside water wells, shelters, and fruit trees
Once delighted travellers traversing ancient cities!

Free lunches are natural and universal!
As the sun's rays illuminate all unconditional
Grasses grow for birds and animals
Rains quench thirst for all inlands!
Without the sound of cash registrars -
Earth provides food, shelter, and minerals
Knowing there is no return or remuneration!

Free lunch is joy of giving
Why roses bloom mainly for romanticism
Perennials come out to decorate gardens in spring
Banana grows though not required for own offspring

Giving (Cont.)

Seedless grapes flourish in the vineyards
Bees produce honey while pollinating buds
Cattle produce more milk than needed for the calves
Bacteria work silently to maintain food products
Berries surprise animals in bushes, forests, and parks
Fruits come to trees in season unnoticed to serve
Wild Grasses and Shrubs live for insects and birds!

Without thought of endless private gain
Giving is the best way to cure universal pains!

In a world full of grains, fruits, milk, and honey - one hungry stomach is too many!
In a land filled with corporate space, estates, and money - one homeless without a place is too many! Kolki

If Politicians Could Speak, Media Could Listen, People Could Read

As we embrace 21st Century and hope for a new beginning it is important that we know the very reason of basic world problems despite unthinkable scientific, industrial and commercial achievements. Thus, while every effort and check point must be in place to justify the appropriate use of federal tax dollars of a country we must honestly ask the following basic questions to ourselves:

1. Why some politicians and media are against Gun (Rifle) registration knowing well that the only use of a Gun is to kill a fellow human or worldly being?
2. What is the cost of maintaining Sovereignty guaranteeing a safe united Country?
3. Why there is a constant effort to deprive Citizens from their universal rights ignoring the perils of private health care and energy industry?
4. If privatization of everything is the only solution then why US is in such a bad shape relying on military hegemony to support a fragile economy that requires many US citizens be uninsured, homeless and hungry?

We live in a society where private media seem to be running the course of a country relentlessly analyzing what politician would say, said, could have said, rather constant gossiping complicating simple issues that are meant for universal well being! Which makes politicians constantly worry about non-democratic biased media poll forgetting their once honest obligations inherited during real poll from the ballots of 'We The People'!

If politicians could speak, media could listen and people could read then people would be living happily in a society:
➤ free from Gun related violence and homicides
➤ united to fight against foreign interventions in domestic and military policies
➤ maintaining precious diversity and God given pristine resources
➤ enlightened disregarding propaganda that spreads the virtue of deforestation, privatism and militarism
➤ where conservatism can never rise toward a bigger military government and lesser civilian government, ignoring the fact that a good sufficient government is fundamental to a democratic peace loving society.

If India and China can build civilizations without hegemony what is wrong with USA, Britain, Australia and some NATO countries?

[Hegemony - aggression or expansionism by large nations in an effort to achieve world domination]

Advancements of China and India toward developed country status must be celebrated and appreciated considering that the two Asian giants feed and care for almost half of the world population - without military occupation, and respecting most global treaties and initiatives!

It is another sad note of US/NATO Administrations, few North American & European politicians, as well as media analyst's narrow world vision, together with the cost of 'War of Terror', which are creating a fear in North America & Europe against China and India's ongoing economic growth and social welfare!

The advent of computers, telecommunications, Internet banking and businesses brought to us a tremendous hope toward implementing a global village for 'we the people, by the people and for the people'. All we need now are the goodwill of all nations, leaders and politicians with an open mind redefining nationalism to facilitate removing protectionism.

Even 20 years back very few people on earth dreamt about so much closeness among people around the world whether it is for business, news, travel or cultural exchanges. Yet we see also political moves toward military dominance and protectionism – leading us back to an **'economy of fear'** as well as **'politics of fear'**!

In a global market no country should feel threatened by the growth and development of other countries as long as the trades are fare and without military strategic interests. Because it is the military strategic interest which divides people, country and the world blocking true free trades and human relations! Thus North Americans & Europeans must not be afraid of the recent growth in China and India. It should be good news for the world considering the size of their population and their long-sufferings under repeated foreign invasions and occupations. So, their well being should be welcoming and encouraging.

It is time for the existing military superpowers to understand that friendly diplomacy is much cheaper as well as effective than military strategic interests.

Because most people around the world just want to see and enjoy a united free world where all humans feel equal while respecting every country's political, cultural and religious traditions!

Every process or model would have pros and cons and so **is US style legalized feudal system**, or **Indian style true democracy**, or **China's socialist capitalism**. It is up to the people of that nation to decide what is best for them to sustain economic growth for the benefit of all people.

One size doesn't fit all and so is US style legalized feudal system which still cannot feed and care for all despite inheriting a brand new non exploited continent and all its resources. It is a sad example for the world that 21st century US political campaign themes are still 'tough on crimes', 'more prisons', 'increasing pension age to 70' and 'improving a failing education system'! US politicians must not forget that domestic criminals are also US citizens produced by the existing socio-political environment to fill the need of ever-growing (2.5+ million prisoners) prison industry.

For hundreds of years Indians and Chinese worked in North America and Europe as refugees, immigrants or contract labourers - building infrastructures, helping in farming, industries and academic institutions, which contributed toward developed country status and related fortunes. It is time for the North Americans & Europeans to enjoy India and China being part of their academic, cultural and technological growth while indulging in generous Asian hospitality.

Finally, each country must avoid irresponsible tax cuts and excessive military spending, both are counter-productive to global village! Rather, debt reduction, balanced budget and the promise of sustainable environmentally sound economy would attract domestic as well as foreign investors into North American & European banks and stock markets much needed for vibrant economy without hegemony.

Good economy doesn't necessarily mean a healthy nation. Largest economy doesn't necessarily mean rich nation. It is time to re-think and re-evaluate economic benefit ensuring that it benefits the people whose well being determines the true richness of a nation.

Let us remind the world 'Preaching Domination is Terrorism'! Acting to achieve it is 'War Crime'

⇑ Effect of Domination ⇑   (Photo: Deepak)   ⇑ Natural Growth ⇑

Hegemony
(Dedicated to a world void of (Constitutional) Supremacist Monarchy)

As the only super power joins United Monarchy
Insulting citizens, depriving democracy
Letting Military dictates the Presidency
Making Suicide Bombings Defence Industry -
No one (media) would blame Hitler or Nazi
As Neocons devise American foreign policy
PNAC, the Project of the New American Century
Unfurling 'New Pearl Harbour' for supremacy!

World watches silently
As war machines destroy countries
Creating fear, threats, and censorships

Silencing UN, numbing International Justice
Riding evangelic Biblical Prophecy
Humiliating loving Jesus with Vatican's hypocrisy
The deadly Cross rids the world of old weeds
Guarding felons glorifying victory for security!

Hegemonic adventures pollute civilized 21st Century
Perpetuating misery of slavery
Dehumanizing naturally blessed humanity!

Whenever National Security Prevails Over Individual Freedom A State Is Heading Toward Military Transition! Let us remind the World that preaching Domination is Terrorism, acting to achieve it is War Crime! Kolki

Global Issues – Current and Outstanding, as we celebrate Earth Day

We can celebrate Earth Day, UN Day, Youth Day, Children's Day, Peace Day, etc., year after year! But without resolving core issues causing the very sufferings, abuses, wars, pollutions, hunger, and discriminations on Planet Earth the celebrations end like another yearly ritual.

Here is a short list of global issues current and outstanding – some for long time:

1. Open public investigation for 9/11 US Domestic disaster which gave USA, NATO and Israel power to take unilateral military actions against any nation and individual bypassing Rule-of-Law and Proof-of-Convictions as well as ignoring United Nations and International Court of Justice.

2. Ending illegal Iraqi Occupation by most brutal and abusive US and, so called, allied military as well as private mercenaries that killed 800,000+ civilians, wounded millions, and displaced 5+ millions in 21st Century. Democracy in Iraq can never work while it is occupied and the puppet government is under the supreme military-mercenary guns.

3. War Crimes in Iraq – invasion of peaceful Iraq was illegal as certified by Kofi Anan and Hans Blix based on UN and International Charter! But the war criminals of Bush-Blair-Howard administrations and respective military are still free endangering the world communities and societies.

4. US-British-Israeli Private Mercenaries - UN must sanction against US-Britain-Israel for using private mercenaries in Iraq, Afghanistan, and Palestine with absolute immunity from sovereign laws. Use of private mercenaries in war or as security forces must be totally banned in a civilized world.

5. US/NATO forces must stop all pre-emptive air strikes in Afghanistan and they must be judged under war crimes for all killings of Afghan citizens and destruction just out of mere speculations. We must ask who gave US/NATO

forces license to extra-judicial killings resembling Israel's path of lawlessness.

6. <u>Unknown Detainees</u> must be brought to open public justice system so that world can see them, hear them, and judge them once for all to identify true nature and power of Al-Qaeda

7. <u>900,000 Secret US Federal Employees</u> – Fellow Americans must stand tall for transparency of Democratic Government identifying all secret federal employees trained by CIA/FBI and what they have doing around the world since <u>9/11</u>!

8. <u>Anthrax Perpetrators</u> – UN must help fellow Americans investigate who sent US military grade Anthrax to Democratic Senators, Media critical to Bush Administration. This is important to stop future biological terrorism around the world.

9. <u>Kyoto</u> – All countries must sign and ratify this protocol as a sign of international solidarity against global warming addressing the issue with urgency bypassing politics (US and its worldwide military operation produce 25% of the green house gases, worst polluter, must be the first to sign and obey the protocol as a leader)

10. <u>Democratizing Constitutional Monarchs</u> – as world embraces <u>democracy</u> and democratic values it is time to have true democracies in most NATO countries including United Kingdom, Norway, Sweden, Denmark, Netherlands, Spain, Belgium, Australia, Canada, New Zealand, and Japan. Use of military must be a political decision of sovereign countries where non-elected Constitutional Monarchs are not the Commander in Chief. So, it is time to end all Constitutional Monarchies to secure and sustain worldwide <u>true participatory democracy</u>.

11. Dissolving NATO – West needs a western Gorbachev to dismantle Aggressive/Abusive NATO military alliance voluntarily. Peace can never be achieved when a military alliance attacks and sanctions countries bypassing UN authority. Thus NATO expansion is United Nation's destruction.

12. <u>Freeing Korea, Japan and Germany from US occupation</u> – large US military presence in those countries for half a century works against democracy and national unity. It is time - Korea, Japan and Germany enjoy freedom void of US military occupation.

13. <u>Air India Disaster of 1985</u> Open Public investigation (long outstanding): Since Canadian Government, Justice system, and Media failed to launch an open public investigation into one of the worst terrorist act in airline history masterminded and perpetrated from Canada, UN must help Canadians to full open public investigation serving long outstanding justice to the <u>real perpetrators</u> including <u>CSIS</u> and <u>RCMP</u> officials for destruction of all important audio tapes and many physical evidences related to the disaster.

14. Democratizing UN Security Council reflecting world population and voice to minimise abusive sanctions and convenient wars of supremacy.

15. Last but not least – opening Bilderberg, Trilateral Commission and Swiss Bank to open democratic process and accountabilities. *"World must be ever vigilant to ensure that anti-Semites are not uniting as secretive Bilderberg, Trilateral Commission, Swiss Bank and sprouting off-shore banks, empowered by covert military, mercenaries and intelligence."*

When wise act ignorant world becomes a dangerous place. We must stand tall as world citizens despite all business to ensure these issues get resolved for the benefit of mankind and other sentient being leading to lasting peace and enormous cultural evolutions on <u>Planet Earth</u>.

How much are Intelligence Service's Contributions to Societies So Far? Aren't Hiding Truth & Obstructions to Justice Felonies?

World already know about the incapabilities of CIA, a 30 billion dollars US Intelligence Agency, which failed The Americans on Virginia Tech Killings, 9/11/2001 Disaster, Oklahoma City Bombing, 1993 World Trade Center Bombing, and other international terror related legally unproven incidents affecting world institutions and citizens. CIA couldn't stop the assassinations of only Pulitzer Prize winning US President, John F. Kennedy and his brother Robert Kennedy as well as Nobel Peace Prize Laureate Dr. Martin Luther King, Jr., on the American soil. **Still today CIA couldn't submit a report about its role on September 11, 2001, to the US Senate and Congress, after six (6) years!**

World also know the incapabilities of 776 million pounds British Intelligence Agency (MI6) which couldn't stop the London subway bombing and princes Diana's mysterious death! Examples of intelligence failures are enormous around the world yet the reasons are shrouded with secrecy leaving the citizens in the dark forever with subsequent baseless accusations and rumours!

A community becomes sleepless if a killer is out there! Cities remain terrified when a serial killer is on the loose! Then imagine how countries worry constantly if mass killers can hide beyond justice and accountabilities in the name of National Interests and Securities! Whenever 'National Security' prevails over 'Individual Freedom' a State is heading toward Military transition! Therefore we must ask ourselves whose interests and securities are being served by guarding secrecies with faith in hearsay publicities from the authorities! Citizens must be concerned about any doubt that intelligence may be running military converting democracy to autocracy or monarchy!

Thus, as with the Neo-Conservatism enthusiasm Canadian Security Intelligence Service (CSIS) has been recruiting members for worldwide secret missions, following CIA & MI6 path, let us review what they have done so far to make Canadian life better or safer since its inception in 1984:

1. **It couldn't stop the** Bombing of Air India Flight 182 **on June 23, 1985,** the worst terrorism in Canadian History, killing 280 Canadian citizens, including 82 children, overall 329 passengers and crew aboard.

   Rather CBC report suggests that CSIS had a Mole in the group who were responsible for the meanest attack on Canadians terminating the flight that originated from Toronto over the Atlantic Ocean near Ireland. On June 22nd, 1985, Canadian Pacific Airline agent Jeanne Bakermans checked in two pieces of luggage at the Vancouver International Airport from a clean shaven would be passenger without confirmation connecting to Air India Flight 182. Air India crew suspected unaccompanied luggage at the Mirabel Airport, Montreal, and asked for the Routine International Airline Procedure of baggage identification by onboard passengers. But the attending CSIS & RCMP officials at the Mirabel Airport insisted that the flight must leave immediately citing cost of holding the runway!

   Those two unaccompanied luggage from Vancouver contained Time Bombs that caused fatal termination of Air India Flight 182 as well as killed two baggage handlers at the Narita International Airport, Tokyo, Japan.

   After 22 years, CSIS **is still** blocking the investigation blacking out most intelligence related pages. It even destroyed most important wiretapping tapes **(156) needed to establish truth in the worst terrorist attack on the Canadian soil by still unknown Canadian Terrorists.**

   The destruction of evidence by the Canadian Security Intelligence Service, meanwhile, was singled out by the judge for criticism during the trial as "unacceptable negligence." Why Canadians would pay to maintain Intelligence Agency which seems to destroy evidence, a felony, against Canadian National Security & Interests?

2. **It couldn't stop the suspects,** 2000 New Years Eve Bombers, take a car full of explosives to USA endangering life of all aboard the Ferry from Vancouver to Victoria and Victoria to Port Angeles! Imagine why CSIS, RCMP, FBI would jointly allow a car full of explosives to board Canadian & American Ferries under their careful eyes ignoring possibilities of Canadian and American casualties and cost of rescue, lawsuits as well as related investigations!

3. **It couldn't predict anything about** 9/11 and so far obstructing justice following CIA, FBI, tactics in USA! Most other world intelligences including German, French, Egyptian, warned CIA and US Administration about the attack!

4. **It couldn't stop** killing of four RCMP officers in Alberta and all other RCMP officers being killed since 9/11 around Canada for mysterious reasons which only help the 'Tough on crime' and 'More Defense spending' ideology!

5. **It couldn't help** victims of RCMP killings of Canadians in British Columbia, Alberta and Saskatchewan

6. **It couldn't tell Canadians** why Virgin Atlantic Flight was sending 'I have been hijacked' without the knowledge of the pilot. And definitely it couldn't say anything about the unusual Air France. Flight Termination in Toronto on the runway that followed the Virgin Atlantic test run!

7. **It couldn't shed any light** on the unthinkable BC Ferry disaster hitting rocks on shore way off the route just after putting new GPSS system which made it prone to flight/voyage termination by remote control.

But CSIS along with RCMP were very pre-emptive to arrest mostly Canadian boys and teenagers as suspected militants **guarding them in solitary prison cells without access to lawyers and open public investigation** all in the name of virtual war-on-terror, as far as Canadians are concerned! They have learned to talk like FBI in Oklahoma City bombing blaming it all on Ammonium Nitrate ignoring myriads of clues that a van parked with Ammonium Nitrate could never blow up that building in that way! FBI ignored and covered up all unexploded bombs in the debris!

So, the question is what CSIS will do with the new found power and secrecy? Watch 9/11 type incidents happen in Canadian soil without its knowledge yet naming and arresting all suspects immediately afterwards without a doubt following the path of CIA, FBI and MI6?

This is a real food for thought for the Canadians! I have travelled with welcoming Canadian passport hiding my American identity for fear a lot. But Canadian secret mission in Afghanistan and treatment of detainees like the Americans are putting stains on Canadians as humanitarians worldwide!

Let our instincts help us unify our consciousness so that our intelligence and military do not join the Axis Power in World War III which divisive forces had been actively initiating since mysterious 9/11, ignoring worldwide deaths & destruction, as the non-Semite NORDIC Cross advances toward Promise World humiliating loving Semite Jesus.

End Note: [*Ref: http://en.wikipedia.org/wiki/Black_budget*]

"A black budget is a budget that is secretly collected from the overall income of a country, a corporation, a society of any form, a national department, and so on. A black budget usually covers expenses related to military research. The budget is kept secret for national security reasons.

Philip Schneider claimed that the alleged "Dulce Base" in the U.S. state of New Mexico is run by such budget. Many other programs such as Area 51 in Groom Lake, Nevada, and many experimental or covert military programs as well are said to be run by black budgets.

The United States Defense Department has a "black budget" it uses to fund expenditures it does not want to disclose publicly. Such an expenditure is called a "black project." The annual cost of the United States Defense Department black budget was estimated at $32 billion in 2008 but was increased to an estimated $50 billion in 2009".

Thus a black budget is nothing but hidden military corruption that propagates all levels of Government undermining democratic accountabilities.

CNN – The WAR Media – Prefers Military Analysts Preaching Assassinations Of World Leaders!

Imagine, before September 11, 2001, 9AM, all CNN could show the world viewers was the case of missing U.S. federal intern Chandra Levy and the character assassination of Representative Gary Condit. From Larry King to Wolf Blitzer to Aaron Brown to 'Talk of the Nation', CNN's main coverage was Chandra Levy and Gary Condit! As if, the world was free from unemployment, homelessness, hunger, violence, 40,000,000 plus medically uninsured and 22000 yearly homicides in USA, death of 100,000 Iraqi babies from unilateral US sanctions, death and destruction in Palestine, Iraq, Afghanistan, and global warming!

Their camera and topic changed totally since September 11, 2001, focussing first on the World Trade Center and then Pentagon, spreading the fear of terrorism mobilizing the world opinion toward the destruction of Afghanistan and the delicate Himalayan Eco system and later on the Ancient Iraqi civilization.

Just like the Desert Storm and undeclared war against Yugoslavia, they simplify the bombing related death and destruction with smart bombs, cluster bombs and bunker busters, '**Tactical Nuclear Weapons**'. Some of their Ret. Military Analysts even openly vouch for the validity of using Nuclear Weapons whenever necessary.

CNN openly preached of taking out Arafat, (late) Iraqi President Saddam Hussain and other foreign leaders merely based on speculations. This media has total disrespect for truth and wants to sell mere speculations as truth and sufficient proof to destroy a State/Country committing genocide against innocent people. They became the media of US military and right wing political and evangelical think tanks.

CNN acted like totally impotent instead of being investigative without shedding any light against the Anthrax problem and the truth regarding September 11, 2001 (9/11). It never raised the question about the feasibility and responsibilities behind a broad and sophisticated scheme like 9/11 without the knowledge of the State Department, CIA or FBI! Instead, CNN tried to gather opinion toward military strikes based on non-scientific online polls without informing people about the whole issue.

CNN never covered the true effects of Desert Storm on the Iraqi people and the death of 100,000 Iraqi children per year due to the cowardly sanctions. Neither they show the environmental effect of NATO bombing in Serbia/Kosovo nor they talk anything wrong about so much bombing in Afghanistan destroying the delicate Himalayan Eco system.

CNN has double standard for war too! As Israeli military, paramilitary and security forces destroying Palestinian towns and villages, they prefer to keep the American audience busy with Retired Army General's plan of toppling/killing Iraqi president as well as further character assassination of former Honorable President Bill Clinton.

They never told US citizens who were the Talibans and Al-Qaeda and how they were nurtured by American tax dollars and weapons to secure **Kazakhstan** oil reserve destabilizing Afghanistan, Kashmir, Chechnya, Kosovo and Somalia.

500+ Billion Dollars US Deficit Proves Conservative Tax Cuts as Failing Ignorant Protocol for the World

The Outstanding US Public Debt as of 01 Sep 2009 at 04:45:25 PM GMT is: $11,733,420,383,589.88.
The current estimated population of the United States is 306,841,502 so each citizen's share of this debt is $38,239.30. The National Debt has continued to increase on an average of $3.87 billion per day since September 28, 2007 (Christian Science Monitor)!

Approximately 21% of Canadian Tax dollars going to pay for <u>the Canadian National Debt</u> any apparent budget surplus can never be justified for tax cuts mainly to enrich the rich while praying on usual public greed! After all who doesn't relish a real tax break which minimizes huge gap in earnings and makes tuition affordable to all for national and public interests!

Imagine a corporation giving away its capital back to investors because the CEO doesn't know how to invest for the betterment of the company. That CEO will be fired right away by the Board of Directors! But, unfortunately, when it comes to Public Money and Welfare, that seems to be the Conservative Politician's theory and belief.

World has created many renowned Management Institutions with mostly Public Money for the benefit of all people. But Conservative Think Tanks try to preach two 'Mantras' -Tax Cuts and Interest Rates Cuts as the solution to all social problems.

It used to 'Trickle Down' when the money from irresponsible tax cuts stayed inside the country! But now the end product is Deficit, Smaller Public government, Essential Services cuts, Higher education costs, Larger Military government and endless User fees.
USA under Bush Administration with 500 Billion Dollars Deficit is a perfect example of that failing ignorant Protocol.

In this global economy, most rich, who benefit the most from Conservative Tax Cuts, would never invest their public gift from tax cuts, inside the country when

Bank Interest Rates are low and Return On Investment from Stocks are negligible or negative. Thus, most of the public money lost due to tax cuts would be invested in the markets in other parts of the world, contributing to other country's momentary economy to maximize private profit.

Only the Middle Class would dare to buy goods or invest that money inside the country. While poor probably simply pay a tiny portion of their' existing debts or have a feast for a change.

Thus the usual Conservative Antidote of Tax Cuts and Interest Rate Cuts seem totally counter productive in the global free market economy. Rather, debt reduction, balanced budget and the promise of sustainable environmentally sound economy would attract domestic as well as foreign investors into country's Banks and Stock markets. **Current Canadian Economy is a concrete proof of this hypothesis being strongest among G8 countries.**

Government surplus is good news like the savings in a family. A Government that runs in a deficit cannot help their citizens during natural calamity like Hurricane Katrina. **People elect politicians to spend tax money wisely for the benefit of all**. Thus irresponsible across the board tax cuts only prove a politician's inability to understand the broadness of the Government and its true purpose to marvel a democratic society.

Good economy doesn't necessarily mean a healthy nation. Largest economy doesn't necessarily mean rich nation. It is time to re-think and re-evaluate economic benefit ensuring that it benefits the people whose well being determines the true richness of a nation.

Terrorists can blow up buildings, buses, subway cars. But the effects of Irresponsible Tax Cuts are usually larger and lasting inside a country, and sometime throughout the world.

Why No Soldier Must Go Beyond Border Unless Peace Mission or Being Led by President or Prime Minister

No matter how media covers it, how many flags a president or prime minister arranged behind the podium during speech, how the military generals and analyst fervour patriotic fever to justify sending soldiers beyond border, they are sending our children as **helpless invaders** in a distant hostile territories!

Irrespective of the label on the mission our children are viewed as unwanted enemy unless they are there for a **united peace mission** as invited guests of honour. Imagine our dear child in a distant unknown place and culture afraid of withstanding humiliation, often extreme heat and cold fighting other citizens for **undisclosed national interests**. And while they kill and destroy out of fear our president or prime minister are enjoying life with red carpet treatment, hunting in their ranch or resorts while our foreign and defence ministers enjoying parties and meetings in cozy rooms analyzing geopolitical gains.

There is nothing called 'War on Terror'. Every country has to live with their internal affairs of revolts or social conflicts without blaming a virtual enemy for military ambition. 9/11 disaster never happened with President George Bush's authorization of changing NORAD fighter jets scrambling protocol that very morning and idling all CIA-FBI fighters and helicopters the same day. On 9/11 US military was at the highest state of alert running military exercise 'Global Guardian' jointly with NORAD.

Afghanistan and Iraq had been destroyed killing more than 700,000 people by the same people who masterminded and implemented 9/11 disaster killing their own 3000 American citizens and destroying their World Trade Center. US Military had paramilitary in IRAQ during invasion who are expert in car and house bombing detonating military grade explosives. They used the same special forces for repeated bombing, kidnappings and killings, even reporters and UN personnel. There is every reason to believe US Military purposefully killing their own disgruntle soldiers who are tired seeing killings and destruction while hearing only lies from their superior.

Thus every soldier is at risk of getting hurt or killed in Afghanistan or Iraq most probably by US special forces staging remote controlled suicide bombing or using their trained militants. It is really sad to see NATO forces are doing the dirty work for US aggression and destruction being victims of the hatred of the sufferers which are really meant for the invaders.

No parents in their conscious mind must ever send their children to foreign land as aggressor unless President or Prime Minister is leading the force along with the military cabinet with full explanation of national interests.

If India and China can have civilization without military hegemony US-Britain-NATO countries can certainly follow that path giving world much needed peace and friendliness.

"Out of nothing money came to the world tying its value to mostly useless resources like gold and silver leading to kingships and wars for resources and slaves while perpetuating class system guaranteeing aristocrative dominance and endless slavery preaching evangelical gospels of honour with fear"! **Kolki**

Why We Need Bindustan? Because British Systematically Destroyed United Coexisting Humane Hindustan for Convenience of Domination

[Ref: The Koenraad Elst Site and The Awakening Ray, vol.4, no.5, published by The Gnostic Center (USA)]

Here is an excerpt from the Lord Macaulay's speech in Kolkata (then Calcutta) on 2 February, 1835:
[Source: The Awakening Ray, vol.4, no.5, published by The Gnostic Center (USA)]

"I have traveled across the length and breadth of India and I have not seen one person who is a beggar, who is a thief. Such wealth I have seen in this country, such high moral values, people of such calibre, that I do not think we would ever conquer this country, unless we break the very backbone of this nation, which is her spiritual and cultural heritage, and, therefore, I propose that we replace her old and ancient education system, her culture, for if the Indians think that all that is foreign and English is good and greater than their own, they will lose their self-esteem, their native self-culture and they will become what we want them, a truly dominated nation."

Lord Thomas Babington Macaulay (1800-1859), member of the governing council of the East India Company from 1834 to 1838, successfully advocated the replacement of the native languages (Persian, Arabic and Sanskrit) with English as the medium of education. He formulated his policy proposal in his Minute on Indian Education, delivered in Calcutta (Kolkata) on 2 February 1835. The Governor-General of India, William Bentinck, approved the proposal on 7 March 1835, so that it became the cornerstone of British-Indian educational policy until Independence (and remained largely in force after that as well).

Here is his biographer G.D. Trevelyan: "**A new India was born in 1835. The very foundations of her ancient civilization began to rock and sway. Pillar after pillar in the edifice came crashing down.**"

In 1813, the British Parliament made it mandatory that "the East India Company spend at least Rs. One Lakh, annually, on the education of native Indians". The British officials became divided in two camps over the years: one the powerful Orientalists, who wanted the indigenous system of education to continue, with Sanskrit, Arabic and Persian as media of instruction; the other Anglicist camp, led by Lord Macaulay, argued for the European kind of modern education, with focus on modern sciences. Macaulay won, and the British-type of modern educational system was introduced in India.

Lord Macaulay argued, **'I would at once stop the printing of Arabic and Sanskrit books, I would abolish the Madrassa and the Sanskrit College at Calcutta.'**

Thus it can be concluded that Anglicised Natives and Institutions are still running most part of the Governments in India, Pakistan and Bangladesh having their built-in insecurity and deep rooted loyalty to British Monarchy as well as well established Swiss Bank connections enshrouded in covert intelligence secrecy!

Bindustan

(Dedicated to union of ancient India)

[Like Russia – former united land of India, Pakistan, and Bangladesh can eliminate most terrorist acts driving out all foreign NGOs without proper registration as well as declaration of ownership and source of funds! Kolki]

If divided Germany can be reunited Germans
If Euro can bring together Europeans
If USA, Canada, and Mexico can join as North Americans -
India, Pakistan, and Bangladesh can certainly unite as Bindustan!

Geographical borders remain the same!
Government, Military, would still maintain independence!
But inter parliamentary union guarantees common interests
Combining military and intelligence for united defence
Guarding border with hospitality, caring for victims of uncertain events!

Tourism will flourish rebinding once united hearts!
Common Identification would help rebuild trust -
Recognizing our harmonious ancient past
Revitalized with the message of truth and love
Enjoying cuisines, games, and creative culture!

Let us hope the day is not really far!
When ancient people of undivided India come together
Hug each other, work and share life together,
Ignoring divisive forces that take us apart -
Celebrate events better exchanging compliments and cheers!

Terror Scientists in USA building Earth Penetrating Nuclear Bombs and in Israel Nuclear Land Mines, As Nations Worry about Iranian Nuclear Power Plant

As some North Atlantic Treaty Organisation (NATO[1]) countries are bullying against Iranian Civilian Nuclear Power Plant **Terror Scientists in USA are busy building Earth Penetrating[2] Nuclear Bombs and in Israel implementing Nuclear Land Mines[3] as well as arming submarines[4] with nukes and biological weapons!**

It is very difficult to imagine that in 21st Century surrounded by high-tech global media and supposedly educated world citizens US-Britain-Israel along with NATO can threat and humiliate Iran (Persia)[5] for its effort to build much needed Civilian Nuclear Power Plant like most nations on Earth, including G8 Nations[6] and Israel[7]!

Every country on planet Earth is entitled to enjoy the fruits of clean nuclear power[8] generation especially the desert countries without much plants and vegetation which can help absorb pollution emitted by fossil fuel powered Power Generation Plants! Ironically world seems to be running by the fear of the only Super Power and its strongest allies including NATO all possessing massive Weapons of Mass Destruction!

Isn't it ridiculous that the **Britain (UK) which gave Israel 20 tonnes of heavy[9] water secretly,** violating all UN Nuclear Arms Protocol and even keeping it secret from US Government, now acting double standard humilitaing otherwise wise and concerned British citizens!

World citizens know very well who possess[10] weapons of mass destruction including US-Britain-Israel and who used them and keep on threatening vulnerable nations for hegemony! **USA is the only country on Earth** who dropped[11] two Nuclear Bombs on innocent Japanese civilians without warning annihilating millions and devastating two thriving ancient cultural cities! **Israel is the only country on Earth** who bombed[12] and destroyed Nuclear Power Plant of sovereign Iraq with full support of US government stunning world's helpless intellectual audience!

Imagine how scared Arab nations are living next to Israel possessing[13] all weapons of mass destruction including Nuclear, Chemical and biological! Also imagine how

Canadians and Mexicans feel living next to USA which not only possesses[14] massive Nuclear, Chemical and Biological arsenals, but also uses them and keeps on threatening to use them!

World leaders seems to be running to satisfy what is good for Israel sacrificing often their self interests and even sovereignty forgetting that Israel is a strong military and economic power which can defend itself better than probably any other nation on Earth! The ordinary citizens can only hope and pray that the political leaders have the vision to deliver what is best for the country and the world dissociating from hegemonic ideology!

References:

1. NATO, http://www.nato.int/
2. 'Earth Penetrating Nuclear Bombs', http://www.ucsusa.org/global_security/nuclear_weapons/the-robust-nuclear-earth-penetrator-rnep.html
3. 'Nuclear Land Mines', http://www.thebulletin.org/article_nn.php?art_ofn=so02norris
4. 'Israeli Submarines with Nukes', http://iraqwar.mirror-world.ru/article/81226
5. Iran, http://www.crystalinks.com/iran.html
6. G8 Nations, http://en.wikipedia.org/wiki/G8
7. Israel's Nuclear Programme, http://news.bbc.co.uk/2/hi/middle_east/3340639.stm
8. 'Nuclear Technology', http://www.iaea.org/NewsCenter/Statements/2004/ebsp2004n011.html
9. 'British Secret Deal Helped Israel Go Nuclear', http://www.theage.com.au/news/world/british-secret-deal-helped-israel-go-nuclear/2005/08/04/1123125853300.html
10. 'Known Weapons of Mass Destruction', http://www.kolki.com/peace/known-WMD-text.htm
11. 'US Atom Bombs on Japanese Civilians', http://www.kolki.com/peace/US-Atom-Bombs.htm
12. 'Israel Bombs Baghdad Nuclear Reactor', http://news.bbc.co.uk/onthisday/hi/dates/stories/june/7/newsid_3014000/3014623.stm
13. 'BBC World - Israeli WMD', http://www.rense.com/general38/bbc1.htm
14. 'United States and Weapons of Mass Destruction', http://en.wikipedia.org/wiki/The_United_States_and_weapons_of_mass_destruction

Why Countries With Majority Jesus Loving Democratic People Need Guns Without Control?

Whoever believes in Jesus of Nazareth[1] and his true messages knows the very basic of Christianity – **"Thou Shall Not Kill"**, **"Love Thy Neighbour"**, **"Love Thy Enemy"**. But ironically many politicians in Western Jesus loving societies vouch for the availability of Guns without a National Registration System or Universal Control. More ironically there are also politicians who are "Pro-life -> love for a foetus" in one side and "Pro-War -> hate for human life" on the other side. **Gun registry is worth even if it saves one valued life!**

For those who are not familiar with Buddhism and Buddha's messages must also know the philosophy of the part of the world which more or less believe in **"Killings Are The Beginning of All Human Sufferings"**. We all know that the only use of a gun is to kill or hurt a fellow being.

For those who are not aware of the true Koran (Quran) and Mohammed's (Peace be upon him) messages, beyond most Western media, must know the basic beliefs "Jesus[1] as the True Prophet in Islam" of that part of the world. As an addendum most verses in Koran (Quran) start with "Peace[2]" glorifying "Mercy. **So whoever tries to mislead people using Media linking violence and Islam must have an agenda of their own[3].**

Now let us focus on gun owning and violence[4]. Even if we start to analyse from the time after World War II we would notice a very familiar pattern how unregistered guns have been used in countries around the world. Most often they have been used by the private militia[5] of the tyrants to gun down political opponents and media personnel who believe in Universal well being like Jesus[1] did. This is true[6] even in democratic countries including Sweden, "A Symbol of Peace[2]" and not to mention USA – time and again.

The recent (March 2005) mysterious killing[7] of the four RCMP officers in otherwise peaceful Alberta, Canada, is a very good example of the use of Unregistered Guns. Also Police becomes helpless in investigating terrorizing drive by shootings and motivated killings using weapons which can't be traced.

The point is if we are really serious about peace in a society and the world we must not give the power back to those people who could hammer big rusty nails through the hands and veins of the most loving noble human being known to mankind, "Jesus Christ[1]".

I know like many I also run the risk of being gun down leaving a suicide note beside by dead body! But as a peace loving caring human being I felt it is my duty to write for peace exposing truth leading to trivial "cause and effect" filtering rumours and gossips. Hope God[8] (The Universal loving expression) helps all humans on Earth to be tuned with the loving messages of co-existence eradicating the concept and desire for World Supremacy at the cost of fellow beings.

1. 'Jesus', *Poems by Kolki - Absolutely Humane, June 2007,* Trafford Publishing, Victoria, Canada
2. 'Peace Now', *Poems by Kolki - Absolutely Humane, June 2007,* Trafford Publishing, Victoria, Canada
3. 'Rebuilding America's Defenses', *Project of the New American Century,* Page 63 of 90,
      http://www.newamericancentury.org/RebuildingAmericasDefenses.pdf
4. 'Violence', *Poems by Kolki - Absolutely Humane,* June 2007, Trafford Publishing, Victoria, Canada
5. FORTUNE Magazine,
http://money.cnn.com/magazines/fortune/fortune_archive/2003/03/17/339252/index.htm
6. 'War of Terror', *Poems by Kolki - Absolutely Humane, June 2007,* Trafford Publishing, Victoria, Canada
7. 'Final credits - Alberta RCMP deaths',
http://www.lastlinkontheleft.com/fcalbertarcmpdeaths.html
8. 'God', *Poems by Kolki - Absolutely Humane,* June 2007, Trafford Publishing, Victoria, Canada

War
(Dedicated to brotherly and sisterly world believing in togetherness)

[Ever wonder how invasive war-planers, military generals, strategists, politicians, executives, plan and hurt distant people in cold blood[1] destroying cities & livelihood, disrupting water & electricity with missiles & sorties, yet go home and be loving to their family, friends & pets[2]? Is it because they justify genocidal duty[3] in mind that requires killing[4] and destroying other kind[5]? Kolki]

Imagine invasive wars -
Where presidents or prime ministers are the on-site commanders
Bilderberg[6] guests and volunteers are physical coordinators
Constitutional Monarchs[7] are the lead Tank drivers
Politicians, analysts, strategists, are the foot soldiers
Global industry CEOs are the war time chefs and servers
Defence industry executives are the weapons loaders
Aristocrats are flying sorties over
Lobbyists are mine sweepers
Evangelists steering the Navy carriers
Supremacy Think Tanks are the paratroopers
Media Anchor persons are the fighter jet refuelers
Peace Corp volunteers are Red Cross-Crescent rescuers
Academics are food and drink suppliers
Scholars are war-zone intelligence gatherers
Doctors beyond borders are resurrecting dead as survivors
Judges and Lawyers for secrecy are guarding prisoners
Pope is openly leading as the cross[8] bearer
Stock[9] brokers are victim identifiers
Covert Operations planners are dead body buriers
Weapon builders caring for orphans and widowers
War profiteers[10] are sustaining wars as prison labourers[11]
Military is the reconstructor
United Nations is the military supervisor!
While Commons are enjoying life at home in the backyard

Playing golf, fishing, waving 'support the troops' placards
Writing history deifying peace[12] as the fruit of real labour!

1. 'Inconvenient Truth', *Poems by Kolki – Absolutely Humane*, Trafford Publishing, Victoria, Canada
2. 'Dying', *Poems by Kolki – Absolutely Humane*, Trafford Publishing, Victoria, Canada
3. 'War Crimes', *Poems by Kolki – Absolutely Humane*, Trafford Publishing, Victoria, Canada
4. 'Unknown News', http://www.unknownnews.net/casualties.html
5. 'Prophecy', http://www.kolki.com/peace/Prophecy.htm
6. 'Bilderberg', http://www.cbc.ca/news/background/bilderberg-group/
7. 'Constitutional Monarchs', http://www.kolki.com/peace/Developed-Constitutional-Monarchies.htm
8. 'Cross', *Poems by Kolki – Absolutely Humane*, Trafford Publishing, Victoria, Canada
9. 'Market', *Poems by Kolki – Absolutely Humane*, Trafford Publishing, Victoria, Canada
10. 'War Profiteers', http://iraqforsale.org/
11. 'History Is A Weapon', http://www.historyisaweapon.com/defcon1/hisprislacap.html
12. 'Peace Now', *Poems by Kolki – Absolutely Humane*, Trafford Publishing, Victoria, Canada

Rome Wasn't Built In A Day, So Is USA

Whoever visited the Museum in Valley Forge, Pennsylvania, USA, and watched the documentary film on George Washington would appreciate the pain and sufferings which gave the Americans independence from mighty British Forces. It was cold winter months when George Washington and his army were fighting for freedom against all odds and eating only boiled wheat flower!

Since declaring Independence in 1776 many American leaders, including Abraham Lincoln, Thomas Jefferson, Theodore Roosevelt, Franklin D. Roosevelt, John F. Kennedy and Dr. Martin Luther King, sacrificed their lives to build a United States Of America which world valued as an example of democracy and basic human rights.

The 20ᵗʰ Century America came into being at the cost of a terrible civil war between North and South (**558,052Americans dead)** and Mexican War (**13,283 Americans dead**). Despite its worst treatment of the Native American Indians and the African slaves as well as annexation of Hawaii and major part of Mexico, America came out to be a champion of democracy and human rights.

America's problem started with the formation of powerful private Corporations and Banks which hijacked the Government and legalized the age old slavery in the form of cheap labours forcing people to work for endless hours for basic family needs. Extreme drought, severe storms, fuelled by corporate greed led to the failure of the stock market and major private banks causing a US depression unparalleled in human history.

It was the World War II which helped US to come out of the 1930s depression creating federal military and infrastructure related jobs. **The success in World War II led to the beginning of the American Imperialism. Instead of embracing the world wide peace initiative following Hitler's defeat, US and Britain started redrawing the world map in order to ensure their strategic military interests.** They divided many parts of the world, including Africa, India, Middle East, displacing and dividing people who lived together for centuries contributing to intricate culture and harmony.

Their imperialistic greed led to many wars including Korean and Vietnam killing millions of people and destroying delicate Eco system of South East Asia. Most contemporary international disputes including India-Pakistan-Afghanistan, Iraq-Kuwait, Palestine-Israel, African in-fighting and famines, are a direct product or byproduct of the irresponsible, ill-intentioned, US and British imperialistic policy.

USA, **once the champion of revolution and democracy, became anti-revolutionary and pro-dictatorship to ensure its military strategic interests and supremacy.** Like the Roman Emperor, President George Bush sees the world full of barbarians, 'the virtual Terrorists', ideal pretext to justify military spending and might ignoring the sufferings of a large number of its own people from hunger, homelessness, crimes and imprisonment. President Bush may not know, "Rome wasn't built in day, so is USA"!

Religion
(Dedicated to universal consciousness)

Religion is the culture of a civilization
Along with all celebrations and education
Including practices which may appear superstition
Tied to mythology, history, and natural intuition!

World religions should be like buffet (buh-FAY) vision
Everyone can take a look at them with inquisition
Taste them; practice them for chemistry of acquisition
Enjoying best of everything for self realization
Eventually developing one's own religion
Which is universal within one's boundary conditions!

Evangelism makes slaves out of religion
Barring people from inherited wisdoms
Making one self-censored limited in vision
Arousing baptised-union for victorious mission
Marring Earth with Holy Wars against the very creation!

"How world could be secular and democratic when the most powerful religious institutions on Earth, Vatican and its authoritarian political wing Holy See and military wing Sovereign Military Order of Malta (SMOM) are heavily represented in the United Nations (UN) making UN a non-democratic instrument of spreading Monarchist vision?" Kolki

Regain

(Dedicated to an egalitarian universal world)

[Let us (including military and covert intelligence) celebrate the season the way True Jesus wanted us to: 'Love thy neighbour', 'Love thy enemy', and 'Thou shall not kill'. Kolki]

Its time for the truth fellow citizens
Let us embrace all through!

We have been living in lies
Insulting heavenly eyes
Making dear God sigh
And many God's children cry!
Let us bring back and bring back honesty with joy!

Its time for the love that grows together
Let us express all through!

We have been isolated
Making life full of stresses
Creating gaps in divide
Letting doubts and fear grow wild!
Let us bring back and bring back friendliness on Earth!

Its time for the march to sustain forever
Let us conserve all through!

We have been unwise
Using without compromise
Polluting air, land, water
Letting many species disappear!
Let us bring back and bring back lost heaven on Earth!

Regain (Cont.)

Its time for the joy to feel universal
Let us extend all through!

We have been naïve in denial
World not yet Egalitarian
More pleasures meant more hunger
Coz resources are not shared
Let us share and share with brothers and sisters!
Ensuring the very basis of Human Rights!

9/11 and Bilderberg Connection

9/11 wasn't an isolated event. The motives of secretive aristocrative Bilderberg's 'One World' vision dominated by the 'elites & bankers' and the NECONS' supremacist ideology of ruling the world creating fear using pre-emptive 'military & covert (mercenary)' forces as well as bribing 'world leaders & politicians' to 'support & aid' the process are very similar.

Let us re-iterate the ex-Chairman of Bilderberg and a current member of the steering committee David Rockefeller's speech at the June, 1991 Bilderberger meeting: -

"It would have been impossible for us to develop our plan for the world if we had been subjected to the lights of publicity during those years. But, the world is more sophisticated and prepared to march towards a world government. The supranational sovereignty of an intellectual elite and world bankers is surely preferable to the national autodetermination practiced in past centuries."

This supranational sovereignty using private Defense, Mining, and Mercenary Industries inflicting collateral damages including 9/11 and 'illegal invasion of Afghanistan & Iraq' had been possible with full cooperation of mainstream media, mostly owned by the same group of people, keeping citizens misinformed of the root causes of most world problems including worldwide violent covert intelligence operations? Here is David Rockefeller again:

"We are grateful to the Washington Post, the New York Times, Time Magazine and other great publications whose directors have attended our meetings and respected their promises of discretion for almost forty years."

Thus, secretive Bilderberg along with secretive 'Swiss Bank & Other Worldwide Offshore Banks' and covert wings of Intelligences dominated by 'CIA, MI6 (SIS) & Mossad' running worldwide shadow governments buying politicians and NGOs with money laundering while silencing opponents (good citizens) using private mercenaries and/or character assassination in their media framing false drug related charges, exposing personal private matters in public.

Theodor Herzl, Founder of **Zionism** in **1897**:

"It is essential that the sufferings of Jews. . . become worse. . . this will assist in realization of our plans. . . I have an excellent idea. . . I shall induce anti-semites to liquidate Jewish wealth. . . The anti-semites will assist us thereby in that they will strengthen the persecution and oppression of Jews. The anti-semites shall be our best friends".
-- From Herzl's Diary

[**Notes** : He meant ancient Hebrews settled throughout the once borderless world before the advent of colonialism; Hebrew language doesn't have letter 'J'; Thus the word Jew was coined to separate all true secular Semites (ancient people on Earth) by the evangelical anti-Semites]

"World must be ever vigilant to ensure that anti-Semites are not uniting as secretive Bilderberg, Trilateral Commission, Swiss Bank and sprouting off-shore banks, empowered by covert military, mercenaries and intelligence."
Kolki

9-11 and Vatican using Holy See and SMOM

One day in July 1944, as the Second World War raged throughout Europe, General William "Wild Bill" Donovan was ushered into an ornate chamber in Vatican City for an audience with Pope Pius XII. Donovan bowed his head reverently as the pontiff intoned a ceremonial prayer in Latin and decorated him with the Grand Cross of the Order of Saint Sylvester, the oldest and most prestigious of papal knighthoods. This award has been given to only 100 other men in history, who "by feat of arms, or writings, or outstanding deeds, have spread the Faith, and have safeguarded and championed the Church." Let the pope keep the kingdom and the glory -- the CIA wants the power. —By Martin A. Lee[x]

Once again, we will see that 9/11 wasn't an isolated event conceived and implemented by some unknown terrorists commanded by diabetic cave dweller Bin Laden in hiding as well as 'coordinating & financing' individual terrorist cells using easily traceable cell phones and easily trackable Western monetary system.

9-11 and related tyrannical war on terror blaming Islam and alike deifying loners as executors of spectacular destructive events only helps evangelic Zionist Christians justify medieval crusades in modern times killing and abusing innocents while occupying and dominating more countries around the world under noble's military and financial security. This is a vast topic traversing parts of history books illustrating evolution of Monarchy, private militarism, and feudal elites at the cost of commons sufferings as collateral damages. We will only address it briefly as pertinent for this research in anticipation of more scholarly work for the benefit of a peaceful coexisting world.

Per then CIA Director George Tenet's own admission *"a group of assets from a Middle Eastern service was unknowingly working for the CIA by that time. Out of the more than twenty people in that group, one third was working against al-Qaeda. By September 2001, two assets had successfully penetrated al-Qaeda training camps in Afghanistan."* [TENET, 2007, PP. 145]

Let us hear US Undersecretary of Defense for Intelligence Dr. Stephen Cambone shortly after a pivotal al-Qaeda warning given by the CIA to top officials on July 10, 2001, *"....that al-Qaeda threats were just a grand deception, a clever ploy to tie up our resources and expend our energies on a phantom enemy that lacked both the power and the will to carry the battle to us.*"

Tenet's reply was, *"No, this is not a deception, and, no, I do not need a second opinion.... We are going to get hit. It's only a matter of time."* [TENET, 2007, PP. 154]

The same CIA Director let Pakistan's ISI Director Lt. General Mahmood Ahmed, *who allegedly transferred money to alleged 9/11 mastermind Atta's Florida account*, enter USA (during September 4-11, 2001) for important mysterious meetings at the Pentagon and National Security Council as well as meetings with CIA, unspecified officials at the White House and the Pentagon, and his "most important meeting" with Marc Grossman, US Under Secretary of State for Political Affairs. [NEWS (ISLAMABAD), 9/10/2001]

Thus it is obvious that Islamic terrorists alone could never wage a battle against the formidable US/NATO/Israeli forces especially inside USA (New York and Washington DC) evading super power 'military & intelligence' and derailing all Governmental procedures, protective measures, and related accountabilities.

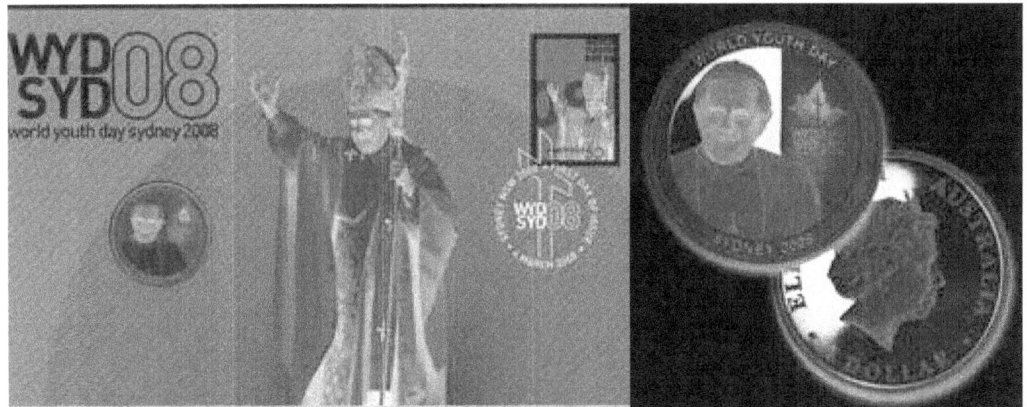

 We have seen the possible Bilderberg, headquartered in Switzerland, and 9/11 connection. It also must be noted that most international organizations (NGOs) including United Nations (UN), World Health Organization (WHO), Red-Cross, Aga Khan Fund, and Trilateral Commission are all based in Switzerland which bears the same NORDIC Cross in their flag as Great Britain and its dominions around the world – as well sharing the same tune for the national anthem. And the appearance of Pope's (Benedict XVI) head along with Queen's head on the 2008 World Youth Day coin suggests the long waited marriage[1] between Vatican and Church of England. This will explain the unconditional support of UK for the illegal (based on the rules set by allied power after WWII) wars against Afghanistan and Iraq without a simple open public investigation diagnosing the very cause of 9/11 respecting rule-of-law and proof-of-conviction.

Now imagine why Mr. Bush and Mr. Blair would be at the Vatican before illegal invasion of Iraq. Imagine then President Bush, who is nothing less than a war criminal in international justice standard, would receive special honour from Vatican's Holy See Pope Benedict XVI. Mr Blair also told BBC 1's Fern Britton Meets, "What your (Catholic) faith does is it sustains you through what is then a very difficult time as you try to implement what you think is right (crusade). What your faith can't do, I'm afraid, is tell you what is the right thing".

"President Bush arrived at the Vatican this morning to a welcome from Pope Benedict XVI so unusually cordial .... In an unprecedented move the pontiff met Mr Bush for their final encounter not in the papal library, as is usual under normally strict Vatican protocol, but at St John's Tower, a restored medieval tower in the Vatican walls used to house the Vatican's VIP guests. As he entered the tower with the Pope, Mr Bush repeatedly exclaimed, 'this is such an honour, such an honour'". - Richard Own in Rome[1A]

Pope John Paul II and Pope Benedict XVI are not ideologically same people as would be obvious from their Coat of Arms:

"When war, as in these days in Iraq, threatens the fate of humanity, it is ever more urgent to proclaim, with a strong and decisive voice, that only peace is the road to follow to construct a more just and united society! Violence and arms can never resolve the problems of man." – Pope John Paul II, opposed war against Iraq

But entertaining those war criminals by Pope Benedict XVI inside Vatican are a total insult and disrespect to that peace loving man and justice around the world.

Pope Benedict XVI – Coat of Arms   Pope John Paul II – Coat of Arms

The Triregnum (the Papal Tiara formed by three crowns symbolizing **the triple power of the Pope: father of kings, governor of the world and Vicar of Christ**) from the XVIII Century, with which the bronze statue of Saint Peter is crowned every June 29th, the feast day of the Saint.

Polish Pope John Paul II voiced his anger against the British-US-Australian led illegal war against Iraq, but the German Pope Benedict XVI has been riding and enjoying the tide towards the New Evangelical World Order embracing the villains of 9/11 and related War Criminals, including Mr. Bush and Mr. Blair.

The Trilateral Commission[2] is a private organization, established to foster closer cooperation among the elites of United States, Europe, and Japan. It was founded in July 1973 at the initiative of David Rockefeller, who was Chairman of the Council on Foreign Relations (CFR) at that time. The Trilateral Commission is widely seen as a counterpart to the Council on Foreign Relations. Funding for the group came from David Rockefeller, the Charles F. Kettering Foundation, and the Ford Foundation.

Speaking at the Chase Manhattan International Financial Forums in London, Brussels, Montreal, and Paris, Rockefeller proposed the creation of an International Commission of Peace and Prosperity in early 1972 (which would later become the Trilateral Commission). At the 1972 Bilderberg meeting, the idea was widely accepted! Founding members included Alan Greenspan and Paul Volcker, both eventually headed the Federal Reserve system of USA.

Let us hear from renowned linguist Noam Chomsky's worries about Trilateral Commission/CFR running US Government.

"Perhaps the most striking feature of the new Administration is the role played in it by the Trilateral Commission. The mass media had little to say about this matter during the Presidential campaign -- in fact, the connection of the Carter group to the Commission was recently selected as "the best censored news story of 1976" -- and it has not received the attention that it might have since the Administration took office. All of the top positions in the government -- the office of President, Vice-President, Secretary of State, Defense and Treasury -- are held by members of the Trilateral Commission, and the National Security Advisor was its director. Many lesser officials also came from this group. It is rare for such an easily identified private group to play such a prominent role in an American Administration." —The Carter Administration: Myth and Reality, Excerpted from Radical Priorities, 1981 Noam Chomsky[2A]

Thus NEOCONS takeover of Bush Administration didn't happen overnight; it started long back and solidified in 80s under the Regan administration which formed the simulated secretive shadow government involving ideologically like minded people including Donald Rumsfeld and Dick Cheney.

The question is **who are these private elites** who have been uniting as secretive **Bilderberg** and **Trilateral Commission** members expediting the path towards their vision of one world using covert CIA, MI6(SIS), and Mossad as well as empowering private mercenaries, militia, and 'shadow governments & institutions'?

NOBILITY, THE NEW WORLD AND THE SOVEREIGN MILITARY ORDER OF MALTA (SMOM) – Military Wing of Vatican In Disguise

The nobility[3] of most of Western Europe had a common origin in the feudal system of early medieval society; the noble class being a relatively small group whose land tenure depended on providing services to their superior lord. The Scottish and Irish Nobilities developed within a tribal structure, descendants of the chiefs being considered noble. In feudal Europe the great magnates held their fiefs directly from the Crown, with lesser knights holding their land from an intermediate lord or minor sovereign. By the fourteenth century proof of descent in the male line from any knight or the possessor of a "knight's fee" came to be considered evidence of nobility, entitling such a person to enjoy the class privileges which had been conferred or confirmed by the Crown.

Although the United States recognizes that "*all men are created equal*", the situation has been getting complicated with the migration of flood of Nobles from Europe following Spanish War, WWI, and WWII having obedience to the mercenary wing of SMOM. Thus even if the United States Congress was to enact a law requiring all public and private organizations not to discriminate in favor of those of noble descent, the SMOM would be exempted from compliance by virtue of the privileged constitutional treatment given to religious organizations (which, for example, exempts the Catholic Church from "equal opportunity" laws that might otherwise require the admission of women to the priesthood).

Officially, the Knights of Malta was a global charity organization. But beginning in the 1940s, knighthood was granted to countless CIA agents, and the organization became a front for intelligence operations. SMOM is ideal for this kind of activity, because it is recognized as the world's only landless sovereignty whose members enjoy diplomatic immunity. This allows agents and supplies to pass through customs without interference from the host country.

Here are some examples of the Knights and Dames of Malta ruling CIA:
• William Casey – CIA Director.
• John McCone – CIA Director.
• William Colby – CIA Director.
• William Donovan – OSS Director (Pre-CIA).

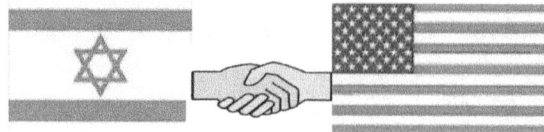

For Zion's Sake: I will not keep silent

Christians United For Israel (CUFI)

Isaiah 62.1: For Zion's sake I will not be silent, for Jerusalem's sake I will not be quiet, Until her vindication shines forth like the dawn and her victory like a burning torch (**Zion (Hebrew: ציון; Tiberian vocalization: Ṣiyyôn; transliterated Zion or Sion)** [Ref: http://cufi.convio.net/site/PageServer]. What CUFI fails to mention that holocausts, world wars and crusades are all Christian affairs!

These evangelic Christians Zionists[4] have nothing to do with loving Jesus, their deity is Cross represented by the Holy See (Seat) – Pope, the King of the United Kingdom of Israel (Church). Most of the 70 million US Evangelic (Zionist) Christians belong to militant John Hagee's CUFI (Christians United For Israel) which is heavily represented by ex-CIA directors and Neocons (members of SMOM).

Unlike most pro-Israel Jews, Christian Zionists emphatically support Israeli settlements and oppose the two-state solution. CUFI supports genocide in Palestine as the vehicle for Christian domination of the world annihilating 2/3 of the people of the ancient world as part of their vision of second coming of Christ that resembles death and destructions under Alexander, Caesar and Hitler.

Following 9/11, Queen Elizabeth II coroneted then New York Mayor Rudolph Giuliani[5] with Knighthood

"When Rudolph Giuliani received his honorary knighthood from Queen Elizabeth II on Wednesday, he joined an exclusive club with a membership dating back to ancient Rome. Giuliani received the award in recognition for his work following the September 11 terrorist attacks in the United States. Honorary knighthoods are awarded by the queen, on the advice of the UK Foreign and Commonwealth Office, to those who have made an important contribution to relations between their country and Britain".

Incidentally, Giuliani was yards away from the London Subway Bombing[6]?

Ever wondered about the Coat of Arms of the Holy See and State of Vatican City?

Coat of Arms of the Holy See and State of Vatican City

up

Since the XIV Century, two crossed Gold and Silver keys surmounted by the tiara7 have been the official insignia of the Holy See. The gold one, on the right, alludes to the power in the kingdom of the heavens, the silver one, on the left, indicates the spiritual authority of the papacy on earth. The mechanisms are turned towards the heaven and the grips turned down, in other words into the hands of the Vicar of Christ. The cord with the bows that unites the grips alludes to the bond between the two powers.

Now imagine a world where those two powers are 'Elites & Bankers' as Vicar of Christ (the power behind the throne) and 'Covert Intelligence & Military' as the authority of Papacy on Earth.

The very basic question people on Earth must ask why religious organization like Vatican and Holy See would use 'Coat of Arms' - a symbol of the medieval crusaders, while claiming as the guardian and beholder of Jesus' love?

Since Holy See activities led to violent persecutions and dominations throughout history since the inception of Christianity it can be interpreted that the Coat of Arms actually symbolizes whoever has control over Gold and Silver deposits on Earth rules the world enslaving commoners forever.

What 61 million Britons or 304 million Americans or 33 million Canadians or 21 million Australians or 4.1 million New Zealanders need to have a good life in their newly found homelands with unexploited enormous resources, unspoilt nature, and hospitable wise and caring natives?

It is time for Britons to take the lead to end Constitutional Monarchy around the world making military and intelligence fully accountable to the participatory democratic process to ensure domestic security eliminating expensive covert intelligence activities which only empower the 'power behind the throne', 'The Vicar of Christ', at the expense of worldwide peace loving humble citizens and other sentient being. Without the expensive brutal inhumane violent covert intelligence activities people will live together in a brotherly and sisterly world embracing cultural and religious differences as well as racial colour blindness.

End Notes: Heraldry is the profession, study, or art of devising, granting, and blazoning  arms and ruling on questions of rank or protocol, as exercised by an officer of arms. *Heraldry* comes from Anglo-Norman *herald*, from the Germanic compound **harja-waldaz*, "army commander". The word, in its most general sense, encompasses all matters relating to the duties and responsibilities of officers of arms. To most, though, heraldry is the practice of designing, displaying, describing, and recording coats of arms and badges. Historically, it has been variously described as "the shorthand of history" and "the floral border in the garden of history." The origins of heraldry lie in the need to distinguish participants in combat when their faces were hidden by iron and steel helmets.

x. Martin A Lee, Their Will Be Done, Conspiracy Central, July/August 1983 Issue

1. World Youth Day Coin 2008, http://www.govmint.com/item/2008-Pope-Benedict-XVI-World-Youth-Day-Coins/POPE08/21

1A. TimesOnline, http://www.timesonline.co.uk/tol/news/world/europe/article4127984.ece

2. Trilateral Commission, http://en.wikipedia.org/wiki/Trilateral_Commission

2A. Noam Chomsky, http://en.wikipedia.org/wiki/Noam_Chomsky

3. Guy Stair Sainty, The Conflict Between British And Continental Concepts Of Nobility And The Order Of Malta, http://www.chivalricorders.org/orders/smom/m-nbprf3.htm

4. Playing the Jesus Card, http://www.foreignpolicy.com/articles/2009/07/24/playing_the_jesus_card

5   Giuliani joins a distinguished club, http://edition.cnn.com/2002/WORLD/europe/02/13/knighthoods/

6. Giuliani Near London Subway Bombing, http://www.daanspeak.com/LondonAttack03Eng.html

7. Papal Tiara, http://www.vatican.va/news_services/press/documentazione/documents/sp_ss_scv/insigne/triregno_en.html

8. The Roman Catholic Church, http://www.jordanmaxwell.com/articles/general-research/pdf/Catholic%20CIA.pdf

Harmony
(Dedicated to a unified world embracing best of humankind)

Imagine a world -
Where Churches are free from the burden of Cross
Smiling Jesus welcoming all with gospels of love!

Temples are free from violent Gods
Enchanting Shiva, Buddha, Krishna, illuminating all
Bhagavad Geeta is Guru Geeta without reference to Mahabharat!

Mosques are spreading loving teachings of Muhammad -
Unitedly praising 'Allah Hu Akbar'!

Synagogues are rejuvenated with ancient Hebrew universal thoughts
Celebrating life as if in the days of wise Solomon
Refreshing knowledge lost in Hebrew-Greek-English translation!

Where people can walk into any religious institution
Knowing their prayers will add to the universal wisdom!

Where self sacrifice stops sacred killings of all forms
No one is suffering from scars of circumcised mutilation!

Knowing religion is a cause for celebration
For everything we achieve for better living condition
Commerce is a mechanism of need based distribution
Science is the vehicle of truth beyond institutions and corporations
Military is for homeland protection not pre-emptive aggression!

Where United Nations is democratic reflecting population
Criminals of War are transparent to legal intuitions -
Irrespective of race, colour, gender, status, and religion!

Where Vatican becomes a religious United Nations
Abandoning all evangelical mission
Promoting global scientific religious vision!

Final Statement

The prime motives and logical circumstantial evidences for 9/11 disasters have been established. If the Americans lived in a country as envisioned by the Founding Fathers then the Government of the United States of America would come forward openly telling the world what really happened on 9/11/2001 that killed so many innocent civilians and military personnel bringing lifetime nightmares for their family and friends! If the Americans had an honest and peace loving Government 9/11 never happened in broad day light evading trillion dollar proactive military, intelligence, and NORAD's preventive measures!

Evidences are circumstantial but more than needed to acquit Bin Laden and 19 proposed nameless dead hijackers and open a public investigation to convict Bush/Cheney Administration and their accomplice!

Pope Benedict XVI's unusual special welcome to Mr. Bush and Mr. Blair who are nothing less than fierce war criminals as the chief architects of the illegal invasion of Afghanistan and Iraq suggests 'war on terror' is another anti-Semitic evangelic crusadic war in 21st century!

World must not forget that Hitler was raised as Catholic and the Jesuit Michael Serafin wrote: "It cannot be denied that [Pope, Pacelli] Pius XII's closest advisors for some time regarded Hitler's armoured divisions as the right hand of God." The Church celebrated Hitler's birthday by ringing bells, flying swastika flags from church towers and holding thanksgiving services for the Fuhrer. When the German army conquered France, the Church bells rang for an entire week, and swastikas flew over the churches for ten days. The greatest surprise from Pope Pius XII was his silence over the Holocaust knowing well it was in progress.

Pope Benedict XVI has been silent about the killings and destruction in Iraq, Afghanistan and Palestine and the worldwide abuses of detainees without justice. World War II annihilated 55 million people from Earth inflicting unthinkable destrcution. **Without 9/11 and related public investigation** the same power may have been gaining steam to hasten 'The end of the world'.

Conclusion

Fellow Americans voted for change with hopes for a better world that respects accountability, rule of law, and proof of conviction. But that change will never materialize if 9/11 perpetrators remain unidentified and unpunished for their treasons allowing them to dictate and pollute the Obama administration mutating as the beholder of American Freedom and Justice. So it is time for North American Politicians, NORAD officials, true patriotic high level Military Authorities and prudent Journalists & Media personnel to come forward and tell the world what really happened on 9/11 in the name of maintaining US/NATO/Israeli military supremacy on Earth, Space, and Cyber Space! Anyone who remain silent and try to make others silent imagining its all good for the security of the NATO Alliance, long term Western Economy, and Holy See committing the greatest crime against humanity letting democratic mass murderers be the worst Frankenstein ruling our world with terror towards overall destruction prophesized as Armageddon. World must ensure that leaders speak truth under oath and minutes of all meetings and conferences including intelligence are public property to sustain open accountable peace loving participatory democracies around the world.

"One has to speak out and stand up for one's convictions. Inaction at a time of conflagration is inexcusable." – Mohandas Gandhi

"When wise act ignorant, or indifferent, world becomes a dangerous place." – Kolki

Let us also hear Democratic Senator Russell Dana Feingold of Wisconsin, the Chairman of the Constitution Subcommittee of the Judiciary Committee: "I recognize this is a different world with different technologies, different issues, and different threats. Yet we must examine every item that is proposed in response to these events to be sure we are not rewarding these terrorists and weakening ourselves by giving up the cherished freedoms that they seek to destroy."

Indian home minister resigned following the Mumbai shootings and massacre, but no one in Bush Administration, Pentagon, CIA, FBI, Counter Terrorism, FAA, NSA, and NORAD resigned or was held accountable for the success of 9/11 like massive spectacular predicted disastrous event. Rather they were all promoted, rewarded, and military higher ups gave themselves extraordinary raises and bonuses – without addressing $2.3 trillion missing Pentagon Funds!

Thus, naturally, encouraged by the success from previous failures the same military, national security, and new homeland security team indulged in failure after failure including Anthrax, DC snipers, Iraqi non-existent WMD, Hurricane Katrina disaster and Virginia Tech massacre – apart from illegal invasion of Afghanistan and Iraq!

Without 9/11 investigation and justice the perpetrators have been very active to make world chaotic! Wall Street Bailout or strengthening the Alliance economic base of secretive Bilderberg for eventual martial law and World War? US Economic problem is just the direct effect of irresponsible trillion dollar tax cuts, trillion dollar increase in military spending, and the outrageous cost of Iraq & Afghan Wars which mostly have been enriching private Defense Contractors & Evangelical Mercenaries making tax payers insolvent! Recovery must have been a post election well thought political decision; but the 9/11 perpetrators and their military Junta only making Government dysfunctional while preparing the crusaders for the martial law enacting another more spectacular Pearl Harbour to officially start Third World War to destroy democracy and our old world!

Let us end this book with a quote from Rear Admiral Chester Ward, a former member of the CFR for 16 years, who warned the American people of the organization's intentions:

"The most powerful clique in these elitist groups have one objective in common — they want to bring about the surrender of the sovereignty of the national independence of the United States. A second clique of international members in the CFR comprises the Wall Street international bankers and their key agents. Primarily, they want the world banking monopoly from whatever power ends up in the control of global government."

What is troublesome for all world citizens that secretive private think tanks in America and Europe with deep-seeded loyalty to Monarchial Alliance had been dictating American Foreign Policy for the benefit of few at the cost of collateral damages like 'New Pearl Harbour', related wars and pandemic virus!

Without 9/11 open public investigation more American God Father like personalities have been vouching for means of continuing ongoing fear from threats to justify US military actions around the world:

"Moreover, as America becomes an increasingly multicultural society, it may find it more difficult to fashion a consensus on foreign policy issues, except in the circumstance of a truly massive and widely perceived direct external threat."

"*The Grand Chessboard: American Primacy and its Geostrategic Imperatives*," by Zbigniew Brzezinski (1997), Ex-Member of CFR, Former Director of Trilateral Commission, National Security Advisor to President Carter and adviser to Presidents Reagan and Bush the First (**nick *named 'Father of Al-Qaeda***).

It would be utopia to live in one world respecting existing open geographical borders; appreciating evolved religions, culture and ancient practices; celebrating festivals breaking the mental barrier; embracing universal values and rights! But that world must be open, just, peace loving pluralistic participatory democratic world governed by "we the people, for the people and by the people".

Thus the only option left to the fellow Americans, void of an honest open public investigation and trial for the treasons, is the American Orange Revolution implemented poetically as follows:

American Orange Revolution

(Dedicated to true American spirit of freedom, peace, and justice for all)

My fellow Americans -
Must have learned form watching television
How quick orange revolution
Thrived around the parts of ancient civilization!

Okalahoma City Bombing and September 11 destruction
All related obstructions of justice sealing documentations
Detentions and abuses disregarding open honest investigations -
Made military, CIA, FBI, NSA, criminal organizations!
Media objective against rule-of-law and proof-of-convictions!

Politicians mute and naïve inactivating political organizations!
Requiring immediate revival of American Orange Revolution!

It may seem unachievable -
But in fact could be very simple!
Without Politicians - who ignore truth as untouchables!
Ideologically bonded to 'The United Kingdom of Israel'!
Fear being labelled as 'soft on crime' and 'too liberal'!
Support troops violating international laws of War Crime Tribunals!
Without Media - that avoid news as unmarketable!
And finally without leaders who whisper Armageddon!

Implementing pre-emptive peaceful mass revolution!
Guarding CIA, FBI, NSA, Pentagon, in Washington!
Releasing all documents for open distribution!
Taking over media like CNN for public television!
Converting FED as open government institution!
Ensuring media reflect population distribution!
And singing in chorus the song for American freedom -
"Then conquer we must, when our cause it is just,
And this be our motto: "In God is our trust."
And the star-spangled banner in triumph shall wave
O'er the land of the free and the home of the brave!".

Finally, rejoicing with American Pride in friendliness!
Reassuring the world -
'The Statue of Liberty' was never meant for military threats!

♥

 It's a fight for Truth & justice against Lies & injustice which is the law of causation! This is a decisive moment in history and all humans must strive to fight for truth with their Heavenly power inside so that they can live heavenly life on Earth with peaceful possessions and truthful vocations! God (universal loving expression) bless our beloved world and all sentient being.☺ Kolki

▲♫▼

When religions coexist, leaders communicate, media respect neutrality, laws not blinded by immunity, and citizens' needs take precedence over profitability - peace becomes reality, world lives in harmony appreciating Human Rights – Kolki

☼
♥

Too much power & money in few like minded group of private hands led to 9/11, related chaos and injustice, insecurity everywhere, failure of the banking & justice systems, almost no accountability, and biased polling by their media to support all that making citizens fight and gossip against each other worldwide. It is time to take back governments from private agencies and outsourcing to live freely as we the people, by the people, and for the people – enjoying true bliss of Participatory Democracy void of Constitutional Monarchy. Kolki

About Kolki (Deepak Sarkar) –

A dual American and Canadian citizen was born in Calcutta, India, on October 17, 1954. A writer, composer, music teacher and performer, photographer besides a Professional Engineer, MBA in Telecommunications Management and Ph.D. candidate at the University of Victoria, British Columbia, Canada. Held IT Management positions in corporations and institutions around North America. Was Honoured with Gold Award from SBC/Pacific Bell 1997.

A converted Vegetarian who believes in non-violence and peace can be achieved throughout the world without military strategic interests while visualizing collateral damages as real death and destructions.

Brought up in Southern Calcutta was always keen to know and learn about the people and their real conditions. A nature and animal lover who maintained his faith in universal well being throughout the career. Travelled extensively in North America and India as well as visited many foreign countries in Europe and Asia.

Also a singer who composed songs like 'Song for One World', 'Song of Equity', 'Regain', 'Canadian Pride', 'Spirit of Victoria', 'Quest', 'Co-existence', 'A Day of Non-Violence', 'Peace Now', 'Life is Simple' and 'New Year'! Directed many Musical shows and performed solo in community fund raising events. Produced music CDs and informational web sites.

Wrote many Peace related articles since 9/11, 2001, which can be accessed online via his poetry WEB Site www.kolki.com. Awarded the International Federation of Animal Welfare 2007.

Writes as Kolki and published a book of poems, **"Poems by Kolki – Absolutely Humane"**, a recipe for better world. Many poems by Kolki had been published in the International Society of Poets anthologies including 'Immortal Verses' and 'Secrets of the Soul', News Media and journals around the world, as well as part of Noble House collections like 'Colours of the Heart' and 'Theatre of the Mind', some winning awards!

Designed and edited a book by renowned art historians Dr. P. Banerjee & R. Banerjee, '**Indian & Central Asian Art** Narrative Interpretations of Unique Fragments'. As Chief Editor of 'Abha Prakashan', Delhi, India, published the maiden issue and Vol. 2 of the annual journal '**Kristi**'.

Working on future books including '**Living with the Lovebirds**', '**Universal Consciousness**', Planet X, and '**Humane Cuisine**' as well as the second edition of **"Poems by Kolki"**.

*'Let us not waste any more time hunting for virtual terrorism! The whole world is hungry for peace and democracy achieved through mutual respect and understanding, not using bombs and missiles. War (irrespective of label) divides and destroys people and civilization, animal and environment, as the ultimate weapons of mass destruction'......***Kolki**.